PRAISE FOR STEVEN DUNNE

'A gripping serial killer story with an exceptional depth of humanity' Stephen Booth

'The highest echelons of writing' *Lancashire Evening Post*

'Fast-paced and thrilling, crime writing at its best' *Sun*

'Well-paced and engrossing' *The Herald,* Dublin
'Truly brilliant' *lizlovesbooks.com*

'Deeply unsettling' *loiteringwithintent.wordpress.com*

'A story that keeps you guessing throughout'
bookaddictshaunco.uk

Follow Steven on Twitter at @ReaperSteven

BLOOD SUMMER

STEVEN DUNNE

BY THE SAME AUTHOR

The Reaper (Reaper - Part 1)
The Disciple (Reaper - Part 2)
Deity
The Unquiet Grave
A Killing Moon
Death Do Us Part
The Ressurection (Reaper - Part 3)

Full details
www.stevendunne.co.uk

1

January 2002 - Chicago, Illinois, USA

Trent gazed out across the skyline from the sixth floor of the Chicago Riverfront hotel on Wacker Street. From his position, he had a postcard's view of the ramrod straight section of the Chicago River, all the way up to Wolf Point, as far as the weather allowed. The river flowed past the old Post Office building on the opposite bank, before branching inland, north and south, away from the heart of downtown through a series of canals.

On every block, a bridge, groaning with crawling traffic and swaddled pedestrians, crossed the river of this heaving metropolis, though Chicago's seasonal snows were doing their best to grind movement to a halt.

Snow fell in fists onto older snow, encrusted with dirt, banked up along the edge of the sidewalk and it was difficult to see the giant banner on the old Chicago-Sun Times building on the opposite bank. The historic waterfront edifice of Chicago's biggest newspaper was due to make way for a colossal skyscraper reaching more than a quarter of a mile into the sky, proposed by New York hotel magnate, Donald Trump.

Concrete plans had been accepted but since the attack on the World Trade Centre, four months ago, all such ventures had been put on hold and Trump Tower was no exception. It seemed the whole country was still in shock about 9/11 and normal service had definitely not been resumed - at least until some Islamic ass was kicked but that looked some way off. Truly, it was winter in America.

Trent's arms extended into a yawn, his chest straining against his service harness so he pulled it over his head, wrapped the harness around the holster and placed his gun onto a high shelf out of reach of the little girl. The scratch of graphite on paper turned his head and he watched Mrs Beaumont's small daughter, Nell, hunched on a chair, her feet in tiny sandals, reaching halfway to the carpet. Tongue out, she was shading a colouring book with a look of concentration that would have been at home on Oppenheimer's face, as he split the atom.

Trent smiled at the top of her head, before resuming scrutiny of his city from a vantage point rarely afforded him. Resting his forehead on the vast window, he could just see the bustling DuSable Bridge on the bend of the river, a line of cars inching along Michigan Avenue onto the Magnificent Mile.

Out of sight, the river waters continued out towards Lakeshore Drive to the grey mass of Lake Michigan although, to the consternation of most tourists, it didn't actually work that way.

'I'm bored,' said Nell. 'Can we go out, mom?' she wailed towards the next room. 'I wanna make a snowman.'

'We have to stay in with Mr Trent, honey,' came the muffled reply. Nell groaned. 'Don't you like Mike?' said the voice. Trent glanced across at her and winked.

'Sure, I do, mom. It's just...'

'Hey kid. Come over here,' said Trent. 'Want to see something cool?'

She hesitated, before slipping off her chair and walking to the window. 'Sure.'

'See the river there,' said Trent.

She stared at him as if he'd lost his mind. 'D'uh.'

Trent grinned. 'That's the Chicago River.'

'I know that, silly,' said Nell, laughing.

'You do?' exclaimed Trent. 'Okay. So, which way is Lake Michigan, genius?'

Nell looked at him, stared down at the river and raised her right arm to point towards the unseen lake.

'Very good,' said Trent. 'So, which way is the river flowing?'

She stared at him with narrowed eyes, took a quick glance down at the DuSable Bridge and pointed in the same direction. 'That way. To the lake.'

Smiling, Trent grunted a two-syllable, game-show sound effect to signal her mistake.

'Wrong?'

'Wrong. The river flows from the lake into Chicago and out to the countryside.'

Nell giggled. 'That's stoopid. Rivers flow *into* lakes. Everyone knows that.'

'Usually, you'd be right. But the Chicago River is different. You see, about eighty years ago, the people of Chicago decided to reverse the water's course and make it flow back through the city.'

'That's silly.' She chuckled again, her untidy blond curls bobbing up and down as she laughed.

'Well, they didn't think so,' said Trent. 'So, they got the best engineers to come up with a plan and now the Chicago River flows from the lake *to* the city and out west, to the plains.'

'Why?'

'Because Lake Michigan provides Chicago's water for drinking and washing and stuff.' Trent glanced up to see, Nell's mother brandishing the coffee percolator. He checked his watch. His shift was almost up, not that Rentoria was likely to be on time and, as he needed to hang around and have words with him, he nodded his thanks. Her smile lingered before she disappeared back into the kitchen to make coffee.

'But why did they need to reverse the water?' asked Nell, tugging on his shirtsleeve.

'Because in the early part of last century, the river flowed through the city picking up pollution from all the homes and businesses on the way, including toilet sewage.'

'Yeeuuw.'

'Exactly. And sewage carries bacteria so people got sick from drinking the water and a lot of them died.'

'Sick from diseases?'

'That's right. Bacteria from what was going in the water, was going into people's bodies. So, to stop pollution flowing into the lake, they reversed the river's course to protect people's health. It was one of the greatest engineering feats in American history. So now, water is pumped from the lake, back up the river and anything harmful is washed back upstream, out along the connected canals they built to spread the water around. In that way, the lake's water supply is always clean and available for public consumption.'

'Don't people get sick in the suburbs?'

'No, because once the water's there, it's specially treated to make it cleaner.'

'Wow.'

'No cream, no sugar, right?' said Mrs Beaumont.

Trent smiled. 'Thank you, ma'am.'

'We've been over this, Mike.'

'Thank you, Gwen.'

'And I'm Nell,' said Nell, holding out her small hand to shake.

'I know that,' said Trent, shaking her hand. She giggled again. 'And it's a beautiful name.'

'Nice to meet you, Mike,' she said.

'Nice to meet you too.'

She chuckled. 'That's funny because we already met.'

'Ah, but now we've been formally introduced.'

Smiling, Nell wandered to the window to stare at the river to process what she'd just learned, hoping to actually see the water moving upstream.

Gwen leaned against the door jamb, gazing pensively at her daughter. She beckoned him over with a long delicate hand and handed him a mug in the compact kitchen. 'Thank you, Mike. You're making this much easier than it might have been.'

'It'll all be over soon,' said Trent, trying to project a confidence he didn't feel.

'Will it?' She closed her eyes in despair and Trent took the opportunity to examine her unblemished face. Her eyes opened and she caught him looking. He dropped his gaze, taking a hurried gulp of coffee. 'I don't know. These people seem pretty pissed and awful determined.'

'Once the trial's over and your testimony is on the record, they'll have no reason to hurt you.'

'Revenge seems like a good reason.'

'They'd have to find you first.' Trent smiled to reassure. 'Mrs Beaumont...Gwen, there's no logic or profit in trying to hurt you once you've testified. Besides, I'm not going to let anything happen to you.'

'I hope you're right. I suppose withdrawing my statement wouldn't help.'

'The people who killed your friend and your boss would take that as a win and unfortunately...'

'Unfortunately, I'd still know what I know and they could never be certain I wouldn't talk in the future.'

Mike nodded. 'I'm afraid so. You're a loose end and people with this little regard for human life are neat freaks about their exposure, especially with serious years in the pen hanging over them. Without your evidence, the court gives them a free pass and the trial is over. And after the fuss has died down all they have to do is wait, knowing the FBI can't keep you under the radar forever. Not without a change of identity and a whole new life.'

'Thank you for your candour, Mike.'

'I'm sorry. I'm not in charge of these things. I wish I was.'

She smiled. 'Don't beat yourself up. No-one could've done more. Your help these last two weeks has been...' Her expression changed and she dropped a soft hand onto his wrist and moved closer, eyes examining the scar that ran from above his right eye, across his forehead before disappearing under his hairline. He looked up at her with longing as she gazed back into his steel grey eyes. At that moment, the doorbell rang and she smiled sheepishly. 'It's just not my year, is it?' She moved towards the door but Trent caught her wrists.

'Hold those horses,' he said, pulling her back and heading for the door.

'But that'll be Agent Rentoria.'

'You can see through doors now?'

'No, but the spyhole...'

'What's rule number one?' he said, cupping his ear theatrically.

She smiled. 'Never answer the door.'

'Never. Answer. The. Door.' He dispensed his reprimand with a smile. 'And Two?'

'Never look through the spyhole,' she said, sighing.

'Top marks. I'm sorry other agents on shift haven't emphasised that as much as they should, but I'm happy to be different. This is our work - please let us do our jobs.'

'Yes, sir,' she said, with a salute.

Trent delicately turned her around, by the shoulders, and directed her towards the lounge. 'With your daughter, please, Gwen.' She obeyed and he followed her in to pull his gun harness from the shelf and over his shoulders. Putting his jacket on over the top, he closed the kitchen door behind him and stood beside the main door.

'Who is it?'

'Housekeeping,' called a female voice, in her second language.

'Just a minute.' Trent took a dinner plate from the

drainer and held it to cover the spyhole, mimicking a head blocking out the light. When no explosion ensued, he opened the door a notch and peered over the chain.

A diminutive, dark-skinned girl smiled a greeting. 'Housekeeping, sir.'

'We're okay today,' said Trent, recognising her.

'You want fresh towels?'

'Leave them by the door, I'm in the middle of something.' He fed a five-dollar bill through the gap and the smiling girl affected a bow of gratitude and arranged the towels on the floor before pushing her trolley towards the next room, wreathed in smiles.

Trent unhooked the chain and retrieved the towels. He glanced testily at his watch and stared down the corridor in both directions. Placing the towels on the kitchen counter, he returned to his coffee.

A minute later, the bell tolled for a second time. 'Who is it?' he said at the door.

'Jose,' was the muffled reply.

Trent opened the door but left the chain on. 'You're late.'

Agent Rentoria shrugged an apology. His cropped black hair was damp with snowmelt and he held a Starbucks coffee cup in his right hand. 'The L was jammed,' he said. 'Had to take a later train.'

Trent slid the chain from its housing but stood to block Rentoria's way, his expression like flint. 'The L was busy, uh? In winter, in rush hour. Who knew?'

Rentoria grinned. 'Yeah, maybe we should call FEMA.'

'You think this is funny, Agent Rentoria?'

Rentoria sighed. 'No, sir. But it is rush hour. What are you gonna do?'

'Gee now,' said Trent, rubbing his chin. 'Would trying for an earlier train be too radical or even, knowing you're running late, skip the Starbucks run?'

'I'm sorry, sir,' said Rentoria, regret the furthest emotion from his face. 'It won't happen again, sir. Can I come in now, sir?'

Trent stepped to the side, eyes glued to his colleague. Rentoria moved past Trent and put down the polystyrene cup to take off his jacket but Trent stepped into him and grabbed the jacket, twisting it hard to immobilise Rentoria's arms in the sleeves before removing his gun from the holster. 'Jeez, Jose. How easy was that? The hell is with you?'

'Get the fuck off me, man,' he wailed, roughly shrugging his jacket back on. 'What's wrong with *you*?'

Trent ejected the clip, spun Rentoria round and handed him the Glock. 'Nothing. I'm doing my job and if you can't do yours properly, you can get the hell off my detail.'

'Your detail?' Rentoria glanced suggestively at the door through to the lounge, raising a lascivious eyebrow. 'You're taking this one way too personal, man.'

'What's that supposed to mean?'

'Come on, Mike. That's one fine looking woman in there. Unattached. Bored.' He winked and leaned into Trent for emphasis. 'I seen you looking.'

'Only friends and valued colleagues get to call me Mike,' snarled Trent.

Rentoria raised his hands. 'Whatever you say, Special Agent. I don't want to step on anyone's toes here.'

'I'm not getting through to you, am I, kid? Let me give you some advice, if you want to make it in the Bureau. You've only just moved up to the big leagues from Shit Kick, Michigan, because Homeland Security has left us short on manpower, nationwide. We get that you're only used to auto theft and pinching college students hustling a little Canadian weed across the border, so we start you off easy. But even with a straightforward babysit, you're not cutting it. You need to get serious about your work or you're heading back to the minors, starting tomorrow. Be on time. To. The. Second. No late train and no coffee run! Capiche.'

'I told you, it won't happen again...'

'Don't tell me!' said Trent, holding up a finger. 'Show me. Turn up late tomorrow and I file paper and you'll be back in Marquette freezing your ass off on campus stakeouts. Am I making myself clear?' Rentoria's head dipped in faint acceptance. *'I can't hear you.'*

'Clear. Wow. Okay! Sorry about today. I got things going on.'

Trent picked up a DO NOT DISTURB sign from the kitchenette counter. 'So much that you can't follow basic instructions.'

'Phillips put that on the door.'

'Then why was it still there when I swung by after your shift started?' Rentoria stared, unable to answer. 'Because you left it there.'

Rentoria sighed. 'I should have taken it down. I'll tell Phillips when he signs in.'

'Tell him what?'

Rentoria took a breath and looked beyond Trent. 'DO NOT DISTURB signs arouse suspicion if they're on the door, all day, every day.'

'And why is that a problem?' demanded Trent.

Rentoria continued in a monotone. 'Because big hotels are great for anonymity but have a higher staff turnover and full background checks on who comes and goes, are impossible.'

Trent patted him on the cheek. 'There you go. You'll be Director in no time.'

2

March 29th 2019 - Mandarin Building, Marina Bay, Singapore

'Tyler's late!' said Carla. 'An hour, you said.'

Harry Renfrew gazed at his wife from his perch on top of his lone suitcase, hoping to make eye contact. He failed. The instant her enquiry was lodged, Carla's mouth reverted to the hard line that had deformed her face since the decision to flee their gilded life in Singapore had been taken. She stood, arms folded, forehead resting on the reinforced glass of the vast corner window of their penthouse apartment, eyes locked onto the twinkling lights of Marina Bay below.

There'd been tears and blazing rows but these had given way to silent anger and frustration and Harry wasn't sure which he preferred. Determined not to answer unless she looked at him, he checked his watch, returning to monitor her profile a second later, her head still inclined to the distant lives being lived forty floors below.

Minute head movements betrayed her changing interest in quotidian events - a boat full of tourists exploring the river with its sites ancient and modern; a couple embracing on a bench on one of the piers; a gaggle of Friday night revellers heading over the Jubilee Bridge to the Esplanade. Thousands of unknown lives being lived, each according to individual preference, even the humblest of them marching to the beat of their own drum and, despite all his money, Harry suspected Carla envied them that.

With a melancholic smile, he remembered their own late-night walks, ambling hand in hand around the bay's promenades when Singaporeans donned T-shirts and shorts and headed outdoors to enjoy the cooler temperatures of what was, after all, reclaimed jungle. He remembered their early nights of courtship, holding her close and exploring her face as they strolled. Carla was twenty years his junior, achingly beautiful and, despite his millions, he'd been under no illusion that he was punching above his weight when he'd finally made her his wife. And everyone he knew agreed.

The first night he'd clapped eyes on her, sashaying towards his table with a tray of Slings, was seared in his memory. He'd been with some of the guys from the trading floor, having a few well-earned sharpeners in a private room at Zouk, a nightclub in The Cannery. Carla had served them. And seeing her sway exotically towards his table, in her short, black pencil skirt and tight-fitting check blouse, he lost the power of speech for a moment. Indeed, time itself seemed to slow through the gears and even the heavy throb of music from the dance floor had been reduced to barely a pulse.

Carla had walked with the poise of a model, comfortable in her own skin. Confidence radiated from every pore and her aura of faint amusement at the attention she received was not for show. That it was her job to play nice with the big money guys, to accept the open-mouthed lust with good humour and patience, was not in doubt. But there was more to her demeanour than that. Carla had been completely undaunted by the unequal power dynamic of a lone waitress attending to a bunch of alcohol-fuelled big shots. Yet not a fibre of her being had implied subservience, not for a second. Rather, she radiated quiet disdain, which Harry's dumbstruck gaping had only compounded. On her own amongst a pack of drunken, lusty rich men, Carla was in complete control of the room.

One of the guys, usually Brad, could be relied on to drop in a crude comment for general amusement so it was a rare event when even he, and another half dozen hard-bitten, financial demi-gods were equally dumbstruck, unable to communicate their appreciation with anything other than an obscene tip. And what was true then was true today - when Carla entered a room, heads turned and the drone of conversation faltered.

Harry broke his gaze to glance at Carla's three suitcases by the door. Having screwed up a life his wife adored, it was clear from the set of her mouth that he wouldn't be forgiven any time soon.

'He's late,' she seethed again, her green eyes finally blazing at him from beneath the blonde fringe. The bureaucratic tone of her first enquiry had been replaced by anger, despair, pleading. *Is this really happening? Do we have to leave?* He fancied he saw a tear glint in her eye. She adored Singapore in all its exotic, fabulous, grimy glory.

For Carla, even the seamier side of life on the island made the glamour more compelling. In Singapore, people lived life to the full and damn the consequences. Live hard or die meek, was Harry's motto. And with the kind of money there was to be made, he'd been true to his word.

Indecent riches were his to command, as they were to all those willing to get their hands dirty, hunched over a terminal, overseeing huge transactions and harvesting eye-watering fees. The trick was to collect only so much dirt that could be safely washed away under a gold-plated tap at the end of the day. Yes, that was the trick and, in that final enterprise, he'd failed.

'It's only five minutes, darling.'

'Five minutes?' she sneered. 'But won't we miss *the plane*?'

The *plane*. There it was. The scorn reserved for scheduled flights on airlines that *poor* people used, squeezed into uncomfortable seats like rats in a sack. By implication, she bemoaned the loss of his private jet, sold a week ago for a fifth of its value to a broker on the twelfth floor of the firm's building.

How Carla had loved that jet. Not just because she could sink into its leather sofas to quaff Cristal - ample reason for most wives and girlfriends - but because, on a whim, it could transport her to all those far-flung places she'd dreamed of visiting, gazing out of the windows of a private school classroom in Surrey.

The Lear had been the trump card in his campaign for Carla's hand. Such a prize hadn't been easily wooed but that only made conquest all the sweeter. Hong Kong. Shanghai. Bangkok. Bali. After months enduring the deafening music in Zouk just to be near her, he'd proposed dinner in Hong Kong, the next night - flying there in his jet. Only then, after months of painfully slow courtship, had Carla finally offered herself up to him, not because he had money but because he used those riches to offer her the world. In a very real sense, that plane had been their engagement ring. And now it was gone.

The entry phone buzzed and Harry leapt up to answer. 'Tyler?' he barked into the microphone.

'*Yes.*'

'Come up. We're ready.'

'Are we?' scoffed Carla.

Harry gathered the cases together and opened the entrance hall door.

Two minutes later, a man, late-forties, tall and lean with grey-streaked, close-cropped hair stepped silently across the threshold. He was simply dressed in black sweater and cargo trousers with a grey jacket slung over his arm and a small rucksack on his back. A scar ran from his right eyebrow, back across his forehead and disappeared under his hairline. He glanced around the apartment, his gaze lingering on his first vision of Carla Renfrew.

'Mrs Renfrew,' he acknowledged, in a soft American accent.

'You're late, Tyler,' complained Renfrew.

'Last minute refinements,' answered Trent, his eye falling on the four monogrammed cases. He removed his rucksack and rummaged inside. 'And while we're pointing fingers, I said one piece of luggage *each,* standard cases. Monogrammed luggage will get you noticed.'

Harry opened his mouth but, before he could apologise, Carla let fly.

'You've got a fucking nerve,' she blazed. 'You're asking us to give up our lives and leave everything behind at the drop of a hat so I don't see what the fuck it matters whether we have two cases or four.'

Trent's response was not the servility her outburst demanded and he stared calmly back. 'I realise this is hard, Mrs Renfrew. But let's get one thing clear. I'm not asking you to do anything. Your husband hired me to help the two of you relocate without, shall we say, eye-catching complications. I appreciate this is all very sudden...'

'Sudden?' shouted Carla. 'Our lives are being turned upside down and you think we should thank you for expecting us to drop everything and walk out of our lives.'

'Honey...' began Renfrew.

'I don't expect thanks, Mrs Renfrew, I take payment,' said Trent, closing the door to soundproof their conversation. 'Once received, I do my job and prepare for your departure. Your husband made a deal with a Russian investment bank.' Renfrew looked at him in surprise. 'The deal went south and the bank are looking for payback on the dough they lost and don't care who they hurt to get it.'

'You...?' stuttered Renfrew.

'Of course, I checked,' interrupted Trent. 'I told you at

our first meeting, I don't work for criminals, I help people in trouble.'

'For a price,' snarled Carla.

'No argument here,' replied Trent.

'Glad to know I passed muster,' said Renfrew.

'Honestly, it was touch and go,' replied Trent. 'But whether I approve of your line of work or not, I do *not* like corporate bullies who think violence can make up for their poor judgement. So, Mrs Renfrew, I'm not here to hold your hand or offer sympathy for your disrupted lives. I understand your pain, I really do. But if you have to disappear to avoid harm, you need my help. This is what I do and I'm very good at it. Now make a choice. Stay or go. Lose two of the cases or I walk but decide now because we're on the clock.'

Carla glared at him. 'People don't talk to me like that.'

'A day of firsts, then,' said Trent.

'You fucking...'

'Carla?' snapped Renfrew. 'Honey.'

'Don't *honey* me,' she said, her eyes filling with tears. 'This is not my fault...'

'Oh, so it's my fault...'

'It's nobody's fault!' barked Trent, his voice like a verbal slap. He stared coolly from wife to husband and back again. 'Shit happens while you're minding your business. You can deal with the consequences or start assigning blame and get consumed in the backdraft. What's it to be?'

Without looking at him, Carla came to a decision and marched sullenly away from the view she loved, picked up two of her cases and marched them into the bedroom, returning without them.

'Good,' said Trent, nodding at the remaining cases. 'No laptops, iPads or other devices in these two?' Carla and Harry shook their heads. 'Jewellery?'

'Safe deposit box, as you suggested,' said Renfrew.

Trent nodded and took a fat roll of black tape from the rucksack and tore off a piece to stick over the lettering on the leather. After doing the same to the other case, he returned the tape to the rucksack.

'You came prepared,' said Renfrew.

'People are in denial right up to the second they walk out of their lives.'

'Don't ordinary people have monogrammed luggage?' demanded Carla.

'Sometimes,' said Trent. 'But, if they're on the run with a new identity, the initials on their luggage may not match their passports and *that* gets noticed.'

Carla speared a fresh dart of anger towards her husband. 'I'm losing my name?'

'It's just for a few months, honey,' soothed her husband. 'Until this blows over.'

'Here,' said Trent, handing over new passports. 'Lies are easier to carry off with a shared truth so you're still English, if that helps.'

'Rule Britannia,' grinned Renfrew, trying to cheer his wife. She returned a look of contempt before examining her new passport.

'Charlotte Butler,' she said, in a voice that would have sent a tremor of fear through all the Charlotte Butlers in the world.

'David Butler,' said Renfrew, turning his new passport over in his hand. 'These look real.'

'They are,' said Trent, taking Carla's case from her. 'You have something for me?' Renfrew handed over a bulging tote bag. 'It's all here?' Renfrew nodded but Trent asked the question anyway. 'All credit and bank cards *with* codes, social media accounts and passwords, iPads, cell phones, chips removed?'

'All there.'

Trent pushed the bag into his rucksack. 'Wait here while I take your bags to the car. I'm certain your building isn't being watched but if it is, the later they see the pair of you leave, the better. I'll brief you in the car about destination and other essentials.'

'You don't know where we're going?' said Carla, eyes wide, to her husband. Powerless to argue, Renfrew stared back helplessly.

'Information he doesn't know can't be passed on,' said Trent.

'It's not like I would have told anyone,' said Renfrew.

'No, but you'd have been tempted to google the area. And if the people threatening you are halfway serious and the same amount competent, they'll be all over your browsing history like a rash when they find out you've gone.' He marched towards the elevators with the cases.

Left alone with her husband, Carla's mouth hardened again. 'He's got the codes for our credit cards?'

'It helps him lay down a false trail,' said Renfrew, moving to embrace her. 'Anybody trying to find us will be following his spending and end up chasing Tyler instead of us. It's going to be okay, baby.'

She shrugged his arms away. 'But if he's got your cards, how are you paying him?'

'I laid out three hundred grand upfront. Cash.'

'How much?' she exclaimed.

'Some of that was for flights and long-term accommodation,' said Harry. 'He claims the balance of his fee on our plastic.'

'So, he's got my cards too?'

'Everything.' He shrugged. 'It's not like we can use them, honey. They'd find us, if we did.'

She nodded, a tear of resignation welling. She took a last look at the apartment, resisting the temptation to return to her vigil by the window.

'David, Charlotte,' said Trent, leaning back into the apartment. 'It's clear. Let's hustle.'

∽

IN THE CAR, travelling along East Coast Park to Changi Airport, Carla's eyes were glued to Trent from the back seat. 'Where to first?'

'The airport.'

'No, I mean you,' said Carla. 'On our dime.'

'That's on a need-to-know basis, Mrs Butler.'

'It's our money,' said Carla. 'And please, call me Charlotte. David and I hate formality.'

Trent smiled, glancing back at her in the driver's mirror. 'That's the spirit.'

'So, where?'

'Honey, he can't...'

'Bermuda,' said Trent.

'Good choice,' said Carla. 'You'll love it there. Great paragliding and rafting.'

'Adrenalin junkie, my wife,' said Renfrew, winking.

'Can you recommend a good hotel?' said Trent.

'We always stay at the Rosewood,' said Renfrew, catching Carla's glare. 'But it's very expensive,' he added meekly.

'If you have history there, I'll steer clear,' said Trent. 'Anywhere else?'

'I hear the Loren at Pink Beach is very good,' said Renfrew. Trent nodded.

'First class all the way?' said Carla.

'If that's how my clients travel,' said Trent. 'A successful smokescreen requires authenticity.'

'I'll bet.'

'Carla...'

'Charlotte,' she growled at her husband.

'It's fine,' said Trent. 'In your situation, I'd be asking the same questions. From this moment, trust no-one.'

'Does that mean, having told us where you're going, you'll have to kill us?' sneered Carla.

'That wouldn't look very good on my CV,' said Trent.

'I promise not to tell,' she said. 'Cross my heart...'

'...and hope to die?' said Trent.

'That wouldn't look good on your CV either,' she said.

'Copy that,' said Trent.

Carla stared out of the window, ruminating on her next barb. 'Sounds like you lead a fabulous life, living it up on other people's money.'

'Isn't that what your husband does?' said Trent.

Renfrew's laughter was loud and hearty. 'He's got you there, Carla.'

'Charlotte,' said Carla and Trent in unison. Harry raised his hands in supplication.

'You haven't answered my question.'

'Whatever you might think, Mrs Butler, this is work,' said Trent. 'Of course, seeing different parts of the world has its pleasures but, if I'm doing my job properly, it involves a lot of sitting around in hotels getting bored, waiting for something to happen.'

'Very expensive hotels,' said Carla.

'If it's any consolation, most of my clients are nowhere near as wealthy as you and your husband. Laying down a trail might involve backpacking around India or sleeping rough in Bangkok.'

'What clients?'

'That's confidential,' he said.

'Broad brush.'

Trent considered. 'A battered wife getting away from a controlling husband, a victim of cyberstalking, a whistle-blower being harassed by a multinational.'

'And if they can't afford you?'

'If they're in danger, they can afford me,' said Trent.

'Oh, the nobility!' shot back Carla, clasping her hands together, voice dripping with sarcasm. 'And I suppose scalping my husband subsidises your pro bono cases.'

'You're entitled to think that,' said Trent. He smiled. 'And you'd be right.'

'It's all deductible, honey,' said Renfrew.

Carla gave him a look of contempt that lowered his gaze. 'Assuming you live to file another tax return.'

'It's my job to ensure he does,' said Trent.

'*And if you say so yourself...*' mocked Carla.

'It's a results business,' said Trent. 'I can't run an ad in the paper, so word-of-mouth recommendations depend on my success.'

'Where did you learn your trade?' she demanded. 'Is there a correspondence course?'

'As I told your husband, I've worked most of my life in security and enforcement which has given me a skill set that few possess. The rewards flow from that.'

'Sounds like you don't need the work.'

'I do and I don't,' said Trent. 'The money's irrelevant but if I don't use my skills, I get rusty.'

'Skills? You mean killing people?' Trent didn't answer. 'What's it like, taking a human life? I've always wanted to know...'

'Honey,' said Harry.

'Do you enjoy it?' said Carla, ignoring her husband's warning.

'Killing people?' said Trent.

'Helping battered wives and whistle blowers,' said Carla.

'The only reason I do it,' said Trent.

Carla studied him. 'Something happened, didn't it? Someone you cared about got hurt and you couldn't protect them. Now you're making up for it.'

Trent glanced at the mirror and their eyes locked briefly. 'It's a dangerous world. People get hurt. My job is to mitigate the risks.'

'But you're still taking a risk, right?' said Carla. 'Pretending to be my husband.'

'I make sure I'm prepared,' said Trent. 'That's why I don't take on law breakers or chancers - the risks are too high.'

'Hear that, *David*,' goaded Carla. 'Mr Tyler doesn't think you're a chancer.'

'Cut it out, Carla,' said Renfrew.

'Charlotte,' she corrected.

Trent glanced at him in the passenger seat. 'She's right. Get used to your new name.'

'Don't worry about me,' said Renfrew. 'If I can memorise a trading spreadsheet...'

'So, this false trail you're laying down,' continued Carla, undaunted. 'How are you going to manage posing as me?' No answer from Trent. 'I mean, you're going to look pretty stupid handing over my card for a pair of Manolos. Are you married?'

Trent glanced at her in the driver's mirror. 'No.'

'But you have a female partner, right?' said Carla. Trent didn't answer and Carla construed his silence as confirmation. 'So, what will she be buying with my credit card?'

Trent considered. 'Whatever you'd buy.'

'I buy designer shoes and clothes.'

'I know.'

'How will you know what sizes I take?'

'Did I mention about being prepared?' said Trent.

Carla rounded on her husband. 'Seriously, Harry...'

'David,' said her husband.

'He's got my measurements?'

'Authenticity,' mumbled Renfrew, unable to look at her.

'I feel violated,' she said.

'It'll pass,' said Trent.

'So, what happens if my shoes and clothes don't fit your partner?' she demanded.

'We give them to charity shops,' said Trent.

Carla closed her eyes in dismay. 'And if your other clients are poor, how do you lay a trail without plastic?'

'Everybody has plastic,' said Trent. 'It's not how much you spend but when and where. And, I'll have your iPhones too. So, when I travel, I post pictures of locations to your social media, pose questions about local attractions, even make Facebook friend requests of locals. In fact, unless you're a law enforcement professional, social media is the simplest way of tracking someone's movements.'

'But the professionals follow the money,' she said.

'Always.'

'So, where will you go after Bermuda?'

'I'll move around every three or four days, then check out, go to the airport, pick another destination and go. Hotel and food go on the credit card when I arrive but transport is paid in cash, so there's no-one waiting at the other end.'

'Like our flights tonight?' said Carla. Trent nodded. 'Smart.'

'You can't hide the fact that you've left but finding out where you've gone will be that much harder.'

'How long have you been doing this?'

'Long enough.'

'And before that?'

'Asked and answered.'

'You're from Chicago,' she said. Trent shot her a quizzical glance. 'Your accent. Harry's friend Brad is from Chicago.'

'You have a good ear,' said Trent.

'You meet all sorts in my line of work,' she said. 'I used to be...' She laughed at Trent's raised eyebrow in the mirror. 'Course. You already know. Cubs or Sox?'

'What's that?' said Trent.

'Brad's first question when he meets a fellow Chicagoan.'

'Bears,' said Trent, pulling into Changi Airport long stay car park. He brought the car to a halt in a free bay and turned to face his passengers, handing them each a baseball cap, with no insignia. 'David. Charlotte. Put these on and listen carefully. From now on use your new names and nothing else. Treat it like a performance and stay in character. I shouldn't see you again until we land but if we do bump into each other on the plane, don't speak to me, you don't know me. And aside from when passport control asks you to take it off, keep the cap on at all times until we clear the airport at the other end. And keep your heads down. Most of the cameras are above you. Understood?' They nodded.

'When we arrive at the destination, I've hired a car and I'll drive you from there. Accommodation has been paid six months in advance and a local bank account has been opened for you with a healthy balance and a cash card in your new name. No credit cards - you pay for everything in cash and when you run out, go to the ATM and get more. ATMs have cameras so, as added security, wear caps and sunglasses whenever you make a withdrawal.

'You'll have two basic, pay-as-you-go burner phones for communicating between the two of you *only*. Nothing with GPS. Avoid texting if you can but, if you absolutely must, stay in character - you never know who might read them. Don't use the phones for any other purpose and, whatever you do, don't call *anybody* from your old life in case their comms are being monitored. And that does mean anybody - parents, work colleagues, best friends - everyone. For their sakes as much as yours. Understood.' Another nod.

'Stay off the internet at all costs. No exceptions. That means don't get cute and buy a laptop, a smart phone or go to an internet café. No emails and no checking social media because you'll leave a trail. Believe me when I tell you, everything you've ever done on the net has been logged which means everything there is to know about you is known because *you* volunteered the information. What you watched on YouTube, what you bought, hobbies, relationships, travel, porn - everything is archived in your digital history. If people knew what data tech companies held on them, there'd be uproar.

'Finally, live modestly, avoid restaurants and bars and do *not* get drunk in public and even at home, take care. Don't go to or throw any parties. If anybody calls at the house and asks you questions try to be relaxed but don't volunteer information either. Without being hermits, you're trying to live quietly and not draw attention.'

'Be difficult with my wife,' said Renfrew, risking a wry smile at her. 'Carla stands out in any crowd.'

'Charlotte!' said Trent and Carla in unison.

'Charlotte,' repeated Renfrew, throwing up his hands. 'Go easy. I'm an old man.'

'You'll adjust,' said Trent. 'Teaching new tricks to old dogs is just a matter of training. And if this was easy, you wouldn't need me. One more thing. When you start hankering after your old life, remember, you're not going to prison here. Most people would give their right arm for the life you're about to lead.'

'I've earned it,' said Renfrew.

'No argument here,' said Trent. 'So, embrace it and get used to living to a different rhythm. Last thing - here are your tickets.' He handed them to Harry and opened the car door. 'Okay, let's move with a purpose. I've left it late because the less time you spend mooching around the Departure Lounge the better.'

Trent removed the two cases from the trunk and handed them to Harry, who set off towards Departures.

'See you in...' Carla looked down at her ticket. 'Nice. I've never been to the South of France before.'

'That's the idea.'

She managed a weak smile and turned to follow her husband but turned back a second later. 'You're not going to Bermuda, are you?'

'No,' said Trent. 'I've been before and I didn't like it.'

'And your name isn't Tyler, is it?'

Trent smiled enigmatically and turned his attention to packing his bulging rucksack into a small travel case.

3

Sunday, March 31ˢᵗ - South of France

Ten minutes after leaving Nice Airport in their hired Citroen, Trent turned west onto the A8 autoroute and Harry and Carla Renfrew finally removed their baseball caps. Carla stretched out in the back seat and shook out her mid-length blond hair in the warm breeze blowing down from the Alpes-Maritime foothills.

'Proper warmth,' said Renfrew, closing his eyes to breathe the clean scented air of Provence. 'Makes a change from the condensation of the Red Dot. What do you say, Charlie?'

Carla grunted her appreciation. 'It's nice.'

'Red Dot?' enquired Trent.

'Ex-pat slang for Singapore,' said Renfrew. 'It's small and full of chinks.' He grinned sheepishly. 'A colleague's description, not mine. Brad,' he explained to Carla when she looked over.

'Immature schoolboy,' muttered Carla. Renfrew held her eyes for a moment then returned to staring out at the passing countryside.

The next half-hour was spent in silence as Trent sped along the motorway and his passengers began to droop from fatigue. On an empty stretch, Trent pulled off the autoroute and headed north, towards the hills, and was soon manoeuvring the car along the sinewy roads bisecting the Lac de Saint-Cassien, its waters dotted with small boats. At a junction, Trent turned west again on the D562, Harry and Carla, feeling the effects of two long flights, were now fast asleep.

After a further half-hour, Trent pulled up at a red light in the small medieval village of Seillans. Carla's eyes opened and she sat up to take in her surroundings. Her husband was still fast asleep, slumped against the window. It was mid-morning and the sun gazed down out of a cornflower blue sky. The main road was dotted with pedestrians and, being a Sunday, the village was moderately busy with churchgoers and a sprinkling of early season tourists sitting at tables enjoying the fine spring weather.

When the lights turned green, Trent drove slowly along the single-file road into the centre of the village and parked. He jumped out of the car, beckoning Carla to stay put. She ignored him and took the opportunity to get out and stretch her legs. Opposite the car, a small fountain bubbled with mountain spring water and she crossed the road to dip her hand in and wipe her brow. A grizzled, middle-aged man, wiping down a table outside a café stopped what he was doing and turned to stare at her.

'Bonjour, madam,' he said, smiling.

Carla replied with her sweetest smile. 'Monsieur. Ça va?'

'Bien, merci.' He indicated a chair at an empty table. 'Un café a Chez Bertrand, peut-être?'

Trent returned carrying two baguettes and a bag of croissants, the butter already staining the paper translucent.

The man in the café eyed him with respect and envy. 'Monsieur.'

Trent returned his greeting with a faint nod. 'Let's go,' he said to Carla.

'Au revoir, monsieur,' said Carla. 'Je roule.' The man muttered another pleasantry and bowed, keeping his eyes trained on her until she was back inside the car.

'You speak French?'

'Un peu,' she replied.

'You seem to have made an impression.'

Carla shrugged. 'He's got eyes, hasn't he?'

For the first time, Trent broke into a grin. 'That, he has. Welcome to Seillans, your nearest village. The house is about a mile away.' He handed her the bag of croissants and she broke off a piece to nibble. 'Baker's shop and the café you've seen. There are a couple of each. The village is compact so you'll find the supermarket easily enough but there's a map in your villa, just in case.'

'Villa? Do we have a pool?'

'You have a pool and you have a view. And if you absolutely have to eat out, there's the Hotel Deux Rocs further up the hill, beyond the church.'

'You've eaten there?'

'I have. The food's good.'

'You don't do things by halves, do you?' Trent shrugged. 'Listen. I'm sorry if I sounded...ungrateful before.'

'Forget it,' said Trent. 'It's a huge wrench for you.'

'That's very gracious of you.' She leaned forward and laid a hand on his shoulder. 'Thank you for helping us.'

Trent drove out of the village and the Citroen began to climb again, winding around a hill but, as soon as the car had crested the rise, Trent turned onto a minor road called Chemin de l'Etang, shaded by mature plane trees. He pulled to a halt, indicating a tiny road on the other side of the D19.

'Shortcut into the village if you've a mind to walk or cycle,' he said. 'It's steep but then the whole commune is built on a hillside and it's good exercise.' He set off again but only two hundred metres further on he drew to a halt on a gravel approach, outside an imposing pair of iron gates. Beyond, a steeply descending concrete drive wound down the hillside and out of sight, behind what appeared to be a hacienda-style villa built from honey-coloured stone with a traditional terracotta roof. Insects buzzed around the many flowers and shrubs. A wooden sign on a wall next to a keypad declared the house to be the Villa Jasmin.

'Home sweet home,' mumbled Carla, getting out of the car. 'Wake up, Davey boy. We're here.' Harry Renfrew sat up and rubbed his eyes while Trent jumped out and keyed in a four-digit code and the gates swung silently back.

He manoeuvred the car down the steep drive and around the corner, below the level of the house, pulling up behind an old Fiat 500. The Fiat was parked on the turn-around next to a padlocked garage built into the bowels of the house.

'Ours?' asked Renfrew.

'Keys in the glove,' answered Trent. 'But use sparingly. Village and back, if absolutely necessary. No day trips. You're not insured for obvious reasons. There are bicycles in the garage if you want to look around.'

Harry got out and stretched as Carla walked down the drive towards them. When Trent had retrieved their cases, he nodded to a path snaking through lush vegetation and led them up towards the back of the house. Moments later, they emerged onto a vast, partially-covered patio area, paved with weathered stone flags. The house was built around the patio with the pool as the fourth wall and two wings of the property jutted out to throw a little shelter onto the warm yard on either side.

In one corner, covered by a beamed and tiled awning, sat a dining table and chairs. In another corner, two bleached, wooden sun-loungers stretched out invitingly. Between the sun-loungers and a view of the Provençal hills, falling steeply away to the coast in the far distance, was an azure blue infinity pool, built into the hillside to take advantage of the stunning views. Its waters sparkled in the burnished light and a swallow dipped at speed towards the pool, its surface rippling minutely as its thirst was quenched. Terracotta steps either side of the pool dropped down towards a mature orchard on the land below.

'Wowser!' said Carla, staring out across the vast emptiness of the valley unfolding beneath them, its gnarled surface draped with the impenetrable scrub of the maquis.

'Double it,' said Renfrew. He reached out an arm to his wife and, after a brief hesitation, she nestled into his embrace.

'Impressive,' said Carla, turning to Trent. 'And not another building in view.'

'There are other houses along the road but they're well spaced-out and invisible from the patio so you're very private,' said Trent. 'It's quiet now but the other villas are mostly hired out for the summer so there'll be a procession of tourists until mid-September.'

'So, fewer permanent residents to get to know us,' said Renfrew.

'And fewer suspicions aroused at who you are and what you're doing here,' said Trent.

'Smart.'

'There are French families nearby but a lot of the houses are second homes and obviously they don't go out of their way to mix with a transient population of foreign holiday-makers,' said Trent. 'Pool guy, Monsieur De Vries, calls every Wednesday to do maintenance but that's it. And he speaks English so mind what you say when he's around.'

'How do we get in?' said Carla, staring up at the Mediterranean blue shutters, covering the windows.

'I'm getting in, right now,' said her husband, unbuttoning his shirt and kicking off his shoes.

Trent headed for a coded key box on a side wall and tapped in four numbers. He extracted a set of keys before disappearing back along the garden path to the drive. From the car, he recovered the luggage, including a small canvas holdall, removed from an airport locker on landing, before collecting the Citroen from airport car rental and picking up Harry and Carla at Arrivals.

He climbed the drive to the shaded front door and let himself in then entered a code to turn off the beeping alarm and made his way to the kitchen. He unlocked the door to the patio, unhinged the shutters then fixed them into position with catches, cemented into the wall. Noonday light and warmth streamed into the cool dark room and Carla stepped inside. Trent carried their cases inside and left them at the bottom of a spiral staircase then returned to show Carla around.

'Kitchen,' said Trent, waving an arm. He opened the largest window and its shutters.

'Small kitchen,' she corrected.

'Functional and adequate,' said Trent. 'Do you cook?'

'I get by.'

'You'll probably only use it for preparing salad and chilling wine as you'll spend most of your day outside.' He pointed to a bone-dry canvas sheet on the far side of the pool, three legs protruding beneath it. 'Barbecue over there.'

'Harry will take care of that,' she said.

'Who?' said Trent, throwing open more shutters.

'David,' she answered with a sigh.

'Top of the class,' said Trent, 'As a reward, I'll take you both out to lunch.'

'Your treat?'

'Technically, it's yours but who's counting?'

Trent moved into the vast living space and opened two sets of French windows, before going outside to fix the shutters in place. Harry was still swimming in the pool, groaning with pleasure, his clothes in a heap on a lounger but Carla dutifully followed Trent through the house.

The intense Provencal light streamed into the main room, falling on a pair of vast, comfortable-looking sofas, arranged in a vague L-shape to face a large log burner and a gigantic TV and DVD player off in one corner. A binder sat on a coffee table in front of the sofas.

'All the information you'll need is in the folder - codes for the alarm, key box, local shops and services, emergency telephone numbers and maps,' said Trent. 'Don't bother looking for the Wi-fi code. I had the owners remove the router.'

'Taking no chances,' said Carla.

He nodded towards the staircase. 'Master bedroom with ensuite bathroom is upstairs. There are two further bedrooms on the ground floor but I'll leave you to open those shutters if you prefer to sleep downstairs. If not, keep both sets of bedroom shutters fixed and close all ground floor shutters at night, just in case.'

'In case of what?'

'There are organised gangs on the Riviera who have been known to gas residents in unprotected villas before breaking in to ransack the place.'

'Seriously?'

'It's rare but it happens,' said Trent. 'But, don't worry. Residents on the coast are much wealthier so the gangs don't usually operate this far inland. But better not to take the risk.'

'Count on it,' said Carla.

While she was admiring the view from the French windows, Trent removed two towels from an adjacent cupboard and took them to drop on a sun lounger then unzipped the canvas holdall. He extracted a shopping bag containing three identical cell phones in their boxes as well as a sealed envelope. He handed the envelope to Carla, when she wandered back in from the patio.

'There's a bank card and ten thousand euros in cash in there, save you going to the ATM for a while.'

'You've counted it?' she enquired.

He ignored her and unpacked the three cell phones and plugged them into nearby sockets to charge.

'Three basic cell phones with no GPS, one for each of us. I'll store the other two numbers in the memory of each phone, using your new names. They're basic burners so you need to top up credit if you use them. But try to avoid it, except in emergencies, obviously.'

'Like if I'm running out of shampoo or something,' nodded Carla.

Trent raised an eyebrow and marched to the shadier side of the living space, Carla following. With a sweep of the arm, he indicated the floor-to-ceiling shelves, full of English language books and DVDs. '*David* told me you both like thrillers and detective novels so, I had a bunch delivered. Apologies if you've already read some of them but there should be enough to keep you going. Top two shelves filled with DVD box sets to while away the nights if you get tired of sitting outside, looking at the stars.'

'Thoughtful,' she said, tilting her head to examine them. 'We don't have a lot of time for TV in Singapore.' She paused. 'Didn't. So, who filled these shelves, left the cash and bought the phones? The owners?'

'That's on a need-to-know basis,' said Trent.

'So, not the owners. Which means someone else knows we're here, besides you. Can we trust them?'

'I arranged everything,' he said. 'You can trust me.'

Carla was about to press him further but Harry walked through the French windows in wet boxers, rubbing a towel through his greying mane. 'Fantastic pool. And what a view. This is alright,' he said, after a few seconds adjusting to the light. 'Rustic, simple and private. Not what we're used to but I've always had a hankering for the simple life, eh, Charlotte?'

'We have a choice?' she said, making an effort to be surly.

'She loves it,' grinned Harry, winking at Trent. 'I don't know about anyone else but I'm bloody famished. Anything to eat?'

'There's a case of wine and some basic foods in the kitchen but if you unpack and change, I'll drive you down to the village for lunch.'

'You're on,' said Renfrew.

Trent indicated the stairs and watched Harry climb

around the corner to the bedroom with the cases, while Carla kept her eyes locked on Trent.

'Better hurry,' said Trent. 'It's a popular restaurant. And empty your suitcases, please. I need them for my travels.'

TRENT FINISHED SETTING up the cell phones and pocketed the one with both Charlotte and David's numbers on speed dial. His number was on both of theirs. He put one of the chargers in his bag and went to the downstairs bathroom to throw cold water on his face and freshen up. Extracting a pair of canvas shorts from his rucksack, he changed quickly, then pulled a large DVD box set from the canvas holdall. He checked that Megan had already inserted a 256-megabyte digital card then attached a powerful new battery to the leads to activate the motion sensor.

Placing the box set on the shelf of DVDs, he adjusted the case to ensure the camera lens was facing the vast room and, beyond, the window of a downstairs bedroom, visible through the doorway. Satisfied that the Renfrews were unlikely to open a boxset of black and white Polish war films, he waved a hand across the little black dot on the spine to store the first photograph to the memory.

Finally, Trent extracted an oily rag from the holdall and unwrapped the gun, ejecting the clip to confirm it was fully loaded and the action smooth. As requested, Megan had stripped and serviced the weapon before returning it to the airport locker so Trent rewrapped the gun in the rag and found a suitable hiding place behind the water tank.

He then did a circuit of the house, testing the shutters from the outside, pleased that most of them squeaked when the handles were turned and the screens opened. The window locks were basic but would deter all but the most determined housebreakers although if Russian gangsters found out where the Renfrews were hiding, no amount of window locks could save them.

.   .   .

HARRY DESCENDED the stairs dressed in rich man's casuals -
Calvin Klein khaki shorts, light green Gap polo shirt and
Conker Marine deck shoes, as though preparing for a week
on a yacht at Cowes. Trent spotted an angry-looking purple
birthmark on his calf so he tossed him a tube of sun block.'

'Thanks,' said Harry. 'I burn like a crisp.'

'Did you get a chance to follow my advice before we left
Singapore?'

'Two lessons,' said Harry.

'Let's hope it's enough.' Trent moved to the downstairs
toilet and, reaching around the water tank, withdrew the
oiled rag concealed behind it. He revealed the pistol and
turned the gun in his hand. 'This is just a point and fire
weapon, so you should be fine.'

'Aren't they all?'

'Yes and no,' said Trent, handing him the gun. 'Sig Sauer
P229 Legion Compact, single action with a custom grip. Feel
the weight.'

Harry took the gun and moulded his hand to it. 'Feels
good. And it's light enough for Car...Charlotte.'

'That's up to you,' said Trent. 'If you think she won't be
freaked out then tell her about it but, if you do, you'll have to
teach her the basics. Watch carefully.' He took the gun back
and ejected the magazine noiselessly then pushed it back
into the butt. 'It's been stripped and serviced, so I know it
works.'

'How did you get it through airport security?'

'I didn't,' said Trent. 'You shouldn't need it but it's good
to know it's there. It fires 9mm ammunition and takes a ten-
round magazine. Not a lot of bullets so don't waste your
shots but, as you won't be robbing any banks, that should be
plenty.'

'If I have to rob a bank, I'd use a computer,' said Harry.

'Too much information,' said Trent. 'Here. Get used to
the low-profile, slide catch lever and try the thumb safety.'

Harry took the gun and fingered the levers, ejected and
reloaded the magazine. With the safety off, he spread his

legs to mimic a firing position then, grinning, raised the gun to Trent's chest.

A split-second later, Trent's body speared towards Harry's stout torso, pushing up the gun arm, bending his wrist back in the same motion. Simultaneously, the heel of his right hand jammed into Harry's chin, sending him reeling backwards before he fell in a heap on the tiles six feet away, the gun stripped from his hand. Trent thumbed the safety back on, rewrapped the gun in the rag and returned it to its hiding place, while Harry lay shocked on the floor.

'Fuck,' spat Renfrew, sitting up, shock turning to anger. He dabbed his tongue for signs of blood.

'Lesson three,' said Trent. '*Never* point a loaded gun at someone unless you're prepared to shoot them.'

Harry's face was like thunder. 'I bit my fucking tongue,' he complained, dabbing fingers on it. 'I've fired people who've only dreamt of doing that to me.'

Trent bent down, smiling inscrutably at his red-faced client, and held out a hand to assist him. 'Lucky I'm not an employee.' Harry glared back until, finally, his features cracked and he accepted the helping hand, pulling himself to his feet and brushing himself down.

He managed a chuckle. 'That was pretty impressive.'

'Muscle memory,' said Trent. 'Luckily, I had a split-second to soften the blow or we'd be picking your teeth off the floor.'

'I don't doubt it,' grinned Renfrew.

Carla appeared at the bottom of the stairs, dressed all in white, her damp blonde highlights just touching her shoulders, long legs flowing from a short cotton skirt into a pair of canvas pumps. A cotton V-neck T-shirt and a wide brim, floppy sun-hat completed the ensemble and she posed for approval as both men turned.

'There's my girl. You married, Trent?'

'Asked and answered,' said Trent.

'Well, I heartily recommend it,' said Renfrew.

'That makes one of us,' sneered Carla.

'Oh, baby,' leered Renfrew. 'You know how to turn me on.'

THE SUN'S arc was waning when Trent skirted Nice airport and pulled the Citroen onto the Promenade Des Anglais, heading for the old town. Ten minutes later, he turned left onto Avenue de Verdun and drove down the ramp into the underground car park, adjacent to the seafront Meridien Hotel.

On the first-floor lobby, Trent produced a passport and credit card, both in the name of Moss Tyler and made his way to his sixth-floor room. He opened and emptied all the alcohol miniatures into the sink then took out his new cell phone and tapped out a long number from memory. The other end picked up on the first ring.

'Megan.'

'Mike. Everything go okay?'

'By the numbers,' said Trent.

'Good. Resources?'

'All good, thanks.'

'The phones are basic model and I serviced and loaded the gun.'

'I noticed.'

'How are Mr and Mrs Renfrew handling it?'

'Adjusting better after seeing the pool.'

'I'm not surprised. It's a great spot. How did you find it?'

'I stayed there once, a long time ago.'

'When?'

'After I left the Bureau. I needed to re-evaluate, recharge. Clear my mind.'

'And did it work?'

Trent hesitated. 'Of course.'

'And now?'

'Now, I'm tired after two long flights in coach.' He

smiled, anticipating her reaction to the change of subject. 'But the sun's helping with that.'

'Oh, is it? Well, it's pissing down here in London, thanks for asking. You're at the hotel?'

'Just arrived.'

A sigh. *'I'd kill for an evening stroll along the Promenade and a swim in the bay.'*

'No such luck. I've got passport photos to change then it's an early night for me. I've got a morning flight back to London and should be there by lunchtime.'

'Excellent. I'll get my comfy shoes on for hitting the shops.' Trent didn't answer. *'Unless there are complications?'*

'Not really.'

'You don't sound too sure.'

'I have a bad feeling about this one.'

'You always say that. Something wrong?'

'I'm just worried.'

'About what?'

'If your background on Renfrew is right, this one could be rough. Russian gangsters don't take prisoners.'

'Nothing you can't handle, Mike.'

'There's always a second time.'

'Then go back and keep an eye on them. I'll cancel the London end.'

'No. Get to the hotel but book in as Wendy. I don't want you taking any chances. Cash deposit for both rooms and I won't start the paper trail until you're safely on your way.'

'Understood. How long?'

'Four nights should do it. And wear a hat where there might be cameras.'

'I've done this before, Mike.'

'I know but...'

'Where?'

'St Pancras Renaissance. Two adjacent suites, if you can get them. Make up a name for the second one.'

'Whoop whoop! Having it large. Beats a roach-infested two-star in Bangkok.'

'That it does. Enjoy the suite tonight but *don't* overdo the mini-bar. Busy day tomorrow.'

'You're no fun.'

'This is news?' he laughed. 'I'll text my ETA. Make sure you bring the usual gear.'

'It'll be there.'

Trent rang off but tapped the phone against his chin. He held his thumb over one of the two stored numbers. A second later, he shook his head, closed the handset and threw it on the bed.

4

1st April 2019 - London, England

Trent jogged up the stone steps and under the lofty arch into the lobby of the St Pancras Renaissance Hotel, carrying Renfrew's monogrammed suitcases - tape removed to display the initials. He'd stayed at the Renaissance before but its gothic splendour always impressed as it loomed imperiously over St Pancras and Kings Cross railway stations. The once-derelict red-brick building had been near to demolition several times but, happily, its listed buildings had been saved from the wrecking ball and it had been lovingly restored as a luxury hotel and a haven of calm at the heart of one of the busiest transport hubs in the country.

He marched through into the magnificent vaulted cathedral of the Hansom Lounge, where guests whiled away time over coffee and cakes, spending much of it staring up at the magnificent ceiling girders and marvelling at its post-industrial chic. Trent spotted Megan immediately, dutifully lingering over a pot of coffee, dark glasses covering her hazel eyes beneath a floppy sun hat, hair fanning out across her shoulders.

Trent pulled out Renfrew's smartphone, turned it on and took a couple of photographs of the lobby for posting on Harry's Facebook page then advanced towards her until it was clear she'd spotted him. With barely a glance in his direction, Megan uncrossed her legs and headed smartly towards the reception desk. Trent followed, standing directly behind her.

'Hi. I'm Wendy Wyatt,' she said, addressing the eager young man behind the counter.

'Yes, Ms Wyatt,' he replied, tapping her details into a computer. 'How can I help?'

'I booked adjacent suites yesterday but I'm afraid my friends have let me down and won't be coming after all, so I'm going to have to cancel the second suite, if that's okay.'

'They were supposed to be staying in the Haywood Suite, yes?'

'Correct.'

'Mr and Mrs Ford.'

'That's them. They can't make it. Their daughter's ill.'

'Sorry to hear that. But you're staying with us for the next three nights, yes?'

'I certainly am.'

'And how are you enjoying your stay?'

'Loving it,' she said. 'It's a remarkable building.'

'Excellent,' said the young man. 'That's all done for you, Miss Wyatt. I've cancelled the Hayward for the next three nights though I'm afraid I can't refund anything for last night.'

'Their loss.' Megan sauntered away with a disinterested glance at Trent, who stepped up to the desk.

'Yes, sir,' enquired the young man, turning his attention to him.

'I'm sorry, I don't have a booking but I've been recommended your hotel and I was wondering if the Hayward suite might be available for a few nights. A friend tells me he wouldn't stay anywhere else.'

The receptionist raised an eyebrow in surprise. 'It *is* available, sir.' He grinned. 'As of thirty actual seconds ago, Mr...'

Trent snapped a credit card onto the counter. 'Renfrew. Harry Renfrew.'

AFTER COLLECTING his key and leaving his cases for the porter, Trent followed Megan through the bar and out onto the upper concourse of St Pancras Station. When she sat on a bench, he joined her and handed her a large padded envelope from his jacket, which she put quickly in her tote bag without opening it.

'Mrs Renfrew's credit cards with codes, passport, iPhone, iPad, social media accounts. Take a few snaps of the hotel to post on her Facebook and Instagram before you go. I've included a few brands she likes plus her sizes...'

'Shoes?'

'38.'

Megan's mouth creased in a lop-sided smile. 'Well, there's a happy coincidence.'

'Don't go in too heavy.'

Megan raised an eyebrow at him. 'Moi?' She checked the passport. 'You've changed the photo?'

'Good to go. So, did Wendy empty the mini-bar last night?'

'Mike, you wound her,' said Megan, clutching her chest with both hands. 'She's not that kind of girl.'

'She has her moments,' said Trent.

'Where to from here? Somewhere blisteringly hot, I hope.'

'Don't pack your bikini yet,' said Trent.

'How can I, I haven't bought it yet.' Megan winked at him and gestured towards Searcy's brasserie. 'Do you have time for lunch?'

'I'd better set up. Renfrew's credit card details are winging their way around the system as we speak. So, you liked the French villa?'

'Ve-ry nice. Just wish I could have hung around for a few days. That's quite some view. Have you stashed someone there before?' Trent looked at her. 'Come on, Mike. The Rappeneau woman didn't turn a hair when I dropped 60k in folding money onto her lap.'

'You see, it's this attention to detail that makes me employ you,' he said.

'Sweet talk me off the subject, why don't you?'

'There's nothing to tell,' said Trent. 'The Rappeneaus are being well compensated to ask no questions and what they don't know can't hurt them.'

'That wasn't my question.'

'All you need to know is, *if* we put this to bed early, the place is all yours until September.'

'Music to my frost-bitten ears.' She gazed inquisitively at him. 'And there it is again.'

'What?'

'That look. You're worried about this one.'

'The richer the client...'

'The higher the stakes, yeah, I know.' She stared at the ground. 'I did all the research, Mike. Everything checked out.'

'I'm not doubting you,' said Trent. 'But you can never cover all the bases. Our work is labour intensive because we have to physically go where our clients would and that always leaves a trail. You and I are going to be on film somewhere - airports, motorways, banks, high-end retail outlets - and no amount of hats, sunglasses, fake IDs and untraceable cells can hide us from view. We *will* leave traces we can't erase and top-end professionals will find them if they look hard enough.'

'You're at the sharp end, Mike,' she said. 'If you don't think I've done the risk assessment properly, we can walk away.'

'I didn't say that,' said Trent. 'I know how thorough you are.' He smiled to reassure her. 'Besides, we're committed. I just want you to be extra vigilant. Any problems or if *anything* feels wrong or suspicious, leave a message on the notice board or WhatsApp me on my cell.'

Megan nodded. 'Always. Speaking of research, Renfrew is British. He'd say mobile not cell.'

Trent shrugged. 'He's a long-time ex-pat which muddies the waters on vocab.' Megan raised an eyebrow. 'But I'll keep it in mind. Key?'

Megan dipped into her bag and handed over her room key. 'A perfectly good suite sitting empty for three nights. I could weep.'

'That's the play,' said Trent. 'If only you could console yourself with a few thousand pounds worth of high-end designer goods.'

She stood, grinning. 'My exit line.'

'Where did you put...?'

'In the safe. Usual code.'

'Would it kill you to memorise four different numbers?'

'Yes,' she said, kissing him on the cheek and turning to leave. 'Wishing you a very dull stay.'

'Fingers crossed.'

'And let me know when and where my bikini is required.'

'Alaska, okay?'

'Don't you dare.'

Trent laughed. 'Megan!' he said, his smile disappearing. 'Watch your six.'

'I always watch my back, Mr Renfrew.'

'Call me Harry.'

She leaned in to whisper in his ear. 'Well, Harry, as you're keen on taking care, perhaps posing as a British bond trader, you should ditch the Desert Storm banter.'

'Copy that,' retorted Trent with a wink. She frowned, aimed an imaginary gun at him and strolled back towards the hotel lobby to take a few photographs with Carla Renfrew's iPhone.

Trent followed her progress until she was out of sight, aware of admiring glances from the men she passed.

ARRIVING IN THE HAYWARD SUITE, Trent spent a diligent five minutes emptying the alcohol from the minibar into the sink then re-filling the bottles with water to discourage replacement by hotel staff. Next, he opened his mono-grammed case and scattered a few clothes around the room, before going next door and letting himself into Megan's adjacent rooms. A sturdy briefcase lay on the bed. Trent tilted it back and selected the usual settings on the security locks to open it and remove a laptop and a large, zip-up bag. After booting up the laptop, he returned to his own suite with the zip-up bag.

Within twenty minutes, a mixture of microphones and mini-cameras, hidden in everyday objects such as air fresh-eners and picture frames, were placed around the various rooms to ensure maximum coverage. Then he turned on Renfrew's iPhone again and, after entering the passcode, posted the pictures he'd taken in the lobby to Renfrew's Facebook page with a suitable comment.

Returning to Megan's adjoining suite, Trent logged on to the laptop and checked the set-up of his spyware. After popping next door to make a few minor adjustments, he was satisfied and returned to Megan's suite, where he repeated his ritual with the minibar. Eating a polished apple from the fruit bowl, he located the safe, keyed in the four-numbered code and extracted his trusty Glock. He checked the maga-zine was full, then replaced it in the safe.

With nothing to do but wait, he spent an hour doing some strength exercises before returning to the St Pancras concourse for a late lunch.

5

April 25th 2019 - Seillans

Carla opened her eyes to the grey light of early morning and saw the pillow beside her was empty. She lifted her head to see Harry standing at the window in his boxers, staring out into the trees, a pair of binoculars raised to his eyes.

'Harry?' said Carla, softly.

Renfrew was startled and lowered the binoculars. 'Did I wake you?'

'No. What are you looking at?'

'Nothing.'

'You're looking at nothing through binoculars?'

Harry smiled. 'There was a deer. It's gone.'

'How long have you been up?' she said, yawning.

'Not long,' he said. 'Lots to do before the party so making an early start.'

'Doing what?'

'Cleaning the barbecue, working out what food to buy, picking up a few cases of very posh grog...'

'Christ, how many have you invited?' said Carla.

'Four, including the two shirt lifters from Surrey...'

Carla frowned. 'Please tell me you won't say that in front of them.'

Harry grinned. 'Would I?'

'Yes, you bloody well would.' Harry laughed. 'I'm not sure about this, Harry. Tyler told us to keep our heads down. He specifically said we shouldn't be throwing parties.'

'Come on, Charlie, we deserve some fun.'

'Didn't we draw enough attention to ourselves at the Deux Rocs the other night?'

'There is no excuse for quaffing cheap champagne,' said Harry. 'None. And it's not a party. It's just a few drinks with neighbours. That's all.'

'Fine. But do we need to do a shop for four guests?'

'Those Brussels Sprouts you invited, makes six.'

'The Willems have got young children,' said Carla. 'Even if they come, they won't stay long. We've got plenty of booze in the house.'

Harry shook his head. 'It's not the amount, it's the quality. I want to make a good impression.'

'I thought that's what I was for.'

'Always, darling. But if our guests see our shitty little car, they might start thinking they're wealthier than us and I can't have that.'

Carla sighed. 'One day we're going to have a long conversation about your childhood.'

'Yes, mother.'

Carla threw back the duvet. 'I'll make coffee.'

'No, I'll do it,' said Harry, pulling on a T-shirt and padding towards the stairs. 'You get some more beauty sleep. Save your energy for the bread run.'

Carla waited for the noise of Harry unfastening the kitchen shutters before jumping out of bed and going to look out of the bedroom window. She picked up the binoculars and scoured the dense vegetation on the other side of the Chemin de l'Etang but there was nothing to see but trees.

6

Thursday May 2nd 2019 - Villa Jasmin, Seillans

The old man pulled his white van to the gates of Villa Jasmin and stepped out, frowning. For the second day running, the Butlers had left the gates closed and unless he could gain access to water them, some of the saplings in the orchard wouldn't survive. And, after eight days, the pool's skimmer and pump baskets would be filling up with debris. If they weren't emptied weekly, problems with the filters would quickly follow. Expensive problems.

He pressed the intercom button. 'Madame Butler. It's Monsieur De Vries.' No answer. He knew the entry code but etiquette demanded he announce himself to the occupants first. A couple of years ago, he'd marched up the path to the patio unbidden and caught an Italian couple screwing on a sun bed. Understandably they, and Madame Rappeneau, had been furious.

After considering his options, he tapped the code into the keypad. Seconds later, the gates swung silently back and De Vries gathered equipment and chemicals from his van and marched to the front door to press the buzzer. After a couple of minutes waiting, he pressed a button to close the gates and marched down the hill to the underground garage. The shabby little Fiat was parked in the shade thrown by the house so De Vries called out. 'Monsieur Butler? Madame Butler?'

A minute later, carrying his equipment, he was on the small path at the rear of the property, climbing warily up to the patio, listening for the noise of occupation. 'Madame Butler?'

A fly hit him on the forehead. Then another. And another.

SERGEANT DANIEL AUGER jumped out of his Peugeot outside the walls of Villa Jasmin and pressed the intercom button. He took a moment to run his eye over the rusting white Renault van parked in front of the gates then fumbled for the scribbled note, giving details of the call.

'Monsieur De Vries,' he mumbled, scratching his three-day beard. Staring at the bars of the gate, he contemplated the best route to climb over then noticed an elderly man near the bend where the drive disappeared below the house. At the edge of the bleached concrete, a border wall of large stones held soil and vegetation at bay and the man sat on a large flat boulder, head down, hand to mouth, unaware of the watching gendarme.

The man was in his sixties, at least - grey-haired and unshaven, wearing a grubby T-shirt, cut-off denim shorts and cheap white trainers with white socks pulled halfway up each calf. His legs and arms sported the kind of deep tan only outdoor work could inflict but, at this moment, a tan was the last thing on the old man's mind and he seemed dazed. A second later, hands clamped against his thighs, he vomited hard onto the drive.

'Monsieur?' called Auger, when he'd finished.

The old man looked up, face white as the concrete. He

picked up a battered straw hat from an adjacent boulder and hauled himself to his feet, tottering towards the gate.

'Monsieur De Vries?'

'Oui,' replied the old man in a foreign accent, croaking out the word through a throat assailed by stomach acid. Near the gate, he drooped against a button on the internal wall and the electric gates began to swing open. 'Gendarmes?'

'Exacte. English, monsieur?'

The man spat remnants of his stomach contents onto the soil next to the drive. 'South African.'

'How did you get in?' asked Auger.

'I have the code. I don't usually enter unannounced but I was worried. I maintain the pool, water the gardens, that sort of thing. I should've done it yesterday but they didn't answer. When they didn't answer today, I let myself in.' His eyes glazed over as his brain reacquainted him with what greeted his arrival.

'*They*?'

'Mr and Mrs Butler. English couple, staying here.'

'Owners?'

'Long-term rental. Been here about a month. Nice people. She...' He shook his head and lowered his eyes. Despite the heat of late morning sun, he began to shiver.

Auger took pity. 'Where?'

De Vries jabbed a thumb over his shoulder. 'Back of the house.'

'Here,' said Auger, touching an arm to guide the old man back to his van, sitting him down on the driver's seat. He located a bottle of water from his car and unscrewed the cap, handing it to De Vries. 'Drink.' The old man positioned his mouth around the neck of the bottle and took a grateful swallow before puffing out his cheeks and reaching for a packet of Gauloises on the passenger seat.

Returning to the Peugeot, Auger removed his uniform jacket and took out his SP2022 service revolver from the glove box and set off down the drive.

. . .

COMMANDANT SERGE BENOIT, of the Police Judiciaire, sat back from a plate of sardine skeletons, lit a cigarette and gazed in forensic detachment at the shaking in his right hand as he ignited the tobacco. He transferred the cigarette to his left hand and gazed out across the glittering bay from his apartment balcony, squeezing his disobedient hand to dispel the trembling.

Spring had given way to early summer and the citizens of Nice were coming out to play and, when he wasn't plunging into the sea himself, Benoit loved to watch his fellow Niçoises enjoying the beach or conveying themselves along the Promenade des Anglais by foot, rollerblade or bicycle.

Unknown to the parade of strangers beneath his balcony, each and every one of them had played a role in Benoit's recovery from a spiralling depression. After a disaffected French-Tunisian criminal had driven a truck into Bastille Day revellers on a balmy night in July, three years before, killing eighty-six men, women and children and seriously injuring many more, Benoit's memories of walking amongst the dead that night had overwhelmed him.

For months, he was haunted by the sights he'd seen, unable to make sense of the carnage, the senseless loss of life. It didn't help that he had personally attended two dozen funerals, fully immersing himself in the grief of his city until, finally, he shut himself away in his apartment, curtains fixed, day and night, to block out the site of the atrocity.

Unable to move on with his life, Benoit had even felt compelled to place his beloved apartment on the market to get away from a city he adored. Situated in the Fabron district of Nice, his apartment may have been nearer the airport than deemed acceptable by the fashionable set but Benoit had always loved the earthier feel of a real neighbourhood where generations of Niçoises had yet to be tempted away by ludicrous property prices.

Just half a mile east, towards the old town, Benoit's two bed, sea-view apartment would cost ten times what he'd paid for it five years ago. Fortunately, in the aftermath of the attack, there'd been no takers and it was difficult now to believe there had ever been a time when he might have abandoned the home he loved.

Instead, Benoit had been forced to confront his emotional problems head-on and, one evening, he discovered he had thousands of unknown allies aiding his recovery - his fellow Niçoises.

Watching them throw themselves back into their own lives every minute of every day, it dawned on Benoit that the sure way to let the terrorists win was to turn his back on the pleasures Nice and, indeed, life had to offer.

Shutting himself away to brood about the horrors of that night was the certain path to self-destruction and Benoit had finally been able to see the folly of such a course and turn his life around. Not that he'd ever forget the things he'd seen that night or the profound sense of loss and violation he'd felt. The emotions he'd experienced would never leave him and were still capable of stealing a night's sleep but, three years on, he had brokered some kind of peace with himself.

So, he watched the real heroes of his retreat from the abyss, strangers oblivious to their role, enjoying the warm spring weather and raised a silent toast to them.

He finished his cigarette and stood to clear away his lunch plate, glancing at the For-Sale sign, wedged behind a pot planter at the far end of his balcony, kept to remind him of those dark days. That, and the tremor in his right hand, were his only mementoes of that terrible night.

The telephone rang. *'Commandant Benoit.'*

He recognised the voice. 'Pierre?'

'I have Directeur Seigner on the line.'

'I'm on a week's leave,' said Benoit. 'She approved it.'

'Should I tell her you're unavailable?'

Benoit smiled. 'No.'

A moment later. *'Serge.'*

'Valerie.'

'I hope you're well rested.' Benoit didn't waste time with a reply. *'I need you and your team right away.'*

'Where?'

'Seillans. It's a small village in the Var foothills.'

'I know it. A bit off the beaten track for our skill set, isn't it?'

'Organised criminals and terrorists respect no boundaries. How soon can you be there?'

'I can be there in under two hours but I can't speak for the rest of my squad. They're scattered to the four winds.'

'Get yourself there and take charge. Now. I'll round up your team for you.'

NINETY MINUTES LATER, Benoit pulled his Citroen onto a small road called the Chemin de l'Etang, a kilometre or two beyond the picturesque medieval commune of Seillans. At a hastily erected checkpoint, a short, middle-aged bald man was arguing with the gendarme on duty. Benoit flashed his ID and the officer saluted before moving the barrier to let his car pass. The bald man took a step towards the Villa Jasmin but the officer put an arm across his path and the argument continued. Benoit drove on towards the gates where another gendarme greeted his arrival.

'Auger?' said Benoit.

'Yes, Commandant Benoit,' said Auger, raising his arm to salute.

'Make that the last time you salute me,' said Benoit, stepping out of his car and pulling on a pair of latex gloves from a carton on the back seat. 'Report.'

'This morning, I answered a report of suspicious deaths, here at the villa. I investigated and found two dead bodies - one male, one female. I think.'

'You think?' Benoit held his eye for a beat. 'And the call?'

'Came from an employee of Villa Jasmin. Monsieur De

Vries, a South African,' added Auger, before Benoit could enquire.

'He discovered the bodies?' Auger nodded. 'You know him?'

'Not personally,' said Auger. 'But he's lived in the community for over a decade. He tends gardens and maintains swimming pools. Lives alone, respectable, law-abiding.'

'And the bodies?'

Auger hesitated. 'De Vries said an English couple were staying here but he couldn't identify them. They're in the pool and...well, you'll see.' He took a deep breath.

'You didn't compromise the scene.'

'As far as that was possible.'

'What does that mean?'

'A lot of evidence is invisible to the eye these days, no?'

Benoit nodded. 'Did you enter the house?'

'Only to check for further victims. A quick sweep but it was empty.'

'You touched nothing?'

'Not so much as a door handle, sir. The place was wide open. I came straight back to the gate, called it in and established a perimeter to preserve the scene for FFP.'

'Good work,' said Benoit, donning a protective suit. He looked across to an old man, wearing a battered straw hat, sitting in a police car, head bowed. A can of Orange Fanta sat nestled between his bare legs. 'De Vries?'

'Yes, sir.'

'The Fanta was a good idea. Yours?'

'Yes, sir,' said Auger. 'Shock depletes blood sugar.'

'Have you taken a statement?'

'I got the bare bones but he was in no condition,' said Auger.

'Then organise a DNA swab and fingerprinting for tomorrow and get someone to drive him home. He's of no use here and will be in shock for a while. We can interview him later but, for now, impress upon De Vries that he is *not* to give out details of what he's seen to *anyone*.'

'He lives alone, sir,' said Auger, beckoning over a young female colleague. 'Costanza, drive Monsieur De Vries home.'

'And make sure he's okay before you leave him,' said Benoit.

'Sir?' enquired the dark-eyed gendarme.

'Put him in a chair,' said Benoit. 'With delayed shock, people can collapse and hurt themselves.'

Costanza saluted. 'Sir.'

A shout from along the road caused Benoit to turn towards the short bald man striding towards them, a gendarme in his wake.

'Who's that?'

'The village's newly-elected mayor,' said Auger, under his breath. 'Monsieur Ruggieri.'

'Sir, you can't be here,' said Benoit, stepping towards the mayor.

Ruggieri came to a halt, held out a hand which Benoit shook. 'Carmine Ruggieri,' he said, allowing himself a pompous sniff of self-regard. 'Maire de Seillans.'

'Commandant Benoit, Serious Crime Squad.'

'Why have you closed the road, Commandant?'

'I didn't.'

'Aren't you in charge here?' said Ruggieri.

Benoit smiled. 'I am now.'

'Then you can't just close a road without permission, you know.'

'Actually, I can,' said Benoit. 'Now, I'm a little busy and this is a crime scene.'

'And the barriers?' said Ruggieri.

'The barriers stay,' said Benoit. 'And you stand on the other side of them. Thank you.'

'I beg your pardon. Did I mention who I am?'

'This is a crime scene, monsieur,' said Benoit. 'If President Macron turned up, he'd be on the other side of those barriers. Auger escort Monsieur Ruggieri away from the crime scene.'

'This way, sir,' said Auger, holding out an arm.

'I know the way,' said Ruggieri, scowling at Auger. 'But you haven't heard the last of this, Commandant.'

'I dare say,' said a disinterested Benoit. Auger tried to suppress a smile as Ruggieri turned on his heel and stalked angrily away.

'You mentioned Forensics?' said Benoit.

'FFP are on their way from Cannes,' said Auger. 'This isn't normal for Seillans. There's a small facility in Draguignan but I don't think it can cope.'

'Your call,' said Benoit, retrieving his gun from the glovebox and holstering it. 'See that no-one else comes through the gate until Forensics or my people get here.' He set off down the steep drive.

'Mind the vomit,' called Auger. Benoit glanced back. 'De Vries lost his breakfast.'

'Did you?'

'Didn't have any.'

Benoit nodded then stepped off the driveway to the sheltered front door, visible from the gate. It was solid oak with ornate iron fittings, including a lever handle, which Benoit tried. It was locked so he resumed his unhurried trudge down the hill.

Rounding the corner of the drive where the house and surrounding shrubbery provided more shade, he saw an elderly Fiat 500, parked outside the closed doors of an underground garage at the end of the drive. The garage was also locked, the car wasn't.

'Not the vehicle of choice at most million-euro properties,' muttered Benoit. *And not a car an English couple, who can afford to rent an exclusive hillside villa in the Riviera, would have driven from the UK.*

Unable to go further on concrete, Benoit spotted the overgrown path, marked by smaller stones, snaking up an incline through lush foliage towards the rear of the house.

He paused to listen, his hearing not the only sense on high alert. He could already smell death, that sickly-sweet odour of decay suffusing and ripening the turgid warm air, intermingled with that coppery note of old blood.

He started up the path and a moment later emerged onto a spacious, partially-covered patio, baking in the afternoon heat. The patio was paved with large stone flags, shiny with age, bordering three sides of an elevated infinity pool. Beyond the pool the wild Provençal countryside dropped dramatically away towards the coast, the sea shimmering in the sun many kilometres into the distance.

Breaking clear of the tangle of plants and shrubs, Benoit began to notice flies darting at and around his head, butting against his skin, seeking the merest hint of salt to feed on. He waved them away, marching purposefully across the patio, better to observe the angry bare flesh of the bloated remains, bobbing in the scarlet waters of the pool. Two bodies nudged above the surface, buttocks in the air, the discoloured, putrefying flesh spotted with animated black dots. More flies.

Judging from blistering on the skin, the bodies had been in the pool and under the unrelenting sun for several days. And the greater the skin damage, the more the flies were able to lay their eggs under the surface of the cracked dermis. Recalling a forensics course last year, Benoit remembered that within twenty-four hours, eggs laid by flies would develop into pale maggots about the size of the nail on a little finger. These maggots fed ravenously on the rotting flesh around them, storing energy for the next stage of their pupal development - transformation into yet more flies. If he remembered correctly, the whole process - egg to fully-developed fly - took around five days.

Benoit's eyes lingered on the impenetrable murk of the dark red waters, on the bodies in cross-section, where the stumps of necks and wrists revealed the ordeal of victims beheaded and hands severed - a level of violence commonplace in organised crime circles on the coast, whether Italian, Russian or Corsican. But, inflicted on an English couple on holiday in the back of beyond, the butchery seemed extreme and incongruous.

The smell of decay drifted across Benoit's nostrils in waves so, eyes scanning the ground, he skirted the large dried bloodstain along the lengthy side of the pool to get himself upwind of the aroma. He passed shards of blackened viscera and torn scraps of flesh, covered in more flies and suggesting a location for the atrocities visited upon the bodies. Beyond this dried puddle, he re-joined the pool's boundary edge, taking care to avoid the red-black paw prints of a cat, no doubt drawn to the scene by the scraps of flesh on offer after the slaughter.

Stepping gingerly along the pool's newer edging slabs, he moved level with the infinity wall and peered down into the run-off basin a couple of metres below. No bodies or parts of bodies were floating there, as far as he could discern in the churning water.

Benoit rang his lieutenant, Gabriel Latour, to check his progress and flag up what awaited.

'Sounds grim,' said Latour. '*You think the gangs are expanding their territory?*'

'Who knows? How long?'

'*I'll be half an hour yet, boss. Dugrippe's on his way but not sure about the others.*'

After pocketing his phone, Benoit turned his gaze to the house. In front of it, a pair of comfortable-looking sun loungers baked in the heat of the sun trap. There was even a half-empty beer bottle sitting underneath one, a pair of dead flies floating in the beer.

Sweeping his eyes across both storeys, all windows were open - upstairs and down. On the ground floor, lace curtains twitched and billowed in the light breeze that had suddenly picked up to exhale welcome fresh air onto the fragrant hillside.

Benoit checked his gun's clip was full and moved towards the open French windows, his disobedient gun hand supported by the other as he stepped cautiously through the curtains. A quick scan of the property showed it was empty, as Auger had attested. It also seemed to be freakishly clean and orderly. The beds had been stripped and all clothes hanging in the wardrobe smelled freshly laundered.

In the kitchen, lights on the washing machine and dishwasher, betrayed recent use and Benoit opened doors to check there was indeed a full load in each. Whoever had done this deed had endeavoured to remove all trace of their visit. Benoit holstered his gun and returned to the drive to climb back to the gates.

ours after the sun had dropped behind nearby hills, covered head to toe in a protective suit, Benoit stood on the edge of the draining pool, watching similarly-attired FFP Officers sloshing around in ankle-high, scarlet water, the blaze of newly-erected arc lights casting a merciless brilliance over their labours.

In all, eight forensic technicians worked methodically on what needed to be done on the slippery tiled floor below, preparing the bloated corpses for their transfer to reinforced body bags.

Tired, after a long afternoon and evening, Benoit's stomach rumbled despite food being far from his thoughts. He knew there'd never be anything to compare with the images of mothers and children, their bodies mangled and crushed by a truck on the promenade in Nice, but this was certainly up there for stomach-churning gore. And, at least the victims in Nice hadn't roasted under a hot sun for days before he'd walked among them.

Gabriel Latour sidled up to Benoit, brandishing a pair of transparent evidence bags each containing a UK passport. Latour was thirty-one, ten years Benoit's junior, and the pair had nearly thirty years in policing between them. But even such experience could never accustom them to the stench of putrefying flesh and both men breathed through nostrils greased with a eucalyptus-based ointment.

Benoit withdrew first one passport, then the other, thumbing through with difficulty in protective gloves. 'David Butler. Charlotte Butler. These look new.'

'Check the date of issue,' said Latour.

Benoit riffled through the booklets again. 'Six weeks old.' He snaked a glance at Latour. 'Both issued on the same day. Fakes?'

'That would be my guess,' said Latour. 'Good ones too.'

'And fake passports mean fake names.'

'So, maybe the Butlers were hiding something.'

'Or hiding *from* something,' said Benoit, lingering over one of the passport photographs. 'Mrs Butler was very attractive.'

'And twenty years younger than her husband,' said Latour, as though this was somehow significant.

'Exit stamp from Singapore, just after midnight on March 30th,' said Benoit.

'Same in both,' said Latour. 'They must have flown out of Changi Airport.'

'And arrived in Nice thirty-six hours later,' said Benoit, examining the entry stamp for Nice Airport.

'Long flight.'

'Two, probably,' said Benoit. 'There's no entry stamp for Singapore. The Butlers were in Singapore when the passports were acquired.'

'So, they're not British tourists who've driven down from Dover.'

'Not in that clapped-out Fiat,' said Benoit.

'And, no way that piece of shit is an airport rental,' said Latour.

'Maybe it comes with the house,' said Benoit. 'Find out. And get these passport pictures to the Singapore authorities, see if they're known and frame them as persons of interest, for now.' He gestured towards the corpses below their feet. 'Without formal ID, don't mention murder and risk a media shitstorm until we know what we're dealing with.'

Latour held up another plastic bag containing a wallet. Benoit removed the wallet and withdrew a thick wad of brand-new hundred-euro notes before pushing them back and glancing inquisitively at his colleague. 'Three thousand,' said Latour, answering the unspoken question. 'So, theft wasn't a motive.'

'With this level of violence, did you think it was?' said Benoit. Returning his attention to the wallet, he extracted the sole plastic card - a BNP Paribas bank card in the name of David Butler.

'See the expiry date?' said Latour. 'Suggests the account was opened very recently.'

'Any other ID?' said Benoit.

'You're looking at it.'

'Fake passports? Virtually no ID? Want to bet the Butlers didn't exist two months ago? How long have they been at Villa Jasmin?'

'They arrived on the Sunday they landed.'

'So, straight from the airport.' Benoit dropped the passports and wallet back into their separate bags. 'Get prints done on these, top priority. Then cross reference against those found in the house.'

'If any,' said Latour. 'Someone's had a serious clean up in there.'

'Let's hope they missed something.'

'They did,' said Latour. 'We've got a hair brush, two toothbrushes and a pair of razors bagged and on the way to the lab. Plus, a half-finished beer bottle which may yield a further sample.'

'Baseline DNA, at least. Any other useful artefacts?'

'Nothing personal apart from freshly laundered clothes,' said Latour. 'No laptops, iPhones, iPads, diaries, cameras or photographs. Weird, right? In fact, the only devices in the entire place are two brand new cell phones and they're basic model burners for texting each other.'

'It's like someone doesn't want us to know who they are,' said Benoit.

'I've lodged enquiries with the British Embassy and Interpol. Early days but, if the passports *are* fake, we won't find the Butlers on any database.'

'Which means we can't even be sure they're British.'

'Then what's their connection to organised crime?'

'Right now, we can't be sure there is one,' said Benoit.

Latour nodded to the bottom of the pool. 'What else but a gangland hit would look like that?'

'I know,' conceded Benoit. 'But if the Butlers had crossed the mafia, why would the killers take hands and heads?'

'Sending a message?'

'Yes, but to who?' said Benoit. 'The mob making an example of people doesn't work so well with unidentified bodies. Going to these lengths makes no sense.'

'Unless victim ID tells us which gang wanted the Butlers dead.'

'It hasn't stopped them before,' said Benoit. 'Knowing who wanted them gone, won't convict anyone and they must know we'll find out eventually.'

'Ah, but how long is eventually?' said Latour.

Benoit sighed, hankering for a cigarette. 'It just feels wrong for the gangs, that's all.'

'Not when you look at the workload,' said Latour. 'There's a lot gone into this. Physically, I mean.'

'You think multiple killers,' nodded Benoit.

'Definitely,' said Latour. 'Another tick for a gangland hit.'

'Then tell me why they took their heads and hands and left the passports?' said Benoit.

'Another reason to suppose the passports and their IDs are fake.'

Benoit shrugged, unconvinced. 'How are we doing locally?'

'Auger's people are going door-to-to, interviewing neighbours though it's little more than taking names and basic data at this stage.' Latour pointed to either side of the patio.

'There are no lines of sight from any neighbouring properties so, unless somebody *heard* something or saw a car parked, we're going to struggle for eye witness testimony.'

'Get names for follow-up, nonetheless. And, get hold of a map or an aerial shot of the neighbourhood so we can locate everyone living on the road.'

'It's the usual mix of locals, second homers and foreign tourists.'

'To be expected. Do we know who owns Villa Jasmin?'

'A Madame Rappeneau,' said Latour, consulting a notebook. 'I've got an address. Lives in the village with her husband. Auger spoke to her briefly and she told him the villa was booked in person, not on the internet...'

'In person? When?'

'About ten days before the Butlers moved in,' said Latour. 'Strange, right?'

'Especially as the Butlers were in Singapore at the time.' Benoit glanced at his watch. 'Get a uniform outside their door. It's too late to follow up tonight. We'll interview first thing tomorrow. Any news on the ICP?'

'The trailer is on its way. Dugrippe says if you want the Command Post right outside the house, you'll have to close the road. There's not much traffic and diversions shouldn't be a problem though the mayor might be.'

'Do it,' said Benoit. 'Dugrippe's here?'

'Half an hour ago.'

'Good. And tonight?'

'It's early season so Auger was able to book a single and a twin at the Hotel Deux Rocs for a couple of nights until we can arrange something longer term. We could draw lots for the single.'

Benoit raised a mocking eyebrow at him. 'Where?'

'Back down the hill. Sharp left at the junction of the main street and follow the road round the top of the village. You can't miss it.'

Benoit nodded. 'Do we know where the bodies are going?'

'Fayence mortuary about five miles away. Post mortem tomorrow at ten. Doc Gueyrande is driving up from Nice to perform.'

'Excellent. Okay. I don't think we can do much more tonight. I've been at it all day and we need to be up with the birds tomorrow.'

'Then why don't you have the single room, boss?' said Latour. 'You've earned it.'

'I have, haven't I?' said Benoit, meeting Latour's reverse psychology head-on.

'I'll share with Dugrippe again,' said Latour. 'Though I probably won't get much sleep, the way he snores.'

'Good that you're used to it though,' said Benoit, unmoved. 'Before you leave, make sure the locals organise regular food and drink for FFP until the trailer gets here then follow me down to the hotel. I'll try and organise a late meal. Any news on the rest of the squad?'

'Caron's driving back from Paris overnight and Gagnon was in Italy. Rolland is coming from Lyon. They should be here by the time we finish at the mortuary tomorrow.'

'Any pushback on their shortened leave?' said Benoit.

'No-one complained to me. Would it have made any difference?'

'Not a jot,' said Benoit.

A photographer in full suit and mask appeared beside them, taking pictures of the pool floor. Drawn by the flash, Benoit's gaze fell on the male torso being painstakingly hoisted into a body bag.

'Wait!' shouted Benoit, above the whine of the generator. He scrambled clumsily down the deep-end ladder and dropped onto the bottom of the pool, the pale red waters now little more than a puddle. Splashing across to the male corpse, he pointed at a deep gouge in the back of the man's right calf muscle. 'What's that?'

'More mutilation,' muttered the forensic technician through his mask. 'Looks clean too. Scalpel, if I had to testify in the next five minutes. See the edges. Clean as a whistle.'

'Post-mortem?'

'Almost certainly,' replied the forensic technician. 'Even without tests.'

'Heads and hands?'

'We'd need more tests for that.'

'Chainsaw? Axe?' The technician's only reply was a weary smile. 'More tests,' echoed Benoit, answering for him. 'Thanks.'

'WHAT WAS THAT ABOUT?' said Latour, stripping off his forensic suit back at Benoit's car. The darkness of the forest enveloped them away from the crime scene and faces were only visible by the flashing blue lights of emergency vehicles.

'A piece of the man's calf removed post mortem,' said Benoit. 'Scalpel, probably.'

'Professional.'

'And unless we have any doctors on our suspect list, evidence of premeditation.'

'What do you think? A tattoo?'

'An identifying mark of some kind. Unlikely to be a tattoo though. He had no other ink on his body and, if he was inclined to decorate himself, it's unlikely he'd start there.'

'Birthmark then?' suggested Latour.

'Birthmark,' nodded Benoit, rolling up his own protective suit and placing the rubber boots on top. He handed the bundle to Latour for bagging, took out his gun and threw it on the passenger seat of his Citroen.

8

Benoit crawled along the dark road to the barrier and acknowledged the salute of the gendarme, before continuing to the main highway. Of Mayor Ruggieri, there was no sign. Descending the hill, he guided the Citroen carefully along the unlit, winding road, his window rolled down for a welcome breath of cooler air.

Not having had a cigarette since lunchtime, he pulled into an untarmacked layby half way down the hill, parking beyond the refuse bins. Out of the car, the rhythmic pulse of cicadas with their nightly symphony, old as the Earth, soothed his overheating brain. He removed a pack of Gitanes from a soft-pack carton in the boot, lit up with a deep sigh and leaned against the car, rubbing his tired eyes.

Hearing a corporeal noise, Benoit squinted up the steep incline behind the layby which rose sharply to an impenetrable tangle of roots and robust shrubs - the maquis, so-called because of its unyielding toughness and durability, a quality lending itself to the French resistance fighters of the same name.

Something, presumably an animal, was moving slowly through the dense brush above him so Benoit flicked on his smartphone torch and scoured its beam towards the noise. As the light fell on the knot of hardy vegetation, whatever had been inching its way through the barely navigable scrub, stopped moving.

Benoit took a final pull on his cigarette and extinguished it under his shoe, turned off his light and prepared to pocket his iPhone. As he did so, a low rolling growl broke the silence before dying in the throat.

Benoit reignited his torch but, unable to locate the source of the noise, he thought no more about it and continued his journey, rolling the half mile around the hill, headlights cutting a triangular swathe through the shadows.

Approaching the village's deserted main street, he turned sharp left at the bend and followed the road as it wound past a public square with its obligatory fountain, mountain spring water weeping gently from its ornate spout. Crossing a bridge, the smell of cooked meats met his nostrils and his appetite began to return.

In another hundred yards, a welcoming scene greeted his eyes - another darkened public square with a more ornate fountain, surrounded by tables, the chairs all vacated and tilted inwards. But convivial lights shone directly outside the hotel and a table of half a dozen diners ate and drank enthusiastically.

Benoit was reminded of Van Gogh's Terrasse de Café La Nuit and surmised the diners were probably staff, eating their late supper after the evening's dinner service.

He parked beyond the Hotel Deux Rocs and removed his ever-present travel bag from the boot, slinging his laptop over his shoulder. He nodded in the direction of the diners, as he ran an eye over their repast - a stew of red meat and vegetables on a bed of rice.

'Hello,' said a well-dressed, middle-aged man, standing. He swallowed a mouthful of food and dropped his linen napkin on his chair. 'Police Judiciaire?'

'Commandant Benoit at your service,' said Benoit. 'You're expecting us, I hope.'

'Yes, but we weren't sure when.' He shook Benoit's hand and ushered him inside, through the empty dining room, towards a small bar that doubled as a counter and stepped behind it. 'I'm Guy Favre, owner of Deux Rocs. Welcome. If I could get your signature on the invoice, monsieur. Your colleagues are not with you?'

'Soon, I hope,' said Benoit, handing back the pen.

'I understand. It must be difficult. Your rooms are ready. I'll have your bags taken up.'

'Excellent. I'll be having the single. I suppose a little supper is out of the question. It's been a long day.'

Favre threw up his hands in regret. 'Service is over I'm afraid.'

'We wouldn't require anything fancy,' said Benoit. 'Just what you've got that's ready to go.'

Favre pondered. 'I could rustle up a salad Niçoise and, afterwards, you're welcome to do as much damage as you can to the cheese board.'

Benoit smiled. 'Perfect, thank you.'

'Wine?' ventured Favre.

'Please.'

He ushered Benoit back outside, indicating the darkened fountain. 'Pick a table. Or would you prefer to dine inside?'

'Al fresco is fine,' said Benoit, his eye taking in the dramatic illumination of spotlights on the evocative buildings of Seillans, beyond the square. This included an imposing church, its sturdy tower looming over the tall, narrow houses surrounding it.

Favre disappeared so Benoit ambled across the road to the fountain and sat down at an adjacent table, lighting another cigarette.

Sleek cats wandered warily from table to table, sniffing for scraps of discarded food and Benoit reclined with a sigh, to watch their foraging. He ran an eye over the floodlit church, looming large on the other side of the compact square then trailed a hand into the fountain's basin and rubbed the cool mountain water across his face.

He lit the tea light on his table as Favre hurried across

the road with a tray of glasses, a carafe of red wine and a water bottle. He poured a glass of each.

'Santé,' said Favre, showing a reluctance to move away. 'Dare I ask what's happened? The village is talking of little else.'

'What does the village say?' asked Benoit, taking a welcome sip of robust red wine.

'Just that old man De Vries found bodies at the Villa Jasmin, up on the hillside, where the English couple were staying.'

'*The* English couple?' enquired Benoit.

'They've been here a few weeks and were set to stay all summer, I gather. Unlike most tourists.'

'So, you noticed them?'

'I confess I did. If you'd seen the English lady...what a great beauty! A real head turner.'

'You spoke to them?'

'They dined here twice, a few weeks apart, I think. The first time, I didn't pay much attention. They were just pale tourists. The second time, it was the fête and it was clear their stay was more than fleeting, so I made conversation.'

'About what?'

Favre shrugged. 'The English. What else but the weather and the food? They were developing good tans by that stage. That hillside is a real sun trap, no?'

'Indeed. Did they stand out for any other reason?'

'Funny you say that,' said Favre. 'The second time they ate here, I noticed they arrived in a battered old Fiat which struck me as odd.'

'Why so?'

'Because Monsieur Butler ordered the most expensive bottle of vintage champagne followed by my best red wine. Their bill came to nearly fifteen hundred euros, most of it for drinks.'

'They drank a lot?'

'Not excessively, no. Quality not quantity, as they say.

The lady only had a glass of champagne. She was driving, I think.'

'Monsieur drank the rest?'

'Yes, he was a bon viveur. Good tipper, too. Wealthy, I'd say. Well, being that much older than his wife, it's to be expected.' He smiled again at the memory of her beauty before his expression changed. 'Terrible to think of her murdered like that.'

'Like what?' said Benoit.

'With her whole life in front of her. Such a waste.'

'How were the Butlers towards each other?' asked Benoit.

'The first time they seemed a lot happier. That was a lunch. I think they'd just arrived because they were pale-skinned so, of course, they were enjoying the sunshine.'

'How did they pay?'

'They didn't. Another man paid.'

Benoit sat forward. 'Another man?'

'Yes. An American, I think - a little older than you but much fitter looking...if you'll forgive me saying.'

'You're forgiven,' replied Benoit. 'What can you tell me about him?'

'Short brown hair, a little grey around the temples, scar across the forehead from his right eye, lean and muscular... he wore shorts and his calves were very well-toned, I noticed. Ex-army from the way he carried himself.' Favre smiled with false modesty. 'I did a year's conscription in the nineties, you know.'

'Thank you for your service,' said Benoit, without irony. 'Any other description?'

Favre shrugged. 'Of him? No, I mostly looked at madame. He was a regular guy, about your height, hand-some if unremarkable features.'

'What about Monsieur Butler?'

'Slightly overweight, jovial, longer brown hair swept back and laced with grey. Oh, and he had a large birthmark on his calf.'

Benoit's expression hardened. 'Did you notice which leg?'

'Right, I think,' nodded Favre, staring into the distance to remember. 'He wore shorts that first time and kept applying sunscreen.'

Benoit nodded. 'How did the American pay?'

'I can go and check receipts, they're still in the drawer. It was right at the start of the season, so shouldn't be hard to find.'

'Please. And perhaps ask your staff if they remember anything about them.'

Favre left the table and returned moments later with a large oval plate of Niçoise, three dinner plates and a basket of bread and cutlery then went to consult his staff.

Benoit speared a large boiled potato and a chunk of tuna then smeared a round of bread into the dressing and savoured the sharp, mustardy vinaigrette. A simple salad had never tasted so good. Favre returned a few minutes later with a receipt.

'This is their lunch bill. It was actually the last Sunday in March, the 31st. The Englishman ordered a steak. I remember because most people pick from the set menu at lunchtime because it's better value.'

Benoit accepted the receipt and examined it briefly. 'Paid in cash.' He raised an enquiring eyebrow at Favre.

'Of course, Commandant. Take it, if it's important. I have a copy.'

Benoit nodded his thanks and pocketed the tariff. 'And your staff?'

'They only remember difficult customers and celebrities, I'm afraid.'

'Understandable. You mentioned the couple were less happy on their second visit.'

'Yes. Nothing to do with the food,' Favre added quickly. 'They were quiet, serious and although they tried not to draw attention, I could see they were having a disagreement.'

'Any idea over what?'

'You ask me, Monsieur was jealous. Madame drew admiring glances wherever she went.' His face betrayed excitement. 'Actually, I have photographs, if you'd like to see them?'

Benoit cocked his head. 'Very much.'

'I help run the village website so I took a lot of pictures from the fête. It was April twenty-second - Easter Monday - and an important local event with a lot of stalls and entertainments. The whole village turned out. It was very crowded. We had a special menu...'

'Can I see the photographs?'

'Of course.' Favre smiled, standing his ground.

Benoit waited another beat. 'Would now be a problem?'

'I'll get my camera,' said Favre, the penny dropping.

A Renault turned the corner and parked. Dugrippe and Latour hauled themselves wearily out of the car. Benoit beckoned them over. 'Leave your bags. Come and eat.'

'Food,' sighed Dugrippe, a tall, well-built young man of twenty-five, dark and handsome, his two eyebrows straining to meet in the middle of a large forehead.

Benoit shook his hand before he sat. 'Sorry about your holiday.'

Having already started munching on a hard-boiled egg, Dugrippe shrugged his indifference. 'Bored already.'

Latour filled their glasses with wine and, after a long pull on the house red, spooned salad onto his plate.

Favre returned with his camera. 'Gentlemen,' he said to the two new arrivals. He handed his digital camera to Benoit to scroll through but it was too dark to see much detail on the small screen. 'Madame Butler,' said Favre softly, pointing at one shot. 'Beautiful, isn't she?'

'Very,' said Benoit, handing back the camera, remembering the bloated, maggot-infested torso in the pool. 'Could you put everything from that night on a memory stick, please?'

'Right away?' said Favre, now attuned to the immediacy of Benoit's needs.

'Please,' said Benoit. 'I want to view the photographs overnight. And, of course, add any incidental costs to the invoice. The Niçoise is delicious by the way.' Approving grunts from the nodding Dugrippe and Latour accompanied.

'Good,' said Favre. 'I'll get the cheeseboard.'

'And more bread,' called Dugrippe, through a mouthful of salad leaves.

Benoit pushed his empty plate aside and sat back to watch them eat. 'Any prelim from Forensics?'

'They ran a lamp over the surrounding gardens and orchard,' said Latour. 'No obvious broken ground. They'll do a proper GPR in the morning but it doesn't look like body parts are buried on site.'

Favre returned with more bread and the cheeseboard and Dugrippe mopped up the vinaigrette from his plate.

'Also, no obvious signs of a break-in,' said Latour, slicing a thick tranche of ripe, golden Saint-Marcellin onto his plate. 'Though the window locks are barely worth the name, so a possible entry point but if the house was as wide-open as we found it, there'd be no need to break in.'

Benoit nodded. 'And the ICP?'

Dugrippe wiped his hands on the napkin and took a swallow of wine to clear his palate. 'The Command Post will be on site tonight and I'll swing by first thing tomorrow to make sure it's powered-up and comms are operational.'

'And after our two nights' accommodation in the lap of luxury?'

Dugrippe nodded towards the floodlit church. 'There's an annex that used to house local novices training for the priesthood. It has a dozen cots, toilets and basic washing facilities.'

'Praise the Lord,' mumbled Benoit, fatigue washing through him. 'Tell the team we brief at eleven in the morning, after Gabriel and I have interviewed Madame Rappeneau and been to the mortuary. Pull together what you can from Forensics and start searching for an American who was with the Butlers when they arrived in Seillans. The three of them had lunch here, according to Favre.'

'He remembers diners from a month ago?' said Latour.

'He especially noticed Madame Butler.'

'Fair point.' Latour withdrew a notebook. 'Any description?'

'Around fifty, lean, my height,' said Benoit. 'Possibly ex-military. So, when you find which flight the Butlers were on, get a manifest and a photo array of all white males in their late forties or early fifties and start whittling them down.'

'You think he was on the same flight?' said Latour.

'Either that or he met them when they landed,' said Benoit. 'But, as we have a witness who can identify him, we should be able to get film and say one way or the other.'

'I'll get the ball rolling with the airport police,' said Dugrippe, thumbing at his phone before jamming it to his ear and walking towards the fountain, picking at food scraps in his teeth.

'Favre says Butler had a birthmark on his right calf,' said Benoit.

'So, the male corpse is Butler,' nodded Latour.

'Looks like it,' said Benoit. Favre returned with a memory stick for Benoit and cleared away their plates. 'Long day tomorrow, Gabriel. Don't be up long. I'm going up to my room to look at these pictures. Breakfast at six.'

'Christ, that's early,' said Latour. Benoit paused to hear further complaint. 'And the best part of the day, it is too.'

'Sleep well.' Benoit pushed back his chair, gesturing a goodnight towards Dugrippe as he trudged towards the hotel.

'I won't,' mumbled Latour, under his breath.

9

Friday May 3rd

The next morning, the sun's light was yet to appear fully over the terracotta rooftops of Seillans as Benoit sat in the shadow cast by the imposing Eglise Saint Leger, the 11th century medieval church across the square. He nursed a jet-black coffee and cigarette at his usual table by the fountain, scrolling again through Favre's photographs on his laptop.

The hotel owner had taken at least two hundred shots over the course of the Easter feast day but Benoit concentrated on the forty snaps taken in the evening, during the dinner service outside his hotel. About half of them featured a glimpse of the Butlers, if only in the background.

He stared at Mrs Butler, that night dining in a mid-length, flower print cotton dress, her blond hair hanging down to her shoulders, her startling emerald eyes beaming out from a tanned face. Zooming in on all pictures containing a view of the Butlers revealed nothing particularly untoward about the couple's manner except that they only seemed to smile when they knew the camera was on them. Otherwise, their demeanour was sober and serious.

One image caused Benoit to linger. While her husband, David, grinned towards Favre's lens, Charlotte Butler's attention was elsewhere, gazing off to the side with an expression of concentration, perhaps even recognition, on her face. Benoit scrolled through again, looking for a different view of the spot at which Charlotte Butler had been staring. He couldn't find one.

But he did notice several other diners taking photographs of their own family group and made a mental note.

Latour wandered out from the hotel, yawning, followed by Favre, carrying a breakfast tray.

'Your coffee,' said Favre, placing a cup and saucer on the table. Latour nodded his gratitude and reached for a pain au chocolat in the pastry basket. He tore off a piece and chewed it mechanically while he wearily booted up his own laptop to check emails.

'Monsieur,' said Benoit. 'I need a list of all the diners eating here on the night of the twenty-second, if you have them.'

'If they're local it'll be easy enough,' said Favre. 'If not...'

'A list of credit and bank card details will help us trace those you don't know,' said Benoit. 'Oh, and monsieur.' He swivelled his laptop around. 'I need a printout of this picture right away, if it's no trouble. You have a printer?'

'Of course,' said Favre, staring sadly at the image of Charlotte and David Butler smiling back at him from the monitor. 'I'll get a copy for you now.'

'Anything overnight?' Benoit asked Latour, when Favre had gone.

'No hits on the Butlers in the UK,' answered Latour. 'As far as their home country is concerned, they don't exist.'

. . .

FIFTEEN MINUTES LATER, Benoit and Latour navigated a narrow, cobbled path amusingly named Grand Rue, one of the steep car-free alleys of Seillans. Halfway down the hill, Latour spotted the gendarme sitting hunched on a rough wooden bench opposite their destination.

'This is it,' he said, turning his face to the warm sun creeping along the narrow lane. 'Knocking them up at cock's crow means they'll be home, at least. Pity that cuts both ways.'

'Best part of the day, you said.'

'Only if you fish,' replied Latour.

Benoit flashed his ID card when the gendarme stood. 'Are they in?'

'Nobody's left the house, sir. I doubt they're up.'

Vaulting up the crooked stone steps, Benoit banged on the door of the narrow, three-storey stone house. A window opened above them and a woman around sixty years of age, with dyed auburn hair and grey roots, blinked blearily down at them, irritation in her voice.

'What time do you call this?'

'Madame Rappeneau? Commandant Benoit of the Serious Crimes Squad,' shouted Benoit, for the entire neighbourhood to hear. He held aloft his ID in the unlikely event she'd be able to see it from her lofty perch. The woman's expression hardened and the window closed.

A few moments passed before the door opened and the stocky figure of Madame Rappeneau, in tightly wrapped gown and shawl, arms folded, peered out at them. 'Yes?'

'Can we talk inside?' said Benoit. After a moment, Madame Rappeneau stepped back from the door and Latour and Benoit passed her into a compact kitchen where the lady of the house busied herself preparing a pot of coffee. 'You're the owner of Villa Jasmin, Madame?'

'With my husband Paul, yes,' she said. 'Terrible news. Terrible. I told Sergeant Auger all I know on the phone last night. But if I can be of further help...'

'You mentioned to Auger the booking of your villa was done in person and not on the internet. Is that correct?'

'Yes,' said Madame Rappeneau. 'A young woman telephoned a couple of weeks before the season started.'

'The season?'

'This year Jasmin is available from March 30th to the end of September,' she explained.

'And she wanted to book the property for the entire six months?'

'Correct.'

'Is that usual?'

'Not really.'

'And even more unusual that a prospective client should apply in person,' said Benoit.

'Indeed,' said Madame. 'Initially, I referred her to the Villa Sud website because that's the normal booking procedure but what could I do? She was in the area and insisted on a face-to-face meeting to discuss terms and look over the property. How could I refuse?'

'She was already in the area, you say?' asked Latour.

'That's what she said and, as she arrived promptly for our meeting, I had no reason to doubt it.'

'She came here?'

'No,' said Rappeneau. 'We live in the villa over winter and here, in Seillans, during summer season. She came directly to Jasmin to look around.'

'And what did you discuss?' said Latour.

'What do you mean?'

'Weren't the terms of rental clear from the website?' said Benoit.

'Apparently not,' said Madame Rappeneau, unable to meet his eyes.

'Or perhaps the lady wanted to propose different terms,' said Latour, after a glance at Benoit. Madame didn't reply.

'Can I infer from your silence that the entire booking was paid in cash?' demanded Benoit.

Madame Rappeneau took a breath before answering in a barely audible squeak. 'It was.'

'The whole six months?' said Latour. 'In advance.'

She hesitated. 'Yes.'

'How much was that exactly?' asked Benoit.

Turning her back to them, Madame Rappeneau shook powdered coffee into a fresh filter paper while she gathered her thoughts. 'Sixty thousand euros,' she croaked, as though hoping they wouldn't hear.

'Sixty thousand euros?' exclaimed Latour. 'And she had the whole amount in cash?'

'She did.'

'And you accepted the booking?'

'Why wouldn't I?' answered Rappeneau, a defensive tone in her voice.

'I checked the Villa Sud website,' said Latour. 'The average rate over the whole season is just under two thousand euros a week. With bookings for a full season, that should come to a little over fifty thousand euros.'

'The money included car rental for six months.'

'The old Fiat?'

Madame nodded. 'She wanted it as a run-around for her clients.'

'Clients?' said Benoit. 'That's the word she used.'

'Yes.'

'An extra ten thousand for a car worth barely five hundred euros?' said Latour.

'There were...complicating factors,' croaked Madame. 'I'd already taken bookings from regulars which I had to cancel to accommodate her.'

'So, she offered a premium for the inconvenience she was causing you,' suggested Latour. Madame nodded.

'And no questions asked,' added Benoit. Madame made no answer. 'Did she give you a name?'

'She said it was Wendy.'

'Surname?'

'She told me but I've forgotten it.'

'Can I see the paperwork?' said Benoit. Her silence provided its own answer. 'You have no paperwork.' She shook her head. 'And no signature.'

An embarrassed pause. 'No.'

'Did you see identification? A passport, a driver's licence?' Again, no answer from Madame Rappeneau. 'So, you only saw the colour of her money.'

'How dare you...?'

'I'm a senior detective investigating a double murder on *your* property, Madame,' barked Benoit. 'So, I do dare without a single qualm and if I don't receive immediate and full co-operation, we'll continue this at the station. Is that clear?'

Unable to speak, Madame lowered her head and nodded.

'Can we see a bank statement to confirm the amount and the date of payment?'

Madame was tight-lipped. 'I...' she began, searching for the words.

'You've been too busy to bank the money,' concluded Benoit.

'Yes.' Her voice was barely a murmur.

Benoit nodded at Latour who donned rubber gloves from a pocket. 'We'll take those bills. All of them.'

'What?' Madame was aghast. 'Why?'

'Evidence,' said Benoit. 'I'll write you a receipt and you'll get the money back in due course.'

'When will that be?'

'In. Due. Course.' Benoit's eyes bored into her. 'Could be months, could be a couple of weeks, depending on the course of the investigation. Then, if you're not too busy, you can bank the money...'

'You think I intended to cheat the taxman...'

'Fetch the bills!' snapped Benoit.

'I don't have the full amount. Some has been spent.'

'How much?'

'A thousand. Maybe two.' She shrugged. 'Legitimate

expenses.'

'Then we'll take what you have.'

They heard the descending chord of footsteps on the stairs.

'In the metal box, bottom cupboard,' said Madame, nodding beyond Latour, who opened the cupboard door and picked out an old tin cashbox. Finding it locked, he glanced up at Madame Rappeneau who removed a small key from her necklace and handed it across.

'Tight security,' said Benoit.

'A precaution against pilfering,' replied Madame, spearing a glance at the bottom of the stairs.

'Just the two of you here, right?' enquired Latour, unlocking the box. She glared at him as he extracted the cash and did a quick count.

Meanwhile, a short, bow-legged man, unshaven with a bald pate emerged from the foot of the stairs. He was about ten years younger than his wife, barefoot, in grubby, ill-fitting jeans and an off-white vest.

'Monsieur Rappeneau?'

'That's right. You here about them murders? Terrible business.'

'They're asking about the woman who hired Jasmin,' said his wife, a sneer distorting her face. 'You remember mademoiselle *Wendy*, don't you?'

'Vaguely,' said Rappeneau, flashing a scowl back at her. Latour finished counting the notes and Rappeneau saw him. 'Here, what the hell are you doing with our money?'

'It's evidence,' said Benoit. 'How much?'

'Fifty-seven thousand,' replied Latour. Madame Rappeneau narrowed her eyes towards her husband.

'But that's our money,' pleaded Monsieur Rappeneau.

'We're not disputing that and you'll probably get it back,' said Benoit.

'Probably?' exclaimed the couple, as one.

'If the money isn't stolen or counterfeit,' explained Latour, holding up a couple of mint condition hundred-euro bills to the light. 'These two notes look genuine, at least.' Latour returned the bills to the cashbox, locked it and bagged the box and key in a clear plastic bag then took out a pad to write a receipt.

'This woman Wendy, who hired the villa,' said Benoit. 'What was the date of her visit?'

Madame Rappeneau turned her thoughts to the question though her eyes stayed on the evidence bag. 'It would have been about ten days before we moved out for the summer.'

'Back to this house?'

'Yes.'

'Can you remember the date?'

'It was a Friday,' said Monsieur Rappeneau. 'We'd just returned from the market, when the phone rang. Remember?'

'That's right,' confirmed Madame.

'The twenty-second of March,' ventured Latour, looking at the calendar on his iPhone. Benoit gestured to him and Latour unfurled the colour printout of David and Charlotte Butler from Favre's photographs. 'Is this the woman who hired the villa?'

Madame stared at the picture. 'No, that's Madame Butler. She and her husband were living at Jasmin. It was another woman. Younger.'

'You know the Butlers?'

'Of course.'

'You met them on arrival at the villa?'

'No. We left them to their own devices. That's how Wendy arranged it. Her clients wanted privacy so I did the cleaning before they arrived and provided sheets, towels and some basic groceries and arranged some books and DVDs onto our shelves that she had delivered. That's it.'

'Then how do you know the Butlers?' said Benoit.

'I don't *know* them. I recognise them. Seillans is a small place so we saw them about the village, at the supermarket and the pharmacy.'

'How did they get into the property? Did Wendy hand over the keys?'

'Nobody did. There's a key box round the back that needs an entry code and it works for the gate too. I gave Wendy the code. Routine.'

'There was something odd though,' said Rappeneau.

'What?'

'Wendy asked us to remove the wi-fi router before the guests arrived.'

'The router?' said Benoit. 'You mean, disable the internet connection.'

'Not just disable it, remove it,' said Rappeneau. 'Odd, right? I mean, even on holiday, most people have iPhones and iPads, even laptops, so they can check their emails and keep in touch.' He shrugged. 'It was a nuisance but I did as she asked.'

'You were very obliging to *Wendy,* weren't you?' sneered Madame.

'Give it a rest, woman,' snapped Rappeneau.

'So, there were no electronic devices left for the Butlers to use,' said Latour.

'Apart from the TV and the music centre, no. We brought our laptop and iPads with us. Phones too.'

'Did you leave a couple of basic pay-as-you-go phones for them to use?' said Latour.

'Not ours,' said Madame, shaking her head.

'Describe Wendy,' said Benoit.

'She spoke English but my husband thought there was a trace of an American accent,' said Madame. 'Well, she was young and blonde, so naturally he hung on her every word.'

'The police are not interested in your paranoid delusions,' growled Rappeneau.

'Delusions? Was I deluded that time...?'

'Woman!' barked Rappeneau, glaring at her and gesturing towards the two detectives. Madame glowered in silence.

'How old, would you say?' said Benoit.

'Younger than Madame Butler,' said Rappeneau. 'Mid-twenties, maybe.'

'Don't forget to tell the officers how pretty she was,' added Madame.

Rappeneau speared a glance at his wife. 'Can't say I noticed.'

A loud snort from Madame. 'My husband couldn't take his eyes off her, Commandant. He could probably tell you her dress size if you ask him nicely.'

Rappeneau smiled sourly back at her, before opening the door. 'I'm going for bread.' He rummaged in his pockets but came up empty and held out a hand to his wife.

'What about all that building work you've been doing?' demanded Madame. 'Haven't you been paid yet?'

'It's for a mate,' explained Rappeneau, not looking at her. 'He'll pay me soon enough.'

'Mate?' said Madame. 'The only mates you have are barmen and bookies. You shelled out five hundred for a brand-new cement mixer and you haven't been paid? Ridiculous. If I find out you've pissed it away at the PMU...'

'Give me some *fucking* money, woman,' seethed Rappeneau. 'And don't speak to me like that in front of company.'

'Don't mind us,' said Benoit.

Stone-faced, Madame produced a small coin purse and handed him three euros.

Pocketing the coins resentfully, Rappeneau headed for the door. 'Have my coffee ready when I get back.' Latour stood across his path but, after a nod from Benoit, stepped aside and Rappeneau left, slamming the door.

'One more thing,' said Benoit. 'I noticed the Jasmin property has an alarm. Have you had a break-in recently?'

'We've never had a break-in,' said Madame, crossing herself to placate the Gods. 'We make sure Jasmin is always occupied. We only put in the alarm to lower the insurance premiums.'

'What about when it's not booked?'

'If there's a free week in summer, we go back for the

week,' said Madame. 'Was there a break-in? Is that how the killers got in?'

'Killers?' said Benoit. 'You think there was more than one?'

'That's how these African gangs operate, isn't it? Sneaking in mob-handed to murder honest Frenchmen in their beds.'

'Thank you for your criminal insights, Madame,' said Benoit. 'We'll be in touch if we have more questions.'

The coffee finished percolating and Madame plucked a pair of mugs from the drainer. Her throat growled and she spat mightily into one of the mugs, filled both, then took a sip of coffee from the unpolluted mug. Benoit and Latour's eyes met.

'What about Jasmin?' she said, as they headed for the door.

'What about it?' said Benoit, though he knew what she was asking.

'When will it be...available?'

'To rent?' said Benoit. Madame nodded curtly. 'In. Due. Course.'

~

TRENT WAS hypervigilant as he ambled out of the Arrivals Hall of Barcelona's El-Prat Airport after his flight from Berlin, ignoring the line of bright yellow taxis waiting for a fare. Pausing to see if he was being watched, he jogged across the three-lane access road with its stream of fast-moving traffic. At the other side of the road, he turned again to be sure nobody was following or paying him undue attention, then made his way to the long-stay car park to take his trusty Range Rover out of mothballs.

One way or another, it always ended in Barcelona - one reason Trent kept so many resources in the city. The sprawling metropolis was a beautiful, gritty, multicultural city, full of tourists all year round, making it easy to go unnoticed amongst the crowds. It was also relatively cheap to store everything he needed for the end of the chase - if indeed, his journey around the globe had ever been one.

He'd been to London, Geneva, Madrid, Toronto, Oslo and Berlin and Megan had joined him for all except the last two. He'd taken more and more risks at each new venue but his stays had been untroubled. So far, there hadn't been even a suggestion of anyone following Renfrew's movements, let alone attempting to commit violence against his person.

Unlocking the Range Rover on the fifth storey of the car park, Trent tossed Renfrew's monogrammed case into the trunk of the left-hand drive vehicle. Checking one more time that he wasn't being watched, he moved to the rear passenger door, opened it and knelt to strip the lining from the inner door, exposing three handguns, clipped in place against the metallic skin of the door. Selecting the Glock 26, Trent ejected and pushed in the magazine to ensure the action was still smooth and the magazine full. He slid the pistol into a side pocket of his laptop case.

Turning to a wad of plastic wallets, he ignored the selection of national passports, instead removing a thick tranche of euros from a bag of different currencies before clipping the lining back into place. He jumped into the driver's seat and drove out of the car park.

On the ten-mile journey from the airport to his hotel, Trent stuck to speed limits and checked his mirrors incessantly but no vehicle seemed to be tailing him. Not that this calmed him. Having gradually amplified the risks to draw Renfrew's enemies towards him, this was the magic hour, the endgame, when adrenalin was Trent's ally and he really came alive.

Beginning this final leg of his round-the-world sojourn, Trent had paid in advance for the flight *and* hotel on Renfrew's plastic and, if an attack was to be launched against him, this was where it would happen.

He lowered the window and felt the warm sea breeze on

his face, the waters of the Balearic Sea glinting seductively on his right. Travelling north along the Catalan coast, he drove past the heavily industrialised port and over the hill, past the infamous Castell de Montjuic, an imposing 18th century fortress which looked down across the city and was the place Franco imprisoned and murdered thousands of his republican enemies during and after the civil war.

Dropping down towards the marina and on towards Barceloneta, the traffic began to build. After passing the aquarium, Trent drove round the short access road that skirted the harbour and, at its end, turned towards the sea where the huge concrete and glass sail that was the lavishly-appointed W Hotel, reared up before him.

The hotel, built on the reclaimed seafront at the apex of the ultra-modern Barceloneta development, was the city's most exclusive hotel and millionaire bond trader Harry Renfrew would have stayed nowhere else. No cheap hostel for Trent on this visit.

Pulling up on the turnaround, Trent left the Range Rover running and slipped a note into the porter's hand in exchange for a tag. Another porter claimed Trent's case from the trunk but a swift ten-euro tip rescued control of his case and he carried it cautiously into the glass-fronted foyer, eyes flicking around for potential threats.

The lobby was buzzing with people, everyone apparently engaged in the normal course of their day, though obviously a professional assassin could have been among them, monitoring Trent's arrival.

Called forward by a receptionist, Trent handed over Renfrew's passport, expertly altered with his own likeness. He snapped Renfrew's credit card down on the counter to confirm his pre-booked suite, keying in the appropriate code on request.

Several weeks since he'd installed Harry and Carla in the heart of rural France and the time had finally come to take the biggest risk of all - spend time in a hotel room with his client's name on it, rather than the room next to it.

Anyone tracking Renfrew's financial transactions would've had more than enough time to plan their attack.

Formalities behind him, Trent waved away all attempts from toadying staff to accompany him to his sea-view suite. If there was to be conflict, the last thing he needed was innocent civilians getting caught in the crossfire.

At the double door to his rooms on the 21st floor, Trent removed his gun from the zipped compartment of his case and placed his key card over the spyhole. As there was no explosion, he waved the card at the censor and pushed open the door.

Crouched low against the door jamb, he pushed his case through the entrance ahead of him, before checking behind the door. Stepping across the threshold, gun held high, he closed it with a heel and advanced into the luxurious apartment.

It took only a couple of minutes to sweep the main living area and, one by one, the rooms leading off it, Trent only lowering his gun arm when he was certain he was alone. He pulled out his phone and tapped in a WhatsApp message to Megan. *In Barca. No welcoming party. Worried now. Where are you? Why don't you answer my messages?*

He unpacked while he waited for her reply. Again, she didn't acknowledge so, with a heavy heart, he set up his laptop and hooked up to the hotel's wi-fi then tapped a few keys to click onto a familiar feed.

He hesitated, his finger hovering over the Return key. 'Don't judge me, Megan. I'm watching your six.' He hit the button and a livestreamed webcam image of the hall in Megan's Chelsea flat loaded. Tapping again, the screen switched to a view of Megan's living room and then her kitchen. Although there was no sign of Megan, the orderly appearance of her flat instilled mild relief.

'Where the hell are you?'

10

'Marriage is a great institution best observed from afar,' said Benoit, outside on the warm cobbles. 'Who said that?'

'I did,' said Benoit.

'Do we believe them?' said Latour. 'About this mystery woman, Wendy, I mean.'

'We do for now but check them out. Get an order for phone records, see where the call from Wendy originated. If Wendy *was* helping the Butlers fly under the radar, it'll be either a public phone or an unregistered cell.'

'But she exists,' said Latour.

'The Butlers didn't arrive in France until the day they moved into Villa Jasmin so, yes. For now, Wendy exists.'

'I'm guessing she wouldn't have hung around either side of hiring the villa.'

'Agreed,' said Benoit, panting at the steepness of the slope. 'Get a list of Wendys entering or leaving the country at Nice Airport. UK flights first.'

'Dates?'

'She met Madame Rappeneau on the 22nd. Assume a couple of days to look around; try the 20th to the 23rd of March and tally against our description.'

'And if we find her?'

'We get a country of departure and footage from airport cameras.'

'And we already have her name.'

'If she has a fake passport as good as the Butlers, that may not mean much,' said Benoit. 'But, with a face and a destination, we have the start of a trail.'

'Do you think she brought the money with her?'

'Unknown,' said Benoit.

'Sixty-thousand euros,' said Latour. 'That's a lot of mattress money. I wonder whether the Rappeneaus will declare it, when they get it back?'

'After our visit, I'd be astonished if they didn't bank it the same day,' said Benoit. He handed over Favre's memory drive. 'Give this to Jerome when he gets here. I want that picture of the Butlers copied onto posters and sent out to Missing Persons. The press too.'

'We're dropping the flag on a search?'

'Until we have official IDs on the victims, we don't have a lot of choice.'

'Interesting the wi-fi being disabled.'

'And no smartphones, iPads or laptops at the house,' agreed Benoit. 'But if the Butlers were in hiding, avoiding devices that can be tracked, starts to make sense and disabling the wi-fi removes the temptation.'

'Unless the killers stole their tech,' said Latour.

'And left a wallet full of cash untouched?' said Benoit, shaking his head. 'This isn't a burglary gone wrong, Gabriel. Their tech wasn't stolen because they didn't have any.'

Latour nodded. 'Which brings us back to a gangland execution.'

'I'm not ruling it out,' said Benoit. 'But the Butlers were English. They came to France from Singapore. If you were running from the Russian, Italian or Corsican mobs, would you fly half way around the world to hole up ninety minutes away from their turf?'

They passed the church and emerged onto the Rue Fontaine D'Amont, where they paused to get their breath back. The hotel basked in the early morning sunshine and breakfast service was picking up.

Guy Favre emerged from the hotel carrying a basket of pastries and hailed them. 'How were your rooms, by the way?'

'Very comfortable, thank you,' said Benoit. Latour merely smiled. 'Monsieur Favre, can I check your hotel register for March please?'

'Of course.' Favre headed indoors and Benoit followed. Latour's mobile rang and he waved Benoit to carry on.

'Any particular day?'

'March 21st or 22nd,' said Benoit. 'I'm wondering if you had a young Englishwoman staying. Christian name, Wendy. No surname.'

Favre tapped a few keys. 'We did,' he said, flipping the monitor around. 'Wendy Wyatt. The 21st. One night only.'

'How did she pay?'

'Cash,' said Favre, examining the log.

Benoit nodded. 'I know it was a long time ago but do you know how she arrived?'

Favre narrowed his eyes then flipped the monitor back round to examine it. 'Well, she didn't drive here or we would have asked for a number plate for security purposes. Now I think about it, she must have arrived in a taxi because the day she checked out, she asked me to order a cab to take her to the airport.'

'Is that usual?'

'Far from it, that's why I remember,' said Favre. 'A local firm took her and I remember asking for a quote and it was two hundred euros *one way*. I told Miss Wyatt she could have hired a car for less but she was unconcerned. Alright for some, eh?'

'I don't suppose you took any photographs of *her*,' asked Benoit. Favre raised an eyebrow. 'Forgive me, I'm aware how that sounds. Just a thought.'

· · ·

'WENDY WYATT'S PASSPORT DETAILS,' said Benoit, walking to the car with Latour. He handed over Favre's note. 'She stayed at the hotel on the 21st and paid cash. Don't bother with the phone records, Wendy rang from her hotel room, met Madame and Monsieur Rappeneau at lunchtime the next day then immediately after booking the villa she left for the airport.'

'Narrows our window.'

'And forget car hire, she took a cab.'

'She's not making this easy,' said Latour. 'Any description?'

'Favre is asking the staff but it was six weeks ago and we should get what we need from passport control.'

Latour called Dugrippe on his phone to brief him.

'Tell Thierry to have Auger supervise another round of door to door,' said Benoit. 'Usual questions but concentrate on tourists staying in rented accommodation.' Benoit started the engine and the car rolled down the hill towards the valley for their appointment in the neighbouring hill town of Fayence.

Latour finished his call. 'The rest of the team are there and working the villa or door-to-door until the briefing.'

'And the ICP?'

'Up and running,' said Latour.

～

IN THE DANK, gloomy mortuary an assistant in protective mask and gown, took a final photograph of the female remains before stepping back. The two headless, handless corpses lay side by side on polished steel trolleys, torsos exposed from the waist up. Both presented with a Y-shaped incision running from both shoulders to the breastbone and then in a straight line down towards the pubis.

Both Benoit and Latour had applied a dot of eucalyptus-based ointment to each nostril, though the smell of putre-faction had been mitigated by the icy temperature and the removal of the victims' internal organs and digestive systems.

Doctor Gueyrande dropped a scalpel into a metal bowl and turned to engage them. 'Serge. Gabriel.' Her breath condensed in the air through her mask and she held up a pair of plastic vials, both topped up with formalin solution to preserve the specimens.

One contained half a dozen cheese-coloured larvae or maggots, the other a similar number of brown-red fly cocoons, the delicate casing shaped like a miniature, fat sausage. 'Sorry about the cold. I had the technician turn the temperature as low as it would go because we haven't had time to remove all the larvae from the flesh.'

'And the cold stunts pupal development,' nodded Benoit.

'Listen to you,' said Gueyrande. 'I'd forgotten you went on a course.'

'Whatever helps with the smell,' said Latour.

'What smell?' she replied.

'Never mind,' said Benoit.

Gueyrande waved a hand at the two trolleys. 'Caucasian male, approximately fifty to fifty-five years old. Caucasian female, twenty-five to thirty-five. The bodies have had an extended immersion in water, floating face down although, as they don't actually have faces, it's more accurate to say buttocks up.' She winked at Benoit and he managed a grunt of amusement. 'Exposed areas of both bodies are infested with blowflies - back and buttocks mainly. When I've finished here, I'll shrink wrap the affected areas and I've ordered a refrigeration unit to transport...'

'You're moving them?' said Latour.

'To a *proper* Post Mortem suite in Nice, yes.'

'Why?'

'Look around you,' said Gueyrande, under her breath. 'The equipment here is Stone Age.'

'Will it allow you to tell us when they died?' said Benoit. Gueyrande frowned. 'We'll take a provisional until you can narrow it down. We need a working timeline.'

'Well,' said Gueyrande. 'Rigor has been and gone - helped by the warm temperatures. And, as you can see from the bloating, discolouration and rupturing of the epidermis and stomach cavity, decomp is well advanced and bacteria and digestive acids have done their work.

'From the extent of larval colonisation and subject to confirmation of current local temperatures, I'd estimate five to six days,' said Gueyrande. 'My bug guy along the corridor in Nice might be able to fine tune that for you but no guarantees, obviously.'

'So, last Friday or Saturday?' said Latour, making a quick note after Gueyrande's nod.

'Cause of death?' said Benoit.

'Based on estimates of blood loss, death occurred when their heads were severed.'

'So, they were alive until then.'

'*Almost* certainly,' said Gueyrande. 'The bodies are virtually exsanguinated, which suggests their hearts were still pumping when lethal trauma was inflicted to the spinal column, trachea and arteries in the neck. Had they died before the heads were severed, their bloods would have had more chance to settle. I can't actually be definitive on that without further tests so don't hold me to it.'

'Chainsaw?'

'I'd say so - certainly something heavy duty and high-powered. Made quick work of their necks and the damage is significant.' She beckoned Benoit and Latour to join her in examining the stump of the female victim's neck, though the pair didn't exactly race to her side. 'See the vertebrae just above the thoracic spine? We call that C6.'

'It's damaged,' said Benoit.

'Exactly. The vertebrae below is C7. It's larger than C6 and both should be a similar shape. But the wing of C6 has been cut clean through, by a single stroke, and is presumably attached to the head, wherever that is.' She looked enquiringly at Benoit, who shook his own head. 'Well, if you find it, you should be able to confirm whether it belongs here by the damage to C6.'

'So, not an axe,' said Latour.

'Even the sharpest axe would involve multiple blows and present a good deal more trauma to the skeleton and flesh. Only La Veuve herself could've made a cleaner cut than what you see.'

'I think even I would have spotted a guillotine at the scene,' said Benoit, stepping back from the corpse. 'Drugs? Alcohol?'

'I've taken fluid samples and tissue from stomach, liver and kidneys so, when I get the organs back to Nice, I'll do full tox screens to test for other substances, for what good it will do after such an extended immersion. I can tell you there were no signs of a struggle on the bodies yet no restraints were used although I'd prefer to examine the hands as they're the most reliable indicator of resistance but, at this stage, it's likely both victims were sedated.'

'Sedated how?'

'Injection,' said Gueyrande. 'I don't know what yet but it's fair to conclude it happened against their will and with the aim of inducing or enhancing passivity. They could, of course, have self-medicated *but* it's more reasonable to assume a barbiturate was introduced by the perpetrator. Unless you found heroin or other psychotropics at the crime scene.'

Benoit shook his head. 'No suggestion anyone connected to the scene were Class A users.'

'I wouldn't have thought so,' said Gueyrande. 'There are no habitual needle marks or the tell-tale ravages of a life spent puncturing veins.' She tried to adjust a spotlight to illuminate the bodies but it wouldn't move so she abandoned the attempt. 'How do they function with this equipment?'

'Did Rembrandt paint on cave walls?' quipped Latour, remembering one of the doctor's regular grumbles.

Gueyrande shot him a wry grin. 'That could be me talking. Next time I'll bring candles.'

'Make sure they're scented,' said Latour.

'Look.' She took out her iPhone and illuminated the male cadaver's arm with the torch, indicating an ovular purple bruise, even more discoloured than the putrefying flesh, just under the right bicep. 'You can see the lesion with the naked eye. The female has a similar puncture wound from another single needle mark.'

'Any thoughts on the sedative?' said Benoit.

Gueyrande shrugged. 'Pentobarbital would be ideal. I'll do the usual tests but it will be problematic without the brain and the vitreous humour. And with a five-to-six-day decomp, substances that may have been present at time of death, like alcohol for instance, will probably have purged. I'll try and get a decent hair follicle from the pubis in the absence of scalp roots and that might be enough to give an indication. You'll send me a full list of meds at the scene?'

'Should be in your Inbox when you get back,' said Benoit. 'Anything else?'

'I can tell you how the killers cut their victims' necks.'

'Killers?'

'Workload suggests at least two perps to me,' said Gueyrande. 'Drugged, the victims would be completely inert and, although resistance would be impossible, their bodies would be dead weight. Heavy lifting would be needed to position the victims.'

'Position them how?'

'A chainsaw is an essential tool in the country but if not used safely, a dangerous one. The victims' necks would need to be suspended off the ground, so the chainsaw could cut through flesh and bone without the blade hitting the ground.'

'In the same way you'd saw a log on a cradle,' said Latour.

'Exactly like that.'

'Blood spatter and staining suggest the victims were mutilated next to the swimming pool,' said Latour.

'That makes sense,' said Gueyrande, taking out a digital camera from a knapsack. 'I took these before we turned the bodies onto their backs because I didn't want to risk excessive movement. The skin is like butter and integrity is suspect.' She scrolled on to find a shot of the female corpse lying on her stomach. 'See those bruises,' she said, indicating two large areas of discoloured skin, side by side between the shoulder blades and about the size of a pair of Easter eggs.

'What are they?' said Benoit.

'At first I thought it was heat blistering but the damage is in the musculature, below the dermis.'

'Not blowflies?' said Benoit.

'Knees.'

'Knees?'

'If the victims' heads *were* severed next to the pool, my suspicion is the killers dragged the victims to the edge, suspended their heads over the water...'

'And knelt on their backs to keep the body steady while removing their heads with a chainsaw,' nodded Benoit.

'Plop,' said Latour.

'I'll need to examine the bruised area with one of my forensic toys back at the lab but that's my confident preliminary,' said Gueyrande.

'It's a theory,' said Benoit. 'Same with the hands?'

'Similar,' said the doctor. 'At which point, the subjects would definitely have been deceased.' Benoit gave her a sideways glance. She shrugged ruefully. 'I work with dead people. Give me a break.'

'What about the mutilation on the male's calf?' said Latour.

'Scalpel,' said Gueyrande. 'Nothing else could have made such an accurate cut. Birthmark?'

'We think so,' said Latour.

'Any medical practitioners on your list of suspects?' said Gueyrande.

'Where were you last Friday and Saturday, doctor?' said Latour.

'At home, writing better jokes than that,' she replied. 'And before you ask, the same scalpel was used to remove the man's penis.'

Benoit and Latour looked at one another. 'Penis?'

Gueyrande's expression lifted. 'Ah, a bombshell. How satisfying. Though not surprising you didn't notice given all the bloating. But, yes, the man's penis was cut off. A *crime passionel* perhaps.'

'Hardly ties in with method,' said Benoit.

'Your area, not mine.' Gueyrande re-covered the bodies with a plastic sheet and stifled a yawn. 'Excuse me.'

'What time did you leave Nice?'

'Before dawn,' said Gueyrande. 'Your Directeur was most insistent.'

'She's certainly that,' said Benoit. 'Sorry to drag you all this way in the middle of the night.'

'Are you kidding? It's lovely getting out the MG, driving up into the hills in Spring and getting paid for the privilege. When I wrap up here, I'll be taking a stroll around the market, enjoying a good lunch before driving back to the lab to wait for the bodies.'

Benoit's tired smile told its own story. 'Sounds appalling.'

OUTSIDE IN THE bustle of market day, the light, colours, sounds and smells of rural France dazzled. Appetites stimulated, Benoit stopped at a baker shop and bought pains au chocolat, croissants and baguettes followed by cheese and pungent black olives at a couple of market stalls.

'Was there a chainsaw on Jasmin's inventory?' asked Benoit, on the way back to the car.

'Not to my knowledge,' said Latour.

'Get Dugrippe to check again. If there isn't, get onto Madame Rappeneau and ask her if there should be.'

Latour tapped out a text to Dugrippe. 'A chainsaw for a crime of passion? But who was the object of desire and who was the jealous lover?'

'I don't like it either. Even assuming their marriage was failing, Butler's only been here a month - hardly enough time to break hearts so badly he deserves to lose his cock.'

'And with his wife on the next slab, we've already lost the most likely suspect,' said Latour.

THE UNIFORMED POLICEMAN lifted aside the barrier laid across the Chemin De l'Etang and shooed away a knot of interested spectators to allow Benoit's car access to the villa.

'Make sure officers on the perimeter wear a bodycam on duty,' he said to Latour. 'I want a morning and evening picture of both barriers to see if anyone's hanging around more than morbid curiosity can excuse. Thank God, there's little or no press yet.'

'Early days,' said Latour. 'We won't be able to keep the lid on much longer.'

Benoit drew the Citroen to a halt next to a vast trailer stretching across the tarmac of the country lane, directly opposite Villa Jasmin's open gates. The prefabricated building was a fully operational, mobile headquarters with integrated satellite communications, wi-fi technology and even chemical toilet facilities, designed for rapid deployment in the field where existing local facilities were likely to be inadequate.

Trying to adapt ancient village halls in remote areas for a complex and lengthy investigation, was a thing of the past for elite law enforcement in France, especially those engaged in the fight against organised crime and terror.

As he stepped from the car, the welcome aroma of fresh coffee hit Benoit's nostrils. An army may march on its stomach, but a police force does its work on coffee and cigarettes

and he hadn't had a hit since breakfast. While Latour
carried the two large bags of pastries, bread and cheese to
the ICP's briefing room, Benoit lit a cigarette and ran his eye
over the hive of activity in front of the house.

Twenty years in the force, three in his current post, and
he'd never ceased to marvel at the commotion generated by
a homicide investigation as dozens of people moved
purposefully around the site. The peaceful sounds of the
forest were no more, the crooning of insects, the song of
birds all now supplanted by the hum of the ICP's generator.

Thick cables ran from the trailer, across the road and
down the drive of the villa to power the huge arc lights
which allowed forensic officers to work round the clock.
Currently those same officers walked calmly up and down
the hill, carrying equipment to and from the house. Some
ferried bagged exhibits to specialist vehicles to be logged
and stored. Others moved methodically around the site,
eyes to the ground.

In taped-off, numbered quadrants potential evidence
was photographed, videoed and catalogued then flagged up
for inspection by numbered rubber markers placed by local
gendarmes, pressganged into fingertip sweeps.

Other local officers manned barricades - checking IDs
and redirecting traffic - while yet more moved along the lane
interviewing neighbours. All this activity co-ordinated and
directed by his experienced Serious Crime Squad investigators, Benoit at the top of the chain of command - in the field,
at least.

He ambled towards the gates, the heat and sunlight radi-
ating from concrete so white it hurt the eyes. The burly
figure of Dugrippe acknowledged him from the bottom of
the drive and Benoit tapped his watch and splayed his hand
twice. Ten minutes.

Dugrippe nodded, cupped a hand to his mouth. 'No
chainsaw on the property.' Benoit nodded and Dugrippe
returned to his conversation with a masked forensics officer.

Lieutenant Nina Caron appeared, walking steadily up

the steep drive towards him, faded jeans, gun clamped to her right hip, hiking shoes and a short-sleeved, V-neck T-shirt, sweat moistening her armpits. She was slim, in her mid-twenties with cropped auburn hair. 'Boss.'

'Nina. Sorry about your holiday.'

She shrugged. 'Honestly, I was bored after a day.' In a gloved hand, she held up plastic bags with the two mobile phones from the house. 'FFP are done with these burners until they can get them to the lab for more tests but there are no prints and both look wipe-down clean.'

'Put a call out to phone shops between here and Nice Airport. Our victims arrived at the start of April and may have bought them after landing. Call log?'

'Only goes back to the start of last month, so looks like you're right about date of purchase. And the two phones *only* called each other twice and for less than a minute each time. No other numbers contacted. However, both handsets have the same third number on speed dial even though neither phone ever called it. Want me to give it a ring?'

'Not yet,' said Benoit. 'But send one handset to the lab, swab the other then hook it up for recording. Briefing in ten, Nina. Go get some coffee and breakfast.'

'Don't mind if I do. Do you know how I like my eggs?' she called over her shoulder.

'From a chicken,' retorted Benoit, spotting Auger talking to Officer Costanza. He walked over to them. 'Anything from door to door?'

'No-one saw or heard anything out of the ordinary,' said Costanza.

'Nothing?'

'These are secluded properties on a quiet road with no through traffic,' said Auger. 'And we're talking about nearly a week ago.'

Benoit raised an eyebrow. 'Are we?'

'I think so,' said Auger. 'The Butlers were definitely alive last Friday night.'

'Dutch couple staying a few doors down, went to Jasmin

for drinks,' said Costanza. 'They left around one in the morning on Saturday and the Butlers were alive and well, if a little drunk.'

'How did they react when you told them the Butlers were dead?'

'Genuinely shocked,' said Costanza.

'We're checking them out, but they consented to elimination prints and swabs and their passports and driving licenses are in order,' said Auger. 'Confirming their Amsterdam address as we speak.'

'Anything about their night with the Butlers?'

'According to the woman, Margo Visser, everything seemed normal,' said Costanza. 'The Butlers were attentive to their guests, good humoured. Drinks and finger food were plentiful and good quality and everyone had a pleasant evening.'

'How many guests are we talking about?'

'Six in total,' said Auger. 'All holidaymakers.' He consulted a notebook. 'A gay English couple, Roger and Ash, staying next door at Villa Lavendre - next door being about fifty metres down the lane. No surnames yet. We're trying to get hold of the owner for more details. Also, there was a Belgian couple, briefly...the Willems staying at Villa Gentillane. They left after an hour to get back to their kids and the gay couple left around midnight because they were leaving for England the next day.'

'So, the Dutch couple were last to see them alive.'

'Apart from the killer,' said Auger.

'Killers,' said Benoit. 'We're thinking there was more than one. Did you ask if anyone heard a chainsaw?'

'We asked about noise but nobody reported hearing a chainsaw,' said Auger.

'Bear in mind, we're on the edge of a forest, Commandant,' said Costanza. 'Chainsaws are background noise at all hours of the day. I doubt locals would even register it.'

'Tourists might.'

'Not the ones we talked to.'

'Okay, thanks,' said Benoit. Costanza walked away. 'What's your name, Auger?'

'Daniel,' said Auger.

'How old are you?'

'Thirty-five, why?'

'Married?'

Auger frowned. 'No. Are you proposing?'

Benoit laughed. 'Not yet.'

'Then why...?'

'Married officers and organised crime don't mix.'

'Is that what this is?'

'That's why my team are here,' said Benoit. 'And the crimes we tackle require a single-mindedness that's incompatible with other attachments.'

Auger nodded. 'I can understand that. So, what are you asking me?'

'You've acquitted yourself well,' said Benoit. 'I need someone on the team who knows the area and can act as local liaison, while we're here. You know the case and your regional commander in Draguignan recommended you. Briefing in five minutes, if you're interested. If so, get coffee and a pastry then collate everything you have for presentation.' Auger stared as though misunderstanding him. 'Unless there's a cat up a tree you have to rescue.'

Auger's surprise turned to pleasure. 'Yes. I mean, no. Thank you.'

11

B enoit took an energising sip of strong black coffee and looked around the room at the familiar faces of his squad - Lieutenants Gabriel Latour, Adele Rolland, Jerome Gagnon and Nina Caron. At thirty-one, Latour was the oldest but all were experienced investigators with a minimum of five years working the most heinous crimes in Southern France for the Police Judiciaire, a branch of the Police Nationale.

Benoit's team were drawn from its brightest and best to form the Serious Crimes Squad, a dedicated unit with a remit to investigate organised crime and terrorism.

It had been a condition of Benoit's appointment to head up the unit, that recruits be young, single and childless. Organised criminals are violent and ruthless, the value of a human life worthless set against activities generating enormous revenue streams and the gangs would stop at nothing to leverage influence against those who got in their way.

For that reason, families were deemed a risk too far for SCS recruits and, in their Nice headquarters, Benoit's unit was inevitably dubbed *Les Intouchables* - The Untouchables - a homage to Eliot Ness and his Prohibition agents in Chicago.

Waiting for Dugrippe to arrive, Benoit watched his team

chatting, reading their briefing notes or studying the photographs adorning two of four floor-to-ceiling display boards. Enlarged passport photographs of David and Charlotte Butler and the shot of them dining at the Deux Rocs were fixed to one board next to two blank portrait rectangles, one with Wendy Wyatt's name underneath, the other...

"AMERICAN MALE (50?)"

ALL NAMES WERE in inverted commas awaiting confirmation.

There were also the first gruesome images of the two corpses floating in the scarlet waters of Villa Jasmin's swimming pool and Auger, perhaps a stranger to such savagery, was especially fixated by them. A final shot looked down on the two corpses in the emptied basin, their grievous wounds and bloated, sagging corpses framed in grisly technicolour close-up.

On the second board, an aerial shot of the road, assembled from Google Earth, showed the layout of neighbouring houses, all with their own pools and a small parcel of land. Auger had written residents' names directly onto the printout next to the various properties. If the names had dates next to them, this denoted tourists and their length of stay. A significant proportion of properties were second homes and marked *Unoccupied* beside absent owners' names.

When Dugrippe hurried in and took his seat, quietly beckoning to Gagnon for a coffee from the pot, Benoit stood to begin the briefing.

'Thank you all for assembling so quickly and apologies for another holiday interrupted.' A low groan emanated from a couple of his squad. 'This is Daniel Auger from the local gendarmerie in Fayence. He'll be attached until further notice.'

Auger swept his eyes around the room and nodded a greeting at the detectives, provoking an answering murmur in return.

'Treat him as a member of the squad and if you have any local enquiries, make Daniel your first port of call. Thierry and Jerome have organised accommodations in the village, so don't leave the site without knowing where you're going at the end of the day.'

'And don't expect luxury,' said Gagnon. 'We're back in barracks.' Another groan circled the room. 'Also, hitch a lift where you can. Seillans is properly medieval so taking your cars into the village is problematic, unless, you drive a horse and cart, like Gabriel.' A chorus of hooting ensued.

'My Renault will still be chugging along when your Alfa garage is screaming for parts,' retorted Latour. More laughter from officers who had been up too late and risen too early.

Benoit held up his hands to signal an end to levity. 'The first pictures of this heinous crime are on the boards and the Directeur is persuaded these killings bear all the hallmarks of organised crime...'

'You're not convinced?' said Rolland.

'I'm convinced by evidence not appearances, Adele,' said Benoit. He nodded at Latour.

'Passports found in Villa Jasmin are in the names of David and Charlotte Butler, fifty-two and thirty-one years of age respectively,' said Latour. 'Age and gender of the two corpses would seem to support the two as our victims but, for the time being, ID is unconfirmed.

'According to Singapore Airlines, Mr and Mrs Butler flew from Changi Airport on standard tickets to Dubai in the early hours of March 30th. Thirty-six hours later, they flew into Nice on a connecting Emirates flight.'

Latour tapped at the keys of his laptop and waved a remote control at a projector above him. Film of David and Charlotte Butler, walking together towards an entry gate at passport control, appeared on the screen. Both removed baseball caps before handing over passports. The officer took extra care to stare at Charlotte Butler before handing back her documents.

'What a waste,' said Dugrippe. Caron rolled her eyes at him. 'What? She had her whole life ahead of her.'

'It would have been less of a waste if she'd weighed a hundred and fifty kilos, right?' said Caron.

'You wound me,' said Dugrippe, feigning offence.

'Interesting they travelled cattle class yet splashed out big money on the villa,' said Gagnon.

'We don't know it was their money,' said Benoit.

'Count on it, he's got money,' said Rolland. 'Someone that old doesn't land a honey like her without serious wealth.'

'Maybe they flew cattle class to stay under the radar,' said Auger.

'Then they weren't trying hard enough,' said Rolland, with a nod at the film. 'That's a Bottega Veneta lambskin tote, Mrs Butler's carrying. Six thousand euros, minimum.'

'Good spot,' said Benoit. 'Is it on the inventory?'

'*Animal skin handbag*,' read Latour. 'Still on the premises.'

'So, theft isn't the motive,' said Caron.

'Not yet,' said Rolland, winking at Caron.

'Don't even think about it,' said Latour, ending the film. 'If these *are* our two victims, cause of death was decapitation.' A wave of laughter rippled around the room. 'Okay, I realise this isn't a bombshell but it is significant because Doctor Gueyrande couldn't find any restraint marks or signs of a struggle, even though she believes both victims were alive at the point their heads were severed.

'Once the victims were dead, their hands were also removed before the killer performed other small mutilations on the male, using a scalpel.'

'What mutilations?'

'An area of flesh was cut from the man's calf,' continued Latour, pointing at the relevant photograph. 'Also, his penis was cut off.'

'Ouch,' said Dugrippe, shifting in his chair. 'That's not a small mutilation.'

'It is after a week in the water,' said Gagnon, provoking another round of laughter.

'Whatever the dimensions, location of all missing body parts is currently unknown,' continued Latour.

'Cock removal suggests sexual revenge,' said Caron.

'Maybe the wife did it,' said Rolland, smiling.

'Murder-suicide,' nodded Dugrippe, provoking more laughter. 'We can all go home.'

'That's enough coffee for you two,' said Benoit, before gesturing at Latour to continue.

'We don't know why his penis was removed,' said Latour. 'But we have a witness who told us Butler had a birthmark on his right calf, so the leg mutilation looks like an attempt to hide ID.'

'And the scalpel suggests premeditation,' said Caron.

Benoit pointed an approving finger at her. 'Important point, Nina. One thing we *do* know is the Butlers were alive at one o'clock in the morning, last Saturday, after a small drinks party they were hosting at Jasmin broke up. The timings tie in with pathology so our current best guess is they died sometime that Saturday morning, maybe even directly after the party. Daniel.'

'A young Dutch couple were at Jasmin until the party finished and, as things stand, were the last people to see them alive,' said Auger, pointing to their names on the makeshift map. 'Piet Janssen and Margo Visser. Both thirty years old, staying down the road at Maison Beaulieu.'

'Oh, to live on a road where every house has a name,' said Caron.

'Visser is a physiotherapist and Janssen an IT engineer,' continued Auger. 'They live in Amsterdam, present as respectable and seem genuinely shocked. We're doing full background but have no reason to doubt their account and they co-operated fully with DNA and fingerprint requests.'

'Any red flags on the pair, let us know,' said Benoit. 'But

the fact they're still here five days later, would suggest they're not our killers.'

'Anyone else at this party?'

'Four other guests, all tourists since departed,' continued Auger. 'A gay English couple, Roger and Ash, surnames unknown for the moment, and a Belgian couple, Mr and Mrs Willems from Wallonia. They were staying in nearby Villa Gentillane and came to the party for an hour but, as they didn't have a sitter for their kids, they left around nine o'clock.'

'Trace the Belgian couple and get a statement over the phone,' said Benoit. 'Confirm that they have kids and, when you do, rule them out for the time being, though ask Belgian police to send us elimination prints and DNA. The two Englishmen are of more immediate interest and we need to track them down as a matter of urgency.'

'What time did they leave the party?' said Rolland.

'Janssen and Visser say the Englishmen left around midnight because they were leaving the next day.'

'Same nationality,' nodded Caron. 'You think they had history with the Butlers?'

'Possible,' said Benoit. 'More compelling is the fact they left the next day.'

'Did anything notable happen at the party?' asked Rolland.

'Not according to Janssen and Visser,' said Auger. 'Anecdotally, they say the evening was pleasant and everyone, including the Butlers, consumed a steady amount of alcohol but not so much they were out of control.'

'Forensics are trying to confirm but because of the length of submersion and an absence of heads, they might struggle to lock down alcohol levels,' said Latour. 'Tests are ongoing.'

'What about recreational drugs?' said Caron.

'Unknown at this point,' said Latour. 'However, it appears the victims were sedated to make them easier to control. Gueyrande identified a single puncture wound on each corpse's right arm suggesting they were injected with something. Barbiturates most likely but unconfirmed.'

'Self-inflicted?' said Auger.

'We can't rule it out but the crime scene and the remains don't paint a portrait of regular drug use, intravenous or otherwise,' said Latour.

'Meds in the house suggest the Butlers were squeaky clean,' said Dugrippe. 'Statins, paracetamol and birth control pills only.'

'Also, muscle tone on the male corpse suggests he was right-handed,' said Latour.

'So, he'd be more likely to inject himself in the left arm,' said Rolland. Latour smiled to confirm.

'Maybe someone drugged the food,' said Caron.

'Too random,' said Rolland. 'Besides, the people who prepped the food ended up in the water.'

'Adele's right but we still need to locate food and drink from that night, if we can,' said Benoit. 'Apart from a half-empty beer bottle, hidden under a sun lounger, there's nothing to suggest the aftermath of a party.'

'No sign of fingerprints on the beer bottle,' said Dugrippe. 'However, the beer was partially consumed so FFP are hopeful of a DNA sample.'

'Someone drank from a bottle but left no prints?' said Benoit. 'Strange to go to the trouble of wiping prints yet leave us possible DNA trace.'

'Unless it's an oversight caused by drunkenness,' suggested Rolland.

'Then it's the only one at the moment,' said Dugrippe. 'Somebody did a thorough clean-up throughout the house - beds stripped, sheets and pillow slips washed, dishes and glasses too. And I could smell bleach in the shower trap. Sinks too. These killers were pros.'

'Waste bins were also emptied, washed out and clean bags put in place,' said Caron. 'Someone must have walked all the trash and bottle bags to the communal bins after the party.'

'Or took them in their car when they left,' said Dugrippe. 'I've suspended waste collection, obviously, but even if the trash was dumped locally, with communal bins there's no telling which bottles belong to which house.'

'We could use the Dutch couples' prints and whatever we find in the house to test against bottles in the trash and go from there,' said Rolland.

'Could take days,' said Dugrippe.

'Get it done,' said Benoit. 'It will help with IDs. We know at least eight people have been in the property since the Butlers arrived, not including the pool guy.'

'It's worse than that,' said Dugrippe. 'Jasmin's a holiday let so any prints that survived the cleaner's cloth could have been left over from last summer's tenants.'

'What about trace on personal artefacts?' said Benoit.

'Nothing with prints on yet but we do have a hair brush, a pair of toothbrushes and a pair of razors, all showing skin and hair roots so we expect DNA,' said Rolland.

'Sounds promising,' said Benoit. 'What about the cell phones, Nina?'

'No obvious prints on the handsets,' said Caron. 'FFP will sample for DNA but they're not hopeful.'

'No prints on the passports either,' said Latour.

'Not making it easy for us, are they?' said Benoit. 'Questions?'

'Who is Wendy Wyatt?' said Gagnon, nodding at the board.

'A young woman, possibly English, who stayed overnight at the Hotel Deux Rocs on March 21st, ten days before the Butlers arrived,' said Latour. 'She arranged to meet Jasmin's owner the next day and offered to pay over the odds to rent the villa for the entire summer season - sixty-thousand in cash to ensure discretion and keep their names off the books.'

'Sixty thousand?' said Caron. A vibration diverted her attention and she fumbled in a pocket for her phone.

'Do we know her movements?' said Gagnon.

'Roughly,' said Dugrippe, clicking his mouse to load a picture of a young woman staring into the camera at Nice Passport Control. She was slim-faced with long blonde hair and hazel eyes. 'Wendy Wyatt, twenty-three years old and from London, according to her UK passport.'

'Another fake?' said Caron.

'Yes and no,' replied Dugrippe. 'The passport was genuine, Wendy isn't. Not sure how that works but the Brits have no records for her and the address on the passport doesn't exist.'

'How can people have real passports for fake IDs?' said Auger.

'Birth and death records in the UK used to be recorded separately,' said Benoit.

'I read about this,' said Dugrippe. 'There was no cross referencing so IRA members used to pick out a dead child's grave, close to their own date of birth, apply for a duplicate birth certificate and create a new identity to travel to the British mainland.'

'Same trick used in The Day of the Jackal,' said Caron.

'I thought they closed that loophole when their records were digitised,' said Latour.

'That may have been *after* someone applied for Wendy's duplicate birth certificate when she was a kid,' said Dugrippe.

'Wouldn't we get a hit on the dead child?' said Rolland.

'In which case, it's more likely a stolen passport, expertly altered with Wendy Wyatt's fake details,' said Latour.

'Whoever she is, Wendy flew into Nice Airport at 09.00 hours on a British Airways flight from Heathrow,' said Dugrippe. 'Later that day she checked into the Hotel Deux Rocs and paid cash for a one-night stay. She took a cab to the airport the next day - a local company confirms - so we're assuming she did the same on the way to Seillans.'

'Not cheap,' said Gagnon.

'But more discreet,' said Dugrippe.

'We know she arrived at the Deux Rocs around midday

so, assuming it took her half an hour to clear passport control and ninety minutes to drive here in a cab, we may be missing a chunk of time out of her schedule,' said Benoit. He nodded for Dugrippe to continue.

'The next day, after completing her business with Jasmin's owner, Madame Rappeneau, Wendy returned to the airport in the evening and flew back to London on a BA flight at 22.00 hours,' said Dugrippe.

'That missing time,' said Caron, staring at her smart-phone. 'It fits my hit on the cell phones. On the morning Wendy landed, a young woman purchased the three identical phones from an Orange store in Antibes.'

'Time?'

'Just after ten o'clock.' Caron reached across the table to hold up one of the phones in its transparent bag. 'Three basic model pay-as-you-go handsets were purchased though we only found two in the house. Both recovered phones have the same third number on speed dial so someone we don't yet know must have the other one. The shop has cameras and is sending film but the serials match.'

Benoit nodded. 'So, Wyatt bought the phones and, given the dates, probably collected Butler's bank card from BNP Paribas where an account had been opened for them. She then contacted Madame Rappeneau and the following day, after meeting her at the villa, rented Jasmin until September...'

'A bit of background here,' interrupted Auger. 'It may be nothing but her husband, Paul Rappeneau, received a caution last year.'

'Was it for a beheading?' said Rolland, provoking laughter.

'No,' said Auger. 'Rappeneau is a local builder and has a reputation for being a little too free with his hands after a drink. Last year, he overstepped the mark at a party and, shall we say, over-enthusiastically embraced the wrong person.'

'And it turned into a police matter?' said Latour.

'The *wrong* person was a thirteen-year-old girl,' said Auger.

'And he got away with a caution?' exclaimed Rolland.

Auger shrugged. 'People were drunk. The girl was up late and tired. The facts were disputed. We took it as far as we could.'

'Sounds like a charmer,' said Caron. 'And Madame?'

'She's a decade older,' said Auger. 'Has her work cut out keeping the marriage going, if you ask me, though it helps that she controls the purse strings which keeps him on the straight and narrow, more than he might wish.'

'We interviewed the Rappeneaus this morning,' said Latour. 'Love's young dreamers, they are not.'

'Village gossip would seem to confirm,' said Auger.

'Gossip isn't evidence,' said Caron.

'No, but out here in the sticks it's currency and it pays to listen,' said Auger.

'Useful background but no more, at this stage,' said Benoit. 'We stay on Wendy. Thierry, get her likeness to the Metropolitan Police in London and Europol, see if you can get them to run her through their facial recognition databases. And get her picture on the briefing board.'

Dugrippe nodded, tapped his laptop keys and the printer sprang into life to produce two copies of Wendy Wyatt's picture.

'Guy Favre at the hotel saw her,' said Benoit. 'Do you mind, Daniel? Your people know their way around better than mine.'

'No problem,' said Auger, stepping to the door of the ICP and shouting. 'Elena!'

'What about Favre, while we're assessing gossip?' said Latour.

'He's honest and upstanding, as far as I know,' said Auger. 'No record and hasn't done anything to merit police attention.'

Dugrippe fixed the image of Wendy onto the space reserved, handing an extra copy to Auger, who transferred it to Costanza with mumbled instructions. She left immediately.

'We'll have confirmation within the hour,' said Auger.

'But if her passport is fake, where does that get us?' said Caron.

'It's a trail,' said Dugrippe.

'What about film from the airport the night she flew home?' said Gagnon. 'With her job done, she may have relaxed and dropped out of character.'

'Good thought,' nodded Dugrippe, tapping at his keyboard.

'What exactly is her connection to the Butlers?' said Rolland.

'This is where it gets interesting,' said Benoit, gesturing at the second blank rectangle. 'The Butlers were met, or possibly escorted on the journey, by an American around fifty years of age. The three of them had lunch at Deux Rocs on their first day in France and Favre said he carried himself like ex-military.'

'Ex-military?' said Caron. 'Are you thinking some kind of bodyguard?'

'If he is, his CV just took a hit,' said Gagnon.

Latour reloaded the film of the Butlers' walking through the airport in Nice and let it play.

'A bodyguard would be sticking closer to them,' said Dugrippe. 'I don't see anyone near them who looks up to the job. Play it again.'

Their first impressions were confirmed. Nobody resembling the American's description accompanied the Butlers.

'Maybe he's more than a bodyguard,' said Caron. 'Someone helping them relocate.'

'Like a security consultant of some kind?' said Gagnon.

'Why not?' said Benoit. 'A person with the skills and the contacts to arrange high quality false passports. Someone, hired by wealthy people looking for privacy, who knows how to move them around the world without attracting attention.'

'Which suggests the Butlers knew they were in danger,' said Rolland.

'They were right,' said Dugrippe.

'If this American exists, it might explain why we've had no hits on the Butlers renting a car or taking a taxi,' said Rolland.

'Any candidates from the passenger manifest?' said Gagnon.

'I'm collating profiles,' said Latour.

'Three cell phones might mean the American has the other one,' said Caron.

'Should we ring him?' said Dugrippe.

'Not until we have some idea who we're talking to,' said Benoit. 'Besides, tomorrow is Saturday - changeover day. Priority is to re-interview any tourists who might be leaving.'

'Janssen and Visser were packing when I interviewed them,' said Auger.

'My first port of call when we finish here,' said Benoit. 'Thierry and Gabriel, man the comms and keep looking at Wendy and the American. I want names. We brief again at six, but this afternoon everyone else is back on the doorstep. We have a clearer window on time of death to frame questions.'

'What about permanent residents?' said Rolland.

'For now, tourists are the priority,' said Benoit.

Rolland gestured towards the images of rotting flesh on the wall. 'But this isn't an argument over a spilled drink or a noisy party. These people had their heads and hands cut off by organised criminals.'

'Yet there's no history of organised crime in the area,' said Benoit.

'Plus, the victimology is wrong for the gangs,' said Latour.

'Got to agree,' said Dugrippe. 'It's too far north for the Italians *and* the Russians in Cannes. All their business is on the Strip. I don't know about Marseille but my CIs are mystified.'

'Nothing from my informants,' said Gagnon. 'Seillans is too remote and too far east for the Shepherds and Sea Breeze. Besides, they're busy fighting for turf in Busserine.'

'Could someone be opening up new markets for product?' said Caron.

'What market?' said Benoit. 'There's nobody here. Most of the young people have already headed off to the coast or Paris.'

'It's true,' said Auger. 'The only drugs we see round here belong to tourists. A little weed, occasionally coke or ecstasy. But only in small quantities and always for personal recreation.'

'Coming from the far east, could the Butlers have been mules?' said Rolland.

'The profile's wrong on that too,' said Latour. 'They'd be poorer, more desperate.'

'Dealers, then,' suggested Gagnon.

'Why would dealers be living where there are no customers?' said Benoit. 'No. Everything we know points to David and Charlotte Butler as wealthy English tourists visiting from Singapore. They have no history in France and no criminal profile...'

'But their passports are fakes,' said Caron. 'They could be anyone.'

'Nina's right,' said Rolland. 'Not all mules are backpackers. They could've been moving product from Singapore - the more respectable they look, the more likely they are to sail through customs.'

'Anything's possible,' said Benoit. 'But Singapore isn't Thailand or Indonesia. Customs at Changi are incredibly tight and corruption levels lower.'

'And even if they *were* mules, what are they doing in Seillans?' said Auger. 'If they were moving product, they'd be in Nice or Cannes.'

'Exactly,' said Latour.

'Is it possible they already delivered their cargo?' said Gagnon.

'And what? Hung around for an expensive six-month holiday?' scoffed Dugrippe. 'You don't risk the death penalty moving gear out of Singapore just to blow it all on a few months in the sun.'

Gagnon shrugged. 'Okay, then maybe they stiffed one of the syndicates and were trying to peddle their shit to another buyer? Original customer got wind and executed them.'

Caron shook her head. 'But any syndicate worth its salt would shout about that from the rooftops as an example to its other dealers. We'd know ID and, sure as shit, we'd know why they were killed.'

'Agreed,' said Benoit. 'If there was an injured party here, they would have sent a message, not thrown a blanket over ID. There's something else at play.'

'Is simple robbery out of the question?' said Rolland. 'I mean, there must be some rich pickings around here.'

'Nothing compared to the coast,' said Benoit. 'And remember the killers left three thousand in cash in David Butler's wallet.'

'And a bank card that could have netted them more,' added Latour. 'It's not a robbery.'

'How much more?' said Caron.

'The account was opened online with BNP Paribas using a bearer bond for a hundred thousand euros,' said Latour. 'A bank card in the name of David Butler was issued to the branch in nearby Montauroux and collected on March 22nd, probably by Wyatt. And that's additional to the sixty-thousand in cash she used to rent the villa.'

'Just a thought, boss, but could this be a witness protection op we haven't been informed about?' said Dugrippe.

'It crossed my mind and I lodged an enquiry,' said Benoit. 'But the DCPJ don't throw these sorts of sums around. I mean, they could *buy* a safe house for the money it cost to rent Jasmin.'

'They might cough up if it was a big financial case - corruption, insider dealing,' said Gagnon. 'If the government stands to make millions in fines and back taxes, a hundred and sixty thousand is chicken feed.'

Benoit shook his head. 'If this was an op, Jerome, there would have been minders or at least people who looked in on them regularly. These people have been dead for nearly a week and no-one batted an eyelid until the pool guy found them.' There was silence around the table.

'So, if it's not organised crime, why are we here?' said Rolland.

'We're here because a cold-blooded double murder has been committed and until we *know* it's not gang-related, we investigate,' said Benoit.

'Who but organised crime would do that?' said Rolland, nodding at the photographs.

'That's what interests me,' said Benoit. 'As you said, this isn't about noisy neighbours. If long-term residents or second-homers killed the Butlers during an argument, it wouldn't have ended like that. We interview everyone who lives on the road, obviously, but unless something screams out at us, residents are likely to be witnesses at best. This was meticulously planned and the violence was deliberately extreme.'

'Too meticulous for organised crime,' said Caron. 'They wouldn't have been this careful.'

'Agreed,' said Dugrippe. 'Gangbangers would have rolled up in a stolen, high-powered car and driven away at high speed, hardly caring who saw or heard them.'

'Seriously?' said Auger.

'Rank and file mob soldiers think they're untouchable,' said Dugrippe. 'As far as they're concerned, there isn't a witness on earth they couldn't intimidate into retracting testimony, especially after making clear the consequences of not doing so.'

'So, we're left with tourists,' said Auger.

'They have the perfect cover,' said Benoit. 'The Butlers are murdered in the early hours of Saturday morning and a few hours later the killers can pack a car and drive away in broad daylight without anyone thinking it strange.'

'And by the time the bodies are discovered, they could be thousands of miles away, in another country,' said Caron.

'Like the two Englishmen,' said Latour.

'And that's why we need to find them,' said Benoit.

12

Benoit stood slightly behind Auger, assessing the young Dutch couple, barely listening to Janssen and Visser's answers.

'...and those spicy sausages,' said Janssen.

'Merguez?' said Auger, making a note.

'That's them,' said Janssen. 'Bloody delicious. We're taking a few kilos back with us. Anything else, Margo?'

The blue-eyed Visser shook her head, glancing at the taciturn Benoit, yet to make a contribution. 'That's all the food I can remember.'

'What about drink?' asked Auger.

'We both had red wine,' said Visser.

'Can you remember the label?'

Both shook their heads. 'It was very nice, expensive, I think,' said Visser.

'Either of you have a beer?' asked Auger. Another shake of heads. 'What about the Butlers?'

'Charlotte drank fizzy white wine, though I don't think it was champagne,' said Visser.

'And David Butler?'

'Bottled beer,' said Janssen. 'Roger and Ash too.'

'What kind?'

'Pelforth, I think,' said Janssen. 'The Belgian couple each had a glass of red, I think.'

'Anybody get really drunk?'

'Mrs Butler, more than anyone,' said Visser. 'She started to get a bit unsteady on her feet after midnight so we left around one in the morning.'

'How did you happen to be invited?' said Auger.

'We met Charlotte on the back road into the village,' said Janssen. 'We used to jog down for our daily baguettes. Great exercise. Charlotte did the same so we saw her most days.'

'She was very friendly,' said Visser.

'And very fit,' said Janssen. 'She swam a lot too. She was very well-toned.' Visser glanced across at him and he looked away. There was an awkward silence so Auger slapped his notebook closed with a glance towards the mute Benoit.

'Were there any drugs at the party?' said Benoit, softly.

'Drugs?' said Visser, not looking at her partner. 'No.'

Benoit's eyebrow raised. 'You speak for everyone there?'

'I mean, I didn't see any.' She turned mechanically to look at Janssen. 'Piet?'

Janssen shook his head. 'Me neither.'

Benoit smiled. 'So, if I empty your luggage and get a sniffer dog to walk through it, we won't find anything?' Visser stared and Janssen licked his lips as Benoit pushed a button on his watch. 'There's an amnesty for full and frank disclosure but it expires in ten seconds.'

Janssen and Visser were temporarily speechless. 'We...' began Janssen, before thinking better of it and lapsing into silence.

'Time's up,' said Benoit, seconds later.

'We have weed,' said Visser, quickly, her throat dry. 'We brought it with us from home. There's only a bit left.'

'You smoked before the party?'

'Yes,' said Janssen.

'What about during?'

'No, that would have been rude.'

'Anyone else take anything at the party or give you the impression that they were high?'

'No,' said Janssen. 'We already said.'

'You didn't take cocaine? Amphetamines? Ecstasy?'

'Nothing like that,' answered Janssen.

'And you don't possess hypodermic needles for drug use?'

'No way,' said Janssen, indignant. 'We like to keep fit. A little weed is as far we go.'

'I'll go and fetch it,' said Visser, eager to please. 'There's only a little...'

'Keep it,' said Benoit. 'Thank you for your candour. One more question. You said the two Englishmen were gay? Did they announce it or did you deduce it from their behaviour?'

Visser and Janssen exchanged a glance.

As the sun began to dip towards the hills, Auger and Benoit ducked under the barrier and headed for the ICP. The crowd seemed to have swelled since the morning and a local journalist took photographs of Auger and Benoit heading for the prefab before shouting a question which both ignored.

'How did you know?' said Auger.

'About the drugs? I didn't.'

'Don't you think you were a little hard on them?'

'Absolutely,' grinned Benoit. 'Which made them concentrate when I asked the more important question.'

'The Englishmen?'

'The Englishmen.'

'You suspect they weren't a couple?' said Auger.

'Suspect? No. But, I think it's easy to make assumptions when two men share the same accommodations.'

'Boss.' Benoit turned to see Dugrippe come panting up the steep drive of Villa Jasmin. 'Something in the house you should see.'

.   .   .

'THERE.' Dugrippe pointed at the bookshelf. Auger and Benoit followed his finger to a tiny camera lens almost invisible on the dark spine of the DVD boxset.

'Is it active?' said Benoit.

'Grace thinks so,' said Dugrippe.

'Grace Coulibaly?' said Benoit.

'You expecting someone else, Sergio?' said a voice behind them. The woman pulled down her mask to reveal a plump black face, multi-coloured spectacles perched on her nose and tufts of wiry hair poking out from the hood of her straining protective suit. 'And please don't touch. We're still dusting.'

'Good to know we're in safe hands,' said Benoit, smiling. 'I don't see any wires or a lead.'

'That's because it's wireless.'

'How does it know when to take pictures?' said Auger.

'It probably keys off a motion sensor,' said Coulibaly.

'And sends the images to a computer?' said Benoit.

'Nope,' said Coulibaly. 'You'd need a router in the house and there isn't one.'

'How close would the router need to be?' said Auger.

'Fifteen, twenty metres,' she said. 'Neighbouring houses are too far away for a signal, if that's what you're thinking.'

'So, without a router?' said Benoit.

'You'd need a connection to a computer on site for storing images,' said Coulibaly.

'There are no computers on site,' said Benoit.

'Exactly.'

'What about a satellite feed?' said Auger.

Coulibaly shook her head. 'Not without a router. And a dish.'

'Then what's the point of the camera?' said Benoit.

'It's a standalone,' she said. 'Which means it's not sending images anywhere. It's storing them, probably onto a SD card.' The officers looked at her. 'Secure Digital.'

'A portable memory,' said Auger.

'Right. You remove the storage card and plug it into a computer or a TV for viewing. It's low tech.'

'But, if it works, we could have our killers on film,' said Benoit. 'What's the power source?'

'Has to be a battery,' said Coulibaly. 'Hopefully a powerful one.'

'Infrared?'

'Depends on the model.'

'It's sounds a bit limited,' said Auger.

'With one obvious drawback,' added Coulibaly.

'The fixed view,' said Benoit. 'Let me know the second you get your hands on the memory card.' Excited, he stood to leave before a thought occurred. 'Where are your people staying, Grace?'

'In a hotel near the forensic lab in Draguignan,' said Coulibaly. 'You?'

'From tomorrow, camp beds in an old church,' sighed Dugrippe.

'Great for team building,' said Coulibaly, winking.

BENOIT, Auger and Dugrippe trudged back up the baking hot drive and poured themselves a cup of lukewarm coffee in the ICP.

'I don't understand,' said Auger. 'Why would the killers leave a camera behind?'

'They didn't,' said Benoit. 'Had they known it was there they would've removed it.'

'Then who put it there?'

'Wendy Wyatt sent boxes of English language books and DVDs to the villa,' said Dugrippe.

'She may have sent them but she wasn't around to set up the camera, make sure it was working and position it on the shelves with the optimal view,' said Benoit. 'And I doubt she'd trust Madame Rappeneau to do it for her.'

'The mystery American!' said Dugrippe. 'He was in Seillans. He must have taken the Butlers to the villa and set up the camera while they weren't looking.'

'Which means it's been taking photographs since the Butlers arrived,' said Auger. 'What a stroke of luck.'

'Assuming it's still working,' said Dugrippe.

'We'll know soon enough,' said Benoit, looking across at Latour. 'Anything from Singapore, Gabriel?'

Latour looked up from his keyboard. 'No records of a David and Charlotte Butler living on the island or of anyone entering Singapore on those passports. The SPF are running the Butler pictures through their Facial Recog software. No hits yet.' He shrugged. 'Different time zone. Different language.'

'And just a Missing Persons enquiry, as far as they're concerned,' said Benoit. 'Okay, scale it up to a murder inquiry and give them everything we have on the Butlers and their movements. We need to inject some urgency and get that ID. We can worry about a media shitstorm later.'

'Ex-Pat Bloodbath in Riviera Beauty Spot!' announced Latour, dramatically.

'There's still time if you prefer to be a journalist,' said Benoit.

'This just in,' quipped Latour. 'Uniform have spoken to the owners of Villa Lavendre.' He handed Benoit a piece of paper. 'Roger Barron and Ashley Cooper. I have a *joint* bank account for them in the UK used to pay for the villa and an address for both of them in Surrey.'

'Address singular?'

'And they're both on the UK's electoral register at that address,' said Latour. 'Looks like they are who they say they are. I've asked British police to check the house and confirm IDs. No word yet.'

'Car?'

'Details soon.'

'Good work,' said Benoit. 'When you get the car, ask Traffic to sift through autoroute film for last Saturday *and* Sunday. Routes from here to the North first. If they find nothing, expand across all autoroute networks in case they broke their journey to Calais. Do we have contact details?'

'I've got a cell phone for Barron from Lavendre's owner but it's dead. Of course, he may have written it down wrong. Checking.'

'And the American?'

'I've got the passenger manifest but no images yet,' said Latour. 'Give me an hour.'

BENOIT FINISHED his ham and cheese baguette and took his freshly brewed coffee outside to smoke a cigarette. The frequency of iPhone camera flashes from the barriers had increased and questions were periodically barked by a growing number of journalists at anyone on the crime scene working within earshot.

Auger was in conversation with Costanza, who sat on a motorbike, about five metres from the barrier. She handed him the plastic wallet containing the image of Wendy Wyatt and Auger headed for the ICP.

'Favre recognised the picture of Wyatt as the girl who stayed at Deux Rocs,' he said to Benoit.

Coulibaly emerged through the gates at the top of the drive, panting, facemask around her neck. She carried the DVD case containing the camera in a large evidence bag and, after catching her breath, struggled towards him. 'Give me a minute,' she panted.

Benoit smiled at the beads of sweat dotting her brow and reached back into the ICP to tear a bottle of water from a palette. 'You're going to be a lot fitter after this case.'

'If I don't die first,' she said, accepting the water and taking a swallow. 'Bad news. No prints on the case and no pictures to show you.'

'I knew it was too good to be true,' said Benoit.

'So, it's not working?' said Dugrippe.

'It's working but the storage card has been removed...'

'Assuming there ever was one,' said Auger.

'The battery has power,' said Coulibaly.

'So, why provide a power source for a camera that can't store the images?' said Benoit.

'Exactly,' said Coulibaly. 'There had to be a memory card and someone took it. In better news, the lab texted. They found DNA samples in the beer bottle, on the hairbrush, toothbrushes and both razors.'

'Progress,' said Benoit. 'Put a rush on them. We need a match to the corpses.'

'You should get word tonight or tomorrow morning,' said Coulibaly.

'What about the villa? Are things slowing down in there, yet?'

'We're getting there,' said Coulibaly. 'It helps that the scene was cleaner than Macron's arse. Someone did a thorough job on it, including the traps. By the way, not sure it's relevant but one of my people found an oiled cloth in the cupboard housing the water tank. He's a weekend hunter and, from the viscosity, he thinks it's gun oil.'

'Gun oil?' said Benoit.

'Unconfirmed. We've sent the cloth for analysis.'

'But no gun.'

'No,' said Coulibaly. 'And no way of telling how long the cloth has been there or if there was ever a weapon wrapped in it.'

'You could say the same for the camera,' said Auger.

'The battery still has power,' said Coulibaly. 'It was set up recently.'

'But no way of knowing who put it there,' said Auger.

'You could ask the owner,' said Coulibaly. 'This is the kind of stunt pulled by sleaze ball landlords. Especially if one of the tenants is an attractive younger woman.'

'Monsieur Rappeneau fits *that* bill,' said Auger.

'Madame Butler too,' said Benoit. 'But wouldn't Rappeneau have put the camera in the bedroom?'

'Depends,' said Coulibaly. 'Easier to hide it in the clutter of living quarters. And, like most people staying as a guest in someone else's house, it's usual to have a fuck in every room.'

Benoit stared at her. 'Remind me never to lend you my apartment.'

Auger pulled out his phone and took a picture of the DVD case before glancing at Benoit.

'Go,' said Benoit. 'And while you're there, ask them whether they own or have ever kept guns at Jasmin. If they produce one, bag it.' Auger headed to his car. 'Grace, what time can you finish in the house?'

'Tonight?' she said. 'Pepe has drains to examine.'

'But nothing that can't wait until morning, right?' said Benoit.

'I suppose we could be out by ten o'clock if I cancel the all-nighters. Why?'

'Can you make that a deadline and secure the place?'

'Secure the house?'

'Leave it as it is and close it up,' explained Benoit.

Coulibaly eyed him suspiciously. 'You havin' a pool party and not inviting me?'

13

January 2002, Chicago

Trent knocked on the door of Room 674 - two sharp raps followed a few seconds later by another. He stood back to gaze at the spyhole, transferred the bag of doughnuts and pointed his gun hand towards the tiny glass aperture. When a shadow fell across the light from inside, he squeezed an imaginary trigger.

'Bang!' he shouted. 'You're dead.'

'Yeah, yeah,' came the muffled reply. 'You got me.'

The door opened. 'You're early,' said Rentoria, walking back into the apartment kitchen to get his coat.

'You complaining?' said Trent, closing the door and securing all the locks.

'Hell, no...what are you doing? I'm leaving in a second.'

'Changeover is a red zone, Jose. But, hey, I left the chain down. That should save you a couple of seconds.'

'I'm gonna need a surgeon if I don't stop laughing soon,' said Rentoria.

'Hi, Mike,' said Gwen, from the doorway.

'Mrs Beaumont,' said Trent, avoiding Rentoria's leering grin.

'Miiiiiiiiiiikkkke!' screamed Nell, running down the corridor to fling her arms around his knees.

'Easy there, tiger.'

'Waddya got? Waddya got?' she begged, looking up at him.

'I haven't got anything,' said Trent, showing her his left hand.

'Other hand, other hand.'

Behind his back, Trent switched the bag of doughnuts and wiggled his empty right hand at her. 'Nothing there either.'

'You switched,' she giggled.

Trent gazed in astonishment at the doughnuts in his left hand. 'How did they get there?'

'Krispy Kremes!' shrieked Nell. Laughing, Trent opened the bag and she removed the unearthly red glaze of a strawberry doughnut and took a bite. 'Mmmmmm.'

'What do you say, Nell?' said Gwen.

'Thank you, Mike,' she shouted, scuttling away to eat her doughnut. Gwen poured Trent a mug of coffee while he emptied the bag of doughnuts onto a plate and held it towards Rentoria.

'Jose?'

'One minute you shoot me in the face, the next you offer me a doughnut,' said Rentoria.

'Your reward for taking down the Do Not Disturb sign.'

'Is a raise out of the question?' said Rentoria, picking a doughnut and taking a bite.

'Wow,' said Trent.

'What?'

'Never figured you for a classic cinnamon man.'

'Full of surprises, me,' said Rentoria, his mouth full. 'Outta here.'

.   .   .

'THANK YOU,' said Gwen, after Rentoria had left.

'For what?' said Trent, sipping his black coffee.

She slid from her kitchen stool and moved into him, kissing him on the cheek. Gazing into his eyes, she moved to his lips and dropped a hand onto his. Trent opened his mouth and they kissed.

Thirty seconds later, Gwen withdrew, her eyes still burning into his.

'For always thinking of us.' She glanced at the door to the next room, a coy smile on her lips. 'Now, if only I could get Nell to go to sleep for an hour.' Trent brandished the Do Not Disturb sign and Gwen laughed. 'Yeah, that'll work.'

'There is another way,' said Trent.

'Does it involve sleeping pills?' said Gwen.

'Better than that.' From a back pocket, Trent withdrew three tickets and held them up.

Gwen stared. 'Tribune Plaza?'

'Ice skating.'

'Sounds great, Mike, but, how can we?'

'Already scoped it out. We take the service elevator to the basement lot where I've got a hire car waiting and the park is just a few minutes' ride.'

Gwen's expression darkened. 'I don't know, Mike. Sounds risky.'

'Your decision, of course,' said Trent. 'But it'll do you both good. We'll be in public view, wrapped up warm in hats and scarves. No-one will even see your face.'

NELL SKATED AWAY from Trent and her mother, leaving the two uncertain adults holding each other up.

'You've done this before,' Trent called after her, trying to balance on the blade. Thrilled, Nell looked back as her mother stumbled but Trent steadied her and they continued uncertainly around the rink, laughing every faltering step of the way.

After twenty minutes the two adults staggered to the

gate and removed their skates. Five minutes after that, they sat huddled under a heater at a rink side table, sipping hot chocolate and nibbling on marshmallows, watching Nell tear around the ice.

When Nell could skate no more, she changed quickly into her shoes so she could drag Trent and her mother off to the nearby Cloud Gate, a smooth, reflective bean-shaped sculpture, like an outdoor hall of mirrors.

'Look at Mike,' giggled Nell, as Trent pulled a face. She ran around the sculpture, kicking up snow, laughing and pointing at her reflection as she went. 'That's funny.'

'Boy, did we need this,' said Gwen. 'I'd forgotten what a normal life was like.'

'You're having a good time?' said Trent.

'Better than that. Thanks for taking the trouble.'

'Trouble?' laughed Trent. 'I'm loving every minute.'

Her smile faded and she covered his hand again. 'Mind if I ask you something, Mike?'

'Marital status or scar?' said Trent.

She laughed. 'Am I that transparent?'

'You've a right to ask. I got married when I was twenty after joining the Marines. It was fine for a while. Sherry and I had fun. We got to travel. But then the Gulf War came along and things were never really the same again. She said I'd changed, that I was...sad, all the time.' He nodded. 'She was right. War and fighting...seeing people die, some of them friends. Luckily, we hadn't gotten around to kids which made the split a whole lot easier.'

'Guess I don't need to ask about the scar now, do I?'

'I was in a Humvee, travelling in convoy through Kuwait. The vehicle in front was hit by a rocket and there was shrapnel. I got hit, spent a month in hospital and was given a ticket home.'

'I'm sorry.'

'Hey, I walked away from it. The guys in the other Humvee were vaporised. The worst thing is there was an intel foul-up. The jet firing the rocket was American.

Friendly fire. What a phrase.' He smiled to close the subject. 'And you?'

'My husband travelled for work. He met someone and had an affair. We divorced two years ago. The American Dream takes another detour.'

'What an idiot,' said Trent. 'You're better off without him.' He flushed with embarrassment. 'I'm sorry...that was stupid.'

'It's fine,' said Gwen, touching his hand. 'How else would I have met you?'

Nell came running towards them, her face red. 'I'm hungry.'

'Want to get some pie?' said Trent. 'I know the best deep-dish joint in the city.'

GWEN FINISHED her third slice of pepperoni and sat back with a groan of pleasure. 'I don't need riches if I can go to the park with my little girl and eat pizza this good.' She ruffled Nell's hair but her daughter didn't look up from colouring in her place mat. A tear rolled down Gwen's face.

'Hey,' said Trent. 'That's enough of that. This *will* end. I gave you my word, didn't I? That means something in this city.'

Gwen put on a brave face. A second later, she looked beyond him. 'Mike? That man's staring at us.'

Trent turned to see a large man in a thick worsted over-coat, sporting a woollen Chicago Bears hat pulled low on his forehead. He stood by the exit and turned to leave when Trent looked in his direction. 'Stay here.'

'Mike!' said Gwen. 'Be careful,' she mouthed, trying not to alarm Nell. Trent nodded reassurance and marched outside.

'Hey, buddy,' he called to the man, following him to a chunky GMC Yukon with blacked out windows. 'Help you with something?'

The man leaned against the driver's door and contemplated Trent. 'Should you be out here like this, Special Agent Trent?'

'Excuse me?'

'Out on the street, with no line of sight on the package.'

'What the fuck...?'

'You can't protect Mrs Beaumont if you can't see her.'

Trent whipped out his service pistol and grabbed the man's overcoat, roughly turning him around. 'Hands on the roof.'

The man chuckled faintly before obeying. 'Anyone ever tell you you're coiled a little tight, Mike?'

'You're the first,' said Trent, stepping into him, pulling out a pair of cuffs and kicking the man's feet apart.

'You're not going to cuff me, Agent Trent,' said the man.

'And why is that?' said Trent, holstering his gun and searching inside the man's jacket.

'I'm not carrying for a start and nor am I dumb enough to meet with you, carrying ID.'

Trent finished his fruitless search. 'Who are you?'

'You can call me Byron.'

Trent paused with the cuffs, span him round. 'Why are you following me, Byron?'

'You know why. I'm working. Like you.'

'On what?' demanded Trent. Byron emitted a chuckle and Trent punched him hard in the stomach, doubling him up for thirty seconds. 'On what?'

'Still in shape, Mike,' said Byron, panting. 'Good to see.'

'How did you find me?'

'Find you?' said Byron, grimacing. 'You've never been out of our sight.'

Trent grabbed his lapels and drew back a fist. 'You fucking...'

'Mike! You need to concentrate on what I'm about to say.' Byron held up his hands to protect his face. Trent's knuckles were white with tension but the punch wasn't thrown and he dropped his hands.

'I'm listening,' said Trent, sliding a hand back to his service weapon.

'The important thing now is to focus on how this ends.'

Trent pulled out his gun. 'You mean with me shooting you in self-defence? Don't worry, *buddy*. I got a spare for your cold, dead hand.'

'I'm sure,' said Byron. 'But *you* don't want the attention that would bring and *we* don't want to kill feds to achieve our goals.' Trent eased off the safety and the urgency in Byron's voice tightened a notch. 'Above all, we do *not* want to harm a child.'

'If you...'

'Listen to me!' said Byron. 'Vested interests need your witness to die and I'm offering you a chance to limit the damage.' Trent's hand tightened on the trigger. 'Take it easy. I'm just the messenger.'

'You're about to become the message, fuckstick,' snarled Trent. 'You think I'd step aside and let you execute a young mother.'

'To avoid greater carnage, yes,' said Byron. 'This is America, Mike. Money wins. Big money that makes the world turn. And you don't have any so you're not in the game. You don't have to like it but that's how it is. Hell, I don't like it. But, Christ, Mike, we're not monsters. We're parents too and we don't want to see a young child...'

'Mike,' shouted Nell, running up to tug on his coat. 'Come quick. We got ice cream.'

Trent hid the gun quickly under his jacket before turning to smile at her.

'Hi, honey,' said Byron, bending down to speak to her before Trent had a chance to stop him. 'How you doing?'

'Hello,' said Nell, warily.

'You got ice cream? What flavour, honey?'

'Chocolate chip,' said Nell, uncertainly.

'What's going on Mike?' said Gwen, walking out without her coat, arms folded against the bitter cold.

Byron fixed a big smile on his face. 'Mike and I were just

catching up, ma'am. We served together in the Gulf. It took me a second to recognise him, sitting there in the booth.'

'I'm not surprised,' said Gwen. 'He had his back to you.'

'Just like in the Humvee, ma'am,' said Byron, without missing a beat. 'I'd recognise those shoulders anywhere.'

'Oh,' said Gwen, relief flooding her features. She grabbed Nell's hand. 'Nice to meet you...'

'Byron,' he said. 'You too, ma'am.'

'Come on, pumpkin. It's cold out here.' Gwen marched her daughter back inside the pizza parlour.

'Nice-looking woman,' said Byron, with genuine regret. 'Such a shame. Cute kid too.' Trent took out his gun and jammed the butt down hard on Byron's nose. Blood spattered across his face and he put a leather-gloved hand to cover his face.

'That's right, Mike,' panted Byron. 'Lash out. Blame others for the bureau leaning on her to testify.' He dropped his hand and speared a malevolent glare towards him. 'But know this. You killed her. You and your colleagues in the Justice Department. You shouldn't pressure the vulnerable when they're in no position to defend themselves. I wish we could rewind the clock but we can't. The damage is done. Stop fighting the inevitable and step aside - save some lives.'

'Get the fuck out of here,' snarled Trent, raising the gun. 'I see you again, I'll kill you.'

Byron smiled, blood coating his teeth. 'You won't see me again, Mike. You won't see anyone.'

TRENT HURRIED BACK into the restaurant, relieved to see Gwen watching Nell tuck into her ice cream. He dropped a wad of bills on the check and flashed his ID at a passing waitress.

'Is there a back way out?' he said. The waitress nodded at a no-entry sign with a keypad security lock. Trent gave her a twenty. 'Open it.' He gathered Gwen and Nell as calmly as possible and led them to the back door, out through the kitchen into a dark alley filled with bins.

After marching Gwen and Nell to the next street, they walked a couple of blocks before he flagged a cab. 'Drive around for half an hour and make sure we're not being followed. There's a fifty in it.'

'You've never met Byron before, have you?' said Gwen, softly into his ear, when the cab was rolling down Michigan five minutes later. Nell was curled up between them, fast asleep.

'No.'

'Was he threatening to kill us, Mike?' Trent's expression told its own story. 'We were alone but they didn't try anything.'

'Too public,' said Trent. 'These people operate in the shadows.'

'What do we do?'

Trent smiled faintly at her, took out his cell, flicked down the speed dial and wrote two numbers onto his hand before breaking the phone apart. 'We go rogue.'

14

'Roger Barron, aged fifty,' said Latour, pointing at the photograph on the left of the split-screen. It was of a tall man with receding grey hair, carrying the weight of prosperity rather than indolence. 'Barron is a law partner in a firm based in Guildford, Surrey, just outside London.' On the right of the screen was a photograph of a fair-haired, slender figure with bright blue eyes. 'Ash Cooper is ten years younger and a chartered surveyor. They married three years ago and share a house which Barron owns.'

'So, they were just another tourist couple on holiday,' said Caron.

'We still need to speak to them,' said Benoit.

'If we can find them,' said Latour. 'Current whereabouts unknown but we're certain they didn't return to England because both were scheduled to return to work at the start of this week yet neither appeared.

'French Transport Police confirm their vehicle hasn't crossed the channel through the tunnel or on any ferry to England since they left Seillans and British police say their house and drive are empty. Neighbours haven't seen them or their car.'

'Maybe they extended their holiday,' said Caron.

'If so, it was last minute because they were booked onto a P&O ferry for *last* Sunday night after leaving Seillans the previous day,' said Latour.

'The day the Butlers were killed?'

Latour nodded. 'As they didn't arrive in Calais, we're widening the search and I've given details of their VW Golf to all autoroute networks. Awaiting sightings and film for our window.'

'Maybe they were delayed or rerouted?' said Rolland.

'If they were, they didn't inform work colleagues or contact family who were expecting them to attend a Bar Mitzvah rehearsal the day after their return,' said Latour. 'Surrey Police have listed them as missing.'

'Finding Barron and Cooper is top priority,' said Benoit. 'They were two of the last people on earth to see the Butlers alive and we treat their disappearance as suspicious.'

'We re-interviewed the Dutch couple,' said Auger, after a glance from Benoit. 'Janssen and Visser remembered there was tension between Barron, Cooper and David Butler at the party.'

'What kind of tension?' said Caron.

'The kind you find in a marriage where one partner gets jealous,' said Auger.

'According to Visser, Cooper was flirting with David Butler and Barron didn't take it well,' said Benoit.

'Did it get physical?' said Rolland.

Auger shook his head. 'Visser said it was no more than awkwardness or they would have told us when first questioned. Nothing was said but apparently Barron was annoyed and itching to leave the party earlier than Cooper wanted.'

'But Butler wasn't gay,' said Rolland.

'He may have married a knockout wife but we don't *know* he was straight,' said Latour. 'These rich guys...'

'You don't need to be gay to enjoy attention from someone of the same sex,' said Dugrippe, looking around the room for support.

'That's our dinner conversation sorted,' said Caron, winking at him.

'Are we seriously suggesting Barron drugged Butler *and* his wife and cut off their heads with a chainsaw because he was jealous?' said Rolland.

'Don't forget slicing off Butler's cock with a handy scalpel, in case his headless rival hadn't got the message,' said Caron. She laughed at the absurdity.

'And, if Barron *was* the killer, he'd have had to wait for the Dutch couple to leave before returning,' said Dugrippe. 'That's hardly a jealous rage.'

'Gave him time to fetch his chainsaw, scalpel and hypodermic, at least,' said Caron.

'Okay,' said Benoit. 'Extreme scepticism noted. And, you're right. What happened to the Butlers had more to do with cold, premeditated evil than passion but, until we find Barron and Cooper and eliminate them from our enquiries, everything's on the table. Nina?'

'Orange sent film of Wendy Wyatt, from their Antibes store,' she said, clicking her mouse. A young woman appeared on the screen, dressed conservatively in khaki chinos and plain white T-shirt, a large straw hat on her head. She waited for her purchases to be bagged, a wad of notes in her hand.

'Shy girl,' said Latour. 'We can't ID her from that.'

'We don't need to,' said Benoit. 'Her passport photograph was positively identified by Madame Rappeneau *and* Guy Favre at the Deux Rocs and the date and time display tallies exactly with the purchase of the three phones left behind in Jasmin.'

'What about the hidden camera?' said Rolland.

'We think the American set it up when he dropped off the Butlers,' said Benoit. 'That's why it has a perfect view of the lounge and the downstairs bedrooms.'

'Entry points,' nodded Dugrippe.

'So, it was storing images?' said Rolland.

'We assume so,' said Benoit. 'But there's no memory card so, if it was taking photographs, someone removed it.'

'Are we sure it's not Rappeneau's camera?' said Caron. 'He wouldn't be the first landlord to be a peeper.'

'We considered it,' said Auger. 'I asked them as diplomatically as possible - both said they'd never seen it before.'

'What else would they say?'

'If Madame even suspected her husband put the camera there, she would have hit the roof,' said Auger. 'She said Wyatt requested the bookcase be cleared when they vacated and restocked with books and DVDs for the Butlers for the length of the tenancy...'

'And, as all the books and most of the DVDs are English, and there's a box of French books in the garage, it looks like she's telling the truth,' said Benoit.

'How did the books and DVDs arrive?' said Latour.

'In boxes four days after Wyatt booked the villa,' said Auger.

'From England?' said Caron.

'Madame threw out the packaging but that's her recollection,' said Auger. 'She put everything from the boxes on the shelves though she doesn't remember the DVD with the camera.'

'And the gun oil?' said Dugrippe.

'Madame said they've never owned a handgun, much less kept one at Jasmin,' said Auger. 'Local licensing records confirm.'

'Doesn't mean they didn't have one,' said Caron. 'And I agree with Adele about Rappeneau and the camera.'

'Then why was there no storage card?' said Benoit.

'Maybe Rappeneau removed it.'

'When?' said Benoit. 'He's had no access since the bodies were discovered.'

'Unless he's one of the killers, in which case he had several days to remove it,' said Dugrippe.

'Then why not take the whole piece of kit?' said Rolland. 'We were always going to find it and ask questions.'

'Adele's right,' said Latour. 'Besides, what can Rappeneau get from a hidden camera that he can't see on the internet? The American set up the camera.'

'Or the Butlers,' said Caron.

'Or the pool guy,' said Gagnon. There was a ripple of laughter. 'We're nowhere, aren't we?'

'But we're getting there quickly,' said Benoit, smiling. 'Thierry?'

'I've got more film from Nice airport,' said Dugrippe. 'I've not seen all of it but I found this view of Wyatt heading to the departure gate to board her return flight to London.'

From a lofty camera position, a young woman wearing Wendy Wyatt's distinctive straw hat ambled towards the cameras carrying a coat and a striking pink and white striped shopping bag.

'Doesn't tell us much,' said Auger.

'Look at the bag,' said Dugrippe, rewinding the film.

'Can you clean it up?' said Gagnon, squinting at the screen.

'I can try,' said Dugrippe.

Rolland and Caron exchanged a smile. 'It's no wonder you guys are single,' said Caron. 'That's a Victoria's Secret bag.'

'Victoria's secret what?' said Latour, provoking mockery and head shaking.

'High-end, sexy underwear and lingerie,' explained Rolland. 'Men. Honestly.'

'Is there a store in Terminal One?' said Latour.

'Yes,' said Rolland.

'You might be on to something,' said Benoit, squinting at the time display. 'Time on the film is 21.15. Get onto the store and have them check all purchases in the previous hour. And ask them to back it up with security film, if they've got it. I want a list of credit card details for customers. If we're lucky, Wendy got careless and used her own plastic and, if there's a name to be had, I want it on the board tonight.'

Dugrippe nodded, tapping at his keyboard. 'Their

website has a phone number. I'll ring them now.' He fumbled for his phone, keyed in the number and leapt up to leave the ICP.

Benoit looked around at his expectant team. 'Questions?' When no-one answered, he gestured to Latour.

'We have eleven Caucasian adult males, around fifty years of age, travelling alone on the same Dubai to Nice flight as the Butlers,' said Latour. 'I took out three who weren't also on the Singapore leg, which leaves eight.' He tapped a key. Eight passport photographs appeared on the screen in two ranks of four. 'None of them American though.'

Benoit studied the faces. 'Get rid of him and him,' he said, pointing at two hefty men with sagging jowls. 'What's left?'

'Three French, two British and one Canadian.'

'Canadian?' said Benoit, looking at the picture of Trent with his short brown hair and steel grey eyes. 'Name?'

'Moss Tyler. An IT specialist from Toronto.'

Benoit nodded. 'And Favre's description?'

'Short brown hair, greying at the temples, scar across the forehead, lean and muscular,' said Latour. 'Hard to gauge physique but there's no spare flesh around the face.'

'And there's the scar,' said Benoit. Latour nodded. 'That's our man. Give me a hard copy to show Favre when we get to the hotel. Throw in the two Brits to make a line-up but I'm putting his picture on the wall.'

'I'll start running him through all the recognition protocols,' said Latour. 'Should I contact the Canadians?'

'I'll wager Moss Tyler is another fake ID.' Benoit considered further. 'But ask Passport Control if they have a record of Tyler travelling on from Nice.'

'You don't think he's in France?' said Gagnon.

'I'd be amazed if he was,' said Benoit. 'And, if he killed the Butlers, he'd be as far away as possible.' He glanced at Caron.

'The third phone is somewhere in Northern Spain,

according to the network,' said Caron. 'That's as close as it gets, without GPS and serious call time and there's no guarantee Tyler even has it in his possession.'

'But now we have a face and a name to match,' said Benoit, pulling on a protective glove. 'Time to drop a pebble into the pond and watch the ripples.'

With a gloved hand, Caron plucked the cell phone from an evidence bag, attached a couple of leads then passed it to Benoit. She began tapping at her laptop, before pointing a finger at Benoit.

Benoit turned on the phone, scrolled down the speed dial screen and flicked at the unknown number.

TRENT SAT on the banquette of his corner suite, training shoes kicked off, eyes switching between the black expanse of sea far below his floor-to-ceiling window and the WhatsApp message to Megan on his smartphone. Wearing shorts, T-shirt and a towel around his neck to soak up the sweat from his two-hour gym session, he glared at the unbroken series of messages, sent to her over the last thirty-six hours. It was the same story on their message board on the dark web.

Where are you? Few more days in B. No sign of hostiles. Speak to me.

He sent the message into the ether and stared pensively out to sea where, on the horizon, the lights of container ships were moving south along the Catalan coast. He stood to go for a shower but was halted by an unfamiliar ringtone. After a second to locate the source, he leapt to his rucksack, took out the cell phone and flipped it open to read the screen.

'Charlotte.' Trent pressed a button and put the phone to his ear but didn't speak. The other end of the line was equally silent. After ten seconds, Trent prepared to ring off.

'Moss Tyler?' An unknown male voice. Trent's veins turned to ice. He grabbed his Blancpain Fifty Fathoms watch from the bed and started the timer. *'This is Comman-dant Serge Benoit of the Alpes-Maritimes Serious Crimes Squad.'* The voice spoke softly and slowly, enunciating each conso-nant to drag out the time. *'I'm speaking to you from Villa Jasmin. In Seillans. You know where that is, don't you, monsieur?'* Another pause. *'As does your attractive young friend, Wendy.'*

Trent gripped the handset tighter. Instinctively, he opened his mouth to reply but resisted. Seillans was blown. The Renfrews were blown. And a man called Benoit was using Carla Renfrew's phone to goad him into an indis-cretion.

'Are you there, monsieur?'

Wendy and not Megan. Benoit didn't know Megan's name. He was fishing with insufficient bait. Was he even a policeman? It was an odd lie, if not. Then again, a hostile would *never* call to gloat about discovering and killing his clients. What purpose would it serve? Trent's expression hardened and he moved a thumb to disconnect.

'I'm speaking to you on Charlotte Butler's cell phone,' continued Benoit. *'Have you nothing to say? Don't you want to know what's happened to Charlotte and David?'*

Butler not Renfrew! Benoit had nothing. Trent glanced at the timer on his watch. Five seconds. He hesitated, plans firming in his mind, thumb hovering to end the call before they had a chance to narrow down his location. A second later, he decided to let the call play out. He wouldn't be in Barcelona long enough for it to matter. Let them waste their time trying to locate him. In fact, it might work to his advantage.

'Fly to Nice tomorrow and surrender yourself to the Airport Police so we can talk. Just ring back or text us your flight number and we'll meet you. Monsieur Tyler?'

Trent imagined a colleague beside Benoit, giving him the thumbs up on a trace so he finally terminated the call and removed the SIM card. He broke the phone apart, throwing the casing into the bin and flushed the SIM card down the toilet, wrapped in tissue. Three minutes later,

Trent was packed and waiting for the lift. He sent a message to Megan.

Ground zero blown. Immediate Dust off. Arrival ZD30. Assume worst. All artefacts in burn bag NOW. Going dark. Confirm.

∼

BENOIT CLOSED the phone and dropped it into the evidence bag, deep in thought.

'Cool customer,' said Latour.

'Or too stunned to answer.' Benoit raised an eyebrow at Caron.

'Barcelona,' she said. 'That's all without GPS.'

'That's close enough,' said Benoit.

'Bit careless staying on that long,' said Gagnon.

'I doubt that,' said Benoit. 'I think he wanted us to know he was there because he soon won't be.'

'Think he'll ring back?' said Caron.

Benoit shook his head. 'He's already destroyed the phone and packed a bag.'

'And then where?' said Caron. 'Back to Canada?'

'Even if he's Canadian, he won't go there,' said Benoit. 'He answered Charlotte Butler's call and, unless I'm mistaken, he's going to want to know why I've got her phone.'

'Doesn't answering the call tell us he didn't kill the Butlers?' said Gagnon.

'I think it does,' said Benoit.

'You honestly think he'll give himself up at the airport?'

'We'll see,' said Benoit.

Dugrippe charged into the briefing room, beaming. 'Got her.'

TRENT GUNNED the Range Rover south, along the coast road towards Barcelona Airport to catch the next flight to

London, his features like granite. He passed Franco's noto-
rious prison in the dark, spotlights throwing its austere
walls into dramatic relief. He had a flash of Charlotte
Butler's hand squeezing his shoulder on that first morning
in Seillans, could picture her grateful expression, as she
thanked him for his help.

A minute later, he slapped the steering wheel with the
palm of his hand and pulled off at the upcoming exit. At the
junction, he glared at his watch and made the calculation,
then pulled onto the roundabout and took the road north
towards Girona.

15

'You're certain?' said Benoit.

Favre laid the photograph of Tyler on the table. 'That's the man who had lunch with the Butlers.'

Benoit nodded and lit a cigarette, blowing smoke into the warm night air. Nina Caron was also smoking but the rest of his squad were nibbling on a piece of bread, tired after a long day.

'You haven't ordered drinks,' said Favre.

'We're fine with water,' said Benoit, looking at his colleagues one after the other. Favre looked round at the officers, who nodded unconvincingly.

'Just water,' mumbled Rolland, staring back.

Favre shrugged. 'I'll get your starters.'

Dugrippe walked out of the shadows to pull up a chair, pocketing his phone. 'I've alerted Immigration but there are no flights from Barcelona into Nice until ten in the morning. Full reception committee on alert.'

'And Megan Matteson?' said Latour.

'I started the ball rolling with the Brits,' said Dugrippe. 'We'll know if it's another phoney ID tomorrow.' He sat down and wrapped his large fist around a piece of bread. 'Where's the wine?'

'We don't want wine,' muttered Rolland.

'We don't?' Dugrippe looked at her raised eyebrow, then at Benoit relishing a long pull on his water before putting his glass down with an exaggerated sigh of pleasure. 'That's right, we don't.' Dugrippe threw bread into his mouth and chewed mightily. 'Water's fine.'

AFTER A STARTER of coarse pate de campagne and a main course of Poulet de Bresse a la Crème with Pommes Boulangere, washed down by copious amounts of spring water, the effects of a long day began to take its toll and heads drooped. Rolland and Caron made their excuses first, heading across the square to the old church for their first night in barracks.

'Set your alarms,' Benoit called after them. Caron raised an acknowledging arm without looking back. Gagnon followed a minute later then Dugrippe pushed back his chair to go in the direction of the rustic hotel's comparative luxury. 'Coming to bed, darling? Last night on a soft mattress.'

'In a moment, my sweet,' replied Latour, not bothering to look up.

'Well, don't wake me if you're staying up late with your men friends,' growled Dugrippe, lumbering away towards the hotel.

The other tables were deserted, chairs tilted into the centre and even the staff table was empty except for Favre sitting with a coffee and a cognac, thumbing through the night's receipts.

Auger got to his feet next. 'See you in the morning.'

'Goodnight,' said Benoit. 'Daniel,' he said sharply, as Auger moved away. 'I've just realised, we don't know where you live.'

'I rent an apartment about two minutes down the hill. Rue du Valat, past the town hall and first left.'

'Convenient.'

'I like it,' nodded Auger. 'Lots of room and great views over the valley.' He turned away.

'Daniel,' said Benoit. Auger turned again. 'Define lots of room.'

'Two large bedrooms, kitchen, dining room, lounge, roof terrace.'

In his peripheral vision, Benoit noticed Latour's eyes narrow. '*Two* bedrooms?' said Benoit.

Auger smacked his forehead. 'Of course, Commandant. You must come and stay with me rather than move into barracks. I have plenty of room.'

'Really?'

'Absolutely. Better than sleeping on a cot like a novice.'

'Far better,' observed Latour.

'I don't know,' said Benoit, rubbing his chin.

'I insist,' said Auger. 'I don't know why I didn't think of it before.'

'You've been very busy,' said Latour.

'That's true,' said Auger. 'Well, Commandant? It would be an honour to have you stay.'

Benoit shrugged, as though resistance would be rude. 'Well, if you insist, Daniel.'

'Absolutely.'

'He does insist,' confirmed Latour, helpfully.

'It's settled then,' said Auger. 'I'll go and make up your duvet and air the room for tomorrow. I hope you're okay with feather pillows?'

'Feather pillows okay for you, boss?' enquired Latour, with an air of excessive solicitude.

'I will endure,' said Benoit, stoically. 'Thank you, Daniel.' Auger smiled, bade his farewells and walked down the hill into the night, Benoit following his progress to avoid Latour's laconic stare. Finally, he was unable to avoid his subordinate's gaze any longer. 'What?'

. . .

THREE HOURS LATER, Trent had left the Spanish border far behind and was speeding north-east past Montpelier on the A9 - La Languedocienne - towards Nimes. Soon, he would turn off onto the road cutting across the Camargue wetlands, heading due east, past Arles, to pick up the A7 and all points for the Riviera coast. It was still half an hour shy of midnight so he'd made excellent time but he kept the needle nudging 160kph.

An hour later, beyond Arles, he pulled into a service station, filled up with fuel and revived himself with a couple of double espressos from an automated dispenser. He checked his phone but there was no reply from Megan.

'I told her to go dark, after all,' he muttered, in a vain attempt to reassure himself. He resisted the urge to message her again.

A FEW MINUTES before four in the morning, Trent eased the Range Rover to a standstill in a layby on the D19, just outside Seillans, and killed the engine. He picked up his night vision field glasses from the passenger seat and jumped down onto the tarmac, closing the driver's door softly. In the gloom, he opened the trunk and extracted his Glock then locked the car.

Extinguishing the lights plunged him into darkness and he waited for a moment while his eyes adjusted. The silence of the forest was deep, the sense of stillness, of a planet gently respiring, total. He paused to be sure of his bearings, inhaling the Earth's lavender sigh, before advancing into the trees to find a good vantage point.

Nestling behind a shrub moments later, he put the binoculars to his eyes to sweep the entrance to Villa Jasmin, below his position. To his surprise, he couldn't see the villa's gates from where he was, even in the stark wash of the Moon's unobstructed radiance.

Before he'd left the Butlers to their life of ease, he'd scoped the entire property and, from his present location, he should have had line of sight on the gate and the windows at the back of the villa. It took a moment to work out that a large structure was blocking his view and a further second to conclude that the structure must be some kind of portable building.

He moved down the hill to his right, catching a glimpse of two gendarmes either side of a road barrier, engaged in desultory conversation and pulling on cigarettes. Trent's worst fears were confirmed. Villa Jasmin was a crime scene.

After checking the magazine in his Glock, he struck out through the wood to skirt the lane until he arrived at a position invisible to the gendarmes. Reaching the asphalt, he leaned against a tree to plot his path. The high stone wall on the other side of the lane turned a corner and descended the hill, its downhill section marking the western limit of Jasmin's grounds. Trent could see the trees of the orchard beyond.

In a trice, he ran noiselessly across the lane and moved along an overgrown track, following the wall until fully cloaked by shadows thrown by the unchecked growth of bushes. A second later, he heaved himself up and over the wall, dropping softly onto thick grass on the other side.

After a moment on his haunches, surveying the house, he approached the honey-coloured stone building bathing in the sulphurous moonlight. At the corner of the patio, he noticed the absence of water in the pool. The black stain on one edging slab added to his disquiet but it was too out in the open for closer inspection.

Instead, he moved to the ground floor bedroom window on the west wall, the one directly in line with the hidden camera set up all those weeks ago. The shutters were fastened but, from previous inspection, he knew they were the only ones that didn't squeak when opened.

He withdrew a thin blade from a pocket and slid it into the gap between shutters, lifting the tool until he met resistance then knocking the catch sharply upwards. The shutters sighed and the tension between them relaxed. Trent prised them open.

The window's catch was unfastened and Trent paused. This was too easy. He stopped to consider his options. He should walk away and drive straight to Nice Airport, leave his Range Rover, with all its resources, in a Long Stay car park then return in a hire car and maintain a vigil, scope out the site properly from the cover of trees for a day or two. If this French cop, Benoit, had really parked himself at Airport Arrivals to await the first morning flight from Barcelona, their paths were unlikely to cross and risk would be minimal.

However, Charlotte Butler's grateful expression flashed through his mind again so, against his better judgement, Trent pulled on his protective gloves, smoothly pushed up the window and climbed inside.

He crept noiselessly across the bedroom to the open door and stared across the expanse of the lounge towards the dimly visible bookshelf. The DVD case with the hidden camera was where he'd left it so he scurried across to open it.

A whiff of chemicals confirmed it had been tested for prints. And, if the police had examined it, he could also expect them to have spotted the camera and removed the storage card. He established its absence before returning the case to the shelf.

Trent was uneasy but, if this was a trap it was already too late so he crept to the bottom of the stairs then through to the kitchen before approaching the downstairs toilet where he opened the adjacent cupboard and reached around the back of the water tank for the gun. It wasn't there.

It wasn't a noise that told him he was no longer alone but a tremor of movement in the turgid air. Resigned to conflict, Trent slipped a hand into his breast pocket and, head level with the water tank, reached as far round as he could to drop his phone behind the cylinder then stood back and peeled off his gloves to be ready. Despite his situation, he couldn't help but be impressed by the deftness of the trap.

A light snapped on and Trent turned to see a man's hand withdraw from the switch, his other hand aiming a gun at him - a SIG Sauer - the weapon of choice for the French Police. He also noticed a slight tremor in his gun hand until his left hand arrived to support it.

'Hands up!' ordered the man, gesturing towards the ceiling with his gun. Trent recognised the voice from the phone call the previous evening. He raised his arms, suddenly feeling hands at his back, one pushing a gun into his spine, the other ripping the Glock from his belt.

Instinctively, Trent grabbed both of the man's hands and pulled them past each hip, gripping and bending the wrists hard to loosen his assailant's grip.

Simultaneously, he pushed firmly back with both feet and snapped his neck back in a reverse headbutt, feeling the gratifying grind of damaged cartilage on the back of his skull, followed by a shout of pain.

The man was strong, however, and Trent couldn't free the gun from his assailant's hand which, in the struggle, discharged a round at Benoit, advancing towards him. In shock, Benoit looked at the bullet hole in the wall behind him then grimly aimed his weapon.

Fortunately, he'd strayed a fraction too far into Trent's arc and he was able to lever his legs into the air, using the man holding him from behind, as a pivot. With a swift kick, Trent caught Benoit on the head and the policeman staggered and fell to the floor with a grunt, his gun flying across the tiles.

Without Benoit to distract him, Trent pulled on the arms of the man behind him until he could feel his stomach on his back then he heaved himself back onto the toilet door. On the rebound, he jerked him forward before collapsing a knee to launch the man over his shoulder, stripping both guns from the big man's grip as he landed heavily.

Trent righted himself but was caught by a rapid volley of

punches that sent him reeling backwards. A wiry figure, dressed head to toe in black hit him again, then aimed a kick into his chest that sent Trent crashing against the wall. Without pause, his assailant kicked out at his hand, knocking one of the guns from Trent's grasp. In turn, he raised his Glock, only to feel another strong pair of hands pull his gun arm behind his back, forcing him to swivel round until he faced his opponent, a woman with cropped auburn hair, which she shoved into his face in a swift headbutt.

As he staggered backwards, she tried to sweep his legs from under him but Trent managed to free his arm from her grip and flat hand her under the chin to unbalance her and send her crashing back against a lamp, knocking it to the floor. By now the big guy was back on his feet and lumbering towards him, blood streaming from his nose.

Trent jumped up to regain his balance but the wiry figure, a blond woman, caught him with another pair of rapid punches to the side of the head. Fortunately, he managed to ride the second punch to minimise the impact but the big man threw out a meaty hand to grab Trent by the throat and the blond kicked his knee to put him on his haunches.

'Get him down,' shouted Benoit, advancing in support. Trent tried to raise the Glock but the big man fell on his arm and pinned it to the ground, knocking the gun from his grip. Meanwhile the blond tried to pull his other arm down but Trent grabbed her hair and yanked her down onto the cool tiles, shouting in pain.

He spied a gun on the floor, let go of the woman's hair and swung a punch at the big man's head to give him more freedom to reach for it. When Benoit also tried to drop onto him, Trent planted his left foot into Benoit's chest and levered him backwards against the bookshelf.

Straining every sinew, Trent put his hand on the Sig Sauer but a loud shot rent the air and a sharp pain nipped at his hand.

Everything stopped at that moment, the only motion the filling of lungs, the only sound, the panting of combatants. All eyes turned to the younger man in the gendarme's trousers and shirt, holding a gun on Trent, the faintest wisp of smoke rising from the barrel.

'Alive, Auger,' shouted Benoit, holding up a hand to his colleague.

'That depends on Monsieur Tyler,' said Auger, his eyes boring into Trent, gun held in tight pose, left hand supporting right.

Trent looked down at his bloodied hand. The bullet had grazed the fleshy part of the hand between little finger and wrist.

The big man rolled away, taking Trent's Glock with him and the blond, on her knees, scrambled away too, neither wanting to get in the line of fire or be used as a human shield.

Trent stared at the gun and, while Auger circled round for a better shot, moved his hand towards the Sig Sauer again. Another shot rang out and Trent felt a stinging pain in his ear and blood splashed his neck. He put a hand up to feel his earlobe bleeding.

'That's just the lobe,' said Auger. 'Do you want to lose the whole ear?'

Trent stared into Auger's fierce gaze, weighing the loss, before withdrawing his hand from the gun and lying back on the terracotta tiles in submission.

The two women pounced, the blond one preparing cuffs, turning him over and snapping them onto his wrists. The big guy was already on his feet, looming over Trent, spots of blood falling onto Trent's trousers from his nose. He took a short run-up and launched a kick into Trent's ribs, doubling him up around his foot, coughing and spluttering. Dugrippe drew back his foot for a second instalment.

'That's enough,' snapped Benoit. Dugrippe paused but held his position, panting hard. 'We're not in Paris, Thierry.'

Dugrippe took as deep a breath as his broken nose

would allow. 'Boss,' he acknowledged, before stalking away to the front door, pulling it open and plunging out into the warm night air. Holding the right side of his head, Benoit gestured at Rolland and Caron to wrestle the prisoner to his feet.

DUGRIPPE MARCHED SOURLY THROUGH the gates of Villa Jasmin clutching a handkerchief over his nose. Gagnon stood by the door of the ICP and Latour joined him after switching on one of the powerful arc lamps.

'Thanks for your help,' snarled Dugrippe, marching past them into the prefab and ripping open the door of the small fridge in a vain search for ice.

'We were searching the subject's vehicle and prepping the ICP,' said Latour. 'As ordered.'

'How many of them were there, champ?' said Gagnon. Dugrippe fixed him with a malevolent eye and raised his middle finger.

'We thought it was just the one,' said Latour, with a wink towards Gagnon.

'Do we need to see the other guy before declaring a winner?' quipped Gagnon.

Dugrippe opened his mouth to impart a foul-mouthed riposte but the sound of footfall turned their heads as Benoit, Rolland, Caron and Auger panted up the steep drive, escorting the now-compliant prisoner, hands cuffed behind his back.

Apart from Auger, they all carried the wear and tear of recent battle, each nursing or massaging an affected body part. The prisoner also had trickles of blood weeping from his left ear lobe, the run-off spattering onto the shoulder of his khaki shirt.

Auger called his gendarme colleagues to leave the road barriers to take an arm of the prisoner.

'There's a first aid kit in the briefing room,' said Benoit, eyes locking on to Latour, who nodded faintly in return.

'Patch up the prisoner then take him to the station and get him a doctor.'

Latour beckoned the gendarmes to escort Trent into the ICP and indicated a chair facing the photo array. The gendarmes sat the prisoner down and held a gun on him while Latour snapped on the light and pretended to rummage around for the first aid kit.

Out of his peripheral vision, he watched while the man they knew as Moss Tyler interrogated the wall display with impassive grey eyes, transfixed by the photographs of Wendy Wyatt, walking towards the departure gate at the airport. His eyes widened at the words below.

WENDY WYATT AKA MEGAN MATTESON

LATOUR BUSIED himself with the first aid box, tearing wrappers from a couple of sticking plasters and allowing the prisoner ample time to examine the column of seven names, in stark isolation on their own whiteboard.

The names of Moss Tyler and Harry Renfrew were at the top beside a picture of Tyler, waiting at Nice passport control. Latour had only just finished copying out all the names from the assortment of passports recovered from Tyler's car before the prisoner was delivered to the ICP. In fact, the ink on the board was still damp though Tyler wasn't to know that.

Tending to Tyler's ear, Latour felt the prisoner's head turn minutely to stare at the pictures of the two mutilated bodies, covered in flies, bobbing on the surface of the swimming pool. Tyler was impressively cool throughout but seeing images so shocking and brutal, Latour detected the man's breathing quicken. Tyler's laptop, two spare guns, the selection of passports and bundles of different currencies lay on a desk in full view and also drew the eye. He made no attempt to speak.

When he'd finished patching the ear, Latour pinched the plaster onto the earlobe as payback for his colleagues' injuries and Tyler winced at the sharp pain.

'Get him out of here,' said Latour to the two gendarmes, who bundled him roughly out of the chair and out onto the tarmac.

BENOIT WAS SMOKING a cigarette and probing his swollen jaw when Tyler was escorted to the waiting wagon. 'Stop,' he called out.

Tyler stared coolly at Benoit, a disinterested smirk playing around his lips, waiting for questions. But Benoit had other ideas. After seeing the ICP display, Tyler would have a head full of his own unanswered questions and the longer he had to think about them, the better. 'Strict security. No-one to see him without my say-so. No exceptions.'

'I want a lawyer,' said Trent, speaking for the first time.

Benoit's gaze locked onto Trent's eyes. 'No exceptions,' he repeated, quietly.

As the gendarmes secured the prisoner in the wagon's interior cage, Latour sidled up to Benoit.

'Okay?' said Benoit.

'He's fully prepped.'

'Good. Go with them. Grace is at the station with a DNA kit. And when he's printed get enquiries in the works with Washington and Ottawa, then get to work on the laptop and the guns.'

'You think Tyler knows he's being played?'

'Doesn't matter,' said Benoit. 'It's a stacked deck.'

TRENT STOOD impassive as the red-faced gendarme fixed the shackles around his legs in the detention area, swearing and gesticulating angrily at both the prisoner and his two colleagues. With their help, Trent was finally frogmarched to the processing suite at a speed designed to ensure the metal took a painful bite out of his ankles.

In the compact suite, a stout black woman dressed in white coveralls and protective gloves, supervised the mugshots and fingerprinting. When she'd finished, the detective who'd dressed his wounds in the portacabin opposite Villa Jasmin, set to work on a computer keyboard, no doubt lodging his prints with law enforcement databases around the world.

Trent also knew his likeness would soon be winging its way into the ether and the only question was whether the IAFIS database or the Facial Analysis Comparison and Evaluation (FACE) unit, pioneering Facial Recog at the FBI's Clarksburg complex, would identify him first. Either way, his fate was sealed unless he could find a way to escape and, with a second failed attempt behind him, his chains were becoming increasingly onerous.

The detective opened and examined Trent's laptop. 'Can I have the passcode to your laptop?' Trent didn't bother to reply so the detective closed and packed the laptop and carried it to the door. 'The courier for the DNA sample is waiting outside, Grace.'

The CSI nodded and the detective left. 'Open wide,' she said, pushing a buccal swab towards his mouth. Trent kept his jaw firmly closed.

The blow from the red-faced gendarme landed in Trent's midriff and he doubled over, gasping for breath.

'Are you deaf?' he said.

'Is that necessary?' said Coulibaly, frowning.

'He kicked me in the bollocks when I was taking him off the wagon,' replied the gendarme, yanking Trent up by the hair and pulling his head back. 'Open your mouth for the lady, or I'll kick your teeth out, shitface.'

Trent stared sideways at him, a grim smile deforming his face, mouth resolutely shut until he puckered up and blew the gendarme a kiss.

'You fucker,' exploded the gendarme, clenching his fists.

'Outside,' said Coulibaly, pushing between the pair and easing the gendarme towards the door. 'We're wasting time. Let me do my work.'

'You're not in charge here...'

'Would you like me to speak to who is?' she demanded, hands moving sassily to her broad hips. 'Because me and Danny Auger are tighter than a week-old turd and if you give me any shit, I'll have him play another tune on your bollocks.' She glared, her mouth an angry line. 'Now, vamoose.'

There was a breathless silence as the gendarme's colleagues controlled their grins behind his back. 'Come on, Pascal,' said one, into his ear. 'Let's grab a smoke.'

With a look of unrestrained violence at Trent, Pascal left the room, followed by his colleagues, one winking at Grace.

'Thank you, Grace,' said Trent.

'Don't dare use my name, fucker,' she snarled, removing a fresh cotton swab from its sealed packaging and holding it up to his face. 'Don't even speak to me. I saw what happened to those poor people at the villa and if you don't open your mouth right away, I'll call Pascal and his friends back in here to kick your ass all the way to Sunday.'

After a pause, Trent opened his mouth and Coulibaly rubbed the swab up and down the inside of his cheek for a few seconds. She did the same on his other cheek then removed the swab, pushing it into a tube with a few millilitres of clear liquid, breaking off the handle and capping the tube. She took a pen to label the sample and sealed it in a special casket filled with ice.

'I realise it doesn't amount to much but I didn't kill those people,' said Trent.

Coulibaly stared at him then knocked on the door. 'You're right. Nothing is exactly what it's worth.'

IN HIS CELL, after an unenthusiastic beating from Pascal and colleagues, Trent sat in the dark on his plastic mattress, knees bent up to his chin. He banged his forehead against them, cursing his decision to drive straight to Seillans without stashing his car at the airport. Now, Benoit had his passports - including Renfrew's - his guns and his laptop.

I'm speaking to you on Charlotte Butler's cell phone.

Benoit's words reverberated around his brain as he tried to assess the damage. They hadn't yet identified the Renfrews - understandable from what he'd seen of the crime scene photographs. But now they had Harry's passport which was a gamechanger. With Trent's photograph in it, the document was a direct connection to the victim of a brutal double murder and clear evidence that Trent was their killer, a man who murdered his victims and stole their credit cards to travel the world, living the high life, on Harry's dime. He shook his head. Only a fool would believe that and Benoit was clearly no fool.

'At least I hope he isn't,' he mumbled.

16

Saturday 4th May

Benoit and Latour didn't arrive back at the hotel until six that morning and the low sun was already creeping along the medieval lanes and passageways, warming the stone buildings in a two-thousand-year-old ritual.

Instead of going up to his room, Benoit slumped down at a breakfast table, nursing a bag of ice against his right cheek and fumbling for a cigarette. His face was swollen and he was leaking blood from a couple of loosened teeth. His hand shook as he moved the cigarette to his mouth and, without a word, Latour took the cigarette, lit it and placed it across an ashtray for him.

'Must have damaged a nerve,' said Benoit, throwing the ice pack on the table so he could support his right hand, as he drew mightily on his cigarette.

'Sure,' said Latour. 'We're checking out in a few hours. I think I'll get a couple of hours sleep while Thierry's having his nose set. God alone knows what that'll do to his snoring.'

Benoit returned a painful smile and took a further pull on his cigarette to deaden the pain. 'You should too, boss.'

'I will,' said Benoit as Latour dragged himself towards the hotel.

Favre emerged a couple of minutes later to prepare the tables for breakfast service, stopping in his tracks when he saw Benoit. 'I hope the other guy looks worse.'

Benoit saw no value in answering. 'I'll order that drink now.'

'Painkiller?' said Favre. 'I've got just the thing.' He returned a moment later with an unlabelled bottle of clear liquid and a pair of shot glasses, filling them both. 'Homemade eau de vie. The breakfast of champions.' Benoit raised an inquisitive eyebrow. 'I forget whose home.'

Benoit chuckled then winced at the accompanying pain. He accepted the glass and sniffed at the pungent liquor. His sinuses cleared immediately so he ventured a sip and a gasp of blood danced in the clear liquid.

Swilling the potion around his loosened teeth, he swallowed, the fire burning its way to his stomach. Favre drank his shot in one go and left the glass upturned. When Benoit had drained his glass, he began coughing and tapping the table for a refill.

'Sure, you don't want some food first?' said Favre.

'Not on an empty stomach,' said Benoit. Favre poured another shot which Benoit downed with a grimace of pain and pleasure.

'Commandant, I hope you don't mind me interfering,' said Favre, pulling a memory stick from his pocket and placing it on the table. 'But I contacted all the Easter diners that I *personally* know and had them email their photographs. Thought it might be quicker than going through channels.'

Benoit nodded. 'Pour me some more moonshine and I'll overlook it.'

. . .

In HIS HOTEL ROOM, Benoit sat at his rustic table, scrolling through the hundreds of photographs taken of Easter Monday diners at the Hotel Deux Rocs, nearly two weeks before. It was a thankless task and Benoit's eyes began to droop at the endless parade of smiling faces, raising glasses in front of tables laden with food.

Flicking through the last batch of pictures, and on the cusp of heading to his bed for a nap, he finally found something. Beyond the inevitable middle-aged couple, grinning and brandishing alcohol, Benoit caught a glimpse of the Butlers' table. He knew from Favre's receipts that their meal had lasted from eight to ten-thirty that evening.

At ten o'clock, according to the digital time stamp, Benoit spotted Charlotte Butler in the background of a photograph, sitting alone at her table. What interested Benoit was that she'd also been alone fifteen minutes earlier in another batch of photographs. He'd thought nothing of it, assuming a toilet break for her husband but, scrolling on, Benoit found a shot of David Butler, returning to the table at five minutes past ten.

Judging from the church in the background, the photographer was positioned between the hotel and the Butlers' table which meant David Butler was returning to the table from the village and not the hotel toilet.

'Where did you go, David?' Benoit isolated a copy of the picture then moved onto the next batch. Three photographs later, he lingered over a startling image taken at five minutes *before* ten.

A soft knocking at the door and Latour entered on Benoit's command.

'Had a sleep yet?' said Latour. Benoit shook his head. 'You should. We check out in three hours. Take the edge off before we interview Tyler.'

'Tyler can wait,' said Benoit. 'Look at this.' He scrolled through the series of pictures.

'Butler left the table,' shrugged Latour. 'So, he went to the toilet.'

'For twenty minutes?' said Benoit. 'Besides, he's walking back from the village. And then there's this.' He clicked on the photograph of a different man embracing Charlotte Butler in the background to a snapshot of a family gathering.

'Who's that?' said Latour, staring at Charlotte Butler kissing an unknown man on the cheek.

'Hard to tell with her head covering his face.'

'Probably nothing more than hello.'

'Even so, who would she know that well after just three weeks in France?'

'You think it's somebody she knew before she came here,' said Latour.

'I don't know,' said Benoit. 'But she's English yet she's embracing a man like she's French so my guess is it's someone local.'

'How old is the guy? Forty-five?'

'Fifty, at the most,' said Benoit.

'There can't be many candidates. Too young to be the pool guy, De Vries, and it's not Favre. Who else would she know?'

'We know she went to the baker's every day,' said Benoit.

'Add in shopkeepers, bar owners...'

'Daniel can take a look. Favre too. He may even have seen him approach Mrs Butler's table.' Benoit removed the memory stick and closed his laptop. 'And we need to widen the scope on this.'

'What do you mean?'

'I want to know what Butler was doing in those twenty minutes,' said Benoit. 'So, I want all the photographs taken by people *anywhere* in Seillans that night.'

'It was a bank holiday,' said Latour. 'That could be thousands of people, even assuming the local force know who to ask.'

'They can ask everyone in the village for a start. Then identify other people from their photographs and move on from there. While we're at it, we might as well go the whole hog and compile all village CCTV from shops and businesses.'

'And Tyler?'

'He can stew in his juices until we're ready,' said Benoit, flexing his swollen jaw. 'Is Nina working his laptop?'

Latour nodded. 'She's running a trace on the guns too.'

'Probably pointless,' said Benoit. 'Tyler's too professional to carry a traceable weapon.'

'Not careful enough to avoid getting caught with a car full of cash and passports,' said Latour.

'Time pressures. He let us know he was in Barcelona, hoping we'd sit around at Nice airport waiting for him.'

'And fell straight into our trap.'

Benoit frowned. 'You weren't there, Gabriel. It didn't feel like we had him cornered. Did we find a phone on him?'

'Destroyed straight after your call, you said.'

'That was a burner for contacting the Butlers,' said Benoit. 'This man would need his own phone to contact Megan Matteson.'

'We've stripped the car,' said Latour. 'It's not there.'

'He may have hidden it,' said Benoit, handing the memory stick to Latour. 'Search the grounds where he came in. Here. Take a copy for Forensics then give it to Auger and Jerome to go through. Enlarge any photographs of interest and then follow up where appropriate.

'I also want hard copies of Mrs Butler's unknown suitor. You stay on Tyler. Work his passports, all of them. I want to know who he is but, more importantly, where he's been for the last month, what name he was using and where he was when the Butlers died. Keep Thierry on the Matteson girl, when he gets back from hospital. Whoever Tyler is, she's the pressure point.'

He yawned mightily. 'Now, if you don't mind...'

∾

THREE HOURS LATER, Benoit stood on the roof terrace of Auger's apartment, gazing out across the plains of the distant Esterel and beyond, the coastal town of Frejus basking in the afternoon heat.

'This is wonderful, Daniel,' said Benoit, turning back to the large living space, drawn by the aroma of fresh coffee.

'Wonderful,' echoed Latour, not looking up from his laptop.

Auger poured strong black coffee into three espresso cups. 'I like it. The rent's controlled and the views...well, as you see.'

Benoit sipped the powerful beverage, glad of the stimulant after only two hours' sleep and a breakfast of alcohol. 'Any better views of our mystery man, Gabriel?'

'None,' sighed Latour.

'Didn't Favre see him?' said Auger.

'He was busy in the kitchens,' said Latour, closing his laptop. He handed Auger the duplicate memory stick. 'Good hunting.'

'Do you want some lunch before we get back to work?' said Auger. 'I could knock up a salad.'

'No time,' said Benoit, running his eye over pictures on the wall, one a sepia-tinged, framed photograph of two elderly people standing arm in arm, looking uncomfortably at the lens. The grey-bearded man carried a hunting rifle and presented as an older version of Auger in both facial features and physique. A black ribbon was affixed across a corner of the frame.

'When do we speak to Tyler?' said Latour.

'Tonight, if we get a hit on his ID,' said Benoit. 'Speaking of Tyler, where on earth did you learn to shoot like that, Daniel?'

'I got lucky,' said Auger.

'Twice in two shots?' said Benoit.

'Do you want to lose the whole ear?' said Latour, in a threatening voice.

'They don't teach shooting like that on municipal courses,' said Benoit.

Auger smiled modestly. 'I suppose not.'

Benoit nodded at the old photograph in its new frame. 'Your father taught you.'

'He did,' said Auger. 'I grew up on a hill farm, on the escarpment beyond Saint-Cézaire. It's barren soil and a hard life so we depended on livestock to get us through the winter. To lose a sheep or a goat was a serious problem so dad made sure I could handle a rifle.'

'You had rustlers?' enquired Latour.

Auger shook his head. 'Wolves.'

'Wolves?' said Latour. 'This far west?'

'You'd be surprised,' said Auger. 'The wolf population has soared since they became a protected species in the seventies. The pack come down from the high Alps in the height of winter, looking for food...'

'You see wolf packs this far from the mountains?' said Benoit.

'No but outcasts behave differently,' said Auger. 'I've seen lone wolves walking through the lanes of Seillans in the dead of night as recently as last December.'

'Doing what?'

'Looking for food, scavenging what they can from bins.'

'Bins, eh?' said Benoit. 'A couple of nights ago, I stopped for a smoke near some refuse bins and there was something moving around in the brush above the embankment. Not sure what it was but it was growling.'

'Where was this?' said Auger.

'A small layby on the way down to the village,' said Benoit. 'The bins stank of rotting food which might have attracted it.'

'Probably a stray dog,' said Auger.

'Of course, it was,' agreed Latour. 'It's too warm for wolves.'

'That's what the experts say but lone wolves are unpredictable,' said Auger. 'It's not unknown for a loner to stake out turf with a reliable food supply, regardless of conditions. Local farmers call it a Blood Summer.'

'And the food supply on your farm was your livestock,' concluded Benoit.

'Not with dad keeping watch,' said Auger. 'He was a true marksman. When I was old enough to hold a gun, he taught me. Then, when he wasn't there, it was my job to protect the animals.'

'But aren't wolves protected?' said Latour.

'They are but I found a way round that,' said Auger, straightening the framed photograph of his parents. 'I learned to shoot them in the ear to scare them off before they could do any damage.'

'So, last night wasn't a lucky shot,' said Latour.

'I guess not,' said Auger.

'Your parents are gone?' said Benoit.

'Dad died three years ago, my mother last year.'

'I'm sorry.'

'No need,' said Auger. 'They were old and when they became too infirm to run the farm, they had to sell up to pay the bills. Dad had lived there his whole life but mum was only there for forty years.' He was silent for a moment. 'Only. They went downhill quickly after they moved away, in all senses of the word.' He smiled. 'I got to scatter their ashes at the farm, at least.'

Latour's phone pinged. 'Thierry's at the ICP.'

Benoit slid the spare apartment key from the table into his pocket. 'Thanks for this, Daniel. I'll see you back at the ICP. I'm going to get some background on the Butlers.'

OLD MAN DE VRIES placed the two coffees onto the patio table, lit a cigarette and sank into his padded chair to resume his thousand-yard stare across neat rows of vegetables starting to emerge from the arid red soil of his small plot.

'Thank you,' said Benoit, running his eye over De Vries'

doughty stone cottage, with its honey-coloured walls and weathered terracotta roof tiles. The dwelling seemed to have grown organically out of the sun-scorched landscape, built to absorb and repel all extremes of weather in the Provence-Alpes foothills. Benoit imagined it would have looked exactly the same two hundred years ago.

A rifle reclined against the ancient stone and, hooked onto a beam under the eaves, two dead rabbits hung by their tied feet, their bloodied heads shrouded in plastic bags to collect the blood. In the garden, bees hovered lazily over the plant life and, as the sun moved into late afternoon, Benoit was glad of the shade under a lifeless canvas awning. He took a sip of his passable grand crème and shot a glance at De Vries. Dark rings had formed under the old man's blood-shot eyes.

'Sleeping okay?' he asked.

'Not really,' answered De Vries, in his strangled Afrikaans accent. 'I keep seeing...' He broke off, further words redundant.

'It'll pass.'

'But what a thing to happen. That poor woman.'

'Madame Butler? What about Monsieur Butler?'

'Him too, of course,' said De Vries. 'But he was...older. Mrs Butler had her whole life in front of her. I'm not making much sense, am I?'

'You liked her.'

De Vries conceded the point with a silent chuckle. 'Better than her husband. Not that I knew her,' he hastened to add. 'But she was cheerful and pleasant and made me coffee when I called to do my work.'

'And Butler?'

'Don't get me wrong,' said De Vries. 'He wasn't unpleasant. Just that he had that rich man's habit of treating everyone else as...underlings.' He shrugged. 'I'm the pool guy - you get used to it.'

'Did he mistreat you?'

'Don't misunderstand,' said De Vries. 'He didn't do

anything because it was like I wasn't there. He didn't say good morning or talk about the weather and, when he was around, I learned to simply get on with it. Mrs Butler was different. She was pleasant and sociable. And anyone who met her in the village would say the same.'

Benoit narrowed his eyes. 'Anyone in particular? A man around her husband's age, say.'

'You mean an affair?' said De Vries. 'I wouldn't know about that but she was very beautiful. She walked down that hill and back for bread every single morning, said it was her open-air gym. She really looked after herself.'

'She walked down the main highway?'

'There's a back lane that runs straight down the hill,' said De Vries. 'You pick it up opposite the junction but it's still a good half hour each way and it's steep.'

'Did she talk about people she met or shops she visited in the village?'

'Apart from a couple of bakeries, there aren't many shops except the supermarket and she went with her husband in the car, for that.'

'What about restaurants, bars, excursions in the car?'

'I wouldn't know,' said De Vries. 'She didn't do that kind of small talk. I know they ate out at the Deux Rocs on Easter Monday because I saw them.'

'Did you speak to them?'

'Not with Mr Butler there. I just waved.'

'I don't suppose you saw Monsieur Butler elsewhere that night, perhaps in the village, maybe talking to someone?'

'No, only at the hotel.'

'How were the Butlers towards each other?'

'People behave differently around the hired help,' said De Vries. 'They didn't say much in front of me beyond practical matters so I couldn't get a sense of their relationship.'

'But they seemed happy.'

'Content would be a better word.' De Vries hesitated. 'They had a nice life but I don't think she loved him.' Benoit raised an eyebrow. 'She didn't show him any affection. I know that's hardly proof of anything but...' De Vries looked uncomfortable.

'What?'

'I don't go in much for village gossip.'

'So, there were rumours?'

'This is a small community, Commandant,' said De Vries. 'There are always rumours in a place like this. Nothing better to do, some people.'

'Rumours that Mrs Butler had a lover.'

'You've heard?'

'No,' said Benoit. 'But that's usually a topic to get idle tongues wagging. And beautiful women inspire much envy.'

'You're right there. Talk was that Mrs Butler had taken a lover in the village.'

'Any idea who?' De Vries shook his head. 'Anybody who might know?'

'No-one who mentioned it to me, at least,' said De Vries. 'Look, it was just talk. Although...'

'What?'

'The last time I saw them alive at the villa, Mrs Butler seemed nervous. Kept looking out of the kitchen windows toward the gates as though she was expecting someone.'

'Who?'

'I've no idea.'

'Do you remember when that was?'

'The Thursday before last.' De Vries raised a finger in excitement. 'They were having a drinks party the following night. Mr Butler was cleaning the barbecue and she was preparing food. Did you know about that?'

Benoit nodded. 'Were you invited?'

De Vries laughed. 'What do *you* think?'

'Do you know who was?'

'Sorry, no, though Mrs Butler often chatted to people on her daily walk to the village. Commandant, do you have any idea who might have done this terrible thing?'

'Not yet. But we will.' Benoit unzipped his laptop case and withdrew a plastic wallet to show to De Vries. 'I don't suppose you know who this man is. Unfortunately, his face is hidden.'

De Vries turned the photograph in his hand, peered closely at the man embracing Charlotte Butler then touched a finger to the man's arm, before passing it back.

'Sorry. The whole village was at the fête and more besides. Could be anyone.'

'Did you take photographs?' asked Benoit.

'What am I? Twelve?' he snorted, a look of disgust invading his features. 'At my age you just enjoy the moment.'

Benoit smiled and rose to leave. De Vries returned his gaze to the vegetables. 'Thanks for the coffee.'

At the car, Benoit's phone rang. 'Gabriel?'

'Singapore have names for us,' said Latour. *'Harry and Carla Renfrew.'*

'Renfrew? Sounds familiar.'

'One of Tyler's passports. Renfrew was a UK citizen and multi-millionaire bond trader. He was reported missing by a Brad Webber of Merlion Park Securities, a month ago. Renfrew was the chief executive.'

'Was?'

'I googled them. The ID checks out. It's David and Charlotte Butler.'

'Progress. Do we have a reason why they dropped out of sight?'

'Nothing solid though Webber told the SPF that Renfrew said a Russian bank had threatened him over a trade that went sour. Apparently, the bank lost a couple of hundred million.'

'Russian?' repeated Benoit, his heart sinking.

'Only a rumour. The authorities investigated but couldn't corroborate and the bank denied any such trade took place. Well, they would, wouldn't they? Thierry's chasing it up with his contacts in Cannes and I've sent an email to Brad Webber in Singapore. No reply yet.'

'How did you leave it with the SPF?'

'I asked if they could access Renfrew's apartment for forensic tests. They're getting back to me.'

'What did you give them from our end?'

'Everything we have. After helping us, I didn't feel I had a choice. Did I do wrong?'

'No, but we should brace for a feeding frenzy.'

'Already happening. The barriers are groaning with press and TV.'

'Can't be helped. Anything else?'

'No hits on Tyler's Glocks though FFP pulled a latent from the clip. It's a match to the prints we took from him last night.'

'Any response from across the pond?'

'The FBI are running it through IAFIS, the Canadians haven't replied.'

'So much for fraternal brotherhood.'

'What do you expect from an organisation calling itself Mounted Police and hoping to be taken seriously?'

'Ask again. Make sure they understand this is a murder inquiry.'

Benoit rang off as De Vries came down the path, hailing him.

'Could I have another look at that picture?' said De Vries. 'I think I know who it is.' Benoit slipped a hand into his case and handed over the plastic wallet. The old man pulled a magnifying glass out of his pocket and held it to the mystery man's arm before handing the glass to Benoit. 'See that circular mark just below the sleeve.'

Benoit looked closely, moving the glass back and forth. 'Barely.'

De Vries rolled up his own sleeve to reveal a tattoo of a ring with flame ascending from it. 'The grenade emblem.'

'You were in the Foreign Legion?'

'In the seventies. That's how I got citizenship.' De Vries pointed to the man's arm on the picture. 'You can only see a partial but he's got the same tattoo!'

17

January 2002, Chicago

Gwen kissed the gently snoring Nell and pulled the blanket over her. After turning off the lights, she left the room but didn't fully close the door in case her daughter woke in the night and became disorientated and frightened.

'Okay?' said Trent, when she emerged.

'She'd sleep through an earthquake after today.'

Trent reached for his coat and moved to the door. 'Try to get some rest yourself.'

'Mike!' said Gwen. Trent turned. 'I don't know what we'd have done without you. Come back safe.'

'We're not out of the woods yet,' he said. He opened the door and looked up and down the corridor before stepping outside. 'Keep this locked. Don't open the door to anyone and don't look through the spyhole. A professional will see the shadow. If you're in any doubt it's me, don't open the door. To anyone. I'll knock three times, pause, then knock three more times.'

She kissed him on the lips and he reluctantly held her away and closed the door.

TRENT WALKED out of the busy lobby of the Godfrey Hotel and straight into a cab.

Ten minutes later, the cab pulled off Wacker Street and onto the Chicago Riverfront Hotel forecourt. It was snowing again and bitterly cold so Trent walked smartly through the lobby to the elevators, scanning for suspicious movements or someone taking even a mild interest in his passing.

Arriving on the seventh floor, he headed for the emergency stairs and descended watchfully to the sixth floor. Encountering no-one, he proceeded to the room he'd left that very morning with Gwen and Nell, excited to be going out for some fresh air and exercise. It seemed like a lifetime ago.

Inside Room 674, he pulled Gwen's two large bags from the wardrobe and packed her and Nell's things quickly and left them beside the door.

Returning to the lobby, he located a row of payphones, fed in some coins and called Phillips to tell him he wouldn't be needed for his overnight shift. Nothing more. He then dialled Rentoria's number to give him a heads-up for the morning, looking around all the while to be sure he wasn't being overheard. His eye fell on a man glancing over a newspaper at him from an easy chair near the check-in desk. The newspaper was raised immediately.

'Rentoria. It's Trent.'

'It's late.'

'Shut up and listen. Take a couple of extra hours tomorrow. I'll have things covered until eleven.'

'Great...'

'Also, there's a change of venue...'

'What?'

'Don't write down the address, just remember it and tell no-one.'

'*You switched hotels? Why?*'

'Tell you tomorrow at eleven, sharp! I'm at the Godfrey Hotel, West Huron Street, Room 429. Don't be late.'

'*But...*'

Trent put down the phone, fed in more coins then rang his own apartment for no other reason than to erase Rentoria's number from the last number redial. The man with the newspaper stood up and left the hotel. Trent let the number ring until his answering machine kicked in then ended the call, returned to his room, fastened all the locks and sat on the bed, gun beside him.

HE WOKE AROUND SIX, fully clothed on the double bed that smelled luxuriously of Gwen. He rose, doused his face in cold water then left the apartment with the two zipped up bags. Paying for the room at the Godfrey had left him short of cash so Trent took out more from the Riverfront Hotel's ATM, in the lobby.

It was dark outside when his cab pulled up at the Godfrey after a couple of detours to make sure he wasn't being followed. He could smell breakfast being prepared by the kitchens as he wheeled the bags to the elevators.

After pressing the button, he heard a heavy door swing open and two hefty, middle-aged men in baseball caps and voluminous coats emerged from the stairwell. Trent heard the embers of a conversation which died the moment they saw him. He recognised the Russian word *zavtrak* - breakfast - and his pulse quickened.

Forgetting about the bags, Trent followed the now mute pair towards the service stairs leading to the basement. Both men kept their heads lowered and moved quickly without appearing to hurry. But even keeping his head down couldn't hide the cauliflower ears and missing eyebrows of the second man who, Trent noticed, had moved a hand inside his coat until they were in the stairwell and the heavy door had shut loudly behind them.

Trent's hand went immediately to his gun and he moved to follow but was distracted by a trace of what looked like blood on the carpet and, although it petered out, Trent could track its origins to the bottom of the emergency stairs. He pushed open the heavy door of the service stairwell. Footsteps were descending rapidly now, accompanied by heated verbal exchanges in Russian so Trent leapt down the steps to follow the two men.

A second later, he came to a dead stop, a voice in his head battering its way out of his subconscious. *Gwen!*

He turned on his heel and sprinted back up to the elevators and ran into the capsule, pushing repeatedly on the fourth-floor button. On arrival, he pulled the doors open and ran out onto the corridor.

Fear gripped his heart as he sprinted to Room 429 and his breathing quickened again when he saw the door. It was closed but a large hole about the size of an orange had replaced the spyhole, its circumference shattered by a small explosion.

'No, no, no.' Not daring to see a preview, Trent pushed at the unlocked door but he couldn't move it more than a foot. Dread pulled on his gut as he heaved his shoulder against the door, creating enough space to squeeze through the aperture, gun in hand.

His legs turned to jelly at the sight of Gwen's inert body behind the damaged door and he stumbled back against it, slamming it closed, before sliding down its polished surface to sit beside her body.

Through hot tears, he lay his gun aside and put a hand on her still-warm ankle. Her face was beautiful, peaceful in repose. At least the half that was still there. Her left eye had taken the full impact of a bullet and the side of her skull had been blown apart, its contents leeching down the wall behind her.

Trent buried his face in his hands before his swirling thoughts coalesced around a single word. 'Nell.'

He clambered to his feet, picked up his gun and moved

quickly into the apartment. A young Asian woman's body in a maid's uniform lay face down in the lounge. Trent turned her over and knelt to feel for a pulse but she was dead. Blood oozed from the double tap wounds in her chest. The lanyard holding her key card master had been torn from her uniform and lay beside her, blood pooling around it. Her name was Yin.

Trent continued to the bedroom. 'Nell?' he called through the closed bedroom door. He pushed it open, almost unable to look. Both twin beds had been slept in but there was no body and no blood.

'Nell? It's Mike.' He heard a slight noise from the wardrobe and pounced on the handle. Opening it, he found Nell lying on the floor, swaddled by a duvet, sobbing gently. She was uninjured but distressed. He knelt down and she jumped into his arms as the floodgates opened.

'Bad men hurt my mommy,' she wailed. 'Help her, Mike. Help mommy. They hurt her.'

'I know, sweetie.' Tears welled in his eyes but he blinked them away to focus. 'They're not hurting her anymore.'

The apartment phone rang and Trent sat on the bed to answer, freeing one hand from his embrace.

'Special Agent Trent,' said a voice he recognised. Byron.

'Jesus,' seethed Trent. 'What the...'

'If you want to save the girl, shut up and listen,' snapped Byron. Trent was panting with fury but held his tongue. *'You do not fuck with business. It's un-American. This was business, Mike, and now it's done. You should've stepped aside when I asked. The Bureau may have killed Mrs Beaumont but you killed the maid.'*

'I'm going to...'

'I said listen! I see you had feelings for Mrs Beaumont and I'm sorry it had to end like this. But, for the sake of the child, you need to draw a line. The girl saw nothing. She can't hurt us and if this ends today, she gets to live her life...'

'If you so much...'

'Stop thinking with your dick. We can get to the kid any time

we want and there's nothing you can do about it. But that's not who we are. So, I need you to do something, Mike. I need you to tell me it's over, right now, then we can all be on our way.'

Trent's breathing was ragged and he ached with pent-up rage. Nell tried to wriggle from his grip and head for the door but he held on tight.

'I need you to say it, Special Agent. I need to know our business is concluded or the kid's life is forfeit. Decide now.'

Trent glanced at Nell. Her eyes were filling with tears again, her cheeks were streaked with salt. He took a deep breath and closed his eyes. 'Our business is concluded.' The phone clicked and Trent dropped the receiver on the bed. Nell finally wriggled free, scrambling for the bedroom door but Trent was there first and stood in her way. He held her away with both hands, kneeling to speak to her.

'Nell. I need you to be very grown up for the next few minutes.'

'I want mommy.'

Trent took a deep breath. 'I'm going to take care of mommy and I need you to stay in here while I'm gone. Can you do that?'

Nell stared at him, her lip wobbling. Finally, she nodded. Trent gave her a kiss then carried her to the bed before leaving the room to make the call. Outside, he quietly locked the door and dialled the field office.

18

Benoit drove back to the ICP but this time the crowd at the barriers was four deep and many were journalists who barked questions at his hastily-raised driver's window as his Citroen crawled through human traffic. Mayor Ruggieri was talking to a reporter from a TV station.

Beyond the barrier, he saw a well-known France 24 reporter doing a piece to camera at the opposite road block. Benoit marched into the ICP, ignoring more shouted questions from journalists.

'One feeding frenzy, as ordered,' said Latour, looking over his monitor.

'Inevitable,' said Benoit. He glanced across at the boards to confirm Latour had updated the victim details.

'Seigner's on the way.'

'When?'

'She'll be here this evening,' said Latour.

'Maybe no bad thing,' said Benoit. 'The Directeur is better with the media and she can give us some breathing space to get on with our jobs. Any more on the Renfrews?'

'Just background,' said Latour. 'Renfrew was originally from East London and became a big financial beast after trading all over the world. According to the SPF, he raked in huge fees from bond dealing and he and Carla lived in a multi-million-dollar, top-floor penthouse apartment overlooking Marina Bay.

'His wife was once a hostess in an exclusive nightclub called Zouk, born in Surrey, comfortable background, private school-educated, left school at eighteen to travel the world. Keen on water sports and sky-diving. They married two years ago. The week before they disappeared, he sold his private jet...'

'Tying up loose ends,' said Benoit.

'Seems so but it makes you wonder why he'd need Tyler to help him disappear. He could have gone anywhere.'

'But a jet has to file flight plans,' said Benoit. Auger and Gagnon were staring at a monitor, sifting through the photographs of Easter celebrations in Seillans. 'Daniel, anything you can tell me about a Patrice Bertrand? He owns a bar in the village.'

'Former Legionnaire,' said Auger. 'Bit of a loner. Runs Chez Bertrand as a tight ship and keeps his customers in order and we rarely get called out to the place. Why?'

'I talked to De Vries and he mentioned rumours that Carla Renfrew had taken a lover...'

'Bertrand?' said Auger.

'Who knows,' said Benoit, nodding at the boards. 'But De Vries thinks Bertrand is the mystery man in the picture with Carla Renfrew.'

'He's got good eyes,' said Auger.

'De Vries was in the Legion too and recognised Bertrand's tattoo,' said Benoit, tapping the partial image on Bertrand's right arm.

'Want me to bring him in?' said Auger.

'No, I don't want him on the defensive,' said Benoit. 'I'll pay him a visit at the bar.'

'I'll come with you,' said Auger, standing.

'No, I need you here working the photographs. But before that, can you get your people to move the barriers back another fifty metres in both directions?'

Auger reached for his phone. 'Do you want more bodies on crowd control?'

'If you've got them. And, I'd like to establish a perimeter all the way round the property and set up patrols. When the media blow hot on a story, nothing is off-limits.' Auger headed for the exit, tapping a number into his phone. 'By the way, are you as good with a rifle as you are with a pistol?'

'Better,' said Auger. 'Why?'

'Keep one handy,' said Benoit. Puzzled, Auger glanced at Latour for enlightenment but Latour was impassive.

'I hope you're not planning what I think you're planning,' said Latour, when Auger had left the ICP.

'That depends on the media,' said Benoit.

'The Directeur won't be happy if the networks start bending her ear again,' said Latour.

'Then the networks need to follow protocol,' said Benoit. 'Any sign of Tyler's phone yet? I need more leverage before we sit down with him.'

'We searched the car again. Nothing.'

'Double check the house. Maybe it was kicked under a chair in the struggle.'

'Nina's looking now.'

Dugrippe arrived from the kitchenette carrying a tray of black coffees.

'How's the nose?' said Benoit, seeing Dugrippe's swollen proboscis, bruised purple with black eyes to match.

'They think I'll need an op,' said Dugrippe, sullenly.

'Is it painful?'

'Only when I breathe,' said Dugrippe.

'Try sharing a room with it,' said Latour, winking. Dugrippe extended his middle finger.

'Ignore him, Thierry,' said Benoit. 'I think it adds character.'

'As long as you don't mind your nose looking like a week-old croissant,' said Latour.

'Never did Depardieu any harm,' said Rolland.

'Is this supposed to be helping?' said Dugrippe.

'Think how bad it might have been without Nina and Adele there to protect us,' said Benoit.

'I resent the implication that we're just hired muscle,' said Rolland.

'When you've all finished laughing about my disfigurement, I've got news on Megan Matteson,' said Dugrippe. 'She's back in France.'

Benoit's smile vanished. 'When?'

'April twenty-fourth,' said Dugrippe. 'Travelling as Wendy Wyatt, she drove her Audi A3 off the ramp of an early morning ferry arriving in Calais from Dover.'

'That's three days before the Renfrews were killed,' said Rolland.

'Where from Calais?' enquired Benoit.

'The last road toll camera we have, puts her near Dijon, travelling south on the A31,' said Dugrippe. 'And that was only six hours after she landed.'

'She was in a hurry,' said Benoit.

'Do you think she was coming here?' said Rolland.

'I wouldn't bet against it,' said Benoit. 'Get me hard copies of her ferry ticket and film of her car going through tolls to show Tyler. And put out a nationwide alert.'

～

'WHAT THE HELL sort of a party did you have last night?' said Coulibaly, in the lounge of Villa Jasmin, indicating the lamp, broken apart on the floor, the upturned table and the water tank door hanging from a hinge.

'Things got a little boisterous,' said Benoit.

Coulibaly gestured towards the bullet hole in the wall. 'Boisterous? Do I need to process any of this shit? No-one's said.'

'None of it,' said Benoit. 'The bullet was ours and we got our man.'

'Man singular?'

'And five of us.'

'Hardly fair.'

'We overcame the odds.' Coulibaly laughed. 'Thanks for processing the prisoner last night, Grace. You've had a lot of late nights and early starts.'

'Another dinner you owe me.'

'Put it on the tab.'

'Did you see the email from Nice?' said Coulibaly. 'They've got results.'

'I've been busy. Give me a verbal.'

'The DNA sample from saliva in the beer bottle is identical to epithelial trace recovered from the man's razor *and* buccal tissue from one of the toothbrushes. And, all three samples are a match to the male victim's DNA. Plus, the female victim's DNA is a match to tissue samples on the second toothbrush and ladies' razor. Your residents *were* your victims.'

'Progress,' mumbled Benoit.

Caron walked through the patio doors, pulling her T-shirt away from her torso as panes of sweat ate their way around her armpits. 'Warm out there.'

'Any sign?'

'Nothing,' she said. 'You're sure he had a phone?'

'Not certain, no. But everyone does.'

'If he suspected he was walking into a trap, he might have stashed it *en route*.'

'He didn't have time.'

'How do you know?'

'Because he would have stashed his fake passports, guns and laptop in the same place?'

'Good point,' said Caron.

Benoit took out a cigarette but, after Coulibaly's warning eyebrow, strolled outside to the patio to light up. As he inhaled, he glanced skyward, into the bluest sky. There was barely a breath of wind. A noise above diverted him and, shielding his eyes, he scanned the heavens for the source.

· · ·

'OKAY, Daniel. Find plenty of cover and make sure no-one sees you or the rifle,' he said into his phone a moment later. Benoit ended the call then trooped back into the villa, through the kitchen, coming to a halt to stare at the damaged door of the water tank cupboard.

A broad smile spread across his face and he leaned into the dark cupboard, stretching to peer behind the water tank as Tyler had done. Benoit flashed his iPhone torch into the cobwebbed corners, spotted the black tablet and stood upright to pull on protective gloves. 'Nina! Bag.' Caron shook out an evidence bag for him and he recovered the iPhone and dropped it in the bag.

'Forensics?' said Caron.

'Not yet. It can only be Tyler's and I'm more interested in contacts and contents.'

'Hack job?' nodded Caron.

'Please.'

They walked briskly up the drive to the door of the ICP as a gunshot rang out from the grounds of Villa Jasmin and Caron clutched a hand to her holster.

'It's fine,' said Benoit, putting an arm across her. 'Sorry, I should have warned you. Unwanted attention again.'

Caron smiled. 'To be expected, I suppose. One shot?'

Benoit shrugged. 'They'll know it wasn't me at least.'

BENOIT LOCKED his car near the Hotel Deux Rocs and strolled through the cobbled maze of Seillans' steep streets down to the village's main artery. Sleek cats adorned every nook, cranny and windowsill, unfazed by Benoit's descent through the heart of the ancient village.

At the main road, a modest corner bar called Chez Bertrand plied its trade with small tables and chairs scattered around its exterior. A sprinkling of tourists and locals sat drinking beverages in the shade of the building so Benoit located an unoccupied table next to a babbling fountain and installed himself onto the stiff-backed wooden chair.

'Monsieur?' enquired a grizzled man of about fifty, brown hair, peppered with grey. His face sported a deep leathery tan and his gravelled voice suggested a lifetime's love affair with tobacco. He wiped down the table as he waited.

'Café,' said Benoit. When the man returned to the bowels of the building, Benoit took out his ID and the photograph of the man embracing Carla Renfrew at the fête and lay them both on the table, while he lit a cigarette. The man returned and, placing the cup and saucer and a clean ashtray on the table, he darted a glance at the picture.

Benoit examined the man's arm below the short sleeve shirt but couldn't see the tattoo. 'Sit down, Monsieur Bertrand.'

Bertrand gazed steadily at Benoit, his watery blue eyes revealing a temptation to decline. 'I'm busy.'

Benoit's smile was implacable and Bertrand relented, slumping sullenly onto the opposite chair.

'What do you want?'

'You knew Madame Butler,' said Benoit. 'That's you, embracing her at the Easter fête.'

'Is it?' said Bertrand. 'You must have X-ray vision, monsieur.'

Benoit took a sip of coffee. He took out a second picture, a close-up of the partial tattoo on the man's arm. 'That's the lower part of a Foreign Legion tattoo, the Grenade Emblem. Lift up your sleeve and make a fool of me.'

Bertrand stared then gestured at Benoit's cigarettes, shaking one out of the pack after a nod of permission. 'Yes, that's me in the photograph with Charlotte. What of it?'

'First name terms?' exclaimed Benoit.

'Of course,' said Bertrand. 'She was a regular. She walked into the village every day to get bread. I'd wish her bonjour, offer her coffee. She'd politely refuse and set off back up the hill to the villa.'

'So, you knew where she lived?'

'Everyone in the village knew.'

Benoit's eyes bored into Bertrand's. 'The greeting you gave Madame at the fête suggests something more intimate.'

Bertrand took a huge belt of smoke, composing a reply. 'Very well. Yes, we were lovers,' he said, fighting off a smile. 'There's no shame in that.'

'She stopped politely refusing your attentions then?'

'Obviously.'

'How did it start?'

'One day, she bought bread and, as she passed, I saw she was upset so I sat her down, brought her coffee and tried to comfort her.' Benoit raised an eyebrow. Bertrand stiffened. 'She was upset,' he insisted.

'And, of course, you took care of her like any chivalrous ex-soldier would,' said Benoit.

Bertrand took a pull on his cigarette, unable to meet Benoit's piercing gaze. 'That's right.'

'And then?'

Bertrand shrugged. 'And, sometime later, we became intimate.'

'How much time later?'

Bertrand hesitated. 'Maybe half an hour.' Another raised eyebrow raised Bertrand hackles. 'It wasn't planned...'

'But being a military man, you saw your opportunity and took it.'

Bertrand's expression hardened and he replied through gritted teeth. 'It wasn't like that.'

'No?'

'I hope you don't think I had a hand in her death.'

'Why would I think that?' said Benoit.

'You're investigating their murder and now you're here,' said Bertrand. 'I didn't kill her, Commandant. That's the truth.'

'Your assurances aren't facts,' said Benoit.

'I don't know what else I can tell you?'

'You can tell me everything about your relationship with Charlotte Butler.'

'It was hardly that.'

'What was it then?'

'A fling. An *amour fou*. Temporary comfort was all she wanted.'

'Did you want something different?'

'Why would I?' said Bertrand. 'Besides, she didn't have the time or the opportunity. She had to get back to the villa. The short time we had together, she always worried her husband would miss her and ask questions.'

'She was worried he might find out?' said Benoit.

'It was more than worry. She was afraid.'

'Did she say why?'

'Only that her husband was in trouble and they had to get away from their old life.'

'She said that?' said Benoit. Bertrand shrugged. 'What kind of trouble?'

'She didn't say but she was worried their house was being watched. And she said, if anyone asked after them, I was to say nothing.'

'You didn't press her on what they were running away from?'

'It wasn't my business.'

Benoit stared at Bertrand. '*Did* anyone ask after them?'

'No, I kept her secret,' said Bertrand.

'An extraordinary level of confidence to place in a bar owner you barely know, don't you think?' said Benoit.

Something boastful played around Bertrand's eyes. 'Women are drawn to me because I'm a good listener. She needed to talk - I listened.'

'Did she speak about her relationship with her husband?' said Benoit.

Bertrand turned to the young woman standing behind the bar and signalled for a drink with a finger and a thumb. 'What was there to say? She was unfaithful. Clearly, she was unhappy.'

'Because she had to leave her old life or was there something else?'

'I couldn't say.'

'Do you think her husband knew about you?'

'Charlotte said not and I had no reason to disbelieve her.'

'And you told no-one about your affair?'

'Not a living soul.'

'I would have thought a woman that beautiful was a conquest to boast about.'

'To do so would have been a betrayal.'

'So noble,' sneered Benoit.

Anger flashed across Bertrand's eyes. 'I was in the Legion, *putain*. How have you served your country?'

'By hunting killers and putting them in prison,' growled Benoit. He leaned forward with menace. 'Provided they survive the hunt.'

'I have work...' snapped Bertrand, standing up.

'Sit down!' barked Benoit. He laid a note on the table. 'You've not had your drink. My treat.'

A young woman emerged with a generous measure of cognac and set it down on the table. Bertrand sat, wrapped his fist around the glass and took a calming sip.

'What else did Madame Butler talk about?'

'The weather, the villa, the pace of life, the food. She loved Seillans and France.'

'But something was wrong.'

'I was her escape from all that. We didn't speak of it.'

'Was she bored? Homesick? Did she even tell you where home was?'

'Commandant, I barely knew her...'

'Yet you claim you were lovers,' said Benoit.

'For a handful of snatched hours.'

'I need dates and times.'

Bertrand nodded at the photograph. 'It started the week before the Easter feast. After she became upset, I invited her back into the apartment to compose herself...'

'To take full advantage of her distress...'

'It wasn't like that!' shouted Bertrand, standing abruptly, his chair hurtling backwards. The hum of conversation ceased. Bertrand looked around at all the curious faces awaiting further drama, righted his chair and sat down. He was silent until people resumed their conversations. 'That's not the way it happened. I'm a soldier. There are rules of engagement.'

Benoit considered him. 'But you were bold enough to embrace her in public at the fête.'

'The village was full of revellers and her husband had gone for a walk.'

'Did she say where?'

'No.' A strange smile hovered around Bertrand's lips. 'Although, on my way through the village, I saw Monsieur Butler in the square.'

'So, you knew him?'

'I'd seen him around.'

'Did he know you?'

'No.'

'What was he doing?'

Bertrand smiled again. 'Talking to someone.'

Benoit leaned forward. 'Who?'

'I couldn't say.'

'Someone from the village?'

'He had his back to me. I couldn't see. But they knew each other.'

'Why do you say that?'

'The way they were talking. The lack of stiffness, formality.'

'Like friends?'

'Not friends, exactly. Close colleagues maybe. And Butler was doing most of the talking, like he was in charge.'

'Describe the other man.'

Bertrand drank more cognac. The sun was dipping behind buildings and the evening light draped a golden glow over Seillans' ancient structures. 'I wasn't close enough.'

'Tall, short, old, young?'

'Taller than Butler. Well built. Not old but not young.

And he was wearing a baseball cap and a dark sweatshirt. I remember that much.'

'Any insignia on the cap?'

Bertrand shrugged. 'I only saw the back of his head.'

'Did you ask Charlotte who it might be?'

'I didn't mention I'd seen him. We only had a moment and I didn't want to spend it talking about her husband.'

'When was the last time you saw her?'

Bertrand finished his cognac and gestured for a refill. 'In the morning, Friday before last. She bought bread, more than usual, but didn't sit for coffee. She said she was too busy.'

Benoit made the calculation. 'April 26th.' *The day of the drinks party.*

19

Benoit drove back to the ICP, the light failing quickly, though the day's heat was barely diminished in the absence of a breeze. Long before the turn-off to the villa, Benoit saw the lights of vehicles, including TV trucks, lined up along the tiny lane all the way from the junction to the barrier, now further removed from the crime scene.

When he turned onto the single-file lane, onlookers blocked the road and Benoit was forced to crawl past the crowds to the barrier, all the while hounded by journalists calling out questions and taking photographs as he passed. Beyond the barrier, he pulled up beside a high-powered Mercedes and its owner, Directeur Seigner, was listening intently to Latour's briefing, arms folded, her face a mask of concentration.

'Serge,' she called, when she saw him.

'Valerie,' said Benoit, greeting her with a kiss on both cheeks.

'Gabriel has brought me up to speed. I see the media have become a nuisance. You haven't given them anything?'

'We're still collating information.'

'Serge, Serge,' she sighed. 'If you don't feed the rats, they'll eat you instead. You know this.'

'It's recent,' said Benoit. 'Since victim ID this morning.'

'Killing wealthy tourists is always big news,' said Seigner. 'And I hear you've been annoying local dignitaries as well.'

'Not intentionally,' said Benoit.

'I'll bet,' said Seigner. 'I've told the mayor to stand next to me when I speak to the media, help smooth things over.'

'If you think it's necessary,' said Benoit.

Dugrippe emerged from the ICP, the colour around his nose and eyes resembling an overripe pear. 'Gabriel,' said Dugrippe, signalling a phone call at Latour, who excused himself to follow Dugrippe inside.

'Never did Depardieu any harm,' observed Seigner.

'My exact words,' said Benoit.

'Where are we on the case?'

'We've ruled out robbery,' said Benoit. 'We're pursuing all leads, including possible mob connections.'

'A bit too well-planned for a gangland killing, no?' said Seigner.

'How do you mean?'

'When they execute their enemies, the mafia usually want people to know about it.'

'I hadn't thought of that,' said Benoit.

'Yes, you had,' said Seigner. 'And if you've ruled out the mobs, this starts to look like a routine murder enquiry.'

'It's anything but that.'

'Don't mistake me, Serge. I'm not stupid enough to pull your team off a murder as heinous as this. You've detained a Canadian suspect, I hear.'

'Moss Tyler,' confirmed Benoit. 'We're holding him under an anti-terror warrant but he's not a suspect.'

'He broke into the crime scene and assaulted your officers.'

'But he didn't kill the Renfrews,' said Benoit. 'If he had, there was no valid reason to return. I think the Renfrews were clients and his actions motivated by a duty of care.'

'Clients, how?'

'He helped them disappear from their life in Singapore.'

'He didn't do a very good job.'

'That's not a crime.'

'Is this to do with this Russian bank Gabriel was telling me about?'

'On the face of it.'

'So, this...Tyler came back to find out what went wrong? What does he have to say?'

'Nothing, yet. I haven't interviewed him.'

'What's the hold-up?'

'Moss Tyler is an alias,' said Benoit. 'That's the hold-up.'

'Have you tried asking him who he is?'

'He had a car full of fake passports, Valerie, including that of the male victim. Deceit is the default setting for this guy. I'll ask him who he is when I know.'

Seigner smiled. 'Never ask a question to which you don't know the answer.' Benoit shrugged. 'Is he a professional?'

'From the fight he put up, I suspect he's ex-army. Marines? Special Forces?'

'So, his prints will be in the system somewhere.'

'We expect a hit soon,' said Benoit.

'From the look of Dugrippe's face, I assume Tyler has skills.'

'It took five of us to subdue him and if we hadn't had Daniel with us, we might still have lost.'

'Daniel?'

'Auger. Local gendarmerie and our liaison in Seillans,' said Benoit. 'A good man in a fight.'

'The marksman I've been hearing about?' said Seigner. Benoit gave a faint nod, bracing himself. 'Talking of marksmanship, Serge, do you know anything about a TV network drone being shot down this afternoon?'

'Drone?' he said, trying not to overdo the curiosity.

'Like the drone shot down when you investigated that terror cell in Villefranche six months ago.'

'I remember that,' said Benoit. 'Channel One got wind of our destination and flew a drone over the suspects' location then broadcast it live on national television. The suspects were gone when we got there.'

'I appreciate...'

'Took us an extra week to hunt them down and we were lucky nobody got killed in the meantime,' continued Benoit. 'Has somebody lost a drone?'

'France24 had one shot down earlier today, according to their lawyers.'

'Where?' said Benoit.

'Flying over the crime scene,' said Seigner. She held up a hand to forestall his objection. 'Don't bother. Their press officer felt the full force of my indignation, believe me. But there are protocols to be followed on our side too, Serge. We *cannot* have people shooting drones out of the sky.'

'Quite right,' said Benoit. 'Do you want me to make enquiries?' He waved an arm at the dense trees behind the ICP. 'This is hunting country. A stray shot...'

'Don't shovel it too hard, Serge, you'll hurt your back,' replied Seigner. 'But if one more drone gets shot down, you're on your own.' She looked at her watch. 'Come on. It's time to throw the rat pack some scraps and tell them where to get all their future meals.'

~

BENOIT WATCHED on from the shadows as Seigner, with Mayor Ruggieri standing close beside her, spoke to the assembled cameras and microphones at the barrier. The unearthly light from the media's cameras threw grotesque shapes onto the trees.

Seigner gave them the bare bones of the case as well as confirming victim ID and made an appeal for witnesses to phone the usual helpline that press and TV would display on their bulletins. She concluded with a promise to give daily evening briefings on the case at Police Judiciaire Headquarters on Avenue Marechal Foch in Nice and made a point of thanking Mayor Ruggieri for all his help.

'I will be in constant contact with Mayor Ruggieri and Commandant Benoit so I'll have up-to-the-minute information daily. There will be *no* further briefings from Seillans. The victims' remains have been removed to Nice for further examination and most of the investigative work will follow.

'Blocking access to the crime scene and relentlessly questioning busy officers, who have difficult and skilled work to do, will be fruitless. Thank you for your cooperation.'

Hands were raised in the throng.

After ten minutes of questions that Seigner answered with the same information in a variety of different ways, the impromptu press conference was over and Benoit walked Seigner to her car.

'Thank you.'

'I was overdue a visit,' said Seigner. 'Besides, it's a pleasure to get out of the sprawl for a day.'

'Join us for dinner,' said Benoit. 'The restaurant is pleasingly bucolic.'

'And have everyone in your team on their best behaviour?' She shook her head with a measure of regret. 'I wouldn't do that to them. The way you drive your people, they'll need to unwind.'

'They'd love to see you.'

'Didn't I tell you to stop shovelling? Speaking of which...'

'Mayor Ruggieri,' nodded Benoit.

'Make the effort,' said Seigner. 'It helps them help you.'

'I couldn't do your job.'

'We both know you could do it in your sleep,' said Seigner. 'You just wouldn't enjoy it. If things had been different...'

'Life happens while you're making plans, Valerie.'

'Death too.' She blushed. 'Sorry. You know what I mean.'

'Death is my craft,' said Benoit. 'Pointless denying it.'

She kissed him on both cheeks. When she withdrew, Seigner pointed an accusatory finger. 'No more shooting at drones and daily contact, you hear?'

'I'll have Gabriel email developments every day.'

Benoit watched as she drove away in her sleek Mercedes, through the dispersing crowd.

BACK AT THE ICP, Latour was waiting in the shadows by Benoit's car.

'Got him. Michael Trent from Chicago, late forties, a former marine who did a tour in the first Gulf War,' said Latour. 'Sent home after being wounded by shrapnel, hence the scar.'

'Good work,' said Benoit.

'That's just it,' said Latour. 'All I did was file a request through channels but, when they got a hit on the prints, the FBI phoned *me*. I just finished speaking with them.'

'He's on their wanted list?'

'Try *Most Wanted*,' said Latour. 'After leaving the Marines, Trent became a decorated FBI field agent in Chicago. He was suspended then dismissed in 2002, after a witness protection detail went bad.'

'What happened?'

'There were deaths, including the witness.' Latour glanced at a notebook. 'Gwen Beaumont - shot to death in a hotel room in Chicago. Also, a maid who was in the wrong place at the wrong time. Trent took full responsibility, was suspended then sacked and a few months later he dropped off the grid and left the country for Canada.'

'Doesn't explain why the FBI want him so badly,' said Benoit.

'No and they're not telling,' said Latour. 'But they want us to hold him under maximum security until we can put him on a plane. Boss, Trent's a killer and the FBI are being cagey because...'

'...France doesn't extradite prisoners who might face the death penalty,' said Benoit, nodding.

'Exactly,' said Latour.

'Request more information about a possible charge and, if they continue stalling, refer them to the Directeur,' said

Benoit. 'If they want him that badly, they'll have to talk to us.'

Half an hour later, the two detectives got into the Citroen and set off into the darkness, through the thinning crowd to the main highway, heading for the village.

On the curve of a bend, a large furry animal shot powerfully across the car headlights and Benoit slammed on the brakes.

Fortunately, there was no sickening thud and, after a pause to catch his breath, he and Latour jumped out to confirm the car had missed the animal. Despite flashing their iPhone torches into the thick vegetation, the creature was nowhere to be seen. Benoit climbed back into the car, with a quick glance at the layby where he'd stopped for a smoke on his first night in Seillans.

'What was that?' said Latour.

'A dog scavenging in the bins.'

'Or one of Daniel's summer wolves,' suggested Latour, with a grin.

DINNER WAS a muted affair as the previous night's exertions had taken their toll and the team mostly sat in silence throughout a meal that opened with a vegetable terrine with pungent shards of truffle, followed by a perfectly cooked magret de canard - crisp skin and pink meat - scented with honey and rosemary and served with garlic potatoes.

Fortunately, this was all washed down by several carafes of hearty red wine and, after a few glasses, spirits began to revive so Benoit went around the table to make sure everyone was up to date with the progress of enquiries.

'Did you believe Bertrand?' said Auger.

'Not entirely,' said Benoit. 'He knew Charlotte Butler, as he knew her, was running away from something but he was too quick to volunteer their intimacy.'

'Put a photograph of him next to one of her and you'll see he's lying,' said Caron. 'No way they were lovers.'

'I don't know,' said Dugrippe. 'Stress does funny things to people.'

'Assuming you believe him about Madame Renfrew being afraid.'

'Remember her husband was a similar age to Bertrand,' said Gagnon. 'And he was no oil painting.'

'But Renfrew had money,' said Rolland. 'Bertrand is an underachieving, middle-aged sex pest.'

'Beauty is in the eye of the beholder, Adele,' said Latour.

'Yeah?' sneered Rolland. 'Well, when I walked past Bertrand's bar yesterday, he was doing plenty of beholding, believe me. Especially my arse and my tits. Gave me the creeps.'

'Everyone gives you the creeps,' mocked Dugrippe.

'That's because we're miles from civilisation and the men around here haven't been taught not to stare and drool at the same time,' said Rolland, provoking laughter.

'What else did Bertrand say?' said Auger.

'He claimed to have seen Renfrew talking to someone in the square,' said Benoit.

'Did he say who?' said Auger.

'He said he couldn't see though I'm not sure I believed him,' said Benoit. 'He seemed to want to tell me something.'

'Any description?' said Latour.

'Taller than Butler,' said Benoit. 'Well built. Not old but not young. Wearing a baseball cap.'

'Not much help,' said Gagnon. 'Hopefully we'll get more photographs taken in the square.'

'Did he say what Madame Renfrew was afraid of?' said Auger.

'No,' said Benoit. 'Just that she was spooked *before* the party and thought someone was watching the house. Given what transpired, that's not a surprise - a crime this well-executed would need plenty of prep.'

'Who?' said Rolland. 'The Matteson girl?'

'We know she was heading for Lyon,' said Dugrippe. 'From there she could drive to Grenoble and onto the back roads over the mountains, staying off-grid.'

'But why hire Jasmin as a hideaway for the Renfrews, fly back to England then drive all the way back to spy on the house?' said Caron.

'None of this makes much sense yet,' said Benoit.

'If Matteson *was* watching the villa, she could be involved in the killings,' said Auger.

'Unless she was keeping an eye on the Butlers because they were in danger,' said Dugrippe.

'In this backwater?' said Caron.

'They were killed in this backwater, Nina,' said Dugrippe.

'But until we found the bodies, no-one knew they were in danger,' said Caron.

'Bertrand knew,' said Latour.

'Trent and Matteson knew and so did the Renfrews,' said Benoit.

'But if Matteson was watching the house, why didn't she raise the alarm or try to intervene?' said Rolland.

'Maybe she did,' said Gagnon. The diners fell silent, weighing the implications.

'And the two Englishmen?' said Rolland.

'Still missing,' said Dugrippe. 'We haven't found their car on any autoroute film going north. It didn't get on a ferry or make a border crossing. In fact, as far as I can tell, Barron's car didn't even get on the A8 at the local Lac de Saint-Cassien junction. No ticket was issued to Barron at the barrier for the entire week after they left their villa. They could have driven over the mountains, I suppose...'

'Nightmare traffic on a weekend,' said Gagnon.

Dugrippe shrugged. 'Agreed. But either they drove cross country or...'

'Or they're still in the area,' said Benoit.

'Unless they switched cars,' said Latour.

'Or took a plane.'

'No hits on their passports at any border controls,' said Dugrippe. 'We're canvassing local car rental but if they hired a different vehicle and used alternate passports, we don't have a prayer.'

'How's it going with the Easter photographs, Jerome?' said Benoit.

'Slowly,' said Gagnon.

'I've appealed to most of the villagers, asking them for any shots they may have taken,' said Auger. 'They're trickling in.'

'Inject some urgency and get bodies to follow up,' said Benoit. 'Go door-to-door with a bag of pen drives if you have to. I want to know who Renfrew was talking to that night in the square.'

Favre arrived with a tray of rum babas and a bottle of Rhum Agricole to soak into the sponge and was greeted with a round of appreciative sighs.

IT WAS APPROACHING midnight when Benoit and Auger were last to leave the table. They made their way wearily down the cobbled lanes and steep passageways towards Auger's building, their footsteps echoing through the narrow streets.

Three scrawny cats hurtled up the hill towards them and skittered past the two men. Benoit and Auger turned to watch the skinny beasts dive into various drains and tiny gaps in walls before poking out wary heads to monitor the lane.

Resuming their journey, Benoit and Auger took a few more steps before coming to a halt.

A large wolf padded towards them along the deserted alley and came to a stop in front of them.

'Don't move,' hissed Auger.

'Don't worry,' whispered Benoit, standing like a statue.

The wolf sat on its haunches and contemplated the pair, its startling blue eyes moving from man to man. The eyes fixed on Auger and it started to growl, its long fangs gleaming in the golden light, the noise rising like the throttle on a motorbike. Benoit noticed a hole in the cartilage of its left ear.

'Friend of yours?' muttered Benoit, still training his gaze on the beast.

'Looks like it,' said Auger, his eyes not straying from the animal's long face.

'Blood Summer,' said Benoit, slowly moving his right hand to his gun.

'Don't!' said Auger. 'Man is the bigger beast. A lone wolf is no match for two healthy adult males. Give him a second to work it out.'

The wolf took a step towards Auger and crouched low as though about to pounce, lips drawn back over its gums. The whole of its jaw seemed to distend, making the sharp teeth appear longer and even more fearsome.

'You sure?' mumbled Benoit. 'He seems to have a hard-on for you.' A second later, Benoit heard more growling and for a split-second thought there might be a second wolf circling behind them before realising it came from his colleague.

The noise in Auger's throat grew and he pulled his own teeth back into a snarl and the wolf cocked a disbelieving ear.

Then, without warning, Auger raised both hands to mimic aiming a rifle and the wolf darted back down the alley and along a narrow path away from them. The sound of its padded feet skidding on ancient stone, faded into the distance.

'That was…interesting,' said Benoit.

20

4th floor, Godfrey Hotel, Chicago 2002

'The Riverfront was compromised and the principals were in danger,' said Trent. 'I made a judgement call to move hotels. It was my decision.'

'Not another word on that until debrief,' said Supervising Special Agent, Lisa Petronelli, a forty-year-old, eighteen-year FBI veteran. 'Right now, I need your badge, your gun and everything you've got on the perps.'

The two agents were in the corridor, opposite Room 429, and Trent found it hard to avert his eyes from the blood and viscera staining carpets and walls. The door had been removed by CSIs in protective suits and, after extensive examination and bagging of head and hands to preserve potential trace, Gwen's body had followed.

Trent had watched the ambulance crew lift her remains onto a gurney for the short journey to Cook County morgue and the vacuum caused by her departure was filled by more forensic investigators, gathering, scraping and photographing evidence of her murder.

An urgent last touch of her blood-spattered hand before

the body bag was zipped, drew a frown of disapproval from Petronelli. When the maid's body had also been removed, Child Services finally emerged with Nell, screaming like a banshee, struggling every inch of the way and calling for her *mommy*.

Trent knelt to speak to her again, to tell her to go with *these nice people* and that he would see her soon. He'd fought back his own emotions, watching her being dragged away, inconsolable. 'Where are they taking her?'

'Let's not get into that, Mike,' said Petronelli. 'I asked for your badge and gun.'

Numbed, Trent handed over both without complaint. 'Somebody leaked the new location.'

'Have I been unclear, Mike?' said Petronelli, her expression hardening. 'When I say not another word, I mean shut the fuck up! Do not speak to *anyone* until your rep or a lawyer is standing next to you. This little shooting party is going to end a trial that's already cost the federal courts millions of dollars, not to mention the blowback we can expect on the Bureau's competence.

'I like you, Mike. I do. You're a fine agent but the OPR is going to want someone's head for this and right now yours is on the block. So, when the ASAC gets here, exercise your rights and keep your mouth shut about why you switched hotel rooms and why the package was alone...'

'Gwen wasn't a package...'

'And that's another thing,' she interrupted. 'If you want to keep your job, I suggest you downplay your personal involvement with the witness...'

'We weren't involved,' said Trent.

'That's not what it looks like.'

'We were *not* involved,' said Trent, quick to anger.

'Your detail will back you up on that?' she said. Trent didn't reply. 'Good. Don't answer that. All I want from you now is a description of the two men.'

'I'll do what I can but I didn't get a good look. And they used the service stairs to avoid lobby cameras.'

'Double tap on the maid tells me they were pros.'

'Russian pros,' said Trent.

'You sure?'

'I heard one of them speak before they saw me.'

'Great,' sighed Petronelli. 'What are the odds they're already out of the country? Distinguishing features?'

Trent pictured the cauliflower ears and missing eyebrows of the second man. 'Nothing out of the ordinary,' he said. 'But there was another man, the fixer. He called himself Byron.'

'Was he at the scene?'

'No.'

'Then how do you know him?'

'It's complicated.'

'Uncomplicate it for me,' insisted Petronelli. Trent hesitated. 'Jesus. Okay. You need to write it all down. And when we get back to the field office, you look at mugshots. If necessary, we'll get an artist in. If they're pros, we're probably not going to find them but, from here on, we need to do everything by the numbers, if only to salvage a little credibility.'

At that moment, Rentoria turned the corner, replacing his badge in a pocket, accompanied by another Supervisor in blue windcheater and baseball cap, the letters FBI emblazoned across both garments in bright yellow. They were deep in conversation and Rentoria was shaking his head, a Starbucks coffee in his hand.

The supervisor put an arm across to direct him away from the crime scene for a debrief and, coming to a halt, Rentoria looked across and caught Trent's gaze. Their eyes locked for a split-second before the younger man looked away, nodding at a question asked of him.

For the first time since discovering Gwen's body, Trent's mind turned to detection. How did the killers know where to find her? Had he been followed? Had they overheard him talking to Rentoria on the payphone? Replaying the events of the last twelve hours in ten seconds, he was certain he hadn't made a mistake.

Okay, Byron had found him at the pizza restaurant but it wasn't hard to believe the Chicago Waterfront Hotel was blown with so many people in the loop. Too many people knew about the op so it was conceivable that Byron's people had followed the three of them from the hotel. But finding the Godfrey Hotel so quickly with no-one else in the loop?

Finally, Trent answered his own question and, with the solution to hand, it took all his willpower to allow Petronelli to usher him into an empty room across the corridor to write his statement.

'Friendly fire,' he mumbled, as he picked up the pen.

'What's that, Mike?'

Trent was finding simple communication difficult but he managed to shake his head and squeeze out a word. 'Nothing.'

21

July 31st 2002 - Chicago

Trent sat in his rented car, eyes glued to the worshippers filing out from the warmth and light of St Nicholas Catholic Cathedral. A large man in a voluminous worsted overcoat, plodded across the length of Trent's windshield, halting briefly at the sidewalk to check for traffic. With the road clear, he hurried across West Rice Street in Chicago's West Town district, sometimes known as Ukrainian Village.

On the south side of West Rice, the man continued along Oakley Boulevard, dipping in and out of sight under mature oak trees casting their shadow over the dark sidewalk. Pulling on his rucksack, Trent got out and closed the car door to follow on foot, hugging the buildings in case the man looked round.

Turning south on Oakley, Trent watched the man lumbering into West Chicago Avenue, two blocks down. He already knew where he was going and quickened his step to follow but didn't turn the corner. Instead, he peered around the side of a hot dog stand to confirm his suspicions.

Sure enough, Aleksay Sokolov arrived at the entrance to Old Lviv Restaurant and disappeared under the blue awning for his regular dose of Ukrainian comfort food - the third time that week.

While Sokolov settled into a booth to order his cabbage soup, Trent retraced his steps along Oakley and turned into the alley, running behind the restaurant, and hurried past the kitchens of Old Lviv.

A hundred yards further, on the opposite side of the alley, Trent arrived at a plain three-storey brick building with a solid wooden stairwell running up the side of the property, servicing three identical white doors, one on each floor.

Not having an access key for the security gate, Trent had to haul himself up to the first-floor landing, using the bars of the wrought iron fence enclosing the ground floor property, as leverage.

Once there, he climbed silently to the top floor apartment, extracted a set of bump keys from his coat and manoeuvred one of them into the lock, then drew it back a notch. Turning it slightly, he tapped the back of the key with the palm of his hand until he felt the pins align then unlocked the door and stepped into the dark apartment to prepare.

SITTING IN THE DARK, Trent heard heavy footsteps plodding up the stairs, heading towards the door. The key turned and a draft of fresh air preceded Sokolov's entrance. Light flooded the main room and the door closed behind him but, when he saw the plastic sheet covering the centre of the room, Sokolov's hand went instinctively to his inside breast pocket.

'It's not there,' said Trent, smiling.

The man's dearth of eyebrows, coupled with his cauliflower ears, lent him a comical air but his expression was severe as he contemplated Trent, sitting on a wooden chair, pointing a gun, fitted with a silencer, at him. Trent held up his other hand to show Sokolov his own gun which he tossed to the floor.

Sokolov smiled, dropping his empty right hand to his side. 'Clever,' he said, in a strong accent.

'Not really,' said Trent. 'I figured even assassins think twice about taking a gun to church.'

'You were at the Godfrey Hotel,' said Sokolov. 'You killed my friend, Sergei?'

Trent grunted confirmation and gestured to the identical wooden chair to his own, placed in the middle of the plastic sheet. Sokolov didn't react.

'Sit!' commanded Trent, gripping the gun to encourage compliance.

In slow motion, Sokolov approached the chair, calcu-lating his options as he moved. The plastic sheet squeaked under his feet. Before he reached the chair, he glanced towards the nearby bedroom.

'Don't bother,' said Trent. 'I emptied that one too.'

Sokolov grunted in amusement and sank onto the wooden chair, his eyes glued to the silencer on Trent's gun. 'Why the sheet?'

'I'm a neat freak,' said Trent.

Sokolov's eyes alighted on a heavy-duty plastic shopping bag, straining at the seams, next to Trent's chair. 'What's in the bag?'

'The contents of your chest freezer,' said Trent.

Sokolov took a moment to consider his next utterance. 'I have a son.'

'Let's hope he's a better human being than you.'

Sokolov nodded. 'You too, Yankee. Can I have a cigarette?'

'No.'

'Then what are you waiting for?'

'Where do I find Byron?'

'Who is Byron?'

'You tell me.'

'I do tell you. I don't know Byron. I know Sergei and I know the target.'

'Who was the target at the Godfrey Hotel?'

'A blond woman.'

'What was her name?' said Trent. 'The woman whose head you blew off through the spyhole.'

Sokolov licked his lips. 'I can't remember. I get room number. I go. I shoot.'

Trent's expression of hatred deepened. 'Gwen. Her name was Gwen.'

'If you say so.'

'Where do I find Byron?'

Sokolov burst into wheezy laughter. 'You're funny.'

'I won't ask again.'

'Good, because you're boring me,' said Sokolov. 'Something I do know is they warned you to forget your anger to protect the child and you agreed. That's why we spared the girl. Now you break the deal, so the girl dies.'

'I broke the deal two weeks ago when I killed Sergei but the child is still alive,' said Trent. 'Know what I think, Aleksay? I think you're expendable. Maybe, I'm even doing your employers a favour, cleaning up their mess for them.'

Sokolov nodded. 'When billions of dollars are at stake, nobody is safe. Not me. Not you.'

'I'm an FBI agent,' said Trent.

'You think that protects you?'

'Where do I find Byron?'

Sokolov shook his head. 'I hear voice on telephone. The voice says who, when and where.'

'Whose voice?'

Sokolov grinned. 'You think I go to their house for vodka? The voice hires me. I don't know name. Sergei would say same.' Without warning, Sokolov lunged at Trent but before he had cleared the chair, Trent fired off a round at Sokolov's knee, blowing a crater in his patella. The big man collapsed like a circus elephant, screaming high and short, clutching his leg and gritting his teeth against the pain.

'God!' groaned Sokolov, in agony.

'I hope you spoke to Him earlier and confessed your sins.'

'Fuck you,' panted Sokolov.

Trent aimed his Glock at Sokolov's undamaged kneecap and fired. The big man yelped in distress and began rocking his ample frame back and forth, cooing to himself to cope with the pain.

'Vybliadok,' he spat at Trent.

'My mother's dead,' said Trent. 'Last chance, comrade. Who is Byron and where do I find him?'

A long moan of despair from Sokolov. 'I told you. Voice on phone.' Trent regripped the gun handle, again preparing to fire at his crotch. 'Go ahead. I tell you if I know but I don't. You can't reach these people, Yankee. Face this. I get phone call. That's it.'

Trent sighed. 'We moved hotel. How did you know where to find her?'

Sokolov managed to grin through the agony. 'I need to tell you this, Yankee?'

'No.' Trent's expression was like granite and he raised the gun for the last time. 'But tell me anyway.'

Trent listened as Sokolov told him what he needed to know and when the Ukrainian had finished, he put a bullet in his head and the big man sagged lifelessly onto the sheet.

Moments later, the mortal remains of Aleksay Sokolov were tightly wrapped in plastic and Trent shook out the body bag from his rucksack and, feet-first, fed the ample frame of the Ukrainian into it.

22

Sunday May 5th 2019 Fayence, South of France

Latour closed his phone and opened the passenger-side window to allow early morning air to cool his face. 'It's done,' he said to Benoit. 'Thierry's rousing Coulibaly's team and they should be in place within the hour. Auger's people will close the road and he's smoothing it over with the mayor.'

'Good,' said Benoit. 'It'll be tough going so better done while it's still cool.'

'What exactly are they looking for?'

Benoit considered his answer. 'Food,' he replied with a cryptic smile.

Before Latour could enquire further, Benoit pulled the Citroen to a halt outside the functional concrete Gendarmerie in Fayence, a jarring presence amidst centuries-old buildings in the beautiful market town.

TRENT DRAINED the bitter black coffee to wash down the baguette and jam, dispirited after his second night in custody. Not because he wasn't used to such privation but because it was clear Benoit was letting him stew until he had enough information to apply pressure. And, at the top of that list would be the hit his fingerprints would register at the FBI. That was the ball game.

He placed the plastic cup on his plastic breakfast tray next to the plastic knife and tried to imagine the reaction of barely remembered colleagues when his prints landed at the Bureau, seventeen years after fleeing his country. Would they shrug and write him off to history or scramble their worldwide network to bring him home? Trent smiled, all too aware of the answer.

Before he had time to resume his exercises, footsteps approached and keys turned in locks. Trent stood ready, gathering his wits. Showtime.

≈

BENOIT AND LATOUR sat on hard chairs at a metal table bolted to the floor. Bulletins lined the walls and, while Latour placed a briefcase on the table and organised the evidence bags, Benoit read the notices absently. A barbecue evening for local officers and families. A picture of a missing female backpacker. A security message about unlocked windows. A poster to warn drivers against leaving pets in hot cars.

The door opened and Trent was hauled into the bright lights of the interview suite, blinking under the harsh strips. The face may have been unshaven and the hair tousled but Trent's eyes were clear and rested. The dressings on his hand and ear were fresh though a couple of new abrasions had appeared on his face. Benoit flashed an enquiring glance at Trent's escort, walking the prisoner to the chair, movement restricted by cuffs and leg irons.

'He kicked one of the guards in the nuts,' said the uniformed officer. A smile of accomplishment ghosted across Trent's features as one of the gendarmes unlocked the cuff on his left wrist then closed it through an iron ring on the table. The leg irons were left on.

'Still not accepting your situation, Mr Tyler?' said Benoit, pushing a paper cup towards Trent. 'Remove the cuffs,' he said to the gendarme.

A few seconds later, Trent massaged his wrists in time-honoured fashion, ignored the coffee cup and fixed his eyes defiantly on Benoit. 'I've been locked up without charge for two days. I demand a lawyer.'

'Drink your coffee,' said Benoit. 'It's from Starbucks.'

'A little taste of home,' added Latour.

Trent flicked off the lid with a thumb and took a sip. 'It's cold.'

Benoit shrugged. 'Hot coffee is a weapon.'

'Lawyer,' repeated Trent.

'I want some answers first.'

'Don't you have laws in France?'

Benoit glanced at Latour, who spread out seven plastic wallets across the table, each containing a passport sporting Trent's photograph. Benoit watched to see whether Trent flicked a glance towards Harry Renfrew's passport but the American was stoically maintaining eye contact with his two interrogators.

'Those laws only apply to real people,' said Benoit. He dropped a finger on the Canadian passport. 'Moss Tyler from Canada. Marco Trentin from Italy. Matteus Trautmann from Germany. Mark Tompkins from the UK.' Benoit nodded to the rest. 'And three other very convincing passports, each bearing your likeness.' A pause. 'Sprechen Sie Deutsch, Herr Trautmann?'

'I get by,' said Trent.

'You see our problem,' said Latour. 'You're a ghost. We have no idea who you are or which embassy to contact.'

'I'm not talking until I get a lawyer.'

'Then listen,' said Benoit. 'You entered France carrying false travel documents and armed with not one, but three unlicensed weapons, their serial numbers filed off. That makes you a potential terrorist...'

'I'm not a terrorist,' said Trent.

Benoit smiled. 'I know that. But the mere suspicion allows me to do what I want with you and, as in most countries in a post-9/11 world, the law allows me to keep you in a deep dark hole for as long as I please.'

'What about my rights?' said Trent, enunciating each consonant.

Benoit sighed. 'Rights?' A memory flashed through his mind - a tiny hand, a glass-eyed teddy bear soaked in blood, a wailing father, on his knees. 'I live in Nice, Monsieur Tyler. In an apartment on the seafront on the Promenade des Anglais.

'Three years ago, Nice joined the list of cities to suffer a major terrorist atrocity and I was there, in person, the night infamy came to my town. It was supposed to be a celebration, a happy night full of good cheer, families strolling by the sea, smiling and joyful.

'Without warning, a lorry was driven at speed into the crowd of tourists and my fellow citizens - men, women and children - mowing them down without mercy.

'Within moments, those happy smiling people were lumps of broken and crushed flesh.' Benoit paused. 'I walked among the victims that night, saw sights no-one should ever see. Sights that made me question my sanity and even my right to live when innocent women and children, even babies in pushchairs, could be brutally flattened, some of them beyond all recognition, even to family members who'd been holding their hand seconds before.'

'I'm sorry,' said Trent.

'Are you? Eighty-six people died that night. And for what? So that a serial loser, a misfit cry-baby, could end his miserable existence in a manner that ensured the whole world would mark his passing. Trust me on this, monsieur; no-one in France gives a *fuck* about your rights, least of all, me.' Benoit contemplated Trent. 'Do you remember the truck driver's name?'

'I confess I don't.'

'You have no idea how happy that makes me.'

'Is there a point to this conversation?' said Trent.

'An important one,' said Benoit. 'I want you to know that if I thought for *one* second that you were a terrorist, you would not be alive to drink my cold coffee.'

Trent stared. 'Would you like to repeat that when my lawyer gets here?'

'Let's start with your real name. I suspect it's not Moss Tyler because all your fake names have the same initials.' Benoit picked up another plastic wallet. 'This passport, however, is different. Harry Renfrew. Is that your real name?' He placed the passport on the table. 'Tell me, Harry, what is your relationship to David and Charlotte Butler?'

'I didn't kill them,' said Trent.

'I know that too,' said Benoit. 'If you'd killed them, you wouldn't have kept the third cell phone or answered the call from Charlotte. I also know that you were in Berlin, posing as Harry Renfrew when the Butlers were murdered.'

'Then, why are you holding me?'

'Because I can,' said Benoit. 'Because a ruthless killer has murdered two people in my jurisdiction and you, and your English lady friend, Megan Matteson, are involved.'

'She's not involved,' said Trent.

'Oh, but she is,' said Benoit. 'It may have been on your orders but she came to Seillans in March, travelling under a false identity, and hired the Villa Jasmin for six months, paying sixty-thousand euros. In cash, up front.

'Her work done, she flew back to her home in London, that same night. The Metropolitan Police gave me her London address, if you're interested. She lives in Chelsea.' Benoit allowed the long pause to play out so Trent would know who was holding all the cards.

'Has she been arrested?' said Trent.

'We tried,' said Latour. 'Unfortunately, the British Police

were too late.' Trent's eyes narrowed. 'She's no longer in London, she's here in France.'

'You're lying,' said Trent.

'Why would we lie?' said Benoit, accepting a folder from Latour and extracting a copy of a screenshot of Trent's unanswered WhatsApp posts. 'It's the reason Megan hasn't answered your increasingly desperate messages. Didn't she mention her travel plans to you, Harry?'

Trent stared at the copy of his messages. 'You're fishing. You don't know where she is.'

'You're right,' said Benoit, pushing a photostat of a ferry ticket across the table, followed by pictures of Megan's Audi A3 rolling off the P&O ferry at Calais. 'But we know where to look.' Further photographs showed Megan behind the wheel, preparing to drive through a variety of autoroute barriers on roads from Calais to the South of France. The final picture was taken at a Peage barrier near Grenoble late in the evening of April 24th.

'See the date?' said Benoit. 'The victims were last seen alive in the early hours of Saturday, April 27th. Our enquiries lead us to believe they were killed within a few hours of that last sighting and Megan was heading for the south coast, *three* days before that.'

'From Grenoble she would take the Route Nationale to Gap, then over the Provence-Alpes to the Cote d'Azur, avoiding the motorway and toll cameras,' said Latour. 'We don't have absolute confirmation yet but there are pinch points in Digne and Castellane and we're checking hotels and cameras along the route. If Wendy Wyatt or Megan Matteson stayed in a hotel, on her way to Seillans, we'll know by tonight.'

Trent examined each photograph in turn before staring at Benoit. 'This doesn't prove she was coming to Seillans.'

'I also have a witness who describes a young woman, matching Megan's description, parked in the very same layby you left your Range Rover,' lied Benoit. 'The young woman in question was seen, gazing through binoculars at Villa Jasmin.'

Benoit turned to Latour, who handed him another evidence bag containing the DVD case. Benoit pointed the camera at Trent. 'Black and white Polish war films. Clever to hide a camera in a box no-one but a Polish war veteran would want to open. When you broke into the villa, you went straight to it to remove the memory card.' He spread his arms wide. 'I wish I could show you a picture of you doing exactly that - or a shot of Megan holding a gun on the Butlers - but I can't.

'Someone removed the storage card before we arrived at Jasmin. Someone who knew the camera was there. You knew it was there but, because you tried to retrieve the memory card, you clearly weren't aware it had been removed. And, until this very second, you would have assumed we removed it. We didn't.' Trent looked to Latour who shook his head in confirmation. 'Who else knew it was there?'

Again, Benoit allowed his question to percolate around Trent's brain before proceeding. 'The victims? Unlikely. Professional killers? Why would they even need the camera? The landlord? Possible but a bit of a longshot. Your associate, Megan Matteson? Without a shadow of doubt.'

Trent jumped to his feet, knocking over the dregs of the coffee, but was constrained by his leg irons and the two gendarmes pulled him back to his seat then reattached the handcuff to the metal ring.

'Megan is not a killer,' seethed Trent. 'We were helping them. She didn't kill Charlotte and David. You must believe that.'

Benoit was silent, letting the storm blow over, while Latour mopped up the coffee with a few tissues. Eventually, Trent's breathing returned to normal and he glared sullenly at the photographs of Megan in her car.

Unruffled, Benoit shook out a cigarette and lit up,

despite the frowns of the two gendarmes. 'Helping them, how?'

'Can I get a drink of water?' said Trent.

Benoit glared at one of the gendarmes, who levered himself reluctantly off the wall and left the room.

Trent received, then emptied, the small bottle of Evian that arrived two minutes later.

'Helping them, how?' said Benoit.

'Release me,' said Trent. 'I've known Megan for a long time. I can help you find her.'

'Helping them, how?' repeated Benoit, stone-faced.

Trent sighed. 'David and Charlotte Butler were fake names for Harry and Carla Renfrew.' Benoit's expression was unchanged. 'But then you already know that, don't you?'

Benoit picked up Renfrew's passport. 'This Harry Renfrew?'

'Yes.'

'Your help included the supply of false passports in the name of David and Charlotte Butler?'

'Yes.'

'Why?'

'They needed to drop out of sight for a while and they hired me to help them.'

'You make people disappear?'

'For a price,' said Trent. 'I have the contacts and the skills. Renfrew is...was a multi-millionaire bond dealer, based in Singapore. Carla was his wife. Both English ex-pats. Renfrew got in over his head on a deal with a Russian bank. Death threats were issued and Renfrew hired me, through Megan. I arranged new identities and escorted the two of them out of Singapore to Nice and from there to the villa. Stop me when I tell you something you don't know.'

'Where is Carla Renfrew's passport?' said Benoit. Trent didn't answer so Benoit turned to Latour. 'Add Carla Renfrew's name to Matteson's list of aliases and re-issue the bulletin.' Latour left the suite, reaching for his phone.

'Megan didn't kill the Renfrews,' said Trent, softly. 'You have to believe me. She doesn't have it in her.'

'But you do,' said Benoit. 'Don't you, Michael?'

Trent smiled. *Michael.* 'How long have I got?'

'Before the FBI come to claim you? That depends on what you did. I'm assuming you killed someone.'

'They didn't tell you?' said Trent.

'Under French law, we can't extradite a prisoner if they might face the death penalty in the petitioning country,' said Benoit. 'Who did you kill?'

'The FBI have no proof I killed anyone.'

'That's not what I asked you,' said Benoit. Latour returned to his chair with a nod of confirmation. 'Who did you kill?'

'I refuse to answer on the grounds it may incriminate me.'

'The Fifth Amendment doesn't apply in France and certainly not to suspected terrorists.'

'I'm not a terrorist,' said Trent.

'That won't help you, if you don't co-operate.'

'So, that's how it is,' said Trent.

'That's how it is.'

Trent took a moment. 'I'll tell you everything I know to help you find Megan and prove she didn't kill the Renfrews. In return, you let her go. You can do whatever you want with me.'

'She's in my country,' said Benoit. 'Why would I need your help?'

'Because I taught her everything she knows,' said Trent. 'Because I want to find whoever did this as much as you do. Because I knew the Renfrews and liked them, especially Carla.'

'Everybody loved Carla,' said Benoit. 'I wonder why that is.'

'She seemed a decent human being.'

'And Renfrew wasn't?'

Trent shrugged. 'He was okay. But you know...'

'Your average rich prick?' said Benoit. Trent didn't disagree. 'You don't bargain for yourself?'

'Would there be any point?'

'None.'

'So, we have a deal?'

'Not unless you tell me who you killed?' said Benoit.

'Off the record?'

Benoit laughed. 'You're a terror suspect, Michael. There is no record until I decide what I want it to say. So, tell me, who did you kill?'

Trent considered his answer. 'Nobody who didn't deserve it.' Benoit gestured to Latour to pack up the evidence bags but Trent interrupted. 'Okay. I was an FBI field agent in Chicago...'

'We know all that.'

'Then you'll know my last assignment was in 2002, protecting a witness...'

'Gwen Beaumont,' said Latour.

Trent nodded. 'She worked for a Russian energy company as a secretary. A friend of hers got her the job. One day her friend confided in her about accounting irregularities - money going missing into shell companies. Bribes. She told Gwen a few details and that she was going to raise it with her boss.

'The next day she was shot to death in an underground car park. Her bag was stolen to add authenticity but it was murder dressed up as a mugging. Gwen came forward to do the right thing...'

'And the killers went after her,' said Benoit. Trent stared at Benoit, a haunted look on his face. 'You were assigned to protect her and when you failed, the case died with her.'

'Yes.'

'Then, like John Wayne, you went looking for the culprits.'

'She was shot in the head by two Ukrainian hitmen while her five-year-old kid was in the apartment,' said Trent.

'A maid who got in the way was executed as well. Do you blame me?'

'You tracked down and killed the two assassins?'

Trent looked at Benoit, Latour and the two gendarmes in turn. 'Let's just say they died suddenly and violently and the FBI want to speak to me about their passing - a conversation we've yet to have. But there's no proof of my involvement and I admit nothing.'

'Why would the FBI put you on their Most Wanted list over a couple of dead assassins?' said Latour.

'I'm rogue FBI and the Bureau doesn't like loose ends,' said Trent. 'Do we have a deal?'

'What guarantees do I have you won't try to escape?' said Benoit.

'Megan's safety is all that matters to me. This is *your* country. Help me find her and I give you my word, cop to cop, I'll place myself completely in your power.'

'Full disclosure?'

'Full disclosure.'

'Then, let's start with the gun at the villa.'

'I left it behind the water tank for Harry and Carla's protection.'

'What kind of gun was it?' said Latour.

'You've got eyes, haven't you?' said Trent.

'We found no gun,' said Benoit.

'Then how...'

'Gun oil from the cloth it was wrapped in,' said Benoit.

Trent took a moment to process the information. 'It was a Sig Sauer P229 Legion Compact.'

'A beginner's gun,' said Latour. 'Could Renfrew handle it?'

'I made him take lessons before leaving Singapore,' said Trent.

'And was it loaded?'

'A full ten-round clip,' said Trent.

'How many people knew it was there?'

Trent hesitated. 'Just me and Renfrew.'

'Mrs Renfrew?'

'That was up to him.'

'And Megan?' said Benoit.

'She prepped the gun for me but she wouldn't know where I hid it.'

'But she knew it was in the house,' said Benoit. 'You searched behind the water tank for a gun that wasn't there so we know you didn't take it. Mr and Mrs Renfrew are dead. That leaves Megan.'

'That doesn't mean...'

'Yes, it does,' said Benoit.

'Maybe Renfrew tried to use it and the killers took it from him,' said Trent.

Benoit smiled. 'How did Megan get the gun into the country?'

'She didn't,' said Trent. 'It was in a storage locker at Nice Airport. She has a key.'

'You put it there?' Trent nodded. 'When?' No answer. 'This isn't your first-time hiding people in our region.'

'Actually, it is,' said Trent. 'But I've been to Seillans before and always thought it would be a good place to hide clients.'

'So, you prepared resources should the need arise,' said Benoit.

'Yes.'

'You have lockers in many airports?'

'What do you care?'

'I'll take that as a yes,' said Benoit. 'What else do you keep in your airport lockers?'

'Some local currency and a gun, as a minimum. It depends. I can't give you a full inventory but you've got my keys - go and look.'

'We will.'

'Your laptop,' said Latour. 'What's the access code?'

'Why?'

'We want to look at your other correspondence with Megan.'

'I can't give you that but if you let me out, I...'

'Full disclosure.' Trent shook his head. 'Our people will break the code eventually.'

'No, they won't. And if you try to access the drive without the code, you should know that will trigger a virus that wipes the drive.'

'Then give me the passcode,' said Benoit. 'If you want to get out of here, that's the deal.'

'I have professional responsibilities to clients who trusted me with their secrets.'

'What kind of secrets?' said Benoit. Trent was implacable. 'For example.'

'The whereabouts of their relocation,' said Trent. 'The identities they're using to hide from a vengeful husband, a litigious employer, an obsessive stalker...'

'We're only interested in Megan.'

'That doesn't mean you're getting access.'

'Then we reach an impasse.'

'Maybe not,' said Trent. 'Give me my laptop. I'll load my correspondence with Megan.'

'Where is it?'

'We have a dark web message board just for our use though the last ten days have been a bit one-sided.'

'She's off the reservation, isn't she?' said Benoit.

Trent lowered his eyes. 'I honestly don't know. When I left Barcelona, I told her to go dark...'

'Go dark?'

'Delete all operational material and suspend all comms in case they were being monitored...'

'But she broke off communications long before that, according to your iPhone,' said Latour.

'That's what's worrying me,' said Trent.

'Then worry no more,' said Benoit. 'Now you know she broke off contact because she'd secretly returned to Seillans.'

'She didn't kill the Renfrews,' said Trent.

'You can't possibly know that,' said Benoit. 'She deceived you about her intentions.'

'I know she left her apartment, leaving her iPhone and laptop behind, and hasn't been back,' said Trent.

'Why would she leave her devices?' said Benoit. Trent lowered his eyes. 'To stop you tracking her. But you were in Berlin when she drove to France. How would you know she wasn't in her apartment without speaking to her?'

'I...keep an eye on her.'

'You bugged her apartment?' said Benoit.

Trent shook his head, unable to meet Benoit's gaze. 'I have cameras.'

'Cameras?' said Benoit.

'In her home?' said Latour. Trent nodded. 'She consented to that?' Trent didn't answer.

'We'll take that as a no,' said Benoit.

'In case you hadn't noticed, we're in a dangerous business,' said Trent, tight-lipped.

'Did you hack her laptop?' said Latour.

'Nothing so crude,' said Trent. 'I set up the system for her.'

'And put in a back door without her knowledge to spy on her,' said Latour.

'For her protection,' said Trent. 'I use it as a last resort. You've seen what can happen in our world.'

'What exactly is your relationship with Megan Matteson?' said Benoit.

Trent paused. 'I'm her father.'

'And you were doing so well.' Benoit gestured to Latour to start packing away the evidence bags. 'We're finished here.'

'Wait,' said Trent, as Benoit stood to leave. 'I need to know. Have you confirmed Carla Renfrew as the female victim?'

'You lie to me and expect privileged information?' said Benoit.

'Please,' said Trent.

'You're worried the female victim might have been Megan,' said Latour.

'Is it possible?' said Trent, a desperate look in his eyes.

Benoit shook his head. 'We confirmed the victims' DNA against samples from a lady's razor, a toothbrush and a hairbrush from Villa Jasmin. Same with Harry. Your clients are dead.'

Trent nodded. 'Thank you.'

'DO WE BELIEVE HIM?' said Latour, as they drove up the adjacent hill back towards Seillans, perched like the decoration on a cake, in the distance.

'Like all good soldiers under interrogation, he gave us a sprinkling of the truth.'

'But he's lying to us.'

'Of course,' said Benoit. 'But, when he says he'd sacrifice himself to protect the Matteson girl, I believe him.'

'Why?'

'Because he has the air of a man who once failed to protect someone he loved and is determined never to repeat that mistake.'

'Are you going to give him access to his laptop?'

'Tempting. We've nothing to lose and we'll be there to supervise.'

'And if he decides to wipe all his data and we can't stop him?' said Latour.

'Then we'll be no worse off than we are now.'

'If we release him, do you take his word he wouldn't try to escape?'

Benoit laughed. 'What do you think?'

CARON EASED past the tough root encroaching on her path, glad of the protective suit, already heavily discoloured by clay. Looking back at Dugrippe and the others, she gave a thumbs-up before plunging into the undergrowth on all fours, wriggling and squirming to avoid sharp stones on the baked ground digging into her ribs.

Despite the early hour, the heat was oppressive under the tangled canopy of the maquis and, under her layers, she sweated copiously, to the delight of freshly-disturbed insects who began nibbling at her face as she tried to move further into the scrub.

Only a couple of metres in and it became so dark that she was forced to flick on her small torch to try and get her bearings and pick out detail on the ground. In the extra illumination, there seemed to be a faint animal track running through the dense shrubbery and about ten metres along, a wider space, free from roots, where she would at least be able to turn around for her return to the layby, should she be unable to penetrate deeper.

Caron hauled herself along the track, panting with the effort, which only excited the insects more, making them dart towards the invisible gasps of carbon dioxide, exhaled in her breath.

At the entrance to the small clearing, she felt something sharp beneath her suit. Feeling around, she picked up a small object and held it up to her torch. With a tremor of disgust, she realised it was the bone of a finger, totally denuded of flesh.

With some difficulty, she retrieved an evidence bag and slid the digit inside.

'*Putain,*' she mumbled, pulling herself into the tight clearing. The heat was unbearable. The insects were unbearable. The confinement was unbearable. With a strenuous effort, in the cramped space, she pivoted around to face the way she'd come in, then buried her face on her arms to get her breath back. She pulled the radio to her mouth.

'It's impossible. We'll have to cut. I'm coming out.'

Preparing to move, she paused when a twig snapped deep in the gloomy tangle of undergrowth behind her.

Caron pivoted to shine her torch at the shadows but saw nothing.

More rustling reached her ear. An animal crawling through the jungle of roots, probably. Again, Caron shone her torch and this time, at the limit of its range, the faint light was thrown back at her by two unblinking eyes, watching her from the shadows.

Caron didn't wait for a better look. She dropped the torch and engaged every sinew to drag herself back towards the sunlight but, in her haste, caught herself on every obstacle successfully navigated on the way in.

Stymied by a particular root, she yanked hard to extricate the sleeve of her suit from its grip and, in so doing, dislodged something held above ground by the canopy of tough branches, which landed in front of her path to freedom with a thud and a half roll in her direction.

PASSING THROUGH SEILLANS, Latour pulled the Citroen up to the barrier closing the D19, just west of the village. A gendarme indicated a back road in the same direction as the 'Deviation' sign but, when Latour held his ID to the window, the barrier was moved aside.

Two minutes later, they drew to a halt behind the welter of Police and FFP vehicles strewn across the carriageway. CSIs were roaming the layby in protective suits, carrying serious cutting equipment. Dugrippe stood apart, talking to Gagnon, Rolland and Coulibaly. He raised an arm in greeting.

'Anything?' said Benoit, staring up at the banked hillside. In daylight, he could see the slope was covered in tough grass which gave way to impenetrable scrub, rising steeply beyond the man-made cutting. Gnarled old roots blocked passage and only a small aperture, suitable for an animal to pass, offered a way into the dense undergrowth.

'We're barely able to get up there with cutting tools, never mind walk around in that stuff,' said Rolland.

'It's thick with lavender, rockroses, tree heather and a dozen other roots,' said Dugrippe. 'It could take days to cut a path and search properly.'

'So, a good place to hide body parts then,' said Benoit.

'Body parts?' said Dugrippe.

'Severed heads and hands,' said Benoit.

'Food?' said Latour. 'You mean the dog we saw last night.'

'It wasn't a dog,' said Benoit. 'It was a wolf.'

'A wolf?' exclaimed Rolland and Dugrippe in unison.

'We only saw it for a split-second, boss,' said Latour.

'I saw it in the village last night, cool as you like,' said Benoit. 'Daniel too. And twice I've encountered it on *this* spot.'

'What's it doing here?'

'I think it's found a food supply and it's sticking around until it's exhausted,' said Benoit.

'Blood Summer,' mumbled Latour.

'Wait,' said Rolland, nodding up the hill. 'Nina's in there.'

'What?' exclaimed Benoit.

'That opening in the roots,' said Rolland, pointing. 'She's the smallest so she volunteered to crawl in and look around.'

'Shit,' said Dugrippe, pulling out his radio.

'Get her out of there,' barked Benoit.

'Nina,' shouted Dugrippe, into the radio. 'Abort. Abort. Can you hear me? Over.'

No reply. The five officers ran to the base of the bank and tried to scramble up the steep slope, shouting Caron's name. At that moment, a blood curdling scream rang out from the undergrowth.

'HERE,' said Benoit, brandishing a bottle of Evian.

'I'd prefer a cognac,' said Caron, sitting cross-legged on the tarmac, smoking a cigarette, her torn and dishevelled protective suit in a ball at her feet. 'Sorry about screaming. It was a shock.'

'I can believe it,' said Benoit.

'Can we tell who it is?'

'The flesh has been gnawed away and insects and birds have eaten the eyes,' said Benoit. 'It looks like she was blond but, for the rest, we'll have to rely on DNA and dental.'

'And the smaller bone?'

'Definitely a human hand, according to Grace.'

'Quick decomp though.'

'Speeded up by the digestive system,' said Benoit. Caron squinted quizzically at him. 'A wolf, judging by the teeth marks.'

Her mouth dropped open but, before she could respond, Coulibaly called him to the huddle of forensic officers working around the canvas sheet.

'Dental is a no-go,' said Coulibaly. Benoit forced himself to look down on the decomposing head, stripped of soft flesh. 'The jawbone's been smashed with a heavy object like a hammer or a crowbar to get at the teeth. They've been destroyed.'

'All of them?'

'Every last one,' said Coulibaly. 'And those they couldn't smash are missing. Pulled out with pliers.'

'Jesus,' said Benoit. 'Still, we'll have DNA.'

'Even if it's a match, that only takes us so far,' said Coulibaly. 'We can do a comparison against what we already have but we need a baseline confirmation from a different source if you want official ID.'

'We're working on it,' said Benoit. 'Meanwhile...'

'Get the head off to Nice and let Gueyrande work her magic,' said Coulibaly, nodding. 'She'll do you a facial recon, get you a likeness. DNA will give us skin pigmentation and eye colour. May take a few days.'

'But it's definitely a woman's head?'

'No doubt,' said Coulibaly. 'Men have thicker bone in

the skull and a more prominent supraorbital ridge. See how smooth the brow is.'

'Age?'

'Fully mature. Mid-twenties to mid-thirties.'

'Any sign of a male head?'

'We'll look as hard as we can but given the terrain, it'll be slow going,' said Coulibaly. 'We've asked for the dogs and we'll send up a drone. If you could avoid shooting it down.'

'Strip the hillside clean if you have to. But find those remains.'

23

Benoit and Latour followed Caron and Rolland's car up the hill and back to the ICP. Inside, Gagnon was alone studying photographs taken on the night of the fête.

'Where's Daniel?'

'Out tracking down more photographs,' said Gagnon, standing to stretch his legs. 'He knows the locals so he skims through what they show him, makes a contact list of people in them and sends someone round with a pen drive. It's cumbersome but methodical.'

'Any shots of Renfrew in the main square?'

'Not yet,' said Gagnon. 'I've set aside half a dozen snaps of Renfrew walking through the village but, so far, no sign of him talking to anyone.'

'And Baseball Cap?'

'I've isolated a few men wearing caps. Nobody jumped out at us.'

'Load them up,' said Benoit, gazing at the display boards where Latour had added Trent's details and history with a mugshot taken after his arrest.

'Ex-marine?' said Rolland, following his gaze.

Caron put an unlit cigarette to her lips. 'Explains how

someone even older than the boss could put up such a fight.'

Benoit snaked a glance in her direction and she winked back. 'How are you doing with the laptop?'

'Trent knows his shit,' replied Caron. 'I've used the two best password software tools I know. Nothing. Want me to get more aggressive?'

'Trent said if we try to access the drive without the code, we'll release a virus and wipe it clean,' said Latour.

'Could be bluffing,' said Caron.

'But it's possible?' said Benoit. Caron shrugged. 'Then you have until tomorrow to crack it.'

'What happens then?' said Caron.

'We make a deal to access his files. If you have nothing by then, I'm sanctioning it.'

'You're letting him walk?' said Caron.

'That's not what he's asking for?'

'He wants to help,' said Latour. 'Claims Matteson's his daughter and he's only concerned with her safety.'

'You buy that horseshit?' said Caron.

'What do you think?' said Benoit. 'But, if we do need to make the deal, we're going to need a tracker on Trent. Something inconspicuous.'

'What's he got in the way of personal effects?' asked Caron. Benoit looked to Latour.

'He's got one of those chunky Fifty Fathom watches,' said Latour. 'At ten grand a throw, he's not going to let that out of his sight when he gets it back.' He rummaged in a drawer and pulled out a small plastic pack containing a rack of different-sized precision tools like a watchmaker might use and tossed them across to her.

'Ten thousand for a watch?' said Caron, examining the tools. 'I'm in the wrong job. I'll see what I can rustle up but I'll need his watch before the morning.'

'I'll get a uniform to bike it over,' said Benoit. 'And before he's released, we fit him with a regulation ankle bracelet, otherwise he might get suspicious.'

'So much for my break,' said Caron, handing Benoit her cigarette. 'Somebody's going to have to do a food run. I missed breakfast.'

'I'm surprised you can eat after your morning,' said Latour.

'Where are we with Matteson?'

'Hitting a brick wall on history,' said Latour. 'There's not a trace of her before she was five years old. No dental or medical records, no photos. Nothing. From six years onwards, we know schools, colleges, employment, the lot.'

'Another fake identity,' said Caron.

'Created with a duplicate birth certificate for a girl who died when she was five,' said Latour.

'Which must mean she had help,' said Caron.

Benoit nodded. 'And her movements in France?'

'Still waiting for hotels and Traffic.'

'Boss,' said Gagnon, switching on the projector and scrolling through six photographs. The first five showed Renfrew in the distance in various locations around the village. None showed his face, though his voluminous white cotton shirt and khaki chinos were easy to pick out as was his swept back hair. The final shot showed Renfrew walking up the busy Grand Rue, away from the bright lights of Chez Bertrand, groaning with festive drinkers.

'Copy of that last one on the boards and give me a hard copy, please, Jerome.'

Latour pointed at the screen to another man, seated at a table of the bar. 'For what it's worth, that's Paul Rappeneau.'

Benoit followed his finger to Villa Jasmin's owner, leaning across tables to speak to a young woman, whose disinterest in his attentions was palpable. 'Could be coincidence. Rappeneau said he only knew Renfrew by sight but they never met.'

Gagnon opened a folder and loaded pictures of men wearing baseball caps onto the screen.

Benoit shook his head. 'I don't recognise anyone. Ask Daniel if he can put names to them.'

'He has,' said Gagnon. 'Says they're all local to the area. Couple of misdemeanours in there but nothing eye catching.'

Discouraged, Benoit left the ICP and lit Caron's cigarette.

'We're not doing very well, are we?' said Rolland, joining him with her own cigarette.

'The clever ones take longer to catch,' said Benoit. 'That's what makes them interesting.'

'What's next?'

'Nothing fancy. We wait for the science, do the legwork. Hope something shakes out.'

'Think it will?'

Benoit smiled. 'It always does.'

Auger drove up. 'I just heard about the layby. Horrible. Who was it?'

'We only know it was a mature female, right age range, killed recently so...'

'You can't tell from a visual?' said Auger.

'Animals, insects and microbes have had a good go at her,' said Benoit. 'Eyes and teeth are gone.'

'Teeth?'

'Smashed by a crowbar and removed with pliers,' added Rolland.

'Christ!' said Auger, picking up a carrier bag from the passenger seat. 'Commandant, how the hell did you know to look in there?'

Benoit shrugged. 'Detection. Deduction.'

'Please don't tell him how great he is, Daniel,' groaned Rolland. 'He already knows. Is that what I think it is?'

'Lunch, if you can stomach it.' Auger held out the bag of filled baguettes for their inspection. 'And I made couscous.'

Rolland tossed her cigarette and pounced on a baguette. 'You're a bloody lifesaver.'

AFTER LUNCH, Benoit drove back to the village alone, calling in at the search site to check progress but the hunt for further body parts was still in its early stages. Driving on to the village, the heat had eased slightly and the ancient buildings bathed in the sun's dying fire. Seillans was Sunday-quiet except for the church bells summoning the faithful and Benoit parked in the shade of a larch tree and pulled out his mobile.

He conversed with Directeur Seigner about the discovery of human remains and, after ringing off, headed for the Rappeneau house. On the way, he spotted Paul Rappeneau sitting alone at Chez Bertrand in his Sunday best, a glass of beer and a cigarette in hand. He was at the same table as the picture of him at the fête, two weeks before.

'Monsieur,' said Benoit, gesturing at a seat at Rappeneau's table but not waiting for an invitation. He spotted Bertrand lurking in the bar's dark interior.

Rappeneau surveyed him with suspicion. 'Commandant.'

A young woman emerged from the bar to take his order.

'*Un demi*,' said Benoit. 'Monsieur?'

Rappeneau dipped his head in thanks. 'Same.'

Without further ado, Benoit spread out the photograph of Renfrew walking away from Chez Bertrand, Rappeneau seated in the background. 'This was taken on the night of the fête,' said Benoit, pointing at Rappeneau. The diminutive builder's mouth opened and his breathing quickened followed quickly by a long pull on his beer and an urgent tug on his cigarette. 'You said you didn't know Butler.'

Rappeneau's head jerked up, his eyes like saucers. 'What?'

'Your tenant at Villa Jasmin,' said Benoit, tapping the likeness of Renfrew on the photograph. 'You told us you'd never spoken to him but here you both are, at Chez Bertrand.'

Rappeneau drained his beer. 'I'm sorry. Yes, I did speak to him that one time. At the fête. But only to introduce myself and ask him how much he liked the villa.'

The barmaid arrived with two beers and a dish of peanuts. Curious, Benoit contemplated Rappeneau. 'Did he mention the problem with the electric gates?'

'The what?'

'Monsieur De Vries told us the gates weren't opening properly and your tenant was going to contact you about it.'

Rappeneau raised a finger. 'Yes, he did mention it. Are they still not working?'

'No, they're fine now.'

Rappeneau nodded, eyes trained on the table. 'When will you...?'

'When we're finished at Jasmin, you'll be the first to know.' Benoit gathered up the photocopy, threw down a ten-euro note and returned to his car.

Rappeneau tipped Benoit's beer into his empty glass and pocketed the note then squinted at the dark bar where Bertrand, polishing a glass, stared back.

'DANIEL, I want everything you have on Paul Rappeneau,' said Benoit, sitting back in his chair at the ICP, gazing at the photo array.

'Any particular reason?' said Auger.

Benoit nodded at the boards. 'I showed him the picture of Renfrew outside Chez Bertrand and he panicked and told me a pack of lies about them having a conversation.'

'What lies?'

'About them having a conversation,' said Benoit. 'I made up some garbage about Jasmin's gates not working and Rappeneau claimed Renfrew mentioned it to him.'

'Which tells you what exactly?' said Auger.

'That he didn't speak to Renfrew that night and never has.'

'Then why invent a conversation he didn't have?' said Latour.

'A very good question.' Benoit put his hands behind his head. 'Jerome, send that picture over to my monitor. I want a closer look.' Gagnon was engrossed in something and didn't respond. 'Jerome!' Gagnon looked up and Benoit repeated his request.

A moment later, Benoit loaded the picture. Ignoring Renfrew, he zoomed in on Rappeneau and found himself staring at the face of the girl at the next table. She seemed to be alone and doing her best to ignore Rappeneau's attentions.

Benoit's eyes narrowed. 'Gabriel. Come look at this.' Benoit pointed at the young woman. 'Isn't that the missing backpacker?'

'Backpacker?' said Auger, from across the room.

'There was a missing persons poster on the wall in the station,' said Benoit. 'I noticed it before we interviewed Trent. Remember?'

Latour gazed at the picture. 'Boss, I think you're right.'

'Daniel?' said Benoit. Auger hurried over to the monitor. 'There's Rappeneau. There's the young woman he's trying to chat up. What do you think? Is it her?'

'I've no idea,' said Auger. 'We get these all the time and I don't take much notice.'

'How long has she been missing?' said Rolland.

'A couple of weeks, I think,' replied Auger. He tapped his head and turned to Benoit in shock. 'Since the fête.'

'Why are we just hearing about this?' said Rolland, glaring at Auger.

'Seriously?' said Auger. 'Thousands of young people wander around the Cote d'Azur every summer. We get dozens of these reports every year. Kids who drop off the face of the earth for months at a time, then resurface when college starts or they go home and their parents forget to tell us. Most don't have a lot of money so they're bumming around off grid, hitchhiking, camping rough...it's a rite of passage.'

'But this woman made it all the way to a missing persons poster,' said Rolland.

'Then someone credible must have reported it,' said Auger.

'Where was she last seen?' said Caron.

Auger sat down at a keyboard. A moment later, 'Mougins.'

'That's forty kilometres away,' said Benoit.

'Nearer Cannes than here,' agreed Auger. 'Eugenie Marchand from Dijon. Twenty-six years old. On holiday. Usual profile for backpackers. I don't want to sound callous but this happens countless times *every* summer and invariably they turn up alive and well.'

'And I suppose she could be anywhere within hundreds of square miles,' said Caron.

'And with *anyone,*' said Auger. 'Camping in the hills with a boy she met, staying at a friend's, hitch-hiking her way back north...'

'Or getting raped in Paul Rappeneau's basement,' said Rolland.

Auger conceded with a shrug and enlarged the poster. 'It's definitely her. Reported missing by the boyfriend she was supposed to be meeting in Draguignan.'

'But she never showed,' said Rolland.

'If she was in Mougins on the way to Draguignan, that's a straight line through Seillans,' said Latour.

'Which might explain why Rappeneau's eyes nearly fell out of his head when he saw this,' said Benoit, standing.

'What are we waiting for?' snarled Rolland, checking her gun. 'Let's go get the fucker.'

'I DON'T KNOW,' wailed Madame Rappeneau, her eyes red, her cheeks tacky with salt. 'I told you, I haven't seen my husband since this morning, when I left for church.'

'What was he doing when you left?' said Benoit.

'Getting ready to go out for a drink.'

'Chez Bertrand?'

'He usually ends up there, yes.'

'When did you get home?' said Rolland.

'I was at church all afternoon,' said Madame. 'There was a function and we had coffee and biscuits afterwards.' Benoit and Rolland waited. 'Six o'clock.'

'And you didn't wonder why your husband wasn't home when you got here.'

'I thought he was,' she said. 'After his Sunday afternoon drink, Paul's usually in bed and doesn't stir until he can smell his evening meal. It was only when you lot arrived that I noticed the car keys and his overnight bag missing.'

'Where would he go?' said Benoit.

'He has a sister in Draguignan. You could try there.'

'Anywhere else?'

Madame shook her head. 'I'm all he has.'

'Sister's contact details,' said Rolland, handing her a blank page of a notebook and a pen.

'What about friends?' said Benoit, as she wrote.

Madame Rappeneau snorted. 'Paul doesn't have friends; he has cronies. Bookies and barmen like Bertrand.'

Latour and Auger walked into the kitchen. 'Rappeneau left Chez Bertrand just after five o'clock, according to the waitress,' said Latour. 'Headed in the direction of his house.'

'Coming home to pick up his car and a bag,' said Benoit.

Rolland handed the page out of her notebook to Costanza. 'Rappeneau's sister in Draguignan. Get eyes on the house, see if his car is there.' Costanza hurried out.

'We've searched the grounds,' said Latour. 'Cellar, outhouses, attic, basement. No sign of him. Unless there's a priest hole we don't know about...'

'Do you or your husband own other property beside Villa Jasmin?' said Rolland.

Madame shook her head. 'You haven't said why you want to speak to Paul.'

Benoit unfolded the picture of Rappeneau talking to Eugenie Marchand. The old woman stared, barely able to breathe. 'This young woman your husband is talking to. Have you seen her before?'

'No,' she croaked. 'Has something happened to her?'

'Why do you ask?'

'Because you're here, asking for Paul. Who is she?'

'Her name is Eugenie Marchand and she's been missing since the fête,' said Auger. Rolland glanced at Benoit. 'We're trying to locate her.'

Madame Rappeneau closed her eyes as though fighting a headache. 'I've never seen her before. Surely you don't think...?'

'I showed this picture to your husband earlier today and now he's missing,' said Benoit.

'We need to ask him about his conversation with this young woman,' said Auger. 'And I'll be honest, Madame. Dropping out of sight does not look like the action of an innocent man. This could go very badly for him unless we find him soon.'

'I don't know where he is,' wailed Madame, on the verge of tears.

~

IT WAS NEARLY dark on the Grande Rue when Benoit and his team finally emerged from the Rappeneau house. The village streets were empty except for scrawny cats, warily assessing each other, shrinking back into nooks and crannies at the sudden appearance of a crowd of people.

'I want plain clothes watching the house, front and back,' said Benoit. 'Same for his sister's and apply to a magistrate for a phone tap. I don't trust Madame's civic instincts where her husband is concerned.'

'All units have Rappeneau's description and license plate,' said Auger. 'Wherever he is, he won't get far.'

'That's what we said about the two Englishmen,' said Rolland.

'What about Jasmin?' said Latour. 'He might try to be clever, thinking it's the last place we'll look.'

'He can't know we've finished at the villa,' said Benoit.

'But, Daniel, make your people aware and have a couple of gendarmes take a look.' Auger nodded and tapped out a text.

'Nina and Thierry are making their way to Deux Rocs,' said Rolland, checking her phone.

Benoit sighed. 'It's late. We better eat. Daniel, a word.' Rolland set off to trudge up the hill but Latour and Gagnon hung back. 'You weren't to know different, but you shouldn't have identified Eugenie Marchand to Madame Rappeneau. We collect information, we don't give it out. If her husband contacts her, she can confirm why we want to interview him.'

'Of course,' said Auger, sheepishly. 'Sorry.'

'No need,' said Benoit, patting his shoulder. 'You've been such an asset, it's easy to forget that you're new to detective work.' He smiled to soften the blow.

'It won't happen again,' said Auger.

'Can I have a word, boss?' said Gagnon, glancing at Latour and Auger.

'I'm going home for a quick shower before we eat,' said Auger, heading up the lane.

'Jerome?' said Benoit, a moment later.

'Boss, I...'

Benoit's phone vibrated in his pocket and he halted Gagnon with a hand. 'Dr Gueyrande.'

'Commandant. Letting you know we received your remains this afternoon and started work on them immediately. I'll have DNA by tomorrow and toxicology from the hair roots the day after but I can confirm the skull is that of a mature white female, aged twenty-five to thirty-five and it's a definite match for your murder victim.'

'How do you know?'

'Remember our conversation about the damaged vertebrae?'

Benoit racked his brains. 'C6 and C7.'

'Right. C6 was damaged and I said you'd find the missing piece on the head when you found it. It's there. The head definitely matches the body from Villa Jasmin.'

'Good work.'

'I assume you want a full facial recon when we finish sampling. I've got fancy new, high-res, 3-D imaging software. I'll still need an artist and a forensic anthropologist but it's quicker than waiting for the beetles to clean the skull.'

'Yes, please,' said Benoit. 'As soon as you can get it to us.'

'On it. Also, I sent you an email with further findings on the two victims.'

'I'd appreciate a quick verbal,' said Benoit.

'I did a colposcopic exam of the female's genital and anal regions and found significant contusions around the fossa navicularis. I'd say she was involved in extensive penetrative sexual activity at least twenty-four hours before she died.'

'She was raped?'

'I can't determine that. But if it was consensual, it was...shall we say, vigorous.'

'Semen?'

'Not a chance,' said Gueyrande. *'There's more. It looks like the male was no stranger to penetration too.'*

'What?' exclaimed Benoit, staring at Latour's curious expression. 'Before or after?'

'Pre-mortem, definitely.'

'Injuries?'

'That's just it. There weren't any. But I'd speculate, the victim was accustomed to regular anal penetration. In fact, do you want to know what I think?'

~

BENOIT DROVE at speed with Latour, back to the ICP, while the rest of the team continued on to the restaurant.

Inside the prefab, Latour fired up the computer and printed the two sets of photographs requested by Benoit, who held them in both hands, his head moving side-to-side.

'What are we looking at, boss?'

Benoit turned the photographs round. 'The Renfrews came to Jasmin for six months, directly from their apartment in Singapore. Compare what they brought with them to offer up their DNA.'

Latour narrowed his eyes at the crowded picture of Carla Renfrew's assorted toiletries - her leather wash bag was Bottega Veneta, an expensive designer brand. Her delicate vanity razor was gold-plated and of the finest quality - even her tooth and hairbrush looked expensive.

Latour turned to Harry Renfrew's toiletries - a canvas washbag containing disposable plastic razors and a cheap, mass-produced toothbrush. 'You'd think a rich man like Renfrew would have something a bit fancier. That's more like a travel kit, something you'd take away for a couple of weeks on holiday at most.'

'Exactly,' said Benoit.

24

D espite hunger and fatigue, the pre-dinner conversation was lively as detectives discussed the case at their alfresco table. It was late and most other diners had long since left or were in the throes of doing so when Benoit's team lowered their weary bones onto chairs. But soon the wine was flowing and, when Auger walked up the hill to join them, freshly showered and changed, Benoit laid out Gueyrande's findings.

'Professional killers don't rape their targets,' said Rolland, when he'd finished.

'They tend not to cut off their cocks either,' said Caron.

'We can't be certain it was rape in either case or that the intercourse happened at the time of the killings,' said Benoit. 'But I'm confident this is not a professional hit even though it's been staged to look like one.'

'And Renfrew?' said Dugrippe. 'If the penetration wasn't part of the assault, you're suggesting he was gay or bisexual.'

'He wouldn't be the first rich man to hide his sexual preferences behind a trophy wife,' said Caron.

'Possibly,' said Benoit. 'But, there's a better explanation.' He looked at each member of his team in turn. 'That isn't Renfrew's body.'

There was silence while the detectives processed the implications.

'But his DNA...'

'...was matched to samples taken from razors and toothbrushes recovered from the villa,' said Benoit.

'Then what's the problem,' said Dugrippe.

'The problem is we can't confirm a definitive match to the Renfrews because their Singapore penthouse has been professionally cleaned. We have no baseline to confirm official ID other than artefacts found at the scene so...' He nodded at Latour, who produced the two photographs and passed them around the table. '...suppose for a minute those artefacts were tampered with.'

'Carla Renfrew's toothbrush, hairbrush and razor,' said Latour, brandishing one photograph. 'They're expensive and personal. Conversely, Harry Renfrew's are the kind of cheap generic disposables you take on a short holiday.'

'They're not his,' said Rolland.

'No,' said Benoit. 'I think someone pulled a switch and we've been led astray.'

'So, whose body is it?' said Dugrippe.

'I think it's Roger Barron,' said Benoit.

'The gay guy from the party?'

'It would explain Gueyrande's findings about habitual anal penetration,' said Latour.

'Plus, he's missing, the right age, build and hair colour,' said Caron.

'You're forgetting the DNA match from the beer bottle,' said Auger.

'Am I?' said Benoit. 'We have DNA from a man's razor and toothbrush matched to the body and saliva found in a beer bottle. Didn't it strike you as odd that it was the *only* beverage left for us to find and it just happened to yield a sample that confirmed our conclusions? Every other glass or bottle drunk from, was either cleaned or removed and that one bottle left for us to find.'

'But it was under the sun lounger,' said Auger. 'The killer didn't see it.'

'Or it was placed there as though forgotten,' said Benoit.

'Which would explain why there were no fingerprints on the bottle,' said Latour.

'I think Renfrew wiped it because Barron's fingerprints were on there but he left the bottle because his DNA was in the beer,' said Benoit.

'Renfrew? I don't understand.'

'If we'd obtained Barron's fingerprints from the bottle and confirmed a match with prints from Barron's home in England, it would have indicated that the DNA in the beer was likely to be Barron's. If that DNA was then a match to the male corpse in the pool...'

'...we'd have surmised the body was Barron's and *not* Renfrew's,' nodded Dugrippe.

'So, Renfrew wiped off the prints but left us Barron's DNA,' said Caron. 'Clever.'

'Who else was drinking beer at the party?' said Rolland.

'According to Piet Janssen, only Barron, Renfrew and Ash Cooper drank beer,' said Auger.

'And Cooper is the wrong age and physical profile for the male corpse,' said Rolland. 'It has to be Barron.'

'So, that's Barron's razor and toothbrush?' said Dugrippe, nodding at the photograph.

'Why not?' said Benoit. 'Their house was less than a hundred metres away. A simple switch for Renfrew's gear and a beer with his DNA and we get a completely different narrative.'

'We've asked the police to get access and gather DNA and fingerprints from Barron's house in England,' said Latour. 'It may take time but should tell us definitively.'

'And Cooper?'

'If that is Barron's body and Cooper wasn't involved in the killings, he's either a witness in hiding or...'

'Collateral damage,' said Caron.

'Aren't we forgetting the birthmark on Renfrew's calf?' said Rolland. 'His leg was mutilated to hide his identity.'

'That's the clever bit,' said Benoit. 'The killer has *correctly* assumed we'll find out about the birthmark, especially as the mutilation draws attention to his leg...'

'So, instead of the mutilation *hiding* Renfrew's identity, it appeared to confirm it,' said Caron.

'Barron was Jewish,' said Gagnon. 'For a male Jew, there's only one body part that can't be mistaken for a gentile.' All eyes turned to him.

'He was circumcised,' exclaimed Caron, banging the table with a fist. 'Renfrew cut off Barron's penis to preserve the narrative that the body was his.'

'Genius,' said Rolland.

'So, Renfrew's alive,' said Dugrippe.

'Nothing is certain,' said Benoit. 'But I'd stake my career that the male body in the pool isn't Renfrew.'

'If you're right, Renfrew must be our killer,' said Rolland.

'So, where is he?' said Gagnon.

'Good question,' said Benoit.

'Wherever he is, he's got Barron's car,' said Dugrippe.

'With Cooper's body in the trunk?' said Rolland.

'A reasonable assumption,' said Benoit. 'Daniel, I want a thorough local search for Barron's vehicle. That means eyes on barns and outbuildings as well as speaking to whoever owns them. And show them pictures of Renfrew - Rappeneau too, while you're at it. Kill two birds with one stone. And I want their pictures on TV.

'Gabriel, Jerome. I want a search done of local hotel registers, holiday and housing lets and give Daniel's people addresses to follow up with a visit and a photograph. Talk to estate agents and get details. If, Renfrew is still in the country, he's lying low somewhere near.'

'How do you know he's near?'

'The further he drives with human remains in a stolen car, the bigger the risk,' said Benoit.

'And, of course, he couldn't risk crossing a border,' said Dugrippe.

'Agreed,' said Benoit. 'So, start within a ten-mile radius and, if you draw a blank, expand the search area.' Auger nodded. 'Jerome will help.'

'I'm still processing the feast day photographs,' said Gagnon. 'And issues arising.'

'You'll have to do both,' said Benoit. 'Sorry. We're all in the same boat.'

'If Renfrew killed his wife and Roger Barron, he's had nearly two weeks' head start,' said Rolland. 'What makes you think he hasn't left the country in another hire car?'

'For one thing, he doesn't have a passport,' said Dugrippe.

'He had one fake passport, what's to stop him getting another?' said Rolland.

'That's possible,' said Benoit. 'But we have to go with what we know. Renfrew and Barron's car are missing. If we find the car, there's a good chance we find Renfrew.'

There was silence for a couple of minutes.

'Supposing Jasmin *is* Renfrew's work,' said Caron. 'Why would he throw his wife's head and hands into the scrub behind the lay-by? Why not leave all the remains in the trunk of Barron's car and simply drive it into a lake or hide it in a barn in the middle of nowhere?'

Benoit shrugged. 'When we find him, we'll ask him.'

'Do we know why Renfrew killed his wife?' said Dugrippe.

'He was being hunted,' said Rolland. 'So, if he dies before he's found…'

'The people hunting him stop looking,' said Latour.

'So, he killed his wife to make his own death look more authentic?' said Rolland.

'Clever,' said Caron. 'And cold as fucking ice.'

'Where does Matteson fit into all this?' said Dugrippe.

'Assuming she did come to Seillans to keep eyes on Jasmin,' said Benoit. 'We have to conclude either she saw something she wasn't meant to see and paid the penalty, or...'

'Or she's helping Renfrew,' said Rolland, nodding.

'Hard to believe she could be complicit in that level of violence,' said Caron.

'Belief isn't evidence,' said Benoit. 'We know, for a fact, Matteson was in France and heading towards Seillans.'

'Trent said Matteson was Renfrew's contact when they took him on as a client,' said Latour. 'My guess, she's up to her neck in this.'

'I don't buy it,' said Caron, shaking her head. 'What happened to the victims was medieval.'

'So, Matteson's too delicate to inflict that kind of violence?' said Dugrippe.

'I'm not saying that,' said Caron. 'Or maybe I am. But I'd need to hear a convincing motive.'

'Maybe Trent's laptop will give us the answers,' said Benoit. 'But Thierry's right. Everything's on the table. Speaking of which...'

'Apologies for the delay,' said Favre, laying down a tray full of plates.

'No need,' said Benoit. 'We've not sat down to eat at the same time all week. It can't be easy for you.'

The conversation dried as they tucked into a meal of escargots followed by slow-cooked lamb shanks on a bed of spicy couscous, washed down by more local red wine.

After dessert, they spent ten minutes, kicking around plans to move the investigation forward before fatigue started to catch up and exhausted detectives began to head for their respective quarters. Only Benoit, Auger and Gagnon remained.

'Another drink?' suggested Auger, looking around at the other deserted tables. Benoit and Gagnon shook their heads. Auger pushed back his chair. 'Time to hit the sack then,' he said, looking expectantly at Benoit.

'Right behind you,' said Benoit.

Auger nodded a goodnight at Gagnon and set off

towards the church and the labyrinth of cobbled streets beyond.

'Something's bothering you, Jerome,' said Benoit, when Auger was out of earshot. 'You've been angling for a word.'

'Boss, I...' A hole opened on Gagnon's chest and the cacophonous report from the gunshot reverberated around the dark square. Blood exploded from the wound and Gagnon's body jack-knifed backwards onto the cobbled ground. A split-second later, Benoit flung himself down, pulling the marble-topped table over in an attempt to shield them both, before applying pressure to the gaping wound.

Auger was caught in the open, staring back at the stricken Gagnon then up at the church tower.

'Get some cover,' Benoit shouted at him.

A bullet struck the ground next to Auger's foot and a second later, he hurtled back to the upturned table and vaulted over it, crashing to the cobbles besides Benoit. Panting, he leaned over Gagnon, feeling for a pulse in his neck. 'Jerome! Jerome!'

'It's bad,' said Benoit, fumbling for his phone with his free hand. 'Did you see the shot?'

Gagnon coughed up blood and Auger rolled him onto his side, grabbing napkins and pressing hard against Benoit's hand over the hole in his chest, blood seeping through both their fingers.

'It came from up high,' panted Auger. 'Church tower, I think.' Another bullet smashed into the marble tabletop. 'Keep your head down.'

Favre was shouting something from the hotel.

'Get inside,' Auger screamed at him. 'Keep your guests away from the windows.'

Benoit barked into his phone, identifying himself with a code and demanding an ambulance and immediate police support. 'Hotel Deux Rocs, Seillans. Shots fired. Active shooter pinning us down. Repeat, active shooter. Scramble armed response and a helicopter now. Ambulance beware. Repeat. Ambulance beware. Shots fired.'

The two detectives peered over the table and another shot hit the cobbles behind them.

'You're right,' said Benoit. 'Church tower.'

'Boss.' Gagnon's strangled whisper turned their heads.

'Don't talk, Jerome,' said Benoit.

Gagnon shook his head. 'Where are the police?'

'On their way,' said Benoit, keeping pressure on the wound. 'Hang on. We'll have you in an ambulance in a few minutes. You're going to be fine.'

Another shot exploded on the upturned table. 'We can't just sit here,' said Auger, drawing his weapon, kneeling like an Olympic sprinter. 'We'll have dead paramedics on our hands, if we don't do something. Cover me.'

'I'll come with you,' said Benoit, drawing his gun.

'One of us has to keep pressure on that wound.'

'Then you stay,' said Benoit. 'This is my responsibility.'

'Do you know how to get up to the church tower in the dark?'

'No,' conceded Benoit, a second later. 'Go. I'll cover you.' He lifted his gun towards the small window of the floodlit bell tower, his hand shaking.

Auger stared at it. 'Okay?'

Benoit clamped his other hand underneath his gun hand and nodded. 'I can hit a building. Go!' He fired four rapid shots, hitting the ancient masonry around the tower window as Auger vaulted over the table and sprinted towards the arch to dip out of sight of the tower. As soon as he was out of the line of fire, Benoit dropped his gun, resuming his pressure on the seeping wound in Gagnon's chest.

AUGER HURRIED to the large panelled door which sat across the church's parabolic arched entrance, barring his way. Although the vast door itself was firmly closed, a small wicket gate had been opened onto the yawning darkness beyond.

Auger stepped carefully towards and through the wicket, into the small narthex, trying to acclimatise his eyes to the blackness. Fortunately, eleventh century churches are compact, simple buildings and, having located the central nave, he hurried down between the rows of wooden pews to the transept and, beyond that, the altar. At the south transept a small side door into the base of the tower stood open and Auger could just make out the bottom of the circular staircase beyond.

He paused to listen but, instead of a noise, a faint light flickered on the circular stairwell, growing stronger by the second. The sound of feet, hurtling down stone steps, followed.

Auger knelt behind the polished dark wood of the first row of seats until the light on the stairs seemed to be blazing its way down from Heaven.

A figure emerged through the door carrying torch and rifle, panting with the exertion of descending the tight stone staircase.

'Drop the rifle or I fire,' shouted Auger, his voice echoing around the stone walls.

25

Monday 6th May

Benoit watched the ambulance containing the stricken Gagnon, roar past a dozen Police vehicles at high speed, sirens piercing the night. The emergency lights cast eerie illumination over the high narrow buildings and residents were silhouetted in windows peering out at the spectacle. More people stood around the front of the hotel - guests and staff - watching on, huddled together, trying to make sense of events. A second ambulance waited for the corpse in the church.

Exhausted, Benoit plunged his hands into the fountain and rinsed off Gagnon's dried blood. He threw water onto his face before making the short journey to the church.

Inside the brightly-lit building, FFP officers were at the far end of the nave, supervising the ambulancemen as they lifted the body onto a trolley and proceeded to wheel it towards the main entrance. Benoit watched the corpse pass, staring at the lived-in, slackened features of Patrice Bertrand being manoeuvred down the aisle, a blood stain over the heart soaking through the sheet.

On a pew, three rows back from the altar, sat Daniel Auger, forehead resting on arms crossed on the backrest in front.

Caron and Latour hurried down the central nave towards Benoit. 'Jerome?'

'He's critical,' said Benoit. 'They're going to stabilise him locally then fly him to the trauma unit at Hospital Pasteur Nice.'

'What are his chances?' said Latour, his voice tight with emotion.

'I honestly don't know,' mumbled Benoit.

'He's strong,' said Latour, looking at Caron for affirmation. 'He'll fight it.'

'Talk me through this,' said Benoit.

'Seems clear cut,' said Caron. 'Adele and I heard two shots from our quarters next to the church and were here inside a minute. Daniel was standing over the body and Bertrand was clearly dead, the rifle next to him. Daniel told us what happened to Jerome and that Bertrand tried to shoot you both.'

'When challenged, Bertrand raised his rifle and Daniel was forced to use deadly force,' said Latour. 'Badge and weapon surrendered without a murmur and he's been sat like that ever since.'

'He's in shock,' said Caron.

'Pity we didn't get to speak to Bertrand,' said Latour.

'He left Daniel no choice,' said Caron.

'Anyone informed the rat squad?' said Benoit.

'Cannes is the nearest IGPN office,' said Caron. 'But I doubt they're even out of bed.'

'Nevertheless, there are procedures,' said Benoit. 'It'll be light in a few hours. Nina, take Thierry and Adele and half a dozen of Daniel's people and get into Bertrand's bar and rip it apart, see if you can shake out a motive for this mess.'

Caron whistled to Dugrippe and Rolland and the three detectives left the church.

Benoit went to sit beside Auger. 'How are you holding up?'

'Don't worry about me,' said Auger. 'Jerome's fighting for his life and I killed the best chance of finding out why.'

'These are split-second decisions, Daniel,' said Benoit. 'You were in fear for your life.'

'Why the hell was Bertrand shooting at us?'

Benoit shook his head. 'We'll find out.' He beckoned Latour. 'Get him over to Fayence and take his statement. I'll speak to Seigner, tell her what's happened and get her to hold off the rat squad for as long as possible. After that, Daniel, you need to get yourself home and take as long as you need...'

'I don't want to leave the investigation,' said Auger, bridling. 'I owe it to Jerome.'

'I know it was self-defence but you just killed a man...'

'Do you think I don't know?' said Auger. 'It was him or me. I don't need counselling. I want to stay on the case.'

Benoit patted his shoulder. 'Then, the sooner you go with Gabriel and write your statement, the sooner we can straighten this out.'

AN HOUR LATER, Benoit stared at the pile of photographs spread across the counter, taken from a locked drawer in Bertrand's private quarters - pictures of distressed young women, in various stages of undress and all either unconscious or close to it. All the shots were taken on a hillside near trees, some in front of a rough barn that seemed to be in various stages of construction over different time periods.

Benoit held up an unblemished new photograph in his gloved hand, brandishing it towards his team. 'Eugenie Marchand.'

'She must have been abducted the night of the fête, probably from Bertrand's bar,' said Rolland.

'She looks out of it,' said Dugrippe. 'And not from drink.'

'Probably slipped her a mickey,' said Rolland.

'A bar on the main road, in the middle of town,' said Benoit. 'The perfect location. Given the right circumstances, every lone female who stopped for a drink was at risk from these animals.'

'You think Rappeneau's involved?' said Rolland.

'After his reaction to the photograph and his subsequent disappearance, I'd count on it,' said Benoit.

'All these women,' growled Dugrippe, picking up a pile of photographs with a gloved hand. 'Why don't we know about this, for God's sake? There must be thirty missing women here.'

'Not that many,' said Caron. 'There are multiple shots of each victim. We're looking at about fifteen women and over several years.'

'Even so,' said Dugrippe.

'As Daniel said, the Cote d'Azur is a playground,' said Benoit. 'Thousands of young people travel around every summer, looking for a good time. They drop off the grid for a while, then go home.'

'And the ones that don't go home?' said Dugrippe.

'Could have fallen off the map at any point within a thousand square kilometres,' said Rolland. 'Impossible to plot their movements.'

'Which Bertrand and Rappeneau would know when choosing their victims,' said Caron.

'Just to add another degree of difficulty, I suspect a high proportion of these women were from other countries too,' said Rolland. 'They were careful.'

'Where is this barn?' said Caron, examining one of the photographs. 'Looks remote.'

'Wherever it is, that's where we find Rappeneau,' said Benoit.

At the other end of the bright bar sat the barmaid, who'd been woken from her slumbers to unlock the metal grille covering the front of the bar. She was perched on a stool and wore a baggy black wool cloak but was visibly shivering when her hand put a cigarette to her mouth. 'Anne-Marie, right?' She nodded. 'This drawer...'

'I've never seen inside it,' she said. 'Never been in his rooms, though he invited me back there a couple of times with his friend. I declined,' she added quickly.

'Invited for what?'

'When Bertrand drinks, he gets horny and when he gets horny, he somehow got it into his head that he was a ladies' man,' she said, taking a long draw on her cigarette.

'His friend?'

'Grotty little man. Builder. You had a beer with him this afternoon...'

'Paul Rappeneau.'

'That's him,' said Anne-Marie. 'Creepy fucker. Never took his eyes off me when he was drinking here, which was often.'

'You're still working here, I notice,' said Rolland.

'Jobs don't grow on trees around here,' said Anne-Marie, defiantly. 'And I can handle a pair of middle-aged school-boys.' She shivered suddenly. 'At least, I thought that's what they were.'

'Did Bertrand have other accommodations, beside these rooms?'

'Not that I'm aware,' she said.

'Or maybe some land in the area?' said Dugrippe. 'A farm with a barn or outbuildings, somewhere remote.'

'I've been here three years and he's never mentioned anywhere like that,' said Anne-Marie. 'Though he used to go off with Rappeneau, off season, and when they came back, they had a trailer full of firewood and a brace of rabbits for the pot.'

'Where?'

'Search me.'

'Did he have other friends he'd go off with?'

'I only know about Rappeneau.'

'What about relatives?'

'None,' said Anne-Marie. 'He took pride in telling me he

was alone in the world, owing nothing to nobody. Never knew his father and his mum died when he was a teenager. That's when he ran off to join the Legion to *become a man,* he said.'

'Did you ever see Bertrand with this woman?' said Benoit, showing her a picture of Carla Renfrew, sitting at the table at Deux Rocs.

'She's been here,' said Anne-Marie. 'That's the one on the news that got butchered, right? She had coffee here a couple of times. Nice lady. Good tipper.' Her eyes widened. 'Did Bertrand kill her too?'

'We don't know,' said Benoit. 'What was her relationship with your employer?'

Anne-Marie snorted. 'Relationship? She stopped for coffee after buying bread, exchanged pleasantries and left.'

'Bertrand claimed they were lovers,' said Rolland.

Anne-Marie laughed. 'Not a chance. The only women Bertrand ever fucked were paralytic from drink.' She gestured at the photograph. 'Nobody in her league. Never.'

'He said they kept it secret,' said Benoit.

'Trust me, if he'd been her lover, I'd have known about it,' said Anne-Marie. 'Whenever Bertrand lured some pissed-up swamp donkey into his bed, he'd brag about it for days. He would have told the newspapers, if he thought they'd print it.' She blew out her cheeks. 'He's really dead?'

'Missing him?' said Rolland.

Anne-Marie glared at her. 'I have a kid to raise. I need my job.'

'I'd start sending out your CV, if I were you,' said Rolland.

'That's enough, Adele,' said Benoit.

Latour walked through from the apartment behind the bar, brandishing an evidence bag. 'One digital camera.'

'Anything on it.'

'I had a quick scroll through but most of the pictures are landscape scenery. No pictures of Bertrand, Rappeneau or any of these women.'

'Which landscape?' said Rolland.

'Beats me,' said Latour. 'Maybe Daniel will recognise the area.'

'Get Costanza to organise circulating the pictures amongst local officers,' said Benoit. 'Daniel's off the rota.'

'How is he?' said Rolland.

'He'll be fine,' said Latour. 'Especially when we show him the vic pics and tell him he's done the world a massive favour.'

Benoit picked up a dog-eared snap from the tangle of analogue photographs and looked at the back. 'These weren't taken on a digital camera yet there's no date stamp on them so they weren't sent for developing.'

'Probably one of those old Polaroid instant cameras,' said Latour. 'It's not here though.'

'What is here?'

'I'm no forensic tech but I'd be surprised if anybody was confined in his apartment,' said Caron. 'It's tidy and clean but very cramped. No sign of restraints, no feminine arte-facts, clothes, shoes, make-up.' She shrugged. 'Obviously, one spray of luminol and a few fingerprints could prove me wrong. Should I buzz Coulibaly?'

Benoit smiled. 'Better I do it.'

'Commandant,' said Officer Costanza, brandishing a clear plastic bag containing dozens of green, sausage-shaped pills in her gloved hand. Benoit took them from her, examining them briefly, then brandished them in front of Anne-Marie.

'What are those?' she said.

'Flunitrazepam, I'd say,' said Rolland.

'Rohypnol to you and me,' said Caron.

'The date-rape drug?' said Anne-Marie. 'Christ. To think...' she shivered again. 'I don't know anything about those tablets, I swear to God. I just serve drinks. Look, it's nearly three and my mum's looking after my kid. Can I go home?'

'Present yourself at the station in Fayence for a formal

statement tomorrow morning,' said Benoit.

She scrambled off the stool but paused at the door, looking pensively out into the night. Benoit gestured to a gendarme to see her safely to her car.

'Unbelievable,' said Rolland, shaking her head in disgust.

'You were too hard on her,' said Benoit.

'She had a serial rapist and murderer right under her nose and never saw it,' said Rolland.

'She doesn't have your training, Adele,' said Dugrippe, looking at the bag of tablets. 'That's a lot of roofies. There must be a hundred tabs in there.'

'They had plans,' said Caron.

'Could other men be involved beside Rappeneau and Bertrand?' said Dugrippe.

'Who knows,' said Benoit. 'But the more participants, the harder it is to keep crimes like this under the radar.'

'And Villa Jasmin?' said Caron.

'What about it?' said Benoit.

'These two must be our killers,' said Caron.

'I'm not so sure. These photographs are trophies of missing women, Nina. Carla Renfrew isn't missing and she's not in the photographs.'

'They target women and the Jasmin vics were drugged and raped,' said Caron.

'We don't know sexual assault was involved,' said Rolland. 'And one of the victims was a man.'

'Adele's right,' said Benoit. 'Hunting couples makes it harder to establish control. Like most rapists, Rappeneau and Bertrand are cowards. From the little we know, they preyed on lone young women who crossed their path. There were two of them yet still spiked their victim's drinks to guarantee submission. I guarantee if Eugenie Marchand had been with her boyfriend that night, Bertrand and Rappeneau wouldn't have gone anywhere near them.'

'And, leaving the bodies in the pool of a house he owns, throws Rappeneau and the whole village into the spotlight,' said Latour. 'For all the years it looks like they've been doing this, no-one's even *looked* for the missing women in Seillans, let alone suspected Bertrand and Rappeneau of snatching them.' Caron conceded with a shrug.

Benoit finished looking through the photographs for a second time. 'That's the lot. No Carla and no Megan.'

'The Matteson girl?'

'She was travelling alone and now she's missing,' said Benoit.

'So, what now?' said Rolland. 'If Rappeneau and Bertrand *aren't* connected to Jasmin, shouldn't we hand this off to the locals?'

'Bertrand was shooting at *us* and I want to know why,' said Benoit. 'Finish up and shut this place down for a forensic sweep and get some rest. Costanza.'

'Commandant?' said the young gendarme, stifling a yawn.

'I need you to go to the Rappeneau house and give Madame ten minutes to move out. Her husband is now a suspect in serial abduction and murder and she can't be there. Stay with her while she packs a bag and escort her to friends or relatives and seal the house for forensic exam.

'Wherever she goes, I want her movements watched, discreetly, and she's to be followed around the clock, in case her husband gets in touch. When that's in hand, I need a compilation of all missing persons reports for young women in the region for the last decade.'

26

Tuesday 7th May

'You get to wear your normal clothes but you're confined to the Command Post during the day, and will remain under SCS supervision,' said Benoit. 'Any problems and you're back to a cell immediately. At night, you're returned to the gendarmerie, where you'll have an evening meal provided by a local restaurant and spend the night in the cells until we pick you up in the morning.'

'Rinse and repeat,' mumbled Trent.

'Pardon?'

'I understand,' said Trent, looking round at the drawn faces in the prefabricated headquarters of the ICP. He strapped on his Fifty Fathoms watch and buttoned up his shirt while Caron set to work on his laptop. 'You guys look wasted.'

'Nothing we can't handle,' replied Benoit.

'In my experience, you don't ever handle one of your guys getting shot,' said Trent. Heads turned. 'There was talk at the station. Is he okay?'

'He's in intensive care,' said Benoit.

'Jerome's a fighter,' declared Rolland. 'He'll pull through.'

'I hope so,' said Trent. 'I know what you're going through.'

'Do you?' growled Dugrippe, arms folded, glaring at him from the back wall.

'I've lost colleagues in the field,' replied Trent. 'Some of them friends.'

'Want to know what you can do with your fake sympathy?' snarled Dugrippe, suddenly looming over him.

'Back off, Thierry,' ordered Benoit. Dugrippe fumed through flared purple and yellow nostrils but moved away.

'How's the nose?' said Trent, smiling.

'Fuck off!' said Dugrippe, flashing an expression of untamed violence towards him.

'If it helps, my ear stings like crazy,' said Trent.

Dugrippe nodded. 'Actually, it does.'

'Are you two finished?' said Benoit.

Caron wheeled her chair over to Trent, brandishing a piece of paper. 'Is that upper or lower case?'

'Lower,' said Trent, reclining on his chair, a white ankle tag, housing an electronic tracking device, perched above the bone.

'You memorized all these letters and symbols?' said Caron.

'The internet is a jungle,' said Trent. 'If you're not careful how you move around, you'll get your throat ripped out by bigger beasts.' He took a sip of his coffee, pulled a paper plate towards him and picked at a day-old croissant, looking around. 'Speaking of my ear, where's Billy the Kid? Auger, is it?'

'Daniel's busy,' said Latour.

'So, Internal Affairs have got their grubby hands on him,' said Trent.

'Internal Affairs?'

'Whatever you call it in France,' said Trent. 'It's IA in the States and, after a cop uses deadly force, they take your badge and gun, place you on suspension then follow up with a series of pointless interviews to make sure you didn't execute the guy because you were having a bad day. And when they think you can't take any more, they throw a psych evaluation at you.'

'How did you know?' said Benoit.

Trent scoffed. 'Please. Cops are family, the world over. When one of your own is shot, you do *not* rest until the perp is in a cell or a body bag. If the shooter was in custody, your buddy Auger would be here. If the shooter got away, you'd be out there, scorching the earth. Conclusion? Your sharp-shooting buddy took out the perp and now he's in a room being asked when he last wet the bed.'

Benoit noticed involuntary amusement appear on the faces of his squad, even Dugrippe.

'Who was the perp?' said Trent.

'Patrice Bertrand,' said Benoit.

'Local?'

'He owned a bar on the high street.'

'Chez Bertrand?' said Trent.

'You know him?'

'First day in Seillans, I stopped for bread and Carla got out to stretch her legs. When I came back, she was talking to some guy, about fifty, deep tan, grizzled expression, former Legionnaire...'

'How did you know he was in the Legion?' said Latour.

'He had a Legion tattoo on his arm,' said Trent.

Benoit glanced at Dugrippe and Rolland who shrugged their grudging respect. 'What were they talking about?'

'Just chit-chat,' said Trent. 'But he liked what he saw of Carla.'

'Most people did,' said Benoit. 'The day before he died, Bertrand claimed he and Carla were lovers.'

'Corroborated?' said a surprised Trent.

'No.'

'Sounds unlikely but you never know,' said Trent. 'Do we know why Bertrand shot Jerome?'

'We?' snarled Dugrippe.

'*We* don't even know he was aiming at Jerome,' said Rolland. 'The boss was next to him and Auger was there too.'

'Then do *you* know why he might have been shooting at you?' said Trent. Silence fell over the room. 'I can't help, if I don't know what's happened.'

Latour glanced at Benoit, who nodded.

TRENT STARED at the enlarged picture of Renfrew, Rappeneau and Eugenie Marchand, taken outside Bertrand's bar. 'How long?'

'The locals are trying to put names to faces but, judging from the age of the photographs, at least a decade, maybe longer,' said Latour.

'Holy shit,' said Trent.

'They chose their victims carefully,' said Rolland. 'It was sheer fluke we picked up the link between Rappeneau and Eugenie.'

Trent nodded. 'But once you did, Rappeneau headed for the hills.'

'Unless Bertrand took matters into his own hands and silenced him,' said Benoit. 'We were at Chez Bertrand when I spoke to Rappeneau on Sunday and he was a nervous wreck. With the right pressure, he would've confessed in a heartbeat and Bertrand probably knew it.'

'Maybe Rappeneau ran knowing Bertrand would be thinking along the same lines,' said Rolland.

'Still doesn't explain why Bertrand was shooting at police,' said Trent.

'I agree there seems little advantage,' said Benoit. 'But that's where we are.'

'And the hunt for Rappeneau?' said Trent.

'Ongoing,' said Benoit. 'Forensics are ripping apart his house, we have eyes on his wife and we're trying to ID a location from Bertrand's trophy photographs.'

'But you think he's still local?'

'It's his best chance,' said Latour. 'This is a big area to hide in and he has the advantage of local knowledge.'

'Okay, I'm in,' said Caron, swivelling the laptop round towards Trent.

'Look through Megan's comms from the end of February through March,' said Trent. 'Same encryption. That's when Renfrew contacted her to hire us and I started prepping their move to France.'

Caron turned back to the keyboard.

'Who is Roger Barron?' said Trent, nodding at the display board.

'A missing English tourist, staying down the road from Villa Jasmin,' said Dugrippe.

'He's also the male victim in the pool,' said Benoit.

'Wait!' exclaimed Trent, standing to point at the bodies in the pool. 'That's not Renfrew? You know that for a fact?'

'Right now, it's just a theory,' answered Benoit.

'A theory that assumes what?' said Trent. 'That Renfrew came here planning to pull a switch and disappear?'

'It's been done before,' said Benoit. 'Renfrew gets in too deep with the wrong people and they want him dead. To get himself off the hook, he can't simply run because the people he owes will find him, sooner or later.'

'But, if he's officially dead, they stop looking,' said Trent, nodding. 'And Carla?'

'Her death lends authenticity to his,' said Latour.

'Even so, to kill her like that...' said Trent, staring at the picture of the bloated corpses.

'Maybe their marriage was in trouble before the move,' said Benoit. 'Add to that, Renfrew would realise how hard it would be for both to disappear and, even if he pulled it off, he could never be completely secure. To be absolutely safe, he has to kill her.'

'Seems extreme,' said Trent.

'Husbands kill their wives every day,' said Rolland.

'Not like that,' said Trent.

'Which is why it's so perfect,' said Rolland. 'Doing that to a stranger is hard enough but to your own wife? Anyone seeing the bodies would assume it was a professional killing.'

'Let's say I buy it,' said Trent, after a moment's thought. 'He'd need someone of similar age, height and body shape to stand in for him.'

'Barron fits the bill,' said Benoit.

'And the guy just fell into Renfrew's lap?' said Trent.

'In a sense, yes,' said Rolland. 'Renfrew would know he had six months to select from a revolving door of tourists, waiting for the right candidate. All he had to do was keep his eyes open and be ready.'

'When Barron and Ash Cooper arrived, Renfrew put his plan in motion,' said Benoit. 'He invites them over for drinks the night *before* they're due to go back to England and a few hours later the killing starts.'

'And, as the Englishmen were due to leave the next day, they won't be missed until they fail to arrive home,' said Trent, stroking his unshaven chin. 'It works as a theory at least. What happens to Cooper in this scenario?'

'Collateral damage,' said Benoit.

'So, where's his body?' said Trent.

'Taken away in the trunk of Barron's missing VW with Barron's head and hands,' said Rolland.

'You think Renfrew killed Barron, Carla *and* Cooper?' said Trent.

'Why not?'

'Because he's outnumbered, three-to-one.'

'But the victims in the pool were drugged before they died,' said Benoit.

'And all three had been drinking,' said Dugrippe.

'Plus, thanks to you, Renfrew was armed,' said Benoit.

Trent grimaced. 'Even so that's a lot of heavy lifting. The Renfrew I saw wasn't in great shape.'

'We're open to the idea he might have had help,' said Benoit.

Trent stared at the photograph of the two mutilated corpses in the swimming pool. 'DNA?'

'The samples from the villa suggested Renfrew and Carla as the victims,' said Benoit. 'However, we couldn't get a baseline to confirm.'

'What about their penthouse in Singapore?' said Trent.

'Blitzed by a professional cleaning company the week after it was vacated,' said Latour. 'Renfrew arranged it.'

'So, the DNA at Jasmin could've been staged,' said Trent.

'We think so,' said Benoit. 'The only evidence Renfrew couldn't manipulate was Roger Barron's penis.'

'Excuse me?'

'Barron's penis was cut off,' said Rolland.

'He was Jewish and circumcised,' said Latour.

'And leaving a circumcised penis on the male corpse would prove the victim couldn't have been Renfrew,' said Trent, nodding.

'After Renfrew rolled the bodies into the pool and switched Barron's razor and toothbrush for his own, he throws the scalpel and chainsaw in the trunk with Cooper and the other body parts, cleans up the crime scene and drives away.'

'Where?' said Trent.

'First stop is the layby down the hill into Seillans to throw Carla's head and hands into the brush,' said Dugrippe.

'And Barron's head?' said Trent.

'No sign yet,' said Rolland. 'But if it's there, we'll find it.'

'And from there?'

'Easier to say where he *doesn't* go,' said Latour. 'Barron's car doesn't join a motorway and hasn't crossed any borders.'

'We've issued national and regional alerts, Interpol and Europol too,' said Benoit. 'The Renfrews are on every bulletin, police website and station wall in the country, not to mention national and international TV.'

'And he doesn't have a passport,' said Trent.

'Unless, he acquired another,' said Latour, staring at Trent.

'He didn't get it from me,' said Trent. 'But, if he *has* planned this in advance, he could have organised one before we left Singapore and brought it with him.'

'All things are possible but the evidence suggests Renfrew's not only in France but local,' said Benoit.

'There must be hundreds of square miles of wilderness in the Var,' said Trent.

'And thousands of remote farms, cottages and outbuildings,' agreed Benoit. 'Not to mention, extensive forest and lakes in which to hide the car.'

'So, we're looking for a needle in a haystack, without being sure there *is* a haystack or if the needle is even in there,' said Trent. Benoit nodded. 'And Megan?'

'For her sake, let's hope she's looking for the same haystack,' said Rolland. 'And not in it.'

'You're certain she wasn't one of Rappeneau and Bertrand's victims?' said Trent.

'As far as we know,' said Benoit.

Trent was thoughtful for a moment. 'But you haven't officially identified Carla's remains?'

'Not yet,' said Rolland.

'Dental records?'

'Her teeth were smashed or pulled,' said Dugrippe.

'Fuck,' said Trent.

'Samples taken from Carla's hair brush and toothbrush, confirm a DNA match with the body in the pool,' said Benoit.

'But there's no baseline DNA from Singapore to make it official,' said Trent. Benoit smiled.

Trent interlaced his hands behind his head. 'Okay, I can see why Renfrew might kill his wife *and* why he might cut off her head. But why dispose of it in the brush and risk it being found?'

'We don't know,' said Benoit. 'Perhaps that was a consequence of their relationship.'

'Meaning?' said Trent.

'Maybe she was unfaithful and he wants a more humiliating, personal revenge,' said Benoit.

'And, what better way to get revenge on a beautiful woman than to obliterate her face and leave it to be consumed by a wolf?' said Rolland.

Trent's eyes narrowed. 'Sorry, did you say wolf?'

'There's a lone wolf in the area,' said Benoit.

'You mean, besides me?' said Trent.

'We're not joking,' said Latour. 'They come down from the Alps in winter.'

'It's not winter, now,' said Trent.

'No, but loners are known to stake out a piece of ground if they find a regular food supply,' said Benoit.

'The locals call it a Blood Summer,' said Latour.

'There's nothing in the email account...' said Caron, softly.

'But a wolf?' laughed Trent.

'I've seen it with my own eyes, here in the village,' said Benoit.

'...in fact, there is no email account,' continued Caron. 'All accounts have been deleted.' Heads turned. 'And recently too.'

'That's impossible,' said Trent. Caron's lip pursed and she flipped the monitor round. Trent stared at the empty black screen. 'Do you know your way around the dark web?'

Caron's expression radiated scorn. 'Er...yes, I know my way around the dark web. I followed the I2P encryption protocols you gave me. There's nothing on your noticeboard and everything in your private account has been wiped, including the archives.'

'I don't understand,' said Trent.

'Don't you?' said Benoit, his mouth a hard line.

'You think I did this?' said Trent.

'Who else had access to the account?' said Benoit. 'To think we shared case-sensitive information...'

'It wasn't me!' insisted Trent. 'Why would I?'

'I can think of several reasons,' said Benoit.

'I didn't do it,' said Trent. 'You have to believe that.'

'A dark web VPN account is virtually impossible to hack,' said Caron. 'Only someone with the passwords could wipe it.'

'So, if it wasn't you, it must have been Megan,' said Rolland.

'Why would she delete all comms on a private encrypted account?' said Caron.

Trent gazed at the monitor. 'I told her to go dark. Break off all comms and drop off the grid to avoid being tracked.'

'Including deleting your encrypted account?' said Benoit.

Trent was silent.

'What about other comms?' said Latour.

'There's nothing except Trent's unanswered messages on WhatsApp,' said Caron. 'Her last contribution was before she took the ferry to France.'

'What about regular email accounts?' said Benoit.

'She has a Hotmail account for appearances but she would never contact me using that,' said Trent.

'I've checked,' said Caron. 'All her email accounts are gone.'

'Is there anything left?' said Benoit.

'Just a folder on her desktop called TRAVEL,' said Caron. 'Should I open it?'

Trent shook his head. 'That's just research on flights and hotels.'

'Open it,' said Benoit. 'We may get clues about her journey through France.'

Caron clicked on the link and a series of sub-folders flooded the screen, all named after a destination, alphabetically ordered from Athens, Barcelona and Berlin through to Reykjavik, Sydney and Tokyo.

'Nothing about France,' said Caron.

'You and your alter-egos get around,' said Benoit. Trent didn't reply, his eyes glaring at the screen. 'What is it?'

'Reykjavik,' mumbled Trent.

'What about it?'

'I've never been there,' said Trent. 'Megan hates the cold and she made me promise never to take her anywhere she couldn't wear a bikini.'

Benoit nodded at Caron, who clicked on the link. Seconds later a picture of a younger, thinner Harry Renfrew appeared, arm in arm with a friend, both men grinning from the observation deck of a skyscraper. Beyond, a sprawling metropolis stretched into the distance. The picture was dated June 2001 and had been captioned by Megan.

HARRY   RENFREW   &   BRYON   LOGAN   (Security Consultant!!)

'IS THAT AMERICA?' said Dugrippe.

'Chicago,' Trent mumbled, sensing Benoit staring at him.

'What else is in the folder?' said Benoit.

While Caron and the rest of the team got to work, poring over documents, detailing Renfrew's senior management role in a Russian oil brokerage, Trent stared at the two men, posing on the Skydeck of the Willis Tower, eighteen years before.

In 2001, it would still have been called the Sears Tower, for twenty-five years the tallest building in the world, surpassing even the World Trade Centre in New York. But more important was the face of the man standing next to Renfrew, a face seared on Trent's memory. Bryon Logan - a man he knew simply as Byron.

Benoit's mobile phone rang. He picked up and listened for a few seconds. 'On our way.'

27

August 17th, 2002 - Northern Michigan

Trent turned his rented BMW onto Battery Street, in the lush outskirts of the small town of Ishpeming, Michigan, about sixteen miles from the shores of Lake Superior and another fifty to the Canadian border. Even at night, it was possible to admire the large plots of land, dotted with two and three-storey detached houses that looked out over Lake Bancroft. Reaching his destination, Trent pulled over to the kerb and silenced the engine.

After lowering his window, he sat for a while, staring at the house through mature trees, listening to the wind rustling leaves and inhaling the scent of a rural summer preparing to shift into autumn. Above the dense treeline, a smear of the Milky Way peeked through from a cloudless sky.

Streetlights were dim and sparse in this part of Ishpeming and cars parked on the road were notable by their absence, the spacious properties being blessed with expansive driveways, most accommodating multiple vehicles.

No lights were on in the house Trent was watching so he pulled on thin leather gloves and picked up the gun on the passenger seat to fit the silencer. He glanced at the two-storey property, dormant except for a pair of coach lights casting their illumination over the drive.

A gleaming Porsche 911 sat proudly on the tarmac, looking black in the night but, having followed it around for nearly a week, Trent knew it was racing green. Next to it sat a chunky Ford truck, adorned with gleaming chrome accessories.

Trent turned to check his cargo on the back seat before easing the driver's door open and climbing out. He closed the door softly, walking quickly but calmly towards the house and arrived at the rear door of the property, invisible from the street, knocking gently on the glass and hiding the gun behind his back while he waited.

A kitchen strip light flickered into life and the door opened moments later.

'Trent?' said Rentoria. 'What the fuck, man?'

'Jose.'

'You know what time it is? I was just turning in.'

Trent smiled. 'I've driven a long way.'

'What the fuck are you even doing here?'

'It's complicated. Can I come in?'

Rentoria considered him but didn't stand aside. 'I heard about your panel. I'm sorry, man. You didn't deserve to get kicked out like that. That was shitty.'

'Two people died, Jose. Millions of dollars of court time went up in smoke. It was my detail and I fucked up. I trusted people I shouldn't have.'

'Yeah?' Rentoria's smile was tight and a gun appeared in his hand, trained at Trent's chest. 'Show me your hands.'

'Welcome to Michigan.'

'Show me your fucking hands!' repeated Rentoria. 'Real easy.' Trent let his hands drop to his sides, his gun trained on the tarmac. 'Fucker. Put it on the ground. *Don't* drop it, lay it down.' Trent crouched to place the gun on the drive.

'Now pick it up by the muzzle and hand it to me.' Trent bent down again and Rentoria accepted the butt of Trent's gun and stepped back. 'Inside.'

Trent walked into a spacious new kitchen where Rentoria stood aside, gesturing him towards the soft lighting of another room.

'You've done well for yourself,' said Trent, reaching the large comfortable lounge.

'You get a lot more bang for your buck out in the boon-docks, compadre,' said Rentoria.

'So, I see. A Porsche, a big lakeside house with land.' Trent pointed through a panoramic window to the dark outline of building work at the back of the house. 'What's that?'

'I'm building a boat house.'

'Nice. You're thriving since transferring back to the Marquette Field Office.'

'Doing okay.' Rentoria tightened his grip on both guns. 'Turn and face the wall.'

'Don't do anything stupid, Jose,' said Trent, turning. Rentoria pushed him to the wall.

'Stupid?' snarled Rentoria, pushing the muzzle into Trent's neck. 'For defending myself against a psycho ex-fed, who comes armed to my home in the middle of the night?'

'You're right,' said Trent, voice strained, attempting to conciliate. 'I underestimated you. You're smarter than I thought.'

'Damn right, I'm smart,' said Rentoria. 'Did you think I wouldn't notice you tailing me around town the last week, that I wouldn't be ready?'

'I guess I've gotten rusty since I got kicked out,' sighed Trent.

'And then some,' said Rentoria. 'Hands on the wall, nice and high.'

Trent placed his hands high up the wall. Rentoria put down Trent's gun and moved into him, kicked his feet apart and moved his hands over Trent's torso, looking for further weapons. Finding none, he pushed Trent against the wall and stepped back, gesturing him towards the sofa.

'Sit on your hands, bitch.' Trent obeyed and Rentoria relaxed. 'A fucking silencer, man? The fuck gives you the right?'

'Just a precaution, Jose. This doesn't have to end in violence.'

'Oh? How should this end?'

'With you giving me the name of your contact and me giving you a free pass,' said Trent.

'What contact?'

'The man who paid you to rat out my detail.'

'What? You think...?'

'Don't insult me, Jose,' said Trent. 'You ratted me out and Gwen died. Someone put you up to it and you got well paid.'

'You got the wrong idea, man. My mom died and left me money.'

'Spare me the cover story. It won't hold. I know you've been smart and kept working, took out a loan to help buy the house, even though you didn't need it...'

'Who says I didn't need it?'

'You think I'm coming at you blind, Jose? I dug deep. You've got bundles of high denomination bills stashed in a safe deposit box at the Michigan State Bank. Sure, you tried to leave it alone but it burned a hole in your pocket. You may be smart but you're also young and impulsive and you got careless. You paid cash on the nose for both the truck and the Porsche.'

Rentoria's mirth dissipated. 'I...got a deal.'

'Cash buyers always get a deal,' said Trent. 'So, throw me a bone. What have you got to lose? You're set for life. Steer me in the right direction and you'll never see me again. The only name I have is Byron but that's as far as I can get without help.'

Rentoria shook his head. 'Never heard of him.'

'Wrong play, Jose. Talk to me. How much did they pay you? I hope it was worth two peoples' lives.'

'You talk too much, amigo.'

'You ratted me out for blood money...'

'You can't prove...'

'You were the only one who knew the hotel and the room number,' said Trent. 'I used a payphone. I was real careful. Nobody followed me there. It was you. You gave up my witness and they executed Gwen and that poor maid. That's on you, brother. Stop denying it so we can make a deal.'

Rentoria stared, licked his lips. 'The kid caught a break though.'

'Having her mother killed in front of her wasn't a break.'

'They could have killed her too.' Rentoria hesitated. 'I told them no. It was a condition.'

'A gesture to decency?' said Trent. 'Or a way to ease your conscience.'

'Fuck you, Trent!' shouted Rentoria. 'I saved her life. There was no saving the mother. With or without me. She should've kept her mouth shut.'

'And the maid?'

'Some no-account migrant?' scoffed Rentoria. 'Collateral damage, man. Shit happens. You should have let things be. Instead, you blunder in here, fucking shit up. They know where the girl is at, man. They find out you're looking for them and they'll kill her just to make the point.'

'They already know.'

'Then you should run.'

'Where would I go?'

'Anywhere,' said Rentoria. 'And I can help you with that. I could give you a taste. I got a couple of thou on me but I can give you...thirty in the morning. You lost your job. Figure I owe you that much.'

'I'm not interested in money, Jose. I want Byron.'

Rentoria shook his head, picked up Trent's gun in his free hand. 'You shouldn't have come. Things were going good.'

'I'm losing patience, Jose.'

'You see I'm holding two guns, right?'

'Give me a name. Last chance.'

Rentoria looked down at Trent's gun and stuffed his own into his waistband. He aimed the silencer at Trent's head. 'I always liked you, Trent. You busted my balls but you were fair. I want you to know this isn't personal.' Trent laughed. 'Something funny, bro?'

'You're going to blow my brains out all over your nice house? Over your nice new sofa? Haven't you learned anything?'

'I've learned plenty,' snarled Rentoria, gesturing to the ceiling with the gun. 'Stand up.' Trent got to his feet. 'Outside. The way you came in. And hands on your head, where I can see them.'

Trent considered his opponent, raised his hands to his head and walked past Rentoria, who backed away to let him pass then followed him to the kitchen. At the door, Rentoria ordered Trent to wait while he rummaged in a drawer for a torch. 'Okay. Outside.'

Trent stepped onto the drive and Rentoria jammed the silencer into Trent's neck.

'Left, towards the water.'

Trent moved slowly towards the darkness, Rentoria at his back. A bright moon glinted on the surface of the lake. 'Where are we going?'

'Head for the boathouse.'

'I thought it wasn't built yet.'

'No, but I've had the foundations dug out,' said Rentoria, shining his torch to direct Trent, through the trees to the water's edge. 'Looks like I'm pouring concrete tomorrow. Thanks for wrecking my weekend, fucker.'

They trudged towards the water in silence. The next-door neighbour's house loomed large on Trent's right and he looked across to it, cloaked in darkness.

'Don't go getting your hopes up,' said Rentoria. 'The neighbours are away for a month.'

'I know,' said Trent.

'Same old Trent,' chuckled Rentoria. 'Every little detail. Only this time I was a step ahead from the get-go. How does that feel, big man?'

'In a strange kind of way, it makes me proud. I had a hand in that.'

'I guess you did,' said Rentoria. 'Thanks, man. That's far enough.'

The pair had arrived at a ladder protruding from a deep pit dug into the gently sloping ground. The bottom of the pit was filled with water.

'Climb down,' ordered Rentoria. Trent hesitated then reached a leg around the ladder to face Rentoria. 'Down!' Trent started descending, his eyes glued to Rentoria.

As Trent disappeared, Rentoria moved to the top of the ladder to shine the torch on Trent's progress. When he reached the bottom, his feet were in water but Trent kept his head down, not moving away from the ladder.

'Good,' said Rentoria. 'I don't want to see your face.' He raised Trent's gun, aiming at the top of Trent's head. 'This is on you, man.'

Trent stepped backwards in the shallow water and raised his face to the torch and Rentoria caught a flash of something dropping into the water. He realised a second too late it was a waterproof plastic bag and he hurriedly squeezed the trigger of Trent's gun. Nothing happened.

In the same instant, Trent's right hand pointed towards Rentoria and a muffled orange explosion sent a bullet tearing into his hip.

The bone shattered and Rentoria fell back, screaming in agony. Instinctively he grabbed for his waistband but before he could clear his own gun from his trousers, Trent was up the ladder firing a second time into his gun hand and the weapon fell from his grip. Trent picked it up as the younger man cried breathlessly in pain.

'Help,' shouted Rentoria.

'The neighbours are away, remember.'

'Fuck you,' screamed Rentoria.

Leaping from the ladder, Trent fell onto the stricken Rentoria and brought the gun butt crashing down on the younger man's skull, knocking him out cold.

~

AFTER THROWING Rentoria's gun into the lake, Trent eased behind the wheel and started his car, drove up onto the apron of Rentoria's drive then reversed towards the back yard as far as the tarmac allowed. He got out and located the outside light switch and extinguished the lamps, plunging the grounds into darkness.

Opening the trunk provided light so Trent picked up the gun from the trunk floor and jammed it into his waistband.

Next, he hoisted out the heavy body bag, manoeuvred the dead man over his shoulder and carried the defrosted body to the back of the house before laying it out on the damp grass where it was easier to drag to the boat house.

At the ladder, Trent stopped heaving and unzipped the body bag. Grunting with the effort, he pulled the heavy-set corpse - a bullet in each knee and one in the head - to the edge of the pit then manoeuvred the bag away from the dead man's legs. With a huge effort he tipped the dead Ukrainian into the pit then scrambled down the ladder to drag him to the far wall to sit him upright.

Trent carried a breeze block up the ladder and placed it in the body bag, zipped it up and hurled it as far out into the lake as he could.

Rentoria was still out cold and losing blood from his groin. His face was white as snow.

'Jose.' Trent slapped his cheek. When Rentoria's eyes opened, pain returned and he began to pant through the gag.

'Hurts like a bitch, I bet,' said Trent, shaking his head in sympathy. He stared into his former colleague's frightened eyes. 'Don't scream when I remove the tape or I put it back and kick you on your hip. Nod if you understand.' Jose nodded furiously. Trent ripped the tape away.

'Please don't kill me,' pleaded Rentoria. 'Please. I'll do anything.'

'I wonder if Gwen had a chance to say that.'

'Please. I'll tell you anything. You said you'd give me a pass.'

'Your contact...'

'Byron,' said Rentoria, through gritted teeth.

'Surname?'

'You think he'd tell me that? His name probably wasn't even Byron but that's what he said. I swear on all that's holy.'

'Describe him.'

'Big guy. Bigger than you. Heavy set. About forty-five. Wore a Bears hat.'

Trent nodded. 'Where do I find him? I won't ask twice.'

Rentoria's eyes closed, squeezing tears onto his cheek. 'I don't know, man. Honest to God, I'd tell you if I did.'

'Try harder.'

Rentoria started to sob. 'I don't know...'

'Then how did he pay you?'

'Briefcase left in a deposit box in Chase Bank on Wicker Park, West North Avenue. He sent a key over by motorbike messenger. That's all I know. I swear.'

'Okay.' Trent sighed. 'Any money in your house?'

'Two thousand in my wallet. It's yours.'

'And the rest?'

'I swear that's all.'

Trent smashed his heel into Rentoria's hip and the younger man squealed in anguish. 'Cookie jar,' Rentoria panted. 'At the bottom. About thirty thou. Thought you weren't interested in the money.'

'Disappearing is expensive,' said Trent.

'What about my free pass. I told you what I know.'

'No Byron, no pass.'

'Fuck, no,' mumbled Rentoria. 'You won't get away with this.'

'You could be right.' Trent smiled. 'Shame you won't be around to gloat.'

'What are you going to do?'

Trent circled behind the prone Rentoria and hoisted him up so he could see the body in the foundations of the boathouse.

'Who's that?'

'His name is Aleksay Sokolov,' said Trent. 'He's a paid assassin. Ukrainian. One of the men who killed Gwen and the maid then went for breakfast.'

'What...what are you going to do?'

'Seriously? You must have gamed scenarios in Theory class, Jose. You tell me.'

Rentoria's smile was strained. He took a breath, swallowed down the pain. 'Bad guys fall out. One wants the other's pay-off and tries to extort money. Guns are drawn, shots fired. The gun you shot me with...will be in his hand and...' His lip quivered and he sobbed quietly '...the gun you shot Sokolov with...'

'Will be in yours,' nodded Trent. 'Top of the class, Jose.'

Trent stood and shot Rentoria in the head and the younger man sank to the ground with a ragged sigh. After placing the guns in the correct hands, Trent unscrewed the silencer on his Glock, with its empty clip, and pocketed both before hurrying back to the house.

In the kitchen, he located Rentoria's wallet and helped himself to the two thousand dollars. He emptied out the cookie jar and bit down on an Oreo then stuffed the crumb-covered envelope into a pocket without bothering to look inside. He took the time to fill a large shopping bag with foodstuffs and soft drinks from the refrigerator.

Eating a second Oreo, he turned off all the lights and stepped out into the darkness, moving swiftly to the driver's door of his car. At that moment, a powerful spotlight dazzled him and he raised an arm against its fierce gaze.

'You done, Mike?'

Trent dropped his arm and stared at a grinning Byron, a

few yards away, woollen Bears hat firmly on his head. Trent stooped to look into the back seat of the BMW. The blanket was unfurled and lying in the footwell. 'Where is she?'

'Safe,' said Byron. Trent marched towards him, fists clenched, eyes darting around to locate Nell. 'Over there.' Byron pointed towards the light source and Trent stopped to look across the road at a familiar GMC Yukon with blacked out windows. Two burly, shaven-headed men leaned against the car body, grinning back at him. One of them pointed a rifle at him, the other directed the spotlight onto the house.

'If you've harmed her, I'll...'

'You'll what, Mike?' enquired Byron, amicably.

Trent didn't answer, forcing himself to accept the balance of power. He unfurled his fists. 'Nothing.'

'Good. Now, answer my question. Are you done?'

Trent's breath slowed and his wits returned. He noticed the Canadian passport in Byron's gloved hand. 'For now.'

'I'm guessing with Aleksay's body in the trunk, you dressed it up as a shootout with no survivors. We should thank you for tying up our loose ends.'

'Who's we?'

Byron grinned. 'Stop, already. How'd you like the nose, by the way?' he said, touching it with a finger. 'Had to have a little work done after our last talk. No hard feelings on my part, Mike. Don't misunderstand me.'

'The cost of doing business,' said Trent.

'There you go,' said Byron, pointing a gloved finger at him. He examined the passport. 'Mark Taylor. Melanie Taylor. Daughter.' He looked up approvingly. 'This looks real.'

'It is.'

Byron laughed. 'Why do dirty cops always make the best criminals?'

'Why don't I put you next to Rentoria so you can ask him?'

Byron grinned. 'I'll miss you, Mike. The border isn't far. Where are you crossing?'

Trent hesitated, before deciding he had nothing worth hiding. 'Sault Ste Marie.'

'Great spot. Good water sports too. Don't you just love the North in late summer? So green, so much space. But you can always smell winter waiting in the wings, ready to bite.'

'What happens now?' said Trent.

'I told you before, Mike, we're not monsters. Blood is bad for business. And what's bad for business is...'

'Un-American,' said Trent.

'Now, you're getting it,' said Byron.

'And Rentoria?'

'Was a greedy little weasel who got what he deserved,' said Byron. 'I mean, a Porsche, for Christ's sake. Would it have killed the guy to show a little class? That said, business being business, we like to carry insurance. So, in twelve hours, an anonymous witness will provide an accurate description of you, the girl and your car which will place you outside this house. It won't take long for the Bureau to connect the dots. You'll be a wanted man.'

'Twelve hours?'

'A head's start to get across. Figure we owe you that much.' Byron held out the passport. Trent hesitated before taking it and jamming it into his jacket pocket. 'If you make it over the border, you can't ever come back, you realise that?'

'And the girl?'

'Escapes a miserable childhood in the system and lives happily ever after, thanks to an all-American hero turned killer.' Byron laughed. 'There's a movie in there somewhere.'

'We can go?'

'When you tell me, you understand one simple fact.'

'What's that?'

'That your life here is over. You burned your bridges, Mike. Time for the pair of you to start afresh elsewhere. Forever.'

'I understand.'

'Good.'

'A favour though?'

Byron's brow furrowed at the suggestion. 'Seriously?'

'Do I look like I'm joking?' said Trent. Byron waved at him to continue. 'Have your witness leave Nell out of the statement. If I go down, I'd rather not take her with me.'

'Child Services will report her missing in a few hours, if they haven't already.'

'I know. But we'll have a better chance of getting away if nobody knows I took her.'

Byron studied him. 'What do we get?'

'My solemn word that it's over and I won't be coming after you or your employer. Nell's future is all that matters now.'

Byron pursed his lips. 'I can't cash your solemn word at a bank, Mike.'

'Whatever happened to trust, Byron?'

Byron chuckled, removed his glove and held out his hand. Trent stared at it, making no move to shake. 'A verbal contract requires a handshake, Mike.'

Just as Byron was about to withdraw, Trent leaned in and shook his hand firmly, staring into Byron's pallid eyes before the big man broke into his trademark grin. With that, Byron gestured across to the Yukon and one of the men opened a rear door. Nell jumped down onto the tarmac. After getting her bearings, she hurtled across the road to Trent and slammed into his body, throwing her arms around his legs, sobbing his name.

'Cute kid.' Byron turned on his heel to cross the road but stopped a second later. 'You're going to miss the Bears. I think we're going all the way this year.'

'Go Bears,' mumbled Trent. After the Yukon had pulled away, Trent bundled the sobbing Nell into the passenger seat of the BMW and drove to the junction of Highway 41. There, he gazed at the road back to Illinois and the departed Yukon. For a moment he considered following before turning his car east towards Lake Superior and the border.

28

'Six bodies?' said Benoit, staring down at the selection of bones and half a dozen shiny, degraded skulls, spread out on canvas. The remains had been picked clean of flesh and weathered over a period of years.

'More,' said Coulibaly. 'We've found eleven different thigh bones so far and the GPR is still covering ground.'

'All female?' said Dugrippe.

'And, apart from the head we found yesterday, the remains have been here for a long time and nature has taken its course,' said Coulibaly.

'No male remains?' said Rolland.

'Not so far,' said Coulibaly. She put a bottle of Evian to her mouth and emptied it.

'How much ground have you surveyed?'

'We've stripped away the front third of the undergrowth which is the most accessible. The further we move up the hill, the fewer remains we expect to find.'

Benoit nodded towards an intact skeletal arm, missing its hand. 'Mutilated?'

'All the bodies were dismembered,' said Coulibaly, walking him over to the bones.

'Chainsaw?'

'Nothing so sophisticated. This arm, for instance - something made a real mess of the Humerus and Ulna at the wrist. See the splintering. That's blunt force trauma caused by repeated striking of the limb to sever the hand. And there's a similar pattern of damage on all the older remains. Almost certainly an axe.'

Benoit nodded. 'Have you got enough people?'

'Now we're winding down at the villa, yes,' said Coulibaly. 'We've got lights rigged and the generator fired so we can work it round the clock.' Benoit glanced up as a drone hovered above the dense maquis. 'Ours,' she said, before he could ask. 'We'll put up marquees just the same. In case of prying eyes.'

A Peugeot drove around the corner and drew to a halt. Auger stepped out.

'Daniel?' said Benoit. 'You can't be here.'

Auger raised two hands in apology. 'I had to get out of the apartment. I'm going crazy staring at four walls. Any news on Jerome?'

'Hanging in there,' said Benoit.

'Thank god,' said Auger. 'I was on my way to the ICP...'

'You're off the rota,' said Benoit. 'You need to go home.'

'I will,' said Auger. 'But with everything going on I thought you might be struggling to get food so I brought baguettes and salad. I'll take them up to the ICP then get out of your way.' His eye wandered across to the canvas sheet. 'Are those...?'

'Human remains from at least eleven victims,' said Dugrippe. 'All female.'

'Eleven?' exclaimed Auger. 'So many?'

'You missed our nocturnal visit to Chez Bertrand,' said Benoit. 'Eugenie Marchand was the tip of the iceberg. We found incriminating material suggesting Bertrand and Rappeneau have abducted at least fifteen young women, over several years. Marchand is the template. All the vics were female backpackers travelling alone, targeted at Bertrand's bar, drugged and abducted.'

'Then raped, tortured, killed and dismembered with an

axe for disposal,' said Rolland, a tremor of anger in her voice.

'Bastards,' said Auger.

'Putting a bullet in Bertrand was a good thing, Daniel,' said Rolland, clapping him on the back.

'That doesn't help,' said Auger. 'This is a disaster for the village. We'll have ghouls sightseeing and taking pictures for years. Any IDs?'

'Not yet,' said Benoit. 'Luckily they took photographs as trophies.'

'And you say the victims were drugged?' said Auger.

'We found Rohypnol in Bertrand's rooms though FFP say the women weren't kept there,' said Dugrippe.

'The pictures suggest they were taken to a rural location,' said Benoit. 'We're looking to see if either man had land or property in the area.'

'I could take a look at local records...'

'In hand,' said Benoit. 'But when you get to the ICP...'

'Of course, I'll look at the photos, see if I recognise the place,' said Auger. 'Is that why Bertrand was shooting at us?'

'We were onto Rappeneau,' said Rolland. 'Bertrand must've known it was only a matter of time.'

'Wouldn't it have been easier for him to dispose of Rappeneau?' said Auger.

'The criminal mind doesn't always think logically under pressure,' said Benoit.

'Or maybe Bertrand had already taken care of him,' said Auger.

Benoit shook his head. 'If so, he wouldn't need to shoot at us.'

'True.' Auger stared at the skeletal remains on the canvas. 'Do you need help with missing persons?'

'Costanza has it in hand but I'm sure the Rat Squad wouldn't object to a little desk work,' said Benoit.

'And Jasmin?' said Auger.

'What about it?'

'If Carla Renfrew's head was dumped in the same location as the others, that's a direct link back to Bertrand and Rappeneau,' said Auger.

'I'd love to tie this up in a neat bow, Daniel, but we're not convinced they're responsible for Jasmin,' said Benoit. 'Bertrand and Rappeneau targeted lone females. Different method, different crime.'

'And the villa is Rappeneau's home,' said Dugrippe. 'He's no Einstein but even he wouldn't be dumb enough to shit on his own doorstep like that.'

Auger nodded. 'I suppose.'

THE TEAM ATE their baguettes in silence, everyone deep in thought, their eyes wandering over the enlarged photographs of fifteen unidentified young women, tacked close together onto the last spare space on the last display wall. The ordeal of their final days was betrayed in their eyes, despite the drugs administered to guarantee docility.

Auger stared at each in turn, trying to focus on the landscape and not the doomed expressions. 'I wish I knew,' he said, shaking his head.

'It's hard when there are no landmarks,' said Caron.

'If only I'd winged Bertrand...'

'Bertrand had a rifle, Daniel,' said Benoit. 'You had no choice.'

Dugrippe finished his sandwich. 'Thanks for the food.'

Auger acknowledged the murmur of gratitude from satisfied detectives and stood to leave the ICP. 'I'd better go.'

'You're still one of the team, Daniel,' said Caron.

'Thank you,' said Auger. 'But I shouldn't have come. I'm putting you in an awkward position.' He rummaged in a pocket for a pen drive. 'A last batch of photographs from the fête.' He hesitated. 'Who do I...?'

'Gabriel and Nina are taking over Jerome's workload,' said Benoit, quietly.

Auger handed the drive to Caron. 'There's a duplicate list of local estate agents and all the websites offering gites and villas for rent. Costanza has a copy and she's co-ordinating contacts and directing uniform visits to question agents, landlords and tenants.' He glanced at the sombre Trent. 'How's your ear?'

'It stings,' crowed Dugrippe, grinning.

Trent touched the dressing on his lobe. 'The worst part is people thinking I've had it pierced.' Even Dugrippe laughed at this.

'You know where I am if you want a matching pair,' said Auger, heading for the door.

'Daniel,' said Benoit, eyeing the American. 'We were in the middle of something before Coulibaly called us away. Hang around for a few minutes. We may need bodies to return Trent to his cell if his answers don't come up to scratch. Gabriel.' Latour reloaded the picture of Renfrew and Bryon Logan on the observation deck of Chicago's Sears Tower.

'Renfrew was in Chicago, eighteen years ago,' said Benoit. 'You were there too. Last chance, Trent. What's the relevance and why was Megan hiding this picture from you?'

'I can't be certain.'

'Then guess.' Benoit folded his arms. 'Full disclosure or you're back in a cell and you won't come out until the FBI get here. First things first. Megan's not your daughter, is she?'

Trent lowered his head. 'No. Megan Matteson is another alias.'

'Why did she hide this picture from you?' said Benoit.

'Maybe this will help,' said Latour. 'I found it while you were out, boss.' Latour loaded a photostat of a death certificate from his monitor onto the big screen. 'I did some background on the man with Renfrew. Bryon Logan, security consultant, born in Bloomington, Illinois in 1956. Died in London in 2017, aged 62.'

Finally, Trent's mask of stone crumbled. 'Byron's dead?'

'Two years ago, in London,' repeated Latour.

'Byron not Bryon?' said Benoit.

'Byron was the name he used in front of me,' said Trent.

'Where? When?'

'Chicago, 2002. I was guarding Gwen...Mrs Beaumont. Byron was a mob fixer. He told me, because of what she knew, Gwen was doomed but if I stepped aside and let them do their work, Gwen's daughter could be spared.'

'You refused, I hope,' said Dugrippe.

Trent's glare was fierce. 'Of course, I refused.'

'Who did Byron work for?' said Benoit.

'I never found out,' said Trent.

'Renfrew?'

'I don't know,' said Trent. 'Though Megan having this picture is suggestive.'

'How did Logan die?' said Benoit.

Latour loaded a page of the London Evening Standard newspaper onto the screen and Logan's older face beamed out next to the text of a story headlined,

AMERICAN BUSINESSMAN DIES IN TUBE ACCIDENT

'HE FELL into the path of an oncoming train at Oxford Circus Underground Station, while on a business trip,' said Latour. 'Died instantly.'

'Fell or was pushed?' enquired Benoit, glancing at Trent.

'I didn't kill him,' said Trent. 'I was in Thailand in 2017.'

'The inquest recorded an open verdict,' said Latour. 'But, when they performed the Post Mortem, they found Logan had an inoperable cancer. The man knew he was on borrowed time.'

'So, it could have been suicide,' said Benoit.

'Two men in a photograph on Megan Matteson's computer, both found dead in suspicious circumstances,' said Caron. 'One, in London where Megan lives, the other in a house which she rented and to which she was travelling, just days before the occupants died. Does that sound accidental to you?'

'I thought we decided Renfrew is alive,' said Dugrippe.

'That's still just a theory,' said Benoit. 'Why did Megan return to France?'

'I have no idea,' said Trent. 'The first I knew of it was when you told me.'

'And hiding these documents from you?'

'She must have had her reasons,' mumbled Trent. 'But I don't know what they are.'

'Reasons like committing murder?' suggested Caron.

'I told you. Megan didn't kill the Renfrews. She's not capable.'

'What about pushing someone under a train?'

'Same answer.'

'But you don't wonder *why* she might have done it,' said Benoit. 'You recognise a motive, at least. Was she in London at that time?'

'She didn't do it,' insisted Trent. 'Any of it. I know her.'

Benoit waited for a beat. 'I'll ask you again. Why might Megan want Logan dead?' Trent was silent. 'Take him...'

'Logan arranged her mother's murder,' said Trent. 'Megan was in the next room when Gwen died.'

'Gwen Beaumont was Megan's mother,' said Benoit. 'So, Megan Matteson is...' he glanced at Latour.

'Nell Beaumont,' said Latour.

'That's right,' said Trent. 'I failed Gwen but I wasn't going to fail Nell. Her mother was dead but Nell was still in danger. So, I did the only thing I could.'

'You took her and ran,' said Benoit.

'And gave up your life, your job and your country to protect her?' said Rolland.

'I didn't think I had much choice.'

'You abducted her,' said Dugrippe.

'Technically,' said Trent. 'But the authorities couldn't protect her in a state orphanage. I could. We crossed the border into Canada and then flew to London.'

'So, who was Megan Matteson?'

'A child in London who died when she was five,' said Trent. 'I found her grave shortly after we arrived and applied for a duplicate birth certificate. From that I was able to reconstruct Nell as Megan - passport, social security, the works.'

'And Gwen's killers?' said Benoit.

'I spent months looking for Byron to find out who gave the order,' said Trent. 'But once I'd smuggled Nell into Canada and then on to London, the search became impossible. Until Nell phoned to tell me Renfrew was hiring us, I'd never even heard his name. I swear.'

'If Renfrew *was* involved in Gwen Beaumont's death, surely he had links to the company she worked for?' said Rolland.

'You're talking about thousands of employees spread across a network of subsidiaries and associated companies,' said Trent.

'How did Renfrew hire you?' said Latour.

'We have a no-frills page on the dark web with a mission statement and a message board to leave contact details,' said Trent. 'It's completely anonymous.'

'So, Renfrew wouldn't know who he was hiring.'

'Not a chance,' said Trent. 'Anyone who needs our services has been referred by word-of-mouth. There are no personnel details, no profiles, no data of any kind on the site that could compromise our operations. I work in the field, laying down a digital and financial trail to obscure the whereabouts of our clients. Nell mostly stays in the background, doing the admin.

'When a potential client makes contact, she fields the initial enquiry, does the vetting and assesses the threat they're facing. But I'm at the sharp end, so I have the final decision. If I sign off, she starts researching destinations and we go from there.'

'How do you choose?' said Benoit.

'We decide between us, depending on the client,' said

Trent. 'Once a destination is chosen, we pick accommodation that matches the client's income and go - mostly just me initially, until I can risk assess. If the client is female, Nell joins me but I'm still in charge.'

'And Renfrew?'

'Should have been a high-level risk, so I mostly worked alone,' said Trent.

'Should've been?' said Benoit.

'I didn't pick up so much as a tail from the airport,' said Trent. 'No-one was trying to find Harry Renfrew. Now I know why.'

'Whose idea was Villa Jasmin?' said Benoit.

'Mine,' replied Trent. 'I stayed there for a couple of months, when I first left the States.'

'Where was Nell?'

'Staying with a friend in London,' said Trent. 'I needed time to think and I was the one with the target on my back so I came here alone. I didn't want Nell exposed. When the Renfrews hired us, Jasmin seemed perfect for them.'

'You had Nell hire the villa as Wendy Wyatt because Madame Rappeneau knew you?' said Auger.

'I didn't think she'd remember me but, being risk averse, yes, I had Nell do it,' said Trent.

'Did you continue looking for Gwen's killer?' said Rolland.

'No. I couldn't go back to the States, so what could I realistically achieve?'

'You could've used one of your fake identities,' said Auger.

'I can change my passport,' said Trent. 'I can't change my fingerprints. Besides, Gwen was gone. Protecting Nell was my only concern.' He shrugged. 'I stopped looking.'

'But Nell didn't,' said Latour.

'So, it seems,' conceded Trent.

'Problem is, there's no smoking gun in these documents,' said Caron. 'Evidence of Renfrew's participation in Gwen Beaumont's murder is non-existent.'

'But not Logan's,' said Trent. 'He approached me in Chicago and Nell saw him briefly. She was five.'

'You think she remembered him?'

'Trauma will do that,' said Trent.

'You were in love with Gwen, I think,' said Rolland.

Trent stared at Rolland then at the floor. 'How did you know?'

'The way you speak her name,' said Rolland.

'We were drawn to each other,' said Trent, after a moment. 'Close confinement can do that.'

'So, Nell found Logan,' said Latour. 'But how did that lead her to Renfrew?'

'Maybe she extracted a confession before she killed him,' said Auger.

'Nell is not a killer,' said Trent. 'I think I may have mentioned that.'

'Keep saying it,' said Dugrippe. 'She may need a character witness at her trial.'

'Pretty long odds, Renfrew receiving death threats and asking the daughter of a woman he murdered, to help him disappear,' said Rolland.

'Want me to field that one, Michael?' said Benoit, when Trent declined to answer. 'There were no death threats. Nell discovered the identity of her mother's killer and invented them as a way to force Renfrew into making a run for it. What I don't yet know is how she offered Renfrew your services without giving the game away.'

'I've been wondering that myself,' said Trent.

'*Cherchez la femme*,' said Benoit. 'Only I suspect this one is alive and well and sunning herself on a beach somewhere, feeling very pleased with herself.'

'I really hope you're right,' said Trent. 'Because Nell did not kill Carla, which means she didn't kill Harry or Roger Barron or whoever the dead man in the pool was. She is *not* a killer.'

'*Witnesses described a young woman in her early twenties standing next to Mr Logan before he fell onto the tracks. They described what appear to be attempts to grab him, in an effort to prevent his fall,'* Latour read from his monitor. 'Interesting article,' he said, raising an eyebrow at Trent before reading on. *'The young woman has not yet been identified and police would ask her to come forward to provide a full statement. Mr Logan...'*

Trent shot his chair from under him, and leapt towards Latour, landing on him with Auger and Dugrippe trying to haul him back by the shoulders. The whole scrum landed with a crash on the floor accompanied by a couple of laptops and the contents of Latour's desktop. Dugrippe, on top of the melee, grabbed a glass paperweight from another desk and smashed it gleefully onto the back of Trent's head.

29

Trent woke with a splitting headache and tried to move a hand to his head to assess the damage. His arm wouldn't obey and he opened his eyes to find himself on the floor, handcuffed to a metal pipe in the toilet cubicle of the ICP, his back against the prefabricated wall.

'You're awake?' said Latour, pushing the door open. 'Here.' Latour handed him a polystyrene cup of water, a tablet fizzing in it. 'Aspirin.'

Trent drained the cup. 'Thanks.' With his free hand, he touched the bump on his head and felt fabric.

'Thierry drew blood so we patched you up.'

'He must have been ecstatic.'

'Hasn't stopped grinning.'

Trent handed back the cup. When Latour left the toilet, Trent moved a hand to his jacket pocket and felt for the tool from Latour's desk, palmed and slipped into his pocket before he'd hit the floor. It was still there. He withdrew the miniature slotted screwdriver, a precision tool more suited to a watchmaker, and pulled his ankle towards him to inspect the tracker bracelet.

. . .

HALF AN HOUR LATER, Benoit pushed open the toilet door, dragging a chair through from the main room. Trent watched him as he sat, curious at first, then shifting with apprehension when Benoit drew out his gun, resting the pistol on his thigh to pacify his trembling hand.

'I never thought I'd die in a men's room,' said Trent.

'I did, once,' said Benoit. 'Oysters. How's the head?'

'Hurts like hell,' said Trent.

'Thierry will be pleased.'

'Sorry I lost my temper.'

'Is that what happened?' said Benoit, glancing at his watch. 'Was thirty minutes long enough?'

'Long enough for what?'

'To see whether the tool you palmed would release the cuffs.'

Trent's smile was thin. He removed his right hand from the handcuffs. 'I was testing your security.'

'Good of you,' said Benoit. 'Can I have it back?' Trent produced the screwdriver from his pocket and made as if to stand. 'Toss it!' barked Benoit, his gun raised. Trent sank back down and slid the screwdriver across the floor then folded his hands onto his lap. 'Thank you. And the tracker?'

Trent pulled up his trouser leg showing the white plastic tracker. 'It's still on.'

'Did you need more time?'

'No. I took it off then replaced it, for appearances. I assume it's still functional.'

Benoit holstered his gun, stood over Trent, put his hand on the plaster covering the wound on his head then ripped it off, producing a sharp yell of pain from Trent. 'Shall we go?'

'Go where?' said Trent, panting.

'That needs stitching.'

FEW SPOKE at the dinner table that night beyond asking for the bread basket or the passing of condiments. The Deux

Rocs restaurant was still closed after Gagnon's shooting and the Serious Crimes Squad dined at an even more bucolic restaurant - if that was possible - La Gloire de Mon Pere.

Tables were arranged around a circular four-tier stone fountain and coloured lights were wound around and between half a dozen gnarled old larch trees, growing through the cobbles of the square. The restaurant was crowded with locals and tourists and the noise of laughter and conviviality was a welcome cloak for the detectives' own moribund efforts at conversation.

As they dined mechanically on ham gazpacho followed by a creamy king prawn risotto, the squad were devoid of the energy to express words they were barely able to summon.

Even Dugrippe's lusty appetite seemed to have deserted him and he gnawed joylessly on a crust of bread as he stared malevolently at Trent. 'I thought he was supposed to eat in his cell.'

'We were delayed at the doctor's surgery,' said Benoit. 'I made an executive decision.'

'He's wearing a tracker, Thierry,' said Caron. 'He's not going anywhere.' Dugrippe grunted.

'I'm grateful for your trust,' said Trent. 'I won't abuse it again.'

'Shut up, Yank!' snapped Dugrippe.

After a dessert of crème brûlée, exhausted detectives began to drift away to their respective quarters, leaving Dugrippe and Benoit with Trent. Dugrippe yawned but showed no sign of moving.

'Go get some sleep,' said Benoit.

'What about...?'

'I'll take him back to Fayence myself.'

'Are you serious?' said Dugrippe. 'He's dangerous.'

'I'll considered myself warned,' said Benoit. 'Go.' Reluctantly, Dugrippe lumbered off into the night, trailing the odour of Gitanes behind him.

Benoit ordered two digestifs and two coffees and leaned back to look at the stars through the trees. 'Beautiful night.'

'What's going on?' said Trent.

'Going on?'

'Why the light touch?' said Trent. 'I'm dangerous, remember?'

Benoit gestured with an arm. 'Feel free. I've decided I'm not going to waste precious time or energy guarding you.'

'I could have this tracker off in minutes.'

'I don't doubt it,' said Benoit. 'But then you'd be outside the investigation, looking for Nell in a strange country with no resources, as well as breaking your word to me.' The drinks arrived and Benoit held up his shot glass. 'To international co-operation.' He put the glass to his lips briefly. 'You prefer a different toast?'

'I don't drink,' said Trent. 'I haven't touched alcohol since...since the last time I was in Seillans, in fact.'

'When you stayed at Jasmin?' said Benoit.

'Seventeen years,' said Trent.

'A cop who doesn't drink,' said Benoit. 'That's not natural.' He downed his glass of eau de vie in one swallow and, gasping at the heat, gestured the waiter for a refill. 'You Americans should think of alcohol not as a crutch but as an old friend distracting you from the pain.'

'Does it distract you?'

'Not entirely,' said Benoit. 'But baggage is part of the game. To keep playing, you carry it as lightly as you can.'

'And the yips are part of your baggage?' said Trent.

'The what?'

Trent shook his right hand in front of Benoit's face. 'The shakes.'

Benoit held out his hand to examine the slight tremor. 'You should have seen me a year ago.'

'Another fifty years, you'll be good as new,' said Trent. Benoit laughed. 'Why don't you get out? You're young enough.'

'Like you did? A stranger to your own country.'

'I didn't choose what happened to me,' said Trent.

'Sure, you did.'

Trent shrugged. 'There is life after police work.'

'But what kind of life and how is it to be lived?' said Benoit. 'Tell me you don't spend part of every day, dwelling on what you've seen as a federal agent and I'll put in my papers tomorrow.' Trent's lips were sealed. 'That's what I thought.'

Benoit took a sip of coffee. 'I've been back in the job nearly two years. I don't sleep as well as I used to but at least I no longer wake up screaming, my sheets soaking wet. That's a good thing. And I'm good at my job. I'm contributing. If I left, what would I do? Would I cope any better? You were a soldier *and* a cop, so you must know how difficult it is for people like us to communicate with civilians. What do we say? How do we explain to those outside the life, what it's like to deal with the horrors we've witnessed?'

Benoit sighed. 'I have neighbours who were caught up in the attack on the promenade. What they saw scarred them forever and they wouldn't be human if it didn't. Yet, that night, the only thing they had to do to make the pain stop was shut their eyes and walk away. You and I never had that luxury. We *have* to do our jobs or twenty other people can't do theirs. Yes?' Trent nodded.

'That night, I walked from body to mangled body, checking for signs of life, each fresh corpse taking a bite out of my soul. Dozens upon dozens of the dead and dying, twisted and warped by the agony of their final moments. Did I have a choice? No. I was trained. I had to function. Onto the next body then the next, trying to make sense, keeping control so I could calm others and tell them what to do. Even after I found my sister and her infant son...' Benoit swallowed the rest of the sentence.

'I didn't know,' said Trent. 'I'm sorry.'

'So am I.' Benoit smiled. Two more shots arrived and he picked up a glass, gazed at the clear liquid. 'But, with the help of old friends, I move forward. Now I only think about the case I'm working, each day, one after the other. It's the way I exist.'

'The old me would drink to that,' said Trent.

Benoit held up his glass. 'To moving forward.'

As Benoit was preparing to drink, Trent picked up his own glass and touched it to Benoit's before sniffing the clear alcohol. When Benoit drank, Trent closed his eyes and tipped the drink down his throat, his face contorting at the fire searing its way down his gullet. He took a deep breath and opened his eyes, like a swimmer resurfacing from a deep pool.

'Hello, old friend,' he said to the glass, cradled in his fingers. He signalled the waiter for a refill. 'Leave the bottle,' he said, when the waiter arrived, downing another shot and refilling his glass. 'There. All caught up.'

'Careful,' said Benoit. 'Artisanal eau de vie is lethal.'

'I know,' said Trent.

'You've had it before?'

'After Nell and I flew to London, I came here. I thought being alone, in the middle of nowhere, would get my head straight so I could get some peace and make sense of it all. Instead, I went on a two-month bender...'

'Bender?'

'A drinking binge,' explained Trent. 'I'd wake up in a chair every morning and start drinking. A couple of beers to get going then onto wine at lunchtime and spirits in the evening until I passed out. Rinse and repeat. I was in a tailspin.'

'How did you pull out?'

'Booze doesn't solve problems, it postpones them,' said Trent, staring affectionately at the shimmer of coloured light through his charged glass. 'I just needed to remind myself of that.'

'So, you just stopped.'

'And never drank another drop.'

'Until now,' said Benoit.

Trent raised his drink. 'To postponement.'

They drank and Trent refilled their glasses.

'Now there are just the two of us, you can tell me who else you killed,' said Benoit. 'And don't give me any horseshit about hitmen. The FBI aren't going to lose sleep over a couple of dead assassins. Off the record, obviously.'

Trent downed the shot of eau-de-vie and his eyes gleamed with the flush of alcohol. 'There is no record, remember.'

Benoit grunted his amusement. 'Then, tell me.'

Trent refilled his glass but didn't drink. 'They shot Gwen through the spyhole of the hotel door. She lost half her face and I had to stand there while CSIs worked around her when all I wanted to do was cradle her in my arms and tell her everything was going to be okay. One of my squad turned up. He tried not to look at me but I guess he couldn't stop himself. When our eyes met, I knew what he'd done. And he knew I knew.'

'What did he do?'

'After the threats from Byron, I moved Gwen and Nell to a different hotel. Only Jose and I knew the new location and he ratted me out...'

'And that suspicion gave you the right to kill him?'

'Not without a confession and not before he'd walked me down to the foundations of his own boathouse to execute *me*.'

'You couldn't have arrested him?'

'I'd been fired. I had no jurisdiction and no evidence. It would've been his word against mine.'

'Even so...' began Benoit.

'Two people died, one a young mother. He betrayed me and everything the FBI stands for and he did it for money.'

'You let your feelings cloud your judgement...'

'How were your feelings when Bertrand was killed?'

'Am I sorry he's dead?' said Benoit. 'No. But I wanted him alive.'

'Easy to say when your colleague is still breathing,' said Trent. Benoit took a sharp intake of breath, but before he could retort, Trent apologised. 'Sorry!' A second later, he leered at Benoit. 'It's the drink talking.'

'I think that's our exit line,' said Benoit, downing his shot and dropping three hundred euros onto the bill. They stood to leave and Trent grabbed the bottle of eau-de-vie, cradling it in his arms all the way to the car.

30

Wednesday 8th May

Madame Rappeneau emerged from her neighbour's house, her home for the next few days while forensics teams examined her own home two doors away. She glanced warily around Madame Bouvard's neat back garden, checking to see if she was being observed. Paul had warned her to take care, that gendarmes might be watching, after he'd gone into hiding.

She'd seen the officer in front of the house but there didn't seem to be anyone watching the back so she scuttled down the steps and out onto Rue du Caire, clutching a bag for market day. At the gate, she peered up and down the hill before hurrying across the cobbled lane and onto a narrow path through trees and out of sight of the lane.

Skirting gardens either side of the path, she emerged behind a basketball court and sat at a bench for a moment, looking back the way she'd come, pleased to see no-one following. She smiled at the excitement of it.

Certain she wasn't being tailed, Madame Rappeneau resumed her journey and minutes later, the smells, noise and colour of the market regaled her as she walked along Promenade Max Ernst to the main square where stalls were squeezed into every inch of the space, groaning with local produce, picked over by villagers and a sprinkling of early-season tourists.

She set about shopping for salamis, bread, cheese, ham, pies, olives, fruit, a few onions and carrots for the pot to flavour whatever game her husband could catch, but mainly she bought food that didn't need cooking. When she finished, she bought a coffee and croissant at a stall and sat down on one of their plastic chairs, scanning for signs that she was being watched.

Reassured, she drained her cup and stepped into a local taxi.

'Take the Route de Mons and the turn-off to Les Combes Longues,' she said, reading the text Paul had sent her the night before. 'I'll direct you when we get closer. And let me know if we're being followed,' she instructed, as an afterthought. The taxi driver raised a mercurial eyebrow then steered his Mercedes carefully through human traffic.

'Do you want me to wait?' said the taxi driver.

Madame Rappeneau looked around at the bleakness of her surroundings. After a half-hour drive, the Mercedes had pulled up in the middle of nowhere, high on a hill, on a barely accessible lane, its ancient tarmac crumbling and potholed. A small wood fringed the lane and a rustic cart track skirted the trees and disappeared out of sight, round the side of the hill. She checked the directions on the phone again.

'Madame?' said the taxi driver.

'Er...no,' she replied. Needing no second invitation, the driver sped away as soon as he'd deposited Madame and her shopping at the roadside. She picked up her supplies and headed towards the track.

. . .

BENOIT WOKE LATER than usual in Auger's spare room and padded through to the kitchen to pour coffee from the percolator and a glass of fresh orange juice from the fridge, which he downed in one. The rooftop patio doors were open so he took his coffee outside to enjoy the endless views while he smoked his first cigarette, scrolling through his messages. He smiled, thinking of Trent's hangover and sent a text to Dugrippe to delay picking up the American from his cell in Fayence until mid-morning. 'Happy postponement,' he toasted with his coffee.

'Daniel?' he called out. No reply from Auger. He hadn't expected one, having heard his host moving around in the apartment earlier that morning. He knew Auger had grown impatient kicking his heels at home and was planning to spend a day at the station, helping to sift through old missing persons reports to match to pictures of victims found at Bertrand's bar.

After his cigarette, Benoit dressed and headed to the door to check in at the excavation site on the D19. His phone rang.

'Adele?' He listened to Rolland for a few seconds then fumbled for a pen. 'Where?' He wrote detailed directions. 'I'll find it. Scramble the team but tell Gabriel to stay at the ICP. He needs to organise the trailer and get it moved to the new site. We're finished at Jasmin.'

TRENT OPENED his eye at the noise of a tray being placed next to his cot, the smell of pastry turning his stomach. Dugrippe stood over him, grinning.

'What time is it?' he croaked, ungumming his lips to speak.

'Ten o'clock,' said Dugrippe. Trent groaned in self-disgust. 'The boss thought you might need your beauty sleep.' Trent closed his eye in the vain hope the pain splitting his skull might cease. Instead, a small packet landed on his face. 'Present for you.'

With some difficulty, Trent deployed an arm to pick up the sachet of soluble aspirin and hold it to his eye for inspection. He sat up slowly, holding his head in both hands, then swung his legs to the hard floor. His brain felt like it was spinning on its axis.

'Thanks,' he croaked, accepting a bottle of Evian and locating the bottle's neck with his hands. He dropped the soluble aspirins into the water and, after a brief shake, downed the entire cloudy concoction before putting a hand over his mouth to ensure ingestion.

Dugrippe lit a Gitanes and blew the blue-brown smoke towards Trent. 'Drink your coffee. We're late.' Trent dutifully picked up the plastic cup for an exploratory sip of the black liquid. 'Are you going to eat that croissant?'

'Not unless you want to see it sprayed over your car,' said Trent. Dugrippe picked up the pastry in his great fist and began gnawing at it.

'Two minutes,' Dugrippe said, with his mouth full.

'I'm ready now,' said Trent, draining the scalding liquid.

Dugrippe marched the unsteady Trent out of the detention area and into the open plan office, gesturing a greeting to Auger, hunched over a pile of missing persons posters. Auger stood to shake Dugrippe's hand.

'We missed you at dinner,' said Dugrippe.

'Keeping my distance.'

'Fucking Rat Squad. How's desk work treating you?'

Auger shrugged. 'Better than nothing. I've written my statement. Just have to wait for the bureaucracy to unwind so I can get back out there.'

'It's a long process,' said Dugrippe. 'They took six weeks to clear me for duty after a dealer I arrested jumped out of my car and crushed both his legs under an oncoming bus.'

'Six weeks?' groaned Auger. He looked at Trent. 'You look like I feel.'

'Glad it's not just me,' answered Trent, eyes glued to the top poster on the pile. 'Zouzou Millault, 21 - disappeared in 2004. Is that another victim?'

'There's a resemblance to one of the earliest photographs, yes,' said Auger. 'And this one we knew about. Went for a walk between Fayence and Seillans and was never seen again.'

'Fifteen years,' mumbled Trent, gazing at the young woman's smiling face. 'Were you around then?'

'The Var is my home,' said Auger. 'Where else would I be?'

'You knew her?' said Dugrippe.

'I knew her,' said Auger. 'We were the same age. She disappeared six months after I joined the Force. She was a nice person. Her family still lives in the village.'

'I know for a fact Rappeneau was here in 2002,' said Trent. 'What about Bertrand?'

'He opened the bar sixteen years ago,' said Auger. 'He was here.'

'So, this could've been the first,' said Trent. 'Was Bertrand ever interviewed?'

'It was local,' said Auger. 'Everyone was interviewed but...'

'No body, no evidence of a crime,' said Trent. Auger nodded.

Dugrippe's phone interrupted the conversation. 'Yes, boss. Taking Trent to the ICP.' He looked at Auger and listened for a few moments. 'I'll find it. Be there as soon as possible.' He ended the call and looked at Trent. 'I've got to go. You're going back to the cells.'

'What's happened?' said Trent.

'Nothing to concern you,' said Dugrippe.

'Then drop me at the ICP, where I can be useful,' said Trent.

'No time,' said Dugrippe.

'I'll take him,' said Auger, dropping the next poster on the pile. 'The dead aren't going anywhere.'

Dugrippe hesitated. 'You're sure?'

.   .   .

UP THE STEEP bank and thirty metres beyond, the vegetation had been stripped down to the topsoil and forensic anthropologists scoured the ground, sifting, brushing and photographing possible remains for transporting down the bank to another besuited CSI for provisional classification.

Auger and Trent stared solemnly at the array of bones laid neatly across the canvas at the roadside. Several more lower leg bones had been unearthed, none connected to the femur and it was clear, despite their condition, that some tibia and fibulae - normally attached - had been cleaved apart by an axe.

Two further human skulls had also been uncovered, one badly cratered above the left eye socket. Smaller bones from toes, fingers and lower ribcages were on a different canvas.

There was even a separate sheet for inorganic artefacts which may, or may not, have been related to the human remains, unearthed in the same ground and gathered for further investigation - a badly frayed rope, small items of jewellery like earrings and studs, badly rotted clothing and even a rucksack. Trent knelt to examine the rope, one end of which seemed to have been chewed.

'Nothing prepares you for a mass grave,' he said, standing.

'You've seen one?' said Auger.

'On the Iraqi border,' said Trent. He nodded towards what looked like a large pile of animal bones, some with identifiable scraps of flesh still clinging to them. 'What are those?' he said to a passing CSI.

The CSI lowered her mask. 'Animal bones.'

'Those look like the T-bones from a steak,' said Trent, peering at her ID lanyard. 'How did a cow get up there, Juliette?'

'I'm told there was a wolf hanging around the lay-by. Now you know why.'

'Wait, someone was feeding it?' said Trent.

'Who knows? But we found leg of lamb, chicken bones, pig's trotters...'

'Foraged from the bins, surely,' said Trent.

'I'm sure some is but we found meat remnants scattered way back, beyond the brow of the hill and caught up in the shrubs. We're pretty sure it was thrown there.'

THE SUN WAS CLIMBING and the temperature with it, as Benoit watched the first ambulance drive cautiously along the rutted ground and back to the lane. Even out of sight, its lights were intermittently visible through the grove of mature trees that bordered the rough track.

The second ambulance waited patiently for the rotting corpse of Paul Rappeneau, still being processed by forensic technicians inside a ramshackle old barn, a rough structure fashioned from a variety of wood, that leaned alarmingly away from the perpendicular.

The ill-fitting doors remained closed to keep out the flies and contain the cloying smell that had filled Benoit's nostrils with the sickly-sweet scent of death.

Rappeneau had been dead for two to three days, judging from the green mottling around his throat, visible either side of the rope suspending him from a high beam. But this was no suicide and it was clear he'd had help getting up there.

Benoit caught the jaundiced flash of a camera from inside the weather worn barn, where Coulibaly and two of her CSIs worked methodically in the stifling heat.

He walked back to the two vehicles parked side by side outside the barn. One was Rappeneau's Renault Twingo, the other a black Audi A3 with English plates. It was registered to Megan Matteson, now known to be Nell Beaumont.

At a patch of flat ground in front of the barn, two further FFP technicians worked. The area had been cleared of tough grass and encircled a huge round cross-section of tree-trunk about a metre high and a little more in diameter. Axe slashes scarred the flat surface from hundreds of impacts, some stained dirty brown, the colour of old blood -

probably the chopping block for Rappeneau and Bertrand to dispatch and dress the animals and birds they hunted for consumption.

It was also where Rappeneau's fingers had been amputated and tossed into a black canvas bag on the ground for his wife to find. Another canvas bag lay on its side, a baguette protruding from it.

The forensics officers processing the amputated fingers worked quickly but methodically, despite the attentions of dozens of black flies. Photographs were taken before each grisly artefact was transferred, one finger at a time, into evidence bags which were placed reverentially in an ice-packed cool box. The bloodied axe, anchored at a jaunty angle in the wood, had already been removed, bagged, tagged and placed in the exhibits van.

Rolland approached with Costanza.

'You followed Madame Rappeneau from her neighbour's house?' said Benoit.

Costanza nodded. 'She was very watchful. Kept stopping to see if anyone was tailing her. When she thought she was safe, she went to the market on the square and did some shopping for bread, cheese and other picnic foods.

'When she sat to have a coffee, I ran back to the house and rode my motorbike to the square. She took a taxi to here and carried her shopping from the road to the barn so I called it in and hung back in the trees. When she saw the bag with her husband's fingers in, she screamed and had some kind of seizure.'

'Shock,' said Benoit.

'The next thing I knew, she'd gone into cardiac arrest,' said Costanza, bowing her head. 'I did my best to revive her but I couldn't save her.'

'You did what you could,' said Benoit. 'Did she see into the barn?'

'No,' said Costanza. 'The door was closed when I got to her. She came straight to the bag and that was that.'

'This is my fault,' said Benoit. 'I put Rappeneau in

danger. I should've interviewed him at the station and, when he ran, put more pressure on Madame to give him up.'

'Wouldn't have done any good, boss,' said Rolland, holding up a cell phone in a plastic bag.

'An unregistered phone we found in her coat,' said Costanza. 'There's a text giving her directions. Until ten o'clock last night, she had no idea this place existed.'

'Last night?' said Benoit. 'Rappeneau's been dead longer than twelve hours. He couldn't have sent the text. Was his phone on his body?'

'Not in his pockets,' said Rolland. 'Thierry's doing a sweep in the barn.'

On cue, the barn door swung open and Dugrippe lumbered out of the barn. When he was clear, he yanked down his protective mask and took a huge pull of clean country air. 'Don't go in there without a dab under your nostrils. Rappeneau did a full evac.'

'Did you find a phone?' said Rolland. Dugrippe shook his head, fumbling for cigarettes under his layers.

'Have we tried ringing it from Madame's phone?' said Benoit.

'It was unattainable,' said Rolland.

'Probably disposed of,' said Benoit. 'Anything from Grace?'

'Only that it's not suicide,' said Dugrippe.

'Provisional time of death?' said Benoit.

'Hard to pin down because of the heat but she thinks between forty-eight and seventy-two hours.'

'Which means Rappeneau died soon after he disappeared,' said Rolland.

'Then who sent the text to his wife?' said Dugrippe.

'His killer,' said Costanza. 'Bertrand?'

Dugrippe shook his head. 'Bertrand died on Sunday night and, when Madame Rappeneau received directions, he was on a slab in Fayence mortuary.'

'There's a third man,' said Rolland, softly.

'And it looks like he's tying up loose ends,' said Benoit.

'But why kill Madame Rappeneau?' said Costanza. 'Surely she wasn't involved in the killings.'

'She wasn't killed,' said Rolland. 'Her death was unintentional.'

'Then why drag her all the way out here?' said Costanza.

'Because whoever lured her here must have known we'd be following,' said Benoit.

'The killer wanted us to find Rappeneau's body,' said Rolland.

'It's a distraction,' said Benoit.

'From what?' said Dugrippe. No-one could come up with an answer.

'There was nothing in Rappeneau or Bertrand's papers about this parcel of land,' said Benoit. 'Can we find out who owns it?'

'Nina's working it,' said Dugrippe, nodding at her walking towards them.

'What about Megan's Audi?' said Benoit.

'It's empty and looks clean but the techs haven't had a chance to process,' said Dugrippe.

'But no luggage?' said Benoit. Dugrippe shook his head.

'Trent's going to have kittens when he finds out those monsters have had their way with her,' said Rolland.

'No, he isn't,' said Benoit. 'We say nothing to him about the car. Thinking she's alive, is the only thing keeping him under control. Any sign of her body?'

'No indications of a fresh grave in the immediate vicinity,' said Costanza. 'When we get more people, we'll do a thorough search of the whole hillside.'

'Let's face it, Megan could have been dumped anywhere between here and Seillans,' said Rolland.

'Does that include the pool at Villa Jasmin?' said Dugrippe. The detectives looked at each other. 'If you can switch DNA once, you can switch it twice.'

'If Grace finds Megan's DNA in the Audi, we compare against Jasmin's female remains,' said Benoit. 'And tell

Gabriel to chase up that baseline sample from the London Police. Speak to me, Nina.'

'It's a co-op,' said Caron, arriving out of breath. 'A few men club together, create a co-operative with a silly name, buy a bit of cheap land in the back of beyond and build a basic shelter so they can meet up at weekends to drink, shoot game, cut wood...'

'...and drug, rape and murder young women,' added Rolland.

'Who's the owner?' said Benoit.

'I can't get through to the land registry,' said Caron.

'You and Elena get down to the town hall and find out,' said Benoit. 'Break down doors if you have to. Better yet, speak to the mayor and promise him more TV if he helps us.'

The barn doors swung open again and Coulibaly and two subordinates walked out in suits, face masks and clear visors. Beyond them, Benoit recognised the shabby backdrop to some of Bertrand's photographic memorabilia - souvenirs of his sickening crimes.

Rappeneau's limp body dangled from the end of a rope. His green-tinged neck had been broken so violently that his head hung at a near right angle to his torso. His eyes bulged out of the sockets and his blackened tongue peeped between cracked lips. What was left of his hands dangled from bloodied sleeves and a chair sat on its side under his feet.

'We're ready to cut him down if you've seen enough,' said Coulibaly.

Benoit nodded. 'Can you say if the axe is what dismembered the female remains found near Seillans?'

'It's suggestive,' said Coulibaly. 'But, until tests confirm, it's just an axe.'

'There was blood on the blade,' said Rolland.

'It's old and could be animal blood,' said Coulibaly.

'Old?' said Benoit. 'Wasn't it used on Rappeneau?'

Coulibaly shook her head. 'The killer used a precision

instrument to cut off the victim's fingers - probably a scalpel. With those hands, he couldn't have pulled the rope around his neck. And there's bruising on his arms and a blow to his head. He had help.'

Benoit nodded. 'Have you got enough...?'

'Don't,' she interrupted, not looking at him. 'I had a dream last night that we were still here six months from now, working new sites with snow on the ground. Is this shit ever going to end?'

'Yes, it is, Grace,' said Benoit. 'How many dinners...?'

'About a thousand,' she sighed. 'But, Sergio, you close this fucker and get me home to my man and my beautiful kids and *I'm* buying.'

31

Trent sipped his black coffee on a chair in the ICP, watching Latour tapping away at his keyboard, Auger next to him, watching him work. Looking around, he noticed the prefab offices were considerably tidier. Desktops had been cleared and monitors not in use had been lain flat and secured. 'The new crime scene?' he said, looking at Latour and Auger's backs in turn. 'Is anyone going to tell me?' The two Frenchmen continued as though he didn't exist, Auger pointing at Latour's monitor, mumbling something inaudible.

'Are you moving the Command Post?' persisted Trent. No reply. 'Course you are. Nothing left to do here.' Trent paused, thinking of a different tack. 'What do you use to move a thing like this? One of those big flatbeds?' He waited in vain for his answer. 'Rappeneau's dead, isn't he?' Finally, Auger and Latour turned to him. 'Where?'

'In the hills, north east of Seillans,' said Latour. 'We move the Command Post tomorrow. Happy now?'

'Killed soon after he dropped off the radar, no doubt,' said Trent.

'Why do you say that?' said Auger.

Trent shrugged. 'He knew too much and had to be silenced.'

'What did he know?' said Auger.

'Same as Bertrand,' said Trent. 'Where the bodies are buried.'

Auger studied him. 'So do we, now.'

'We don't know where Barron and Cooper are buried,' said Trent.

'You think Rappeneau and Bertrand did?' said Auger.

'I suspect Rappeneau did,' said Trent.

'What makes you say that?' said Latour.

'Bertrand didn't run, Rappeneau did. He possessed knowledge that was dangerous to him and he knew it.'

'Maybe Bertrand didn't run because he'd already killed Rappeneau,' suggested Latour.

'If he'd silenced Rappeneau, he wouldn't need to shoot at the police.'

'You're very sure of yourself, aren't you?' said Auger.

'I'm an experienced detective.'

'And we're not?' said Auger.

'Gabriel, maybe,' said Trent, smiling at Auger's offended expression.

'Can we get on with this?' said Latour.

'If you're still looking for local rentals where Renfrew might be hiding, forget it,' said Trent.

'Why?' said Latour, not taking his eyes from the monitor.

'Because, he's committed a double murder and he's on the run,' said Trent. 'He was in no position to start looking for accommodation.'

'But, if he was planning to kill his wife *before* he got here, he could have rented somewhere before they travelled to France,' suggested Latour.

'But Renfrew didn't know he was coming to France until I put them on the plane,' said Trent.

'He's got a point,' said Auger.

'Renfrew had weeks after arriving at Villa Jasmin to scout around before the killing started,' said Latour.

'Maybe,' said Trent. 'But, by that time, I bet most rentals were already booked for the summer.'

'It didn't stop you,' said Latour.

'True,' conceded Trent. 'But I paid a premium.'

'Which Renfrew could also afford,' said Latour.

'Also, true,' said Trent, shrugging. He smiled at Auger. 'Excuse us two experienced detectives riffing about the case.'

Auger scowled. 'As you're so clever, what do *you* think we should be looking for?'

'I'd concentrate on remote empty properties, up for sale rather than rent,' said Trent. 'Something empty and hard to shift, where he could break in, unseen. And I'd have been looking for them as soon as I landed so, if French estate agents are the same as American realtors, the first thing they'd do is take details of interested foreign buyers for their mailing lists.'

Silence apart from the tapping of a keyboard. 'Okay,' said Latour. 'Date?'

'Renfrew arrived at the end of March,' said Auger. 'Look for enquiries from April onwards.'

'Problem is, we can access records for properties on sale and who bought them but, if no money changed hands, we'll have to ask agents for their mailing lists,' said Latour.

'And Renfrew probably gave a false name,' added Auger.

'Welcome to police work!' said Trent.

'Do you want to go back to your cell?' said Latour. Trent held up his hands in apology.

Latour resumed his tapping of the keyboard. 'Hundreds of remote farmhouses,' he mumbled. 'This could take a while.'

'I'll do some ringing round,' said Auger, reaching for his phone.

'Can't allow it, Daniel,' said Latour. 'Strict orders from the boss. You're off the roster. It's only a dozen calls at most. I'll do it.'

. . .

'I'LL MAKE MORE COFFEE,' said Trent, an hour later, standing to stretch his legs. He'd missed his workout that morning and was feeling it. Hunger was starting to bite too so he headed for the small kitchenette to fill the coffee machine and help himself to a croissant.

'Coming up empty,' said Latour, when Trent placed a coffee next to his monitor. 'I'm expanding the search area to a fifty-mile radius.'

'Don't bother,' said Trent. 'He wouldn't risk travelling that far in a strange country in a car he doesn't own with bodies in the trunk. Face it. Renfrew's had nearly two weeks to slip over the border. He's gone...' Trent hesitated '...unless...'

'Unless what?' said Latour.

'Try a search from the beginning of March,' said Trent.'

'But Renfrew didn't know he was coming to France until the end of March,' said Latour.

'Suppose, just for a second, he did know,' said Trent.

'Why the beginning of March?' said Latour.

'Because that's when he told his missing young assistant where he was planning to stash them,' said Auger, smiling. 'And she leaked it to Renfrew.' Latour turned back to his monitor. More tapping of keys.

Trent glared at Auger. 'She didn't leak anything. But if she was hacked...'

'Whoa,' exclaimed Latour. 'Got a hit. A farm, sold on March 3rd to...' he turned to them, excitement in his eyes '...a company in Singapore.'

'Where?' said Trent.

'It's about twenty miles away, up in the hills, north of Saint-Cézaire...wait a minute.' Latour's voice tailed off and his body seemed to stiffen. Auger crashed down the hastily-produced gun onto Latour's head, pointing it at Trent a split-second later, as the American prepared to leap.

'Don't!' warned Auger, as Latour's body crumpled to the floor. 'Not if you want to see Nell again.'

'She's alive?' breathed Trent, poised to attack.

'Yes, but she won't be unless you do *exactly* as I say.'

'I want to see her,' said Trent.

'That's the plan,' said Auger. 'Just follow my instructions.'

'How is...?'

'She's fine,' said Auger. 'Do we have a deal?'

Trent nodded, his body easing back onto the chair. 'How long?'

'How long what?' said Auger, examining Latour's empty holster. He opened the drawer of his desk but Latour's gun wasn't there either.

'You and Renfrew.'

Auger stepped over Latour's unconscious body and opened more drawers. 'Long before you brought him to France,' he said, frowning.

'One gun not enough?' said Trent. 'I'm flattered.'

Auger ignored him, picked up the set of precision screw-drivers and tossed them to Trent. 'Take off the tracker.'

'I don't know how.'

'I don't believe you,' said Auger. 'And if you haven't removed it in sixty seconds, I'll shoot you.' He pressed a timer on his watch.

Trent selected the appropriate tool and got to work on the device around his ankle while Auger scribbled some-thing on a post-it and fixed it to Latour's monitor.

'How the hell did you get hold of Nell?' said Trent, while he worked.

'Renfrew spotted her watching the house from the woods above Villa Jasmin, her car parked in the same lay-by you left your car.'

'He was expecting her?'

'He knew she'd come,' said Auger. 'It was the day before the drinks party so I had to drive over from Fayence and play copper. She had her guard down, tried to pretend she'd broken down. It was easy.'

'Where is she?' said Trent, tossing him the unfastened tracker.

'Safe.' Auger nodded at the stricken Latour. 'Pick him up.'

Trent hesitated. 'Why don't we leave him out of this?'

'Pick him up!' ordered Auger. Reluctantly Trent hoisted the unconscious Latour over his shoulder. 'Wait here.' Auger opened the door of the ICP and peered out, then stepped into the road, quickly opening the trunk of his Peugeot. With furtive glances towards the distant road blocks, he beckoned Trent to place Latour in the trunk.

Closing the trunk on the unconscious Latour, Auger took out a pair of handcuffs and threw them at Trent. 'Put those on and make sure I hear the click.' Trent fixed the cuffs around his wrists and locked them with a flourish. Auger tossed him back the tracker and Trent caught it. He gestured the American to the passenger seat and jumped in on the driver's side.

'Remember, do exactly as I say if you want to see Nell again.' He trained the gun on Trent. 'And as far as my colleague on the road block is concerned, you're going back to your cell. Say and do nothing to contradict that or he dies.'

THEY PASSED the road block without incident and Auger crossed the main highway to avoid the barriers blocking either side of the mass grave site at the bottom of the hill. The single-track lane into the village was a steep and sinuous back road, bordered by expansive houses, set in generous grounds, panoramic pools perched vertiginously on the hillside.

At the end of the diversion, the Peugeot re-emerged onto the D19, beyond the uphill road block and Auger turned towards the centre of Seillans. At the main traffic lights, they both glanced across at the metal grille, pulled down across the darkened façade of Chez Bertrand.

'You didn't have to kill Bertrand, did you?' said Trent. 'You executed him to shut him up.' Auger kept his eyes front.

'Don't you watch the movies, Auger? If you're going to kill me, you owe me an explanation.'

Auger considered. 'I do, don't I? You're right about Bertrand. And Rappeneau knew even more but Bertrand was the more dangerous so I put him down quickly - like a rabid dog - and, given what the two of them did for sport, who can blame me?'

'And Rappeneau?'

Auger smiled at remembered pleasures. 'I took my time with him. By the end he was begging for death.' His expression hardened. 'They were animals. I did the world a favour.'

The sun was beginning to dip so Auger switched on the sidelights and, when the traffic lights turned green, drove down into the valley, towards the main road. At another junction, he retrieved the tracker bracelet from Trent and flung it over a wall into a huge tangle of brambles. He then pulled out a chunky yellow walkie-talkie and depressed his thumb on the side of the casing.

'It's me, over. I've got him. On my way. Get the girl ready. Over.' He stared at Trent. 'If I'm not there in half an hour, kill her. Over and out.' The lights turned green and Auger drove on.

'Why was Bertrand shooting at police?' said Trent. Auger smiled at Trent. 'He wasn't shooting indiscriminately, was he? He was aiming for Gagnon. Jerome was onto you.'

Auger nodded. 'I was collecting the Easter day photographs from locals to pass to him.' He stared at Trent, giving him a few seconds to work it out.

'But not before deleting the ones with you in them,' said Trent. 'The pictures of you talking to Renfrew that night.'

'We met in the square,' said Auger. 'That's what they say, isn't it? Meet where there are plenty of people and no-one will notice.' He grunted in amusement. 'If Favre hadn't taken so many pictures for his damned website, Benoit would never have known Carla was sitting alone for twenty minutes and he wouldn't have thought to search for images of Renfrew in the village.

'I was off duty that night but on the way to meet him, I helped a couple of colleagues break up a fight. There was an arrest, minor shit, but people took pictures - as they do. There was even a paragraph in the local paper. When Jerome found out, he became suspicious, realised there were no pictures in the material I was passing him...'

'And he was on the verge of mentioning it to Benoit.'

'I couldn't allow that,' said Auger. 'I want you to know, I hope he pulls through. Jerome's a good man and I didn't start down this path thinking colleagues were going to get hurt. That wasn't supposed to happen. In spite of everything I've done, I'm still a policeman.'

'You're breaking my heart,' snarled Trent.

'I don't expect you to understand.'

'Trying to kill a fellow officer? Why would I?'

'I told Bertrand I didn't want Jerome dead, just incapacitated,' said Auger. 'I couldn't take the shot myself so I made Bertrand do it. He was a Legionnaire, after all.'

'Jerome nearly died,' said Trent. 'He still might.'

'I know,' said Auger, softly. 'Like I said, I hope he pulls through.'

'If he regains consciousness, you'll be implicated.'

'Will I though?' said Auger. 'I didn't shoot Jerome and Bertrand tried to shoot me too. And I've got deniability on the photographs. I was in them, didn't think they were important, didn't know who Renfrew was at the time...'

'And when I suddenly disappear?' said Trent.

'You've been trying to escape since we arrested you,' said Auger, smiling. 'You finally succeeded. But don't worry, you won't be disappearing...'

'Let me guess. I attacked you, took you hostage and made you drive me away from the ICP at gunpoint. To cover my tracks, I killed Latour but, when I tried to kill you, you got the drop on me. That's why you wanted Latour's gun - to choreograph some kind of shootout.'

'You're good,' said Auger, with genuine appreciation. 'And who wouldn't believe it of a stone-cold killer like you. Someone with a history of murdering cops.' Trent's eyes narrowed. 'Yeah, I know all about it. Renfrew told me.'

'Exactly how *did* you persuade Bertrand to shoot Jerome?' said Trent. Auger stared expectantly at Trent. 'You knew what he and Rappeneau had done to those women.'

'I found out a few months ago,' said Auger. 'I was driving past the lay-by, below where they dumped the body parts. It was dark. There was a car parked and Rappeneau was inside, just sitting there behind the wheel. For some reason, I sensed something wasn't right. I drove on but it troubled me. We'd arrested him for inappropriate sexual contact with a minor the year before and he'd escaped with a caution so I was concerned he might have a kid in the car.

'Down the hill, I pulled over and walked back. When I shone my torch in the car, he was on his own, masturbating. I gave him a warning and sent him on his way. But it bothered me so I did some research. If you're FBI, you'll understand why.'

'Some killers relive their kills by masturbating where they dumped their victims,' said Trent.

'Exactly,' said Auger. 'So, the next morning, I went back to look around. It was tough going and it took me a while, scrabbling around in the undergrowth but, well...you know what I found. When I picked up Rappeneau, he folded like a bedsheet, told me everything, even threw Bertrand's name at me before I thought to ask.'

'But you didn't arrest him,' said Trent.

Auger's smile disappeared. 'No.' He drove over a busy crossroads following signs for Saint-Cézaire. 'Something came up and I suddenly had a use for him.'

'And when his usefulness ended, you delivered a more permanent sentence,' said Trent.

'And left him strung up to rot in the same place he and Bertrand killed those poor women.' Auger nodded with satisfaction. 'That's where Benoit and the others have been all day.'

'Convenient his body being found, leaving you in the ICP with just me and Latour.'

Auger smiled. 'Wasn't it?'

'You arranged that too?'

'I knew Madame Rappeneau was being watched so, last night, I used her husband's phone to text her directions and ask her to bring food the next morning. When she got there, she'd find her worthless husband dead. I knew she'd be followed.'

'And Gabriel?' said Trent. 'He discovered something before you hit him.'

'The farm in the hills above Saint-Cézaire,' said Auger. 'It belonged to my parents. Renfrew bought it a month before you brought him to Seillans. That's when we met. He flew to France in his private jet to complete the sale and look the place over. I was distraught having to sell my birth right to pay off my parents' debts...'

'And he used that against you.'

'One way of looking at it,' said Auger. 'Before he flew back to Singapore, he invited me up for a drink. We got talking and he promised to give me the farm and money besides...'

'On condition you killed his wife and whoever he selected as his body double,' said Trent. 'You butchered five people for a piece-of-shit farm...'

'I was born on that farm,' growled Auger. 'My father too. There's nothing more important than walking on your own land, your own soil. It belongs to my family. It's in my blood.'

'Not much use if you're a fugitive, hiding on the other side of the world.'

'*If* I have to run, wherever I am, I'll know the farm belongs to my family. And I'll have money.'

'How much?'

'Enough.'

'Renfrew's a millionaire many times over.'

Auger snorted. 'It's not about the money.' He seemed to falter before repeating, 'It's not about the money.'

In the dying light, the car drove through the pretty village of Saint-Cézaire and shortly afterwards turned sharply up a hill, climbing along a pot-holed, one-track road, the headlights cutting a swathe through unlit countryside. There were fewer dwellings the higher they climbed, until they breasted the escarpment where the treeless plain stretched out to a desolate horizon.

'When did Renfrew know I was planning to hide them at Villa Jasmin?' said Trent.

'From the moment you suggested it to your little friend,' said Auger. 'And you're right. She didn't leak it. Renfrew knows Russians and they're the best hackers. They hacked into her computer the day after his friend, Logan, fell under that train two years ago. Been monitoring her comms ever since. Her phone too. Every text, email, everything. There's even a network of webcams in her flat they could piggyback. You delivered yourselves into his hands.'

Trent closed his eyes in self-recrimination. 'And the death threats?'

'He knew they were bogus,' said Auger. 'He's known who and where Nell Beaumont was for a very long time, keeping an eye on her in case she became a threat. He's a resourceful man but...'

'But what?'

'He's not a likeable person.'

'Did irony just die?'

'You mock me,' said Auger. 'And, yes, I've killed people like they were livestock because they meant nothing to me. I cut off their heads and their hands and mutilated Barron's corpse because that's what Renfrew paid me to do. It was work. But that doesn't mean I enjoyed it. But Renfrew? His own wife. To want her dead, okay - we all know the end of love can provoke strong feelings. But to want someone you once loved slaughtered like *that*?' Auger shook his head in disgust. 'That's a hatred I can't imagine.'

'It's not hatred,' said Trent. 'Renfrew's a sociopath. He feels nothing. The only reason he wanted her killed like that was to support the narrative of a mafia hit and make his own death seem more convincing.'

'I can believe it,' said Auger. 'It was the hardest thing I've ever had to do. Worse than watching my parents die.'

'It gets easier with practice,' said Trent. 'You'll have no trouble killing Nell and me.'

Auger was unable to meet his eyes. 'You're wrong and I'm sorry it has to end this way. At least you get some time together before you die.'

'She's really alive?'

'I've said so, haven't I?' said Auger, bristling.

'If you've hurt her...'

'Not a scratch, I swear,' said Auger. 'Even though Renfrew wanted her killed.'

'Then why isn't she dead?'

'Because I only kill when it's necessary,' said Auger. 'And I needed Nell to get to you. Renfrew wants you but I *need* you. You're a killer, escaping extradition and my path to the life I want. Before you arrived on the scene, I thought I'd have to run. Now? Maybe not.'

'What about Nell? She's got her whole life in front of her.'

'I'm sorry,' said Auger.

'And I suppose her disappearance will be chalked up to two dead serial killers from your village,' said Trent.

'Already in hand,' said Auger, glancing smugly at Trent. 'I left her car at Rappeneau's barn.'

'You've thought of everything.'

'I flatter myself I have,' said Auger.

'So, where's Renfrew now?'

'What do you mean?'

'If Nell's at the farm, alive, against Renfrew's wishes, then he must be somewhere else.'

Auger smiled. 'All in good time.' He drove the car over a cattle grid and along a dirt track towards an imposing stone farmhouse that loomed out of the darkness. A welcoming light glowed in a downstairs window. Beyond the house, Auger pulled to a halt in the middle of a rough, concrete quadrangle, partially enclosed by outbuildings on all sides.

'We're here.'

32

'Gabriel.' Benoit threw open the ICP door and felt for the light switch. 'Where is everyone?'

The prefabricated cabin flooded with light and Benoit made a beeline to Latour's monitor to peel off the attached note.

We've taken Trent back to Fayence for the night.
We'll meet you at the DR for dinner.

Daniel

'ALRIGHT FOR SOME,' said Rolland.

'I'll make fresh coffee,' growled Dugrippe, marching into the kitchenette.

Benoit absent-mindedly picked a set of car keys from the floor beneath Latour's chair and tossed them on the desk. His phone rang and he sat down to power up his computer, while he answered. 'Directeur. Yes. I was about to ring with developments. When? Let me know when you have a date and I'll have Trent ready to transport.' He then spent several minutes briefing her about the discovery of Rappeneau's body and the background to his, and Bertrand's, crimes.

'Yes, a terrible state of affairs for the village. Residents are going to have a lot to deal with but at least a positive conclusion when you break the news. No, we don't know who killed him and he was tortured first so, whoever did it, took their time. I'll have Gabriel send you a full report. No, I won't,' he corrected himself. 'He's gone to dinner. I'll do it myself.'

Benoit listened then broke into a huge smile. 'Thank you, Valerie. I'll pass it on. They'll be thrilled.' He ended the call and grinned at Dugrippe and Rolland. 'Jerome has stabilised and his vital signs are improving. The surgeon is hopeful he's going to pull through.' Dugrippe and Rolland yelled their pleasure and stomped aggressively around the ICP, concluding with a violent high-five.

'Thank *Christ*,' said Rolland, her fists clenched. She blew out her cheeks after the emotion began to dissipate.

Dugrippe blinked a tear from his eye. 'Wow. There is a God. What was that about Trent?'

'The government has received extradition papers and approved them,' said Benoit. 'The FBI will be sending someone to take him into custody for repatriation.'

'So, he's not facing the death penalty?' said Rolland.

'It's on a Chicago warrant and Illinois don't practice capital punishment,' said Benoit.

Rolland nodded. 'Pity. I was getting used to having him around. He'll be distraught to be hauled away before we find Nell Beaumont's body.'

'Tough shit,' said Dugrippe. 'He gave us what we needed. Fuck him.'

'He was a cop, Thierry,' said Benoit.

'And he's gone rogue,' said Dugrippe.

'Whatever he's done in the past, we only caught him because he came back to Jasmin out of a sense of duty towards his clients,' said Rolland.

'Bullshit!' said Dugrippe. 'When a dog bites its master, you put it down.'

'Remind me not to buy you a puppy for Christmas.'

Caron walked into the ICP clutching papers and the celebrations over Gagnon's improved condition began again.

'You have something from the Land Registry?' said Benoit, when things had calmed down.

'Yes and no,' said Caron. 'Ownership on the co-op is opaque, which apparently is not unusual. The mayor said neither Bertrand nor Rappeneau are on the deeds. But the original owner is dead, so it looks like they paid cash to the widow for access, according to receipts we found going through Rappeneau's papers.'

'Cash isn't proof of ownership,' said Dugrippe.

'No, but it's common practice out here in the sticks,' said Caron. 'Assuming ownership ever fell into dispute or if the widow dies, they produce their signed receipt, get it notarised and they have a legal claim on the land.'

'Meanwhile, their names stay off the register,' said Benoit, gesturing at the sheaf of papers. 'Is that the receipt?'

'Amongst other things,' said Caron. 'We also found interesting papers regarding Rappeneau's recent building work. He's been spending a lot of money the last couple of months, over five thousand euros on building materials in the last four weeks alone, going back to the end of March...'

'...including a new cement mixer,' said Benoit.

'You know about that?' said Caron.

'Gabriel and I were privy to one of their riveting domestic disputes,' said Benoit. 'He's a builder. What of it?'

'First of all, he's building something substantial because he's got through five tons of stone in a month. Second, in amongst his receipts for expenses incurred, I couldn't find any copies of invoices billed to customers and there are no deposits in his financials.'

'He's a builder,' said Dugrippe. 'Maybe he was paid in cash.'

'Possible but we've stripped the Rappeneau house bare,' said Caron. 'If he was hoarding cash, we can't find it.'

'Madame mentioned he was owed money,' said Benoit. 'Maybe he hasn't been paid.'

'Or maybe he spent it at the PMU,' said Rolland. 'He liked a flutter.'

'No clue about where he was working?' said Benoit.

'None,' said Caron. 'No addresses in his records either but he's also been filing hefty receipts for his truck's petrol, which suggests it's not local.'

'What about the builder's merchant where he got the stone?'

'Nothing was delivered to the site,' said Caron. 'Rappeneau collected everything in his truck.'

'It's probably nothing but see where it leads,' said Benoit.

'After I sift through more of Jerome's photographs,' said Caron. The memory of their good news brought back the smiles.

AUGER JUMPED out of the Peugeot and opened the passenger door for Trent before stepping back, taking no chance with Trent's close combat skills and producing his gun and a torch. Trent swung his feet onto the damp concrete and levered himself into a standing position when it became clear Auger wouldn't be helping. Gesturing Trent away from the vehicle, Auger kicked the car door closed.

Night had fallen but the moon was bright and Trent looked around to take in what he could see of his surroundings, searching for potential escape routes should the opportunity present.

As well as the house, there were three separate outbuildings; an ancient row of stables which, although ramshackle, appeared to have been modernised with a new roof; a large barn, extensively restored and an even bigger silo, in a poor state of repair, if not ruin, its metal roof and walls badly holed.

The buildings were arranged in a rough rectangle, providing the farm's inner courtyard with partial shelter from the harsher elements of high-altitude weather but the air was still noticeably cooler. On the breeze, Trent could smell the faint odour of rotting manure though he couldn't hear or see any signs of livestock.

Another note reached his nostrils - the cool earthiness of damp cement. To confirm his sense of smell, he spied the upturned pot-belly of a cement mixer, standing at ease, next to the barn.

With the car engine silenced, they could hear Latour banging and shouting from the boot. Auger flicked the key fob to lock the car.

'What if he can't breathe?' said Trent.

'Then I save a bullet.'

'This, from the man wringing his hands about shooting Gagnon.'

'I don't like this any better than you,' said Auger. 'But I've enough on my plate with you to control and letting Gabriel out to stretch his legs only doubles my problems.'

'Nell!' shouted Trent, at the top of his voice.

'Knock yourself out,' said Auger. 'There's not a soul within five miles to hear you.'

'You promised I'd see her.'

Auger flicked the torch in the direction of the stables. 'That way.'

CARON TOOK a sip of coffee and sank onto her chair, flicking disinterestedly through photographs on the projector. 'Nothing worse than watching people eating and drinking, when you're hungry.' She looked at her watch then at Benoit before clicking onto the next photograph. 'And poor Gabriel and Daniel, drinking wine and eating dinner.'

'Wait until I see the malingering sods,' grumbled Dugrippe.

'Nine o'clock,' said Benoit, glancing at the clock. 'You three go. I've got to finish this briefing for Seigner.'

'We go together, boss,' said Rolland.

'That's odd,' said Caron, squinting at a vehicle on the edge of a photograph, a crowd gathered around. 'Is that what I think it is?'

'Looks like a police wagon,' said Dugrippe, approaching the screen for a closer look. 'Jerome mentioned something about a drunken scuffle in the square.'

'Costanza mentioned it too,' said Caron. 'She said an arrest was made.'

'People drinking all day,' shrugged Dugrippe. 'Always ends the same way.'

'Odd there are no pictures though,' said Caron.

'Not one?'

'No, and you know what people are like with cameras when something kicks off,' said Caron. 'You'd think there'd be one photograph, if only of the aftermath, but no. And, if there was an arrest, where are the police?'

Benoit's head shot up from his monitor. 'What did you say?'

'Where are the police?' repeated Caron. 'If there was an arrest there must be film but there's not a single gendarme on any photograph I've seen.'

'Give Daniel a call,' said Rolland. 'Ask him who was on duty that night.'

'No,' snapped Benoit, his voice reverberating around the room like a crack of thunder. Rolland, Dugrippe and Caron stared. 'Don't ring Daniel,' he added, at normal volume. 'Call Fayence and ask the duty officer. Then text Gabriel and Daniel and tell them to get back here right away. Just that. No details. Understood?'

'Yes, boss,' said Caron, exchanging puzzled glances with Dugrippe and Rolland.

~

TRENT APPROACHED THE STABLE BLOCK, Auger a safe distance
behind, gun at the ready. In the dark, it was difficult to gauge
the ground he'd need to cover before his captor could get off
a shot and, given Auger's prowess with a gun, Trent was
reluctant to try.

A few feet from the stable, his eye was drawn to a large
earthmover in the dark meadow beyond the silo, almost at
the limit of his vision. Its scoop sat poised but inert, behind
a rough pyramid of dirt that dwarfed the bright yellow vehicle. Next to the dirt, Trent saw what looked like a pit, cut into
the slope of the earth, about ten feet wide. He couldn't see
the pit bottom, only a dark wall of cleaved earth beyond the
pit's entrance. But he couldn't fail to notice the double line
of tyre tracks which approached the lip before descending
into the bowels of the earth.

Even in poor light, Trent could see the tracks hadn't been
made by an earthmover's giant tyre. A car had been driven up
to and into the pit and he had a pretty good idea which one.

'Barron,' he muttered, turning to face Auger, ten yards to
his rear. His gun was supported by both hands, raised to fire.
'Barron's car!' he shouted.

'Do you want a prize?' sneered Auger. 'Nell's in the end
stall. I'm doing you a favour. Make the most of it.'

Trent turned back to the stable and opened the door of
the end stall.

'PHILLIPE AND RODRIGUEZ MADE THE ARREST,' said Rolland,
holding her hand over the receiver. 'But Auger was there. He
was off duty but pitched in to help.'

'Get contact numbers for Phillippe and Rodriguez, in
case I need a word,' said Benoit.

'Isn't Rodriguez on the barrier?' said Dugrippe.

'Get him in here,' said Benoit. Dugrippe hurried out of

the ICP to set off down the dark lane. 'Adele, ask the duty officer what time Trent was returned to his cell.'

Rolland put her phone back to her ear to pose the question. Her eyes widened and she nodded slowly then ended the call. 'Trent's not in his cell. They haven't seen him since he left the station with Auger this morning.'

'Ring Gabriel. Now.'

'I have,' said Caron. 'His phone is off.'

'Adele, ring the Deux Rocs. Ask Favre if he's there. Nina! Get Trent's whereabouts from the tracker.'

'Which one?' said Caron.

'Both,' replied Benoit.

Rolland stepped outside to make her call as Dugrippe returned, panting. He ushered in Rodriguez, the gendarme promptly saluting.

'You wanted to speak about the arrest at the fête, Commandant?' said Rodriguez.

'Never mind that now,' said Benoit. 'What time did Auger and Latour leave with Trent?'

Rodriguez looked at his watch. 'I moved the barrier for them about two hours ago but...'

Rolland returned. 'No sign of Gabriel, Auger or Trent at the hotel.'

'Commandant...' began Rodriguez.

'Try Auger's number,' said Benoit.

'I did,' said Rolland. 'His phone is off too.'

'Commandant,' repeated Rodriguez. 'Lieutenant Latour wasn't in the car. It was just Sergeant Auger and the American.'

'But Gabriel's car is here,' said Dugrippe.

'They were in Sergeant Auger's car,' said Rodriguez.

'Who was driving?' barked Benoit.

'Auger,' said Rodriguez.

'Auger's suspended,' said Rolland. 'He doesn't have his service weapon.'

'No, but Latour does,' said Benoit, his face like stone.

'So, maybe Trent took Gabriel's gun and got the drop on Auger,' said Dugrippe.

'If he did, I didn't see Trent holding it,' said Rodriguez. 'And he was cuffed.'

'Put out a bulletin on Auger's vehicle. And emphasise Auger and Trent are to be treated as hostiles...'

'Boss?'

'You heard me. One of them is armed, so consider them both highly dangerous until we know which one - approach with maximum caution. Rodriguez....' Benoit gathered up the set of car keys from Latour's desk and tossed them at the gendarme. 'Check Latour's Renault - make sure he's not in the trunk. If he isn't, rustle up a few officers and sweep the ground around the ICP, including the villa. Gabriel may be hurt. Or worse.' Rodriguez stared, uncomprehending. 'Move!' Rodriguez jumped out of the ICP like a startled cat.

'What the hell's going on, boss?' said Dugrippe.

'*Where are the police?*' said Benoit. 'The last thing Jerome said to me before he slipped into a coma.'

'I don't...'

'It was a message,' said Benoit. 'Jerome was agitated before he was shot. He kept trying to tell me something but Auger was always there. He must have realised the pictures Auger was collecting from locals had been edited.'

'Edited how?' said Rolland.

'Photographs deleted,' said Caron, nodding. 'Incriminating photographs...'

'Of what?' said Dugrippe.

'Of Auger at the fête, having a conversation with Harry Renfrew,' said Benoit.

There was a shocked silence as detectives weighed the implications.

'Auger was Renfrew's hired help,' said Rolland.

'He must have realised Jerome was onto him,' said Dugrippe.

'And you think Auger forced Bertrand to shoot Jerome?' said Caron.

'I don't doubt it,' said Benoit. 'And for that, he'd need a huge amount of leverage and I think we can guess what it was.'

'Then, Auger executed Bertrand to shut him up,' said Rolland.

'Nina!' said Benoit, impatiently. 'We need that location now.'

'Just a few more seconds to triangulate,' said Caron, furiously tapping keys, as the others checked their firearms and gathered car keys. 'The bracelet has him south of Seillans. The other signal is in the hills, north of Saint-Cézaire.'

'Saint-Cézaire?' said Benoit, holstering his gun. 'That's it. Two cars. Nina with me in the lead. Adele, call for back-up and get a helicopter in the air. Use my code.'

They burst out of the ICP. Latour's trunk was open but the space was empty.

'The lieutenant's gun is here, sir,' said Rodriguez, holding Latour's service weapon by the barrel.

Benoit acknowledged as he ran to his car. 'You have your orders.'

The two vehicles were gone in seconds, screaming along the tight lane to the main highway.

Trent stepped inside the dark stable stall, peering into the gloom. 'Nell?' No answer. When his eyes accustomed to the dark, he spotted an indeterminate bundle on the cold concrete floor at the back of the stall. He felt around for a switch on the wall and flooded the stable with light. A yellow walkie-talkie hung from a nail next to the switch. He ran to pull back the thin blankets balled up on a small mattress and found a bare foot, ice cold to the touch.

'Nell?' Throwing off the blankets, he saw it was her and felt for a pulse on her lifeless wrist, rubbing her limbs as well as he could in handcuffs. A few seconds later, he heard a soft moan emanate from her mouth. 'Nell, wake up.' She tried to speak and he leaned in to decipher her mumbling.

'Megan,' she breathed. 'My name's Megan.' His sigh of relief gave way to anger when he saw the needle marks on her arms and he turned to the door to vent his anger on Auger. 'What have you done to her?'

'Given her something to keep her docile...'

Trent jumped to his feet. 'If you or anyone else has...'

'No-one's taken advantage of her,' Auger replied, angrily. He aimed his gun at Nell and Trent froze. 'I don't enable perverts, I execute them.'

'Then why drug her?'

'I'm away, working on a complex investigation,' said Auger. 'And my partner likes the quiet life.'

'Renfrew's here?' said Trent.

'Renfrew? Yes, he's here.' Auger gestured with his gun. 'Come and see.'

'I'm not leaving Nell,' said Trent. 'She's freezing - she needs to be in the warm.'

Auger considered for a second. 'Bring her. He'll be pleased to finally meet her.'

Trent stared at Auger then bent down to the unconscious Nell and gathered her up. Before doing so, he covertly pulled up the mattress to inspect the underside. It was soiled and wet though the stable floor was dry.

PASSING Lac de Saint-Cassien in convoy, Benoit's phone rang in the lead car. 'Get that, Nina,' he said, concentrating on keeping up speed on the dark country roads.

Caron reached into his jacket, extracted his phone. 'Gueyrande,' she said, after a glance at the screen. 'Hello, doctor. It's Nina. This isn't the best time - we're operational and the boss is driving. Okay, quickly.' A pause. 'What?' exclaimed Caron, loud enough to attract Benoit's attention.

'What?' said Benoit.

Caron held up a hand. 'Then who...? Can you send a picture to this phone? Thank you.' She rang off and stared at Benoit, stunned. 'You're not going to believe this...'

33

T rent carried Nell through the stone-flagged kitchen, dipping his head to avoid a couple of low beams. A closed door blocked their way but Auger pushed it open and stepped back to a safe distance, allowing Trent to pass with his burden.

He emerged into a large room, shabbily but comfortably furnished, to be greeted by a blast of heat from a huge, cast-iron log burner, housed inside an ancient brick fireplace with standing room for several people.

The flames licking around a spent log in the hearth should have been the focal point of the room. Instead, Harry Renfrew, seated behind a sturdy desk near the fire, drew the eye.

'You're finally here, Trent,' said the Englishman, smiling broadly. 'Welcome to my home, for a few more hours, at least. Excuse me not getting up.'

Benoit's investigation had raised the possibility that the mutilated male corpse at Villa Jasmin might not be Harry Renfrew but, seeing him alive and in the flesh, was more than enough to tie Trent's tongue.

Renfrew nodded towards a vast old leather sofa behind Trent. 'Sit. Be comfortable. You'll be here a while.'

'If not forever,' said Trent, finding his voice.

'Gallows humour,' said Renfrew. 'I like it.'

Trent lay Nell's unconscious form onto the leather cushions, but stayed on his feet.

'The man said sit,' ordered Auger, pointing the gun. Trent stared down the barrel of the Sig Sauer P229 Legion Compact then lowered himself onto the sofa. Sweat dotted his brow and he loosened his shirt.

'Forgive the heat,' said Renfrew, glancing at the fire. 'I'm not used to mountain temperatures after so long in the Singapore furnace.'

'My heart bleeds,' said Trent.

'Not for another hour,' said Renfrew, laughing. 'Do the honours, Auger.'

Warily, Auger circumnavigated Trent and threw two large logs onto the embers, not daring to put down the gun. He left the glass fronted door slightly ajar to suck in a reviving draught and returned to stand across the entrance to the kitchen.

'It's good to see you,' said Renfrew. 'I've been starved of conversation while Auger's been away, misdirecting your investigation.' For the first time, his gaze fell upon Nell's slackened features. 'Is that who I think it is?'

'The vengeful Nell Beaumont,' said Auger, grinning at Trent's confusion. 'I promised you I wouldn't let harm come to her.'

'Promised?' said Renfrew. 'What am I missing?'

'Nell Beaumont has been at the farm, the entire time,' said Auger.

'What?' said Renfrew. 'You said she was dead.'

'And she will be.'

'I'm paying good money...'

'And you'll get what you paid for,' insisted Auger. 'But I needed her alive. Trent's my fall-guy and Nell was the only way to lure him here on his best behaviour. In case you hadn't noticed, he's a difficult man to control.'

'Oh, I noticed,' said Renfrew, staring at Trent. 'You got much closer than you realised in Chicago, my friend. I wanted you terminated but my clients were wary of the attention *two* dead federal agents would attract. You and Nell have caused me a fair amount of trouble and expense, over the years...'

'You can afford it,' said Trent.

'I confess I can,' said Renfrew. 'But I want to be alive to enjoy it.'

'Haven't your Russian friends taken care of that?' said Trent.

'*Friends*?' Renfrew laughed. 'The Russian mafia are brutal beyond words and they do *not* have friends. They have collaborators or they have enemies. There's no middle ground. Worse, they're massive control freaks. Money and power are all they respect and, if you cross their path, you roll over and do exactly what they say or *you* become their enemy, for however long you can stay alive.

'My client's army of hackers may have helped me dodge a few bullets over the years but having to tell Russian gangsters that a situation they thought resolved seventeen years ago was coming back to haunt them, did very little for my reputation. And those death threats your sleepy young protégé was throwing around on the web have made a certain client review my long-term usefulness. Not a healthy option.'

'So, you're actually fleeing for real,' said Trent.

'I prefer the term retiring,' said Renfrew. 'And the more people think my retirement is terminal, the safer I'll be.'

'How did your wife feel about that?' said Trent.

Renfrew's eyes narrowed. 'That philandering bitch got exactly what she deserved. I gave her the world and she betrayed me with my best friend, Brad - someone else who will soon discover the terrible cost of disloyalty.' He speared a glance at the gendarme. 'Where are your manners, Auger? Pour our guest a drink.'

'You said he doesn't drink.'

'So, I did,' said Renfrew. 'Looks like I'm drinking alone.'

'It's a special occasion,' said Trent. 'I'll have what you're having.'

'Good for you,' said Renfrew, nodding at Auger.

Auger crossed the room and poured two large whiskies from a decanter, warming on a small table by the fire, and placed a leaded glass on the leather blotter in front of Renfrew. He balanced Trent's drink on the arm of the sofa, a respectable distance from his combat arc, before moving away. Trent made no move to reach for his glass.

'Speaking of my wife, I want to thank you,' said Renfrew. 'Jasmin was perfect for our needs and Carla absolutely loved the place. For a while, I even thought we might be reconciled until Auger discovered she was having it off with some coarse bar owner in the village.'

'So that little fiction was your idea, was it?' said Trent, smiling at Auger.

The gendarme raised an amused eyebrow at Renfrew. 'What did I tell you?'

'Auger said you'd try and drive a wedge between us,' said Renfrew. 'Save your breath, Trent. My wife got what she deserved.'

'Nobody deserves that,' said Trent.

Renfrew nodded. 'I'm sure it looked bad but I want you to know, she didn't suffer. I couldn't bear the idea of Carla in pain so, when the time was right, I slipped Rohypnol into her wine - just enough to get her slurring and swaying, help persuade the Dutch couple to leave or they'd have been there all night. And, after Margo and Piet left, Auger gave her an injection to put her completely under. Trust me, she was doped up to the eyeballs when he did the deed.'

'So, you didn't have the balls to kill her yourself,' said Trent.

'Don't waste your last hour trying to guilt trip me,' said Renfrew. 'I work in the financial markets where a conscience is a disability that I dispensed with decades ago. Besides, what's the point of being richer than some actual countries, if you can't leave the dirty work to the little people…no offence, Auger.'

'None taken,' said Auger.

'No, I inflict violence from behind a terminal,' said Renfrew. 'That's why I hired Auger and he hasn't disappointed. Things have gone so smoothly. Even before Piet and Margo had left Jasmin, Auger was at Villa Lavendre giving Barron his tranquiliser and putting a bullet in his little bum boy. While I was still enjoying the party, Auger was stashing the lovely Ash and their luggage in the trunk of Barron's car and stripping my double for his bravura performance in the pool.

'When my Dutch guests left, Auger drove Barron's car to Jasmin, walked Roger up to the pool and fired up the chainsaw while I removed items from Barron's washbag to swap for mine.'

'So, you didn't even see Auger do the deed,' said Trent.

'Fuck, no,' said Renfrew, grimacing. 'I don't have his farmer's stomach for slaughter. No, I sat behind the wheel waiting for Auger to throw the heads and hands into the trunk.' He winked at Trent. 'Plus, a couple of extra bits and pieces from Barron.

'The minute the trunk slammed shut and Auger banged on the roof, I drove back here for a stiff drink and left him to clean up.' He shook his head in wonder. 'I've got to say, Trent, I see why you do what you do. The whole experience that night was exhilarating. By the way, what was the point of that sneaky little camera Auger found hidden amongst the DVDs? Yours?'

'A visual record, in case anything went wrong,' said Trent. 'Normally I'd install a live feed…'

'Which you couldn't do without an internet connection,' said Renfrew, nodding. 'Of course.'

'When did you find it?' said Trent.

'When I was wiping down for prints,' said Auger. 'Don't worry, I destroyed the storage card. You and Nell are the last of the loose ends.'

'And you've even dug our grave,' said Trent, smiling. 'Now, that's planning.'

'Sorry, there won't be a headstone,' said Renfrew. 'I'm impressed how well you're taking this. I could've used a man with your talents.'

'You know where I'll be if you need me,' said Trent.

'I'm not sure I will,' said Renfrew. 'It seems Auger has different plans. I suspect he needs your body found with smoking gun in hand so he can play the avenging hero. Am I right?'

Auger's expression was inscrutable. 'Something like that.'

'You've covered everything then,' said Trent.

'He's a policeman,' said Renfrew. 'I pay handsomely and expect competence.'

'Is that why you didn't check the contents of the trunk when you got back here?' said Trent.

Renfrew shuddered. 'Why the hell would I do that?'

'For one thing, to make sure your wife's head and hands were in there,' said Trent.

'My wife's...?'

'Daniel didn't tell you?'

'Tell me what?' said Renfrew.

Trent smiled. 'Your wife's body parts didn't make it into Barron's car.'

'What?'

'He's lying,' said Auger.

'Why would I lie?' said Trent. 'The car's here. Let's go and see Mrs Renfrew's head to prove me wrong.'

Renfrew stared at Auger. 'What's he talking about? Why wouldn't Carla's head be in the trunk?'

'He's trying to turn us against each other,' said Auger. 'Ignore him.'

'That's right,' said Trent. 'Don't listen to me. Listen to the man who told you Nell was already dead.'

'Auger?' said Renfrew.

'Tell him, Daniel!' said Trent. 'Or I will.'

'Shut up!' said Auger.

'Tell me what?' said Renfrew.

'That Daniel couldn't put your wife's head in the trunk, because he didn't want you to see it,' said Trent.

'I didn't want to see it either,' said Renfrew.

'Ah, but he couldn't take that chance,' said Trent. 'That's why, after sending you on your way, he put her severed head and hands in his own car and dumped them separately.'

'I don't believe you,' said Renfrew.

Trent pointed his cuffed hands at the door. 'The car's fifty metres away.'

Auger aimed the gun at Trent. 'That's enough!'

'If her head's not in the car, where is it?' said Renfrew.

Slowly, Trent rose from the sofa. 'He threw it into the undergrowth near Seillans.'

'Sit down,' said Auger.

'And you know that, how?' said Renfrew.

'Because the police found it,' said Trent.

'What?' said Renfrew. 'Auger?'

Auger regripped the gun. 'He's lying. Don't fall for it.'

'Fifty metres,' said Trent, indicating the door again.

'I want to look in the trunk,' said Renfrew.

'He's buying time,' said Auger. 'Ignore him.'

'You can spare two minutes,' said Trent. 'Come on. Take us to see Carla's head, make a liar out of me.'

'I want to see in the trunk,' said Renfrew. There was silence apart from the spitting and cracking of burning logs. 'Auger?'

Auger licked his lips. 'There wasn't room for both heads in the trunk. I put your wife's head and hands in my car and disposed of them separately.'

Renfrew exploded. 'You mean the police did find Carla's head? Where is it now?'

'In a forensic lab in Nice,' said Trent.

'I don't believe this,' said Renfrew.

'I had no idea the police would find it,' said Auger.

'Yes, he did,' said Trent. 'He was counting on it because

your wife's head and hands weren't the only remains dumped there.'

'I don't understand,' said Renfrew.

'Two local men have been abducting and killing young women for years then discarding their remains in the same spot,' said Trent.

'Shut up,' said Auger.

'Auger found out but instead of arresting them, he used them...'

'Those women deserved to be found,' shouted Auger. 'They deserve a decent burial.'

'Like Zouzou?' said Trent.

'Yes, like Zouzou,' said Auger. 'She was a beautiful person. She didn't deserve to die like that.'

'What the fuck are you talking about?' said Renfrew.

'Two men abducting and murdering young women,' said Auger. 'I killed them both and one of them was fucking your wife so it's all good.'

'But Carla's head...?' said Renfrew.

'...wasn't found until animals and insects had eaten away her face,' said Auger. 'And before I disposed of it, I smashed up all your wife's teeth.'

'You did what?' said Renfrew.

'A precaution to prevent identification,' explained Auger. 'You should thank me for my diligence.'

'Thank you?' said Renfrew, angrily. 'I'm no scientist but even I know they can reconstruct a face from a skull and scraps of DNA. That's what they do. All that planning...'

'I killed her on *your* orders,' said Auger. 'I cut off her head and hands on *your* orders. What do you care what I did with the head? Your wife is dead, Harry. Don't you see? It's actually better that she's identified because her death confirms yours. You're in the clear.'

'Then why didn't he just tell you that instead of lying?' said Trent.

'I don't know,' said Renfrew, reaching for his whisky glass. When he took a sip of the amber liquid, Trent saw the manacles around Renfrew's wrists and turned, in shock to the smiling Auger.

Renfrew jangled his chains like Marley's ghost. 'These? A temporary disagreement about the financial settlement. I've agreed to double the money but Auger thinks I'm gullible enough to transfer the funds before I'm safely over the border. It's just a question of negotiation.' He glared at Auger. 'Though now I'm thinking I should demand a refund.'

'How much are you paying?' said Trent.

'Two million dollars,' said Renfrew.

'Plus, the deeds to the farm,' said Auger.

'Already signed over with half million in cash as an advance,' said Renfrew.

'Then you've signed your death warrant, Harry,' said Trent.

'Don't be absurd,' said Renfrew. 'If Auger kills me, he loses a fortune and has to live out his days on this piece-of-shit scrub instead of a life of ease anywhere in the world.'

'A pity your money hasn't made you smarter,' said Trent. 'Don't you wonder why Auger needs me as a fall-guy if he's heading to a beach on the other side of the world? Or why a man leaving a place forever, needs a builder to renovate a barn? He's not interested in your money, Harry. He wanted the farm. The cash is a bonus he can live without.'

'You're being ridiculous,' said Renfrew.

'The problem with people who worship money,' said Trent, smiling at Auger.

'It's all they understand,' said Auger, nodding. 'They have no soul.'

'Who needs a soul when I've got more money than I can ever spend?' said Renfrew.

'For a start, so you can understand what drives the rest of us,' said Trent. 'Love. Family. Belonging. You die tonight, Harry, and I can't say you don't deserve it.'

'This is getting tiresome,' said Renfrew. 'Kill these two so we can finish our business and be on our way.'

'But I need Trent alive long enough to carry your body to the pit,' said Auger.

'My body?' said Renfrew, laughing. 'You can't kill me. What about the two million?'

'Trent's right,' said Auger. 'I have what I need.'

'You can't be serious.' Renfrew yanked hard at his chains, kicking the chair away and straining against the manacles, held firm by the ancient wood of the heavy desk. 'This has gone far enough. I should've been across the border a week ago, damn it. Release me.' Renfrew's anger increased and he scrabbled at the wood with his fingers. 'Auger!' he shouted. 'Unlock these chains.'

'It's time,' said Auger, gesturing at Nell. 'Pick her up.'

'No,' said Trent.

Auger pointed the gun at Nell. 'Then she dies now.' Trent moved into the line of fire. 'Step aside.'

'Or what?' said Trent.

'Daniel!' shouted Renfrew. 'I'll make it four million. I'll wire you the money from Italy. You'll never have to work again.'

'Daniel's not afraid of work, Harry,' said Trent. 'He's looking forward to returning the farm to its former glory. In fact, you'd be dead already if it wasn't for one thing.'

Auger raised an eyebrow. 'Oh, what's that?'

'You're afraid of losing the woman *you* love if you don't get the money *she* loves,' said Trent.

Auger's stunned expression turned into a smile. 'You're good. But don't underestimate my powers of persuasion. Pick up Nell.'

'Eight million, Daniel,' said Renfrew, breathless. 'Just let me go.'

'You're wasting your breath,' said Trent. 'By now, the police will know the head they found doesn't belong to your wife.'

'What?' exclaimed Harry. 'Then whose...?'

'A missing backpacker called Eugenie Marchand,' said Trent. 'Similar height, hair colour, age. Snatched to order by

Auger's unwilling accomplices, though I dare say they took out their frustrations on poor Eugenie.

'Auger planned everything down to the smallest detail. It's actually a thing of beauty, Harry, and he did it all for love. Something you wouldn't understand if you live to be a hundred.'

'He won't,' said Auger.

'Please,' begged Renfrew, hot tears running down his cheeks. 'Let me go. You can have it all.'

'You bet your life, Harry,' said Trent. 'And you lost. If it's any consolation, love has blinded Daniel as much as your money blinded you.'

'Trent!' pleaded Renfrew, skinning his wrists in a fresh attempt to escape his manacles. 'Get me out of here and *you* get the eight million.'

'Enough.' Auger aimed at Trent's chest and squeezed the trigger. The gun clicked but no bullet fired. Auger's expression darkened and he pulled the trigger again, with the same result.

'That's the gun I left at the villa for Harry's protection,' said Trent. 'Nell's as good as any qualified gunsmith and she prepped the gun before I collected it. It had a full clip - I checked. No doubt you did too. But Nell would know I'd spot blanks from the get-go, so I'm guessing she used a kinetic puller to open the casing and tip out the propellant.

'When she reassembled the bullet, it would look like regular ammo until you pull the trigger.' Trent's expression hardened. 'After all, when you're planning to confront the man who killed your mother, you'd be crazy to leave him a loaded gun, right?'

Auger hurled the weapon at Trent's head but he ducked and the gun hit the wall. The gendarme's sudden rage became a full-on lunge and Trent was knocked off balance and forced to backpedal across the room as Auger clawed at him, trying to get a grip. Eventually, Trent could retreat no further and he collided at speed with the log burner, knocking the whisky decanter over and spilling its contents onto the threadbare rug.

At the hearth, Trent felt the weight of the stove shift under the combined onslaught of the two men as Auger scrabbled furiously at Trent's neck, pushing him back against the hot metal.

Trent felt the back of his leg burn so he jammed his foot against the glass door and levered himself away from the stove, forcing the door to swing open. Glowing embers spilled onto the whisky-soaked rug and it began to smoulder and burn.

Auger tore at Trent's hair, trying to bang his head against the bricks but Trent dropped his cuffed hands then launched them upwards, hitting Auger on the chin and the Frenchman staggered back under the blow.

Now, Trent was on the front foot, following his unstable quarry across the room. Dazed, Auger spat blood from his mouth and tried to land a punch but Trent grabbed his fist and pulled Auger further off balance before swinging a double-fisted punch at Auger's head, catching him flush on the nose, spraying more blood and sending him spiralling backwards, arms whirling furiously through the air.

He crashed into a solid oak sideboard next to the kitchen door and hauled himself back to his feet to make a beeline for the unconscious Nell, staggering towards her like a drunk.

But Trent's advance was swift and his parry of Auger's weak punch, decisive. In the same movement, he stamped down on Auger's hyperextended leg and the crack provoked an evacuation of air from Auger's lungs, as he crumpled to the ground in agony.

A scream turned Trent's head. The rug was now fully on fire and flames were lapping at Renfrew's feet and he tore around in a limited arc like a caged animal, trying to get purchase and use his chains to drag the heavy desk away from the encroaching flames.

'Help me!' screamed Renfrew.

Trent leapt across and tried to help Renfrew smash the solid wood and dislodge his chains. Hot smoke began to seep across the ceiling so Trent scoured the room for something to break up the desk but he was forced to beat a retreat from the flames.

'Auger has the keys,' screamed Renfrew. 'Quick, man.'

Trent turned to see Auger was gone, though the keys to his Peugeot were on the ground, having fallen from a pocket in the struggle. He stooped to gather them then threw Nell over his shoulder to carry her out into the welcome embrace of the cool night air, to the soundtrack of Renfrew's growing distress.

Trent placed the inert Nell on the cold concrete and her eyes opened. He smiled. 'Hey, kid.'

'Mike...' she groaned. But Trent was already on the move towards Auger, at the driver's door of the Peugeot, frantically searching his pockets for the car keys. Seeing Trent sprinting over to him, Auger limped around the car to keep the vehicle between them, desperately looking around for escape routes.

'Keep away from me,' he screamed.

'Give me the keys to Renfrew's chains and you can go,' shouted Trent.

Auger laughed. 'You'd save him? He's a monster.'

'The keys,' repeated Trent.

Auger rummaged in a breast pocket and flung them at Trent. 'I hope you both fry.' He limped away into the darkness, grimacing with every agonising step, blood pouring down his face.

Trent grabbed the keys and ran back into the house.

~

AUGER GLARED across to the barn as he hobbled past the stable block, cursing. Nauseous with the pain and soaked to the skin, sweat blinding him, he scrambled to the lip of the pit. Barron's car was at the bottom of the steep incline which ended at the sheer wall of dirt, dug out by the earthmover.

The ground had dried after more than a week exposed to the air, so clods of earth had started crumbling onto the hood and roof. Auger hobbled down the slope towards the vehicle, trying not to imagine the smell he'd have to endure from its grisly cargo.

Above the roar of flames, consuming his parents' beloved home, Auger heard the unmistakable machine-gun rumble of a helicopter and hurried his step but, a few yards from the vehicle, he slipped on mud and fell on his damaged leg and an excruciating pain knifed through him, nearly taking his consciousness.

He bit his bottom lip to fight the waves of nausea and pain. Panting at the effort, he dragged himself back to his feet only to come face to face with the wolf, sitting calmly on the roof of the car, tongue hanging out, its vivid wild eyes fixed on him. The hole in the wolf's ear winked at Auger.

'Hello, old friend,' said Auger. Despite being unarmed, he assumed the firing position as well as he could manage, left hand supporting right, eye squinting to refine his aim.

But, instead of skittering away in fear, the wolf slowly got to its feet, a full-throated growl rumbling up from its depths, teeth bared in anger.

Auger smiled through bloodstained teeth and pulled something from a pocket, glancing at it before relaxing his hands to stand easy. As the wolf leapt through the air, he managed a final word.

'Carla.'

34

T rent raced into the farmhouse kitchen to be greeted by smoke billowing through the doorway. He examined Auger's keys and unlocked his cuffs. His wrists unshackled, he tore off his jacket, ran to the sink, threw it in and turned on the cold-water tap to soak the material. He wrapped the garment around his hands and held it above his head to push through the smoke and the wall of heat, into the main room.

Flames were licking across the ceiling and, even with his soaked jacket for protection, Trent felt like his head had been plunged into a pan of hot jam. He could barely see Renfrew through the smoke but moved further in, feeling the soles of his shoes beginning to warm on the stone flags.

The aroma of roasting meats reached his nostrils and he saw Renfrew. The Englishman was no longer screaming but was slumped across the desk that confined him, his head a pink-black ball, mouth set in a circular howl of agony.

Feeling serious heat on his head, Trent retraced his steps through the smoke to where he thought the doorway was. Travelling purely on instinct, he felt his way back to the kitchen and, a moment later, emerged into the cool night air, a riot of flashing lights filling his vision.

Thinking he must be losing consciousness, he sank to

his knees next to Nell, coughing and spluttering, smoke and steam rising from clothes and hair. He rubbed hands over his hair to be sure it wasn't alight then looked towards the sound of distant shouting and realised the lights were attached to half a dozen police cars, its occupants swarming over the site.

'Let me see your hands,' said a gruff voice from the shadows. Dugrippe.

'Never thought I'd be glad to see you,' said Trent, between coughs.

'Soon cure that.' Dugrippe grabbed his shoulder and flung him onto his stomach.

Spread-eagled, Trent's arms were roughly pinned behind his back and he felt the familiar pinch of handcuffs on his wrists. Caron advanced towards Nell, pulling off her coat and wrapping it around the shivering young woman, helping her to her feet and drawing her away from Trent.

'No,' screamed Nell, collapsing onto the concrete and scrambling back to Trent on all fours, skinning her knees.

'Where's Gabriel?' said Rolland, shouting over the noise of the helicopter which breasted the brow of the hill, its spotlight picking them out.

'Back pocket,' said Trent, coughing. 'Peugeot keys. In the trunk.' Dugrippe knelt to pull them out. 'He's alive.'

'He'd better be.' Dugrippe lumbered away to release Latour.

'And Auger?' said Benoit, appearing through a thick wave of smoke.

'Unknown,' said Trent. 'But he's unarmed and injured - can't have got far.'

'He was going to kill us,' said Nell, eyes dazed, tears streaming down her face from the smoke.

'He killed Barron and Cooper,' said Trent. 'He also killed the woman in Jasmin's pool but it wasn't Carla...'

'We know,' said Benoit. 'It was Eugenie Marchand.' He nodded to Caron. 'Take off the bracelets. And find them some water.' Caron removed the handcuffs and jogged to a car for bottled water.

'How did you find us?' said Trent, hoarse from smoke inhalation. 'Auger threw away my tracker.'

'Nina put one in your watch,' said Rolland.

Trent squinted at his Five Fathoms. 'Auger didn't know?' Benoit shook his head. 'How long have you suspected him?'

'We didn't. He was elsewhere when we bugged your watch. Where's Renfrew?'

'Dead,' said Trent. 'In the fire.' He pulled Nell to her feet and she slipped unsteadily under his arm for comfort and support. 'I tried to save him.'

'Why?' said Benoit, staring at the farmhouse, now completely engulfed in flames.

Trent considered. 'So, I could show Nell the monster in her dreams was just another emotional cripple.'

~

DUGRIPPE BROKE INTO a wide grin and flashed a thumbs-up from the rear of Auger's Peugeot then offered an arm to the grateful Latour, who scrambled out of the trunk with some difficulty, his muscles cramping.

'Never thought I'd be glad to see your ugly mug,' he said, flexing his limbs.

'You're welcome,' said Dugrippe. Benoit and Rolland jogged over to check Latour's well-being.

'Where's Auger?' snarled Latour. 'I owe him a good kicking.'

'We're looking,' said Dugrippe. 'What about Trent? Just say the word and I'll flatten him.'

'Innocent bystander,' said Latour.

'The barn's clear,' Costanza shouted. 'The stables too.'

More shouting from further up the hill turned their heads and the helicopter flew over to shine its light on the commotion. Caron was waving her torch near the silo. Trent left Nell and sprinted towards her position, the others following.

When Caron reached the lip of the pit, she saw Auger covered in blood, his throat torn open. He wasn't moving. A large wolf stood over him, blood dripping from its mouth, startled by the twin illumination of Caron's torch and the helicopter's searchlight. It began to growl and tensed every muscle in its lean body.

Caron raised her gun as the wolf inched its way out of the pit towards her. She fired but her shot was spoiled by an arm pushing her gun hand into the air as she pulled the trigger. The wolf sprinted away into the darkness.

'What the fuck are you doing?' she demanded.

'It's not the wolf's fault,' said Trent, panting after his yomp up the hill. He pushed past her and descended into the pit, dropping next to Auger's lifeless body to check in vain for a pulse. In his dead hand, Auger gripped a blood-stained copy of a photograph. Trent eased it from his fingers.

Benoit, Dugrippe, Rolland and Costanza arrived, puffing, Latour trailing in their wake.

'He's dead,' said Trent, passing Benoit the photograph. Benoit examined the picture of Carla Renfrew, raising a glass to the camera at her table outside the Deux Rocs. He slipped it into a pocket.

Costanza put a hand to her mouth. 'Oh, Danny. What have you done?'

'I'm sorry,' said Rolland, putting an arm on her shoulder. 'He was your friend.'

'Ours too,' said Dugrippe.

'He was a good man,' said Costanza. 'I want you to know that.' She stared fiercely at his remains. At Benoit's urging, Rolland escorted her away.

'Great,' said Benoit. 'No Auger, no Renfrew, no Bertrand and no Rappeneau. I look forward to the paperwork.'

'We know most of it without them,' said Trent, going through Auger's pockets.

'What are you looking for?' said Benoit.

'Auger had a walkie talkie,' said Trent. 'He spoke to someone on the drive from Seillans. The other handset was in the stables when we arrived.'

'Renfrew, surely.'

'Renfrew was chained to a desk.'

'He what?'

'Auger wanted more money,' said Trent, standing. 'At least, Renfrew thought he did. Must be in the car.'

'Why do you need it?' said Dugrippe.

'I don't,' said Trent. 'But Nell was drugged and unconscious in the stable when we arrived yet she wasn't kept there. It's too cold and the mattress had been dragged across damp concrete. Someone moved her.'

'We've searched the whole place,' said Dugrippe. 'If there was someone else here, they're gone.'

Benoit spotted the cement mixer and glanced at Trent.

'OKAY,' said Benoit, banging on the car roof, an hour later. Costanza started Auger's Peugeot and turned the car around, following all the other police vehicles in single file, heading back down the hill, to the valley. The helicopter had already flown Nell to the hospital and Auger's remains to the morgue in a body bag.

Seconds later, the hushed site was returned to darkness, apart from the pale light of the moon and the glowing embers of the fire from the smoking ruins of a once-imposing farmhouse.

THE SKY TURNED from black to grey to pale gold as the sun rehearsed its entrance behind the distant Alps. Across the quadrangle, opposite the ashes of the smouldering farm-house, the faint sound of a squeaky hinge encroached on nature's silence. Seconds later, the barn door shifted a few centimetres and a head poked out to look around before a figure emerged, carrying a bag.

In the dim light, the figure paused to stare at the ruins of the farmhouse then struck out towards the earthmover and its adjacent pit.

At the edge of the drop into the bowels of the earth, the figure looked around again before disappearing over the lip towards the Volkswagen.

At the sound of the engine starting, Benoit wrenched open the stable door and ran towards the pit, barking into his radio as he moved. 'Go! Go! Go!'

Another car, without lights, flew over the cattle grid from the brow of the hill as Benoit and Trent ran towards the pit and Caron emerged from the dilapidated silo with Rolland. Trent overtook Benoit but Latour and Dugrippe were already there, weapons drawn, having sped from their hiding place behind the earthmover.

'Turn off the engine,' shouted Dugrippe, crouching low, gun aimed at the driver's window. 'Get out of the car.'

If the driver heard the instructions, they were ignored and the reversing lights came on as the car moved backwards, up the slope. Latour and Dugrippe prepared to fire as the car appeared over the rim.

But before the VW could extricate itself from its burial pit, the headlights on Auger's Peugeot snapped on, as it tore up the slope towards the pit, skidding to a halt and shunting into the rear of Barron's car, blocking its exit.

The VW's trunk popped open and Benoit and Trent caught a glimpse of the horrors within before the decomposing head of Roger Barron fell to the ground and rolled to a halt a few yards away.

Meanwhile the vehicle careered forward, into the steep earth wall at the bottom of the pit and several large clods of earth fell onto its bodywork. Costanza leapt out of Auger's car and joined the ring of armed detectives standing in the beam of the Peugeot's headlights, all pointing their weapons at Barron's car.

'Engine off. Out of the car!' shouted Benoit, trying not to glance at the gnarled, rotting flesh in the trunk or Barron's decaying head on the ground.

For a full minute the only sound was the idling engine, broken by intermittent thumps as earth, loosened from the pit wall, fell onto the VW.

'Engine off!' repeated Benoit, firing a shot into the air. A moment later, the car was silenced and the driver's door swung open. The cabin light came on and the driver leaned out over the bare earth and vomited hard onto the ground.

'Out!' repeated Benoit. 'Show me your hands.'

One foot followed the other, then empty hands were held out of the car before the driver emerged and turned towards them, face in shadow.

'Walk towards us, hands up,' instructed Benoit.

The driver walked carefully up the damp slope to the edge of the pit until their eyes met.

'On the ground, Mrs Renfrew,' barked Benoit.

Carla Renfrew stared at Benoit as though about to burst into tears before sinking to her knees. Her eyes darted towards Trent. 'Tyler? Is it over? Please say it's over.' Her voice cracked as she implored him. 'Tell me he can't hurt me anymore.' Tears began to stream down her face and her shoulders shook as she sobbed.

Trent and Benoit exchanged a glance as Rolland jumped down behind Carla, pushed her to the ground and clipped handcuffs to her wrists. 'Save it.'

'Please,' sobbed Carla. 'Don't let him hurt me again.'

'Who?' said Benoit.

'The gendarme,' she screeched, suddenly agitated. Rolland finished frisking her prone body before hauling her to her feet. 'Auger. Is that his name? Have you got him?'

'Daniel Auger?' said Benoit.

'Yes,' she said, voice querulous. Her knees buckled and she sank back to the ground. 'He came to the house one time to speak to Harry and he wouldn't stop staring. Later, we were having a party and the next thing I knew...I was here. He kept me in a windowless cell and made me do things...' She began sobbing again.

'You mean the cell you just walked away from?' said Rolland, raising an eyebrow.

Carla lowered her head, more tears falling, shoulders shuddering with emotion. 'Where's my husband? I want Harry. I want to go home.'

'And the Oscar goes to...' sneered Rolland.

'Take her,' said Benoit.

Rolland yanked Carla Renfrew to her feet and hauled her down the hill. Dugrippe radioed the rest of the cars to return to the site.

'Does she think that shit's going to fly?' said Caron.

'The problem is there's no-one left alive to say different,' said Dugrippe.

'Perhaps Daniel Auger could make a miraculous recovery and give us a statement,' said Trent. 'We can use it to force a confession.'

Benoit frowned. 'We don't fabricate evidence in SCS.'

'It'll be the truth,' argued Trent. 'We have to try something. If this goes to a jury and Carla Renfrew pleads her innocence, she'll wrap them around her little finger.'

'Look what I found,' said Latour, emerging from the passenger side, holding his nose with one hand and a plump doctor's bag in the other. Clear of the stench of putrid flesh, he opened the bag to show them bundle after bundle of one-hundred-euro notes. 'Must be half a million in here.'

'Then we've got her,' said Caron.

35

Monday 13th May

Trent sat on his cot after a strenuous workout in his cell and mopped his brow, feeling a pang of hunger. Nearing lunchtime, footsteps approached but instead of the hatch being opened to pass through his lunch, the cell door opened and Benoit walked in.

'I thought it was tomorrow,' said Trent.

'It is,' said Benoit. 'But the team and I are having a final lunch at Deux Rocs before some of us head back to Nice and we thought, after your contribution, you'd like to join us. Strict security, obviously.'

'So, that's it,' said Trent. 'Carla gets away with it.'

'Unless something turns up to contradict her story,' said Benoit.

'They were lovers, damn it,' said Trent. 'They killed Barron and Cooper and Marchand.'

'We can't prove their conspiracy,' said Benoit. 'I wish we could. There's no forensic evidence to put Carla in Auger's apartment. Same story with his car. Either Auger did a hell of a clean-up or he and Carla got together elsewhere. We interviewed everybody in his building but not a single witness could put the two of them together before the killings.'

'What about the missing photographs from the fête?' said Trent.

'They were on Auger's laptop but they only show him talking to Renfrew. He didn't approach Carla that night.'

'And the bag of money?'

'She claims she thought it was ransom money, paid by her husband,' said Benoit. 'When she finally summoned the courage to escape, she was determined her rapist wouldn't profit from his crimes.'

'Please,' scoffed Trent. 'She's guilty as hell.'

'You don't need to convince me,' said Benoit. 'But without evidence...'

'There must be something,' said Trent. 'They planned it, Benoit. They were lovers. You saw the secret rooms Rappeneau built inside the barn. No locks and just a hidden lever. She could have escaped any time she liked. Auger even chained up Renfrew so she could go outside to take a walk.'

'She says Auger threatened to kill her if she left the barn,' said Benoit. 'And the farm is miles from anywhere. Where would she go? It's credible. Plus, all the physical evidence supports her account. Her injuries...'

'...could've been self-inflicted,' said Trent.

'Obviously,' said Benoit. 'But their existence is ambiguous. What *isn't* ambiguous is the provable fact of Auger and Renfrew's criminal conspiracy, confessed to you and documented in your statement.'

'But Renfrew was in chains,' said Trent. 'Auger double-crossed him.'

'A consequence of Auger's obsession with Carla,' said Benoit. 'He even had her picture in his dying hand. But there's not a scrap of evidence to show his feelings were reciprocated. All the irrefutable proof convicts Auger and Renfrew.

'Renfrew's private jet landing in Nice; Auger's gun used

to kill Ash Cooper; Auger's farm bought by Renfrew then signed over to him. And both confessed to planning and executing the murders at Villa Jasmin and Lavendre *to you!* The fact they fell out doesn't implicate Carla.'

Trent sighed. 'Look, she may not have set this thing in motion but as soon as Auger laid eyes on Carla, everything changed. That was the moment he decided to double cross Renfrew. And, to get Carla to cooperate, he had to tell her what her husband was planning and make her a willing participant.'

'Prove it!' said Benoit. 'Auger had the Marchand girl snatched to order. Auger drugged her and brought her to Jasmin in the trunk of *his* car. We found her DNA.'

'When Renfrew drove away, the two of them killed Barron and Marchand to take Carla's place,' said Trent. 'Then Auger drove her to the farm and smuggled her into the barn until he'd had a chance to shackle Renfrew to the desk.'

'Supposition,' said Benoit. 'Carla claims to have no memory of the party and Renfrew admitted drugging her.'

'With fake Rohypnol supplied by Auger, no doubt,' said Trent.

'Yet guests at the party claim Carla was disorientated,' said Benoit.

'She was faking it,' growled Trent. 'What about Marchand's DNA being on Carla's razor, toothbrush and hairbrush?'

'Auger bought a duplicate set and used them on Marchand before he brought her to the villa,' said Benoit. 'I have the receipts.'

'But who told him what to buy? It had to be Carla.'

'But how do we prove it?' said Benoit. 'We have nothing. If we can't put Auger and Carla together before the night of the killings, there's no conspiracy and we have to release her.'

'So, she gets away with it,' said Trent.

'We haven't given up but, unless something changes,

Carla will be formally cleared tomorrow and return to Singapore a wealthy woman.'

'She's played this beautifully,' said Trent.

'I almost feel sorry for Auger,' said Benoit, nodding. 'He was completely outmatched.'

'Blinded by love,' said Trent. 'I even told him so.'

'What did he say to that?'

'He told me not to underestimate his powers of persuasion,' said Trent. 'Know what I think? I think Auger was all too aware that Carla might be unwilling to live out her days on the farm...'

'Which is why he wanted Renfrew's money,' said Benoit.

'What use is money if you can't leave the farm to spend it?'

'What are you suggesting?'

'I think Auger had some kind of leverage over Carla, in case she threatened to leave.'

'Like what?'

'I wish I knew,' said Trent.

'Well, we only have twenty-four hours to figure it out or accept defeat with good grace,' said Benoit. He held out a pair of handcuffs. 'But now, it's lunchtime.'

Trent smiled. 'You French and your lunches.'

'You Americans and your burgers on the go,' said Benoit. 'If you learn only one thing from your time in France, let it be the power of a good meal to work its magic on the creative juices.'

Trent extended his wrists and was led to the rear of Fayence gendarmerie where Latour waited next to a police wagon.

FIFTEEN MINUTES LATER, the back door of the wagon opened and Latour unlocked the cage and unfastened Trent's handcuffs.

'You're taking a chance, aren't you?' said Trent,

descending the steps onto the tarmac of the Hotel Deux Rocs car park.

'Not really,' said Benoit. 'We haven't formally decided whether or not to charge Mademoiselle Beaumont with attempted murder.'

Trent frowned. 'You can't prove that.'

Benoit beamed at him. 'I take my leverage where I can find it.'

'Low blow,' said Trent, looking across tables filled with lunchtime guests. Nell was alone at a table, trailing her hand in the water of the fountain and Trent turned to Benoit in surprise.

'You said you didn't want her to see you in custody,' said Benoit.

Trent nodded, choking with emotion. 'Thank you.'

As they ambled towards Nell's table, Trent gestured a greeting towards Benoit's squad, conversing over their menus at a large table. Even Dugrippe acknowledged respectfully.

Trent glanced up at the blue sky, inhaling the fresh air scented with lavender and cooked meats. 'I've underrated freedom.'

'Everyone does,' said Benoit.

A couple ate sternly at the table adjacent to Nell, studiously avoiding eye contact. 'How many?' said Trent, smiling.

'Four,' said Benoit. 'Including a sniper in the bell tower.'

Trent laughed but Benoit's severe expression provoked an examination of the church tower's narrow windows. A second later, Nell threw herself into his arms.

'Mike,' she squealed, hugging him.

'Hey, kid.' She buried her head under his chin before both sat, Nell not letting go of his hand.

'I'll leave you two to talk,' said Benoit. 'Oh, and this is my treat. Order whatever you want.'

∾

'WHY WOULDN'T you let me visit?' said Nell, after they'd demolished a starter of foie gras.

'Because,' said Trent. 'And if things go badly in the States, I don't want you visiting me in the pen either. Remember me today then forget me altogether.'

Tears filled her eyes. 'How can you say that?'

'My past has caught up with me and I have to face it,' said Trent. 'I can only do that if I know you're safe and getting on with your life.'

'This is so unfair,' she said, scowling towards Benoit.

'Hey,' said Trent, pulling her chin back and staring deep into her moistening eyes. 'Benoit didn't have to give us this time *or* take off the bracelets. He's doing a good thing.'

Tears rolled down her cheeks. 'This is all my fault. If I hadn't...'

'We've covered this,' said Trent. 'I'm in charge. I took the decision...'

AFTER THEIR MAIN course of roast partridge and dauphinoise potatoes, a bottle of Champagne from Benoit arrived to accompany their dessert. Favre poured Nell a glass and glanced at Trent. When he nodded, Favre filled his flute.

'I've never seen you drink alcohol,' said Nell.

'Today I'm having every fine thing,' he replied, raising his glass. 'To the good things in life.' They touched glasses and drank then Trent gestured a toast towards Benoit, who acknowledged and took a sip of his own champagne.

'How can you celebrate?' said Nell. 'You might be in prison for the rest of your life while that bitch walks away, free as a bird.'

'Maybe she's innocent.'

'You don't believe that for a second.' She leaned towards him. 'Would it help if I testified? I could say I'm starting to have flashbacks of Carla giving me the injections. I could...'

'You were drugged, Nell,' said Trent. 'Even if you could remember, your testimony is easily discredited.'

'We've got to do something. That poor Marchand girl...'

'You're not testifying!' said Trent. 'If you lie on the stand, you'll be torn to pieces. It's not happening. Which brings us onto the subject of you and Byron. And I want the truth.'

Nell looked away. 'I was going to tell you after I'd...'

'After you'd killed Renfrew?' said Trent. 'I'm almost glad your mother isn't alive to hear you say that.'

Angry tears filled her eyes. 'My mother deserves justice.'

'Yes, but she'd be appalled to hear you were planning a murder to achieve it. Your mother wasn't that person, Nell.'

'Don't tell me about my mother,' said Nell. 'You hardly knew her.'

'I knew her well enough to know she'd be devastated to hear you consider taking a human life,' said Trent.

'After the things you've done?'

'You're right,' agreed Trent. 'I'm the hypocrite who killed three people to avenge your mother's death, telling myself it was to keep you safe. But, after killing those men, I discovered something - your mother was still dead and that was never going to change.

'And now, I may lose the rest of *my* life as payment for violence which achieved nothing. I'm pushing fifty, Nell. And on my last day of freedom, I'm mourning its loss. You're twenty-four and you've spent years planning retribution for your mother's murder. That isn't freedom. I want your word that you'll never kill again.'

'Again?' she exclaimed. 'What do you mean?'

'Byron was pushed under that train by someone matching your description,' said Trent. 'You were there, Nell.'

Her shock was real. 'No...' She shook her head. 'I didn't...'

'I've seen the cuttings,' said Trent.

Nell's breathing quickened. 'Yes, I was there. But I didn't kill him. I wanted to but I couldn't.' She began to sob and Trent gripped her hand.

'You were following him.'

'Yes,' gasped Nell.

'Why didn't you tell me?'

'I wanted to,' said Nell. 'But you were in Thailand and you'd already done so much. You gave up your life to protect me. It was my turn to do something for my mother. Me. Her blood. So, after I found him on the internet, the year before, I kept tabs on him and waited. When he came to London on business, I took my chance. I staked out his hotel and followed him. It wasn't hard. Considering he was a security consultant he was very relaxed about wandering around a foreign city on his own. At least that's what I thought.'

'What happened?'

'We were in the station at Oxford Circus, waiting for a train. Byron was at the edge of the platform and I was directly behind him, wondering why he'd never once looked over his shoulder in three days. Then, as the train was pulling in, he turned and looked straight at me and smiled.'

'He recognised you?'

'He didn't recognise me, Mike, he *knew* me. He said *'Hello Nell'*. He knew I was following him and it was like he'd planned the moment.'

'And then?'

'Then he stepped backwards over the white line and said one last thing, clear as day, to make sure I heard...'

'What?'

'Harry Renfrew.' Nell sighed. 'He knew why I was there. He wanted me to know who ordered my mother's death. When he started to fall backwards, I tried to grab him, to pull him to safety but he was too far gone. And all the while he had that strange smile on his face.' She closed her eyes to remember the impact. 'After...I was aware people were speaking to me but I couldn't take it in, so I just ran. I didn't kill him.'

'Thank God,' said Trent. He glanced over at Benoit who was tapping his watch. Trent acknowledged and both men rose from their tables. Nell hurtled into Trent's midriff again.

'Don't go,' she wailed.

'I must,' said Trent.

'Please,' she begged the approaching Benoit. 'Five more minutes.'

'I'm sorry,' said Benoit.

'Don't be,' said Trent. 'And thank you.' He hugged Nell one last time and, on releasing her, Nell's tear ducts opened and Benoit gestured to the couple on the next table to take care of her.

'I did it all for you, kid,' said Trent. 'Make it count.' He turned and walked back to the wagon. 'You'll see she gets safely on the plane to London?'

'Of course,' said Benoit.

Trent nodded his appreciation as the handcuffs snapped around his wrists. 'Is there really a sniper in the bell tower?'

Benoit smiled. 'Still time to find out.'

THAT EVENING, Benoit poured a second glass of wine and gazed at Caron and Latour. Even in the darkness of the deserted square, their exhaustion was palpable. It was always the same after a big case. The adrenalin was spent and the team were on their knees. Rolland and Dugrippe had returned to Nice after lunch and, after draining her sparkling water, Caron stood to do the same.

'Roads should be clear,' said Latour.

'Here's hoping,' said Caron, stifling a yawn. Giving Benoit and Latour a kiss on both cheeks she marched away to her car and sped away.

Guy Favre emerged from the Deux Rocs and made his way across the empty square, trying to tempt the two detectives into a dessert. Without success.

'Big lunch,' explained Benoit. Favre smiled and apologetically laid down an invoice which Benoit signed. After exchanging handshakes, Favre returned to the hotel, turning off the other table lights on the way, leaving Benoit and Latour in the reflected glow of the floodlit church. The fountain trickled relentlessly and the cats moved in to scour for scraps. Both men were easy in their silence before Latour spoke.

'Trent saved my life,' said Latour.

Benoit nodded. 'Then hold a good thought for him.'

'I will. I'm turning in. Early start.' He grinned. 'Let me show you to your cot, boss.'

'I'll find it,' said Benoit. 'I need a few minutes.'

'Give it up,' said Latour. 'We've done all we can.'

'There's always something undone, Gabriel,' said Benoit. 'Go to bed and give thanks Thierry is snoring at home.'

Latour wandered away towards the church and Benoit rummaged in his pockets for a final cigarette. With his pack of Gitanes, he pulled out the key to Auger's apartment and, after a few seconds contemplation, he set off down the hill, his cigarette unlit. 'Cot, my arse.'

Standing outside Auger's apartment, he scored through the crime scene tape and let himself in. The smell of forensic chemicals lingered so Benoit opened the roof terrace windows to freshen the air. Sitting on a cane chair, he gazed out towards the twinkling lights of the coast, lit his cigarette and revelled in the warm breeze. Fatigue washed over him but tomorrow he would swim in the ocean.

Crushing his cigarette into an ashtray, Benoit's eye fell on the portrait of Auger's parents. From his seat on the terrace, he noticed the frame didn't quite sit flush against the wall. Curious, he removed the picture from its nail, turned over the frame and peeled the tape from the back of the housing.

A minute later, Benoit was sprinting up the hill to the car park. Panting, he fumbled for his car keys. Extracting his laptop from the trunk, he powered it up while he rummaged for a card reader in the side pocket. Pulling it out, he inserted the Secure Digital card taken from the picture frame, and slotted it into the USB port.

Double clicking impatiently, Benoit was greeted with a photograph of Carla Renfrew, bikini-clad, on the tiled floor of the living room of Villa Jasmin, the sun streaming through the French windows behind her, caressing her perfect physique in its warmth. The date/time stamp showed the photograph had been taken on April 15th at 3.16 pm.

Excitement surged in Benoit as he scrolled through the timeline to the end of the album. The final picture, taken on April 27th at 03.37 in the morning was of Auger's hand reaching out towards the lens.

Benoit sat on the bench outside the hotel to review the preceding photographs. It didn't take long to find a dozen images of Auger and Carla standing naked together on a plastic sheet, towelling themselves down. The photographs had been taken fifteen minutes before Auger's hand had picked up the camera to remove the memory card from the box.

Benoit sat back with a huge smile on his face and fumbled for his phone.

36

B enoit was outside the cell door when Trent emerged in chains, a gendarme either side of him. He greeted him with a cursory nod. 'Ready?' he enquired.

'All set,' said Trent.

'Sleep well?'

'Like a log.'

'I'm surprised,' said Benoit. 'We arrested a triple murderer last night and she didn't come quietly.' He beckoned a puzzled Trent to the far end of the custody suite and pulled down the hatch on a cell door to reveal Carla Renfrew sitting cross-legged on her plastic mattress. She looked up briefly with those startling green eyes and opened her mouth to protest as Benoit snapped the hatch closed but they could still hear her muffled cry.

'I want my fucking lawyer.'

'How?' said Trent.

'Auger was right. We did underestimate him. I found your camera's missing SD card in his apartment. He had himself and Carla get clean after mutilating Marchand and towel down naked on a plastic sheet in front of the camera.'

'And Auger kept the film as insurance.' Trent smiled and offered his hand to shake. 'Well done.'

Benoit smiled back. 'Time to go.' Trent nodded and the two men walked solemnly to the back entrance of the station, where a familiar figure waited with Directeur Seigner.

'Lisa,' said Trent, warmly. 'I wondered if it would be you. Good to see you.'

'Hello Mike,' said Lisa Petronelli.

'You look great,' said Trent.

'I'm closing on sixty, Mike,' said Petronelli. 'You're my last assignment. Agent Holcomb and I will be your escort for the duration. Plenty of time to talk over old times when we're in the air.'

'Keeping it professional,' said Trent. 'Best way.'

'All set?' Trent nodded. Petronelli gestured to the gendarmes who gave Trent a final pat down then marched him out through the yard and helped him up the steps into the waiting wagon.

'Good luck,' said Benoit.

When the cage and the back door were safely locked, the gendarmes jumped up into the cab next to the driver and Petronelli climbed into a car next to Agent Holcomb, to follow.

The wagon drove out into the warm streets of Fayence followed by the FBI agents in their rented BMW. Benoit's eyes were fixed on the point of departure long after the wagon had disappeared from view and the electric gates had moved smoothly back over the entrance.

'I'm sorry about Trent,' said Seigner. 'I know you were starting to like him.'

'He's not on the plane yet,' said Benoit.

Seigner touched him on the arm. 'Great result, Serge. Take a few days.' She walked back into the gendarmerie. A moment later, Benoit turned and followed to say his good-byes to local officers before climbing into his Citroen and pointing it down the hill towards the coast and his beloved Nice.

FIN

Printed in Great Britain
by Amazon